Jules Verne

I0576276

The Great Explorers of the Nineteenth Century

Outlook

Jules Verne

The Great Explorers of the Nineteenth Century

1. Auflage | ISBN: 978-3-73262-383-9

Erscheinungsort: Frankfurt am Main, Deutschland

Erscheinungsjahr: 2018

Outlook Verlag GmbH, Frankfurt.

Reproduction of the original.

THE GREAT EXPLORERS

OF THE

NINETEENTH CENTURY.

LONDON:
GILBERT AND RIVINGTON, PRINTERS,
ST. JOHN'S SQUARE.

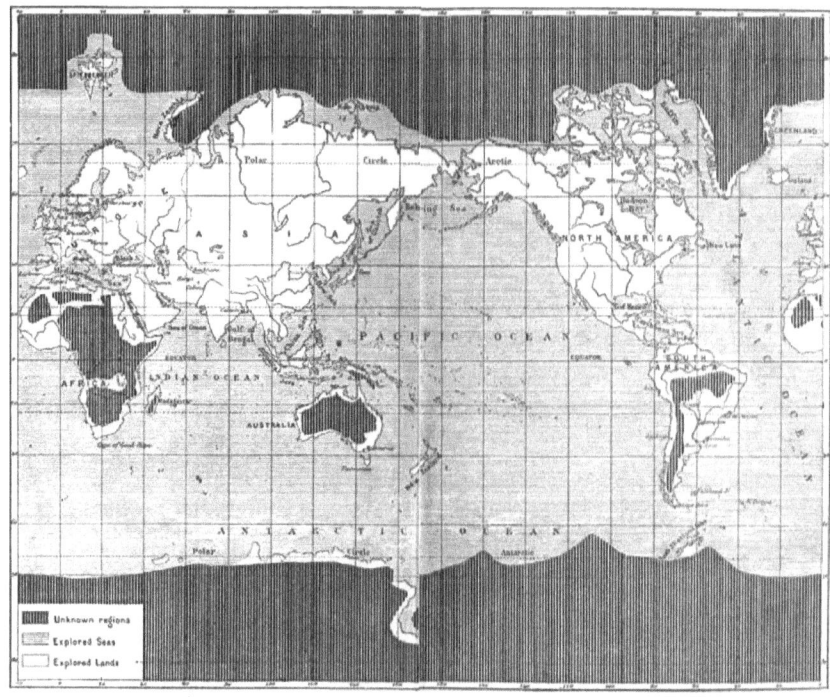

Gravé par E. Morieu 23, r. de Bréa Paris.

Map of the work which had to be done in the 19th Century.

CELEBRATED TRAVELS AND TRAVELLERS.

THE GREAT EXPLORERS

OF THE

NINETEENTH CENTURY.

BY JULES VERNE

TRANSLATED BY

N. D'ANVERS,

AUTHOR OF "HEROES OF NORTH AFRICAN DISCOVERY," "HEROES OF SOUTH AFRICAN DISCOVERY," ETC.

WITH 51 ORIGINAL DRAWINGS BY LÉON BENETT, AND 57 FAC-
SIMILES FROM
EARLY MSS. AND MAPS BY MATTHIS AND MORIEU.

London:
SAMPSON LOW, MARSTON, SEARLE, & RIVINGTON,
CROWN BUILDINGS, 188, FLEET STREET.

1881.

[*All rights reserved.*]

TO

DR. G. G. GARDINER,

I Dedicate this Translation

WITH SINCERE AND GRATEFUL ESTEEM.

N. D'ANVERS.

HENDON, *Christmas, 1880.*

TRANSLATOR'S NOTE.

In offering the present volume to the English public, the Translator wishes to thank the Rev. Andrew Carter for the very great assistance given by him in tracing all quotations from English, German, and other authors to the original sources, and for his untiring aid in the verification of disputed spellings, &c.

THE

GREAT EXPLORERS OF THE 19TH CENTURY.

LIST OF ILLUSTRATIONS AND MAPS

REPRODUCED IN FAC-SIMILE FROM THE ORIGINAL DOCUMENTS, GIVING THE SOURCES WHENCE THEY ARE DERIVED.

TABLE OF CONTENTS.

II.

Clapperton's second journey—Arrival at Badagry—Yariba and its capital Katunga—Boussa—Attempts to get at the truth about Mungo Park's fate —"Nyffé," Yaourie, and Zegzeg—Arrival at Kano—Disappointments— Death of Clapperton—Return of Lander to the coast—Tuckey on the Congo —Bowditch in Ashantee—Mollien at the sources of the Senegal and Gambia —Major Grey—Caillié at Timbuctoo—Laing at the sources of the Niger— Richard and John Lander at the mouth of the Niger—Cailliaud and Letorzec in Egypt, Nubia, and the oasis of Siwâh

CHAPTER III.
THE ORIENTAL SCIENTIFIC MOVEMENT AND AMERICAN DISCOVERIES.

The decipherment of cuneiform inscriptions, and the study of Assyrian remains up to 1840—Ancient Iran and the Avesta—The survey of India and the study of Hindustani—The exploration and measurement of the Himalaya mountains—The Arabian Peninsula—Syria and Palestine—Central Asia and Alexander von Humboldt—Pike at the sources of the Mississippi, Arkansas, and Red River—Major Long's two expeditions—General Cass—Schoolcraft at the sources of the Mississippi—The exploration of New Mexico— Archæological expeditions in Central America—Scientific expeditions in Brazil—Spix and Martin—Prince Maximilian of Wied-Neuwied—D'Orbigny and American Man

SECOND PART.

CHAPTER I.
VOYAGES ROUND THE WORLD, AND POLAR EXPEDITIONS.

The Russian fur trade—Kruzenstern appointed to the command of an expedition—Noukha-Hiva—Nangasaki—Reconnaisance of the coast of Japan —Yezo—The Ainos—Saghalien—Return to Europe—Otto von Kotzebue— Stay at Easter Island—Penrhyn—The Radak Archipelago—Return to Russia

—Changes at Otaheite and the Sandwich Islands—Beechey's Voyage—Easter Island—Pitcairn and the mutineers of the *Bounty*—The Paumoto Islands—Otaheite and the Sandwich Islands—The Bonin Islands—Lütke—The Quebradas of Valparaiso—Holy week in Chili—New Archangel—The Kaloches—Ounalashka—The Caroline Archipelago—The canoes of the Caroline Islanders—Guam, a desert island—Beauty and happy situation of the Bonin Islands—The Tchouktchees: their manners and their conjurors— Return to Russia

CHAPTER II.
FRENCH CIRCUMNAVIGATORS.

The journey of Freycinet—Rio de Janeiro and its gipsy inhabitants—The Cape and its wines—The Bay of Sharks—Stay at Timor—Ombay Island and its cannibal inhabitants—The Papuan Islands—The pile dwellings of the Alfoers—A dinner with the Governor of Guam—Description of the Marianne Islands and their inhabitants—Particulars concerning the Sandwich Islands—Port Jackson and New South Wales—Shipwreck in Berkeley Sound—The Falkland Islands—Return to France—The voyage of the *Coquille* under the command of Duperrey—Martin-Vaz and Trinidad—The Island of St. Catherine—The independence of Brazil—Berkeley Sound and the remains of the *Uranie*—Stay at Conception—The civil war in Chili—The Araucanians—Discoveries in the Dangerous Archipelago—Stay at Otaheite and New Ireland—The Papuans—Stay at Ualan—The Caroline Islands and their inhabitants—Scientific results of the expeditions

II.

Expedition of Baron de Bougainville—Stay at Pondicherry—The "White Town" and the "Black Town"—"Right-hand" and "Left-hand"—Malacca—Singapore and its prosperity—Stay at Manilla—Touron Bay—The monkeys and the people—The marble rocks of Faifoh—Cochin-Chinese diplomacy—The Anambas—The Sultan of Madura—The straits of Madura and Allas—Cloates and the Triad Islands—Tasmania—Botany Bay and New South Wales—Santiago and Valparaiso—Return *viâ* Cape Horn—Expedition of Dumont d'Urville in the *Astrolabe*—The Peak of Teneriffe—Australia—Stay at New Zealand—Tonga-Tabu—Skirmishes—New Britain and New Guinea—First news of the fate of La Pérouse—Vanikoro and its inhabitants—Stay at Guam—Amboyna and Menado—Results of the expedition

CHAPTER III.
POLAR EXPEDITIONS.

Bellinghausen, yet another Russian Explorer—Discovery of the islands of Traversay, Peter I., and Alexander I.—The Whaler, Weddell—The Southern Orkneys—New Shetland—The people of Tierra del Fuego—John Biscoe and the districts of Enderby and Graham—Charles Wilkes and the Antarctic Continent—Captain Balleny— Dumont d'Urville's expedition in the *Astrolabe* and the *Zelée*—Coupvent Desbois and the Peak of Teneriffe—The Straits of Magellan—A new post-office shut in by ice—Louis Philippe's Land —Across Oceania—Adélie and Clarie Lands—New Guinea and Torres Strait —Return to France—James Clark Rosset—Victoria

II.
THE NORTH POLE.

Anjou and Wrangell—The "polynia"—John Ross's first expedition—Baffin's Bay closed—Edward Parry's discoveries on his first voyage—The survey of Hudson's Bay, and the discovery of Fury and Hecla Straits—Parry's third voyage—Fourth voyage—On the ice in sledges in the open sea—Franklin's first trip—Incredible sufferings of the explorers—Second expedition—John Ross—Four winters amongst the ice—Dease and Simpson's expedition

THE GREAT EXPLORERS

OF THE

NINETEENTH CENTURY.

PART I.

CHAPTER I.

THE DAWN OF A CENTURY OF DISCOVERY.

Slackness of discovery during the struggles of the Republic and Empire —Seetzen's voyages in Syria and Palestine—Hauran and the circumnavigation of the Dead Sea—Decapolis—Journey in Arabia—Burckhardt in Syria—Expeditions in Nubia upon the two branches of the Nile—Pilgrimage to Mecca and Medina—The English in India—Webb at the Source of the Ganges—Narrative of a journey in the Punjab—Christie and Pottinger in Scinde—The same explorers cross Beluchistan into Persia—Elphinstone in Afghanistan—Persia according to Gardane, A. Dupré, Morier, Macdonald-Kinneir, Price, and Ouseley—Guldenstædt and Klaproth in the Caucasus—Lewis and Clarke in the Rocky Mountains—Raffles in Sumatra and Java.

A sensible diminution in geographical discovery marks the close of the eighteenth and the beginning of the nineteenth centuries.

We have already noticed the organization of the Expedition sent in search of La Pérouse by the French Republic, and also Captain Baudin's important cruise along the Australian coasts. These are the only instances in which the unrestrained passions and fratricidal struggles of the French nation allowed the government to exhibit interest in geography, a science which is especially favoured by the French.

At a later period, Bonaparte consulted several savants and distinguished artists, and the materials for that grand undertaking which first gave an idea (incomplete though it was) of the ancient civilization of the land of the Pharaohs, were collected together. But when Bonaparte had completely given place to Napoleon, the egotistical monarch, sacrificing all else to his ruling passion for war, would no longer listen to explorations, voyages, or possible discoveries. They represented money and men stolen from him; and his expenditure of those materials was far too great to allow of such futile waste. This was clearly shown, when he ceded the last remnants of French colonial rule in America to the United States for a few millions.

Happily other nations were not oppressed by the same iron hand. Absorbed although they might be in their struggle with France, they could still find volunteers to extend the range of geographical science, to establish archæology upon scientific bases, and to prosecute linguistic and ethnographical enterprise.

The learned geographer Malte-Brun, in an article published by him in the "Nouvelles Annales des Voyages" in 1817, gives a minute account of the condition of French geographical knowledge at the beginning of the nineteenth century, and of the many desiderata of that science. He reviews the progress already made in navigation, astronomy, and languages. The India Company, far from concealing its discoveries, as jealousy had induced the Hudson Bay Company to do, founded academies, published memoirs, and encouraged travellers.

War itself was utilized, for the French army gathered a store of precious material in Egypt. We shall shortly see how emulation spread among the various nations.

From the commencement of the century, one country has taken the lead in great discoveries. German explorers have worked so earnestly, and have proved themselves possessed of will so strong and instinct so sure, that they have left little for their successors to do beyond verifying and completing their discoveries.

The first in order of time was Ulric Jasper Seetzen, born in 1767 in East Friesland; he completed his education at Göttingen, and published some essays upon statistics and the natural sciences, for which he had a natural inclination. These publications attracted the attention of the government, and he was appointed Aulic Councillor in the province of Tever.

Seetzen's ambition, like that of Burckhardt subsequently, was an expedition to Central Africa, but he wished previously to make an exploration of Palestine and Syria, to which countries attention was shortly to be directed by the "Palestine Association," founded in London in 1805.

Seetzen did not wait for this period, but in 1802 set out for Constantinople, furnished with suitable introductions.

Although many pilgrims and travellers had successively visited the Holy Land and Syria, the vaguest notions about these countries prevailed. Their physical geography was not determined, details were wanting, and certain regions, as for example, the Lebanon and the Dead Sea had never been explored.

Comparative geography did not exist. It has taken the unwearied efforts of the English Association and the science of travellers in connexion with it to erect that study into a science. Seetzen, whose studies had been various, found himself admirably prepared to explore a country which, often visited, was still in reality new.

Having travelled through Anatolia, Seetzen reached Aleppo in May, 1802. He remained there a year, devoting himself to the practical study of the Arabic tongue, making extracts from Eastern historians and geographers, verifying the astronomical position of Aleppo, prosecuting his investigations into natural history, collecting manuscripts, and translating many of those popular songs and legends which are such valuable aids to the knowledge of a nation.

Seetzen left Aleppo in 1805 for Damascus. His first expedition led him across the provinces of Hauran and Jaulan, situated to the S.E. of that town. No traveller had as yet visited these two provinces, which in the days of Roman dominion had played an important part in the history of the Jews, under the names of Auranitis and Gaulonitis. Seetzen was the first to give an idea of their geography.

The enterprising traveller explored the Lebanon and Baalbek. He prosecuted his discoveries south of Damascus, and entered Judea, exploring the eastern portion of Hermon, the Jordan, and the Dead Sea. This was the dwelling-place of those races well known to us in Jewish history; the Ammonites, Moabites, and Gileadites. At the time of the Roman conquest, the western portion of this country was known as Perea, and was the centre of the celebrated Decapolis or confederacy of ten cities. No modern traveller had visited these regions, a fact sufficient to induce Seetzen to begin his exploration with them.

His friends at Damascus had tried to dissuade him from the journey, by picturing the difficulties and danger of a route frequented by Bedouins; but nothing could stay him. Before visiting the Decapolis region and investigating the condition of its ruins, Seetzen traversed a small district, named Ladscha, which bore a bad reputation at Damascus on account of the Bedouins who occupied it, but which was said to contain remarkable antiquities.

Leaving Damascus on the 12th of December, 1805, with an Armenian guide who misled him from the first, Seetzen, having prudently provided himself with a passport from the Pasha, proceeded from village to village escorted by an armed attendant.

In a narrative published in the earlier "Annales des Voyages," says the traveller,—

"That portion of Ladscha which I have seen is, like Hauran, entirely formed of basalt, often very porous, and in many districts forming vast stony deserts. The villages, which are mostly in ruins, are built on the sides of the rocks. The black colour of the basalt, the ruined houses, the churches and towers fallen into decay, with the total dearth of trees and verdure, combine to give a sombre aspect to this country, which strikes one almost with dread. In almost every village are either Grecian inscriptions, columns, or other remnants of antiquity; amongst others I copied an inscription of the Emperor Marcus Aurelius. Here, as in Hauran, the doors were of basalt."

Seetzen had scarcely arrived at the village of Gerasa and enjoyed a brief rest, before he was surrounded by half a score of mounted men, who said they had come by order of the vice-governor of Hauran to arrest him. Their master, Omar Aga, having learned that the traveller had been seen in the country the preceding year, and imagining his passports to be forgeries, had sent them to bring him before him.

Resistance was useless. Without allowing himself to be disconcerted by an incident which he regarded as a simple contretemps, Seetzen proceeded in the direction of Hauran, where after a day and a half's journey he met Omar Aga, travelling with the Mecca caravan. The travellers having received a hearty welcome, departed on the morrow, but meeting upon his way with many troops of Arabs, upon whom his demeanour imposed respect, he came to the conclusion that it had been Omar Aga's intention to have him robbed.

Returning to Damascus, Seetzen had great trouble in finding a guide who would accompany him in his expedition along the eastern shore of the Jordan, and around the Dead Sea. At last, a certain Yusuf-al-Milky, a member of the Greek church, who, for some thirty years, had carried on traffic with the Arab tribes, and travelled in the provinces which Seetzen desired to visit, agreed to bear him company.

The two travellers left Damascus on the 19th of January, 1806. Seetzen's entire baggage consisted of a few clothes, some indispensable books, paper for drying plants, and an assortment of drugs, necessary to sustain his assumed character as a physician. He wore the dress of a sheik of secondary rank.

The districts of Rasheiya and Hasbeiya, at the foot of Mount Hermon—whose summit at the time was hidden by snow—were the first explored by Seetzen, for the reason that they were the least known in Syria.

He then visited Achha, a village inhabited by the Druses, upon the opposite side of the mountain; Rasheiya, the residence of the Emir; and Hasbeiya, where he paid a visit to the Greek Bishop of Szur or Szeida, to whom he carried letters of recommendation. The object which chiefly attracted his attention in this mountainous district, was an asphalt-mine, whose produce is there used to protect the vines from insects.

Leaving Hasbeiya, Seetzen proceeded to Bâniâs, the ancient Casaræa Philippi, which is now a mere collection of huts. Even if traces of its fortifications were discoverable, not the smallest remains could be found of the splendid temple erected by Herod in honour of Augustus.

Ancient authorities hold that the river of Bâniâs is the source of the Jordan, but in reality that title belongs to the river Hasbany, which forms the larger branch of the Jordan. Seetzen recognized it, as he also did the Lake of Merom, or the ancient Samachonitis.

Here he was deserted by his muleteers, whom nothing could induce to accompany him so far as the bridge of Jisr-Benat-Yakûb, and also by his guide Yusuf, whom he was forced to send by the open road to await his arrival at Tiberias, while he himself proceeded on foot towards the celebrated bridge, accompanied by a single Arab attendant.

He, however, found no one at Jisr-Benat-Yakûb who was willing to accompany him along the eastern shore of the Jordan, until a native, believing him to be a doctor, begged him to go and see his sheik, who was suffering from ophthalmia, and who lived upon the eastern bank of the Lake of Tiberias.

Seetzen gladly availed himself of this opportunity; and it was well he did so, for he was thus enabled to study the Lake of Tiberias and also the Wady Zemmâk at his leisure, not, however, without risk of being robbed and murdered by his guide. Finally he reached Tiberias, called by the Arabs Tabaria, where he found Yusuf, who had been waiting for him for several days.

"The town of Tiberias," says Seetzen, "is situated upon the lake of the same name. Upon the land side it is surrounded by a good wall of cut basalt rock, but nevertheless, it scarcely deserves to be called a town. No trace of its earlier splendour remains, but the ruins of the more ancient city, which extended to the Thermæ, a league to the eastward, are recognizable.

"The famous Djezar-Pasha caused a bath to be erected above the principal spring. If these baths were in Europe, they would rival all those now existing. The valley in which the lake is situated, is so sheltered, and so warm, that dates, lemon-trees, oranges, and indigo, flourish there, whilst on the high ground surrounding it, the products of more temperate climates might be grown."

South-west of the lake are the remains of the ancient city of Tarichæa. There, between two mountain chains, lies the beautiful plain of El Ghor, poorly cultivated, and overrun by Arab hordes. No incident of moment marked Seetzen's journey to Decapolis, during which he was obliged to dress as a mendicant, to escape the rapacity of the native tribes.

"Over my shirt" he relates, "I wore an old kambas, or dressing-gown, and above that a woman's ragged chemise; my head was covered with rags, and my feet with old sandals. I was protected from cold and wet by an old ragged 'abbaje,'which I wore across my shoulders, and a stick cut from a tree served me as a staff; my guide, who was a Greek Christian, was dressed much in the same style; and together we scoured the country for some ten days, often hindered in our journey by chilling rains, which wetted us to the skin. For my part, I travelled an entire day in the mud with bare feet, because I could not wear my sandals upon sodden ground."

Draa which he reached a little farther on, presented but a mass of desert ruins; and no trace of the monuments which rendered it famous in earlier days,were visible. El-Botthin, the next district, contains hundreds of caverns, hewn in the rocks, which were occupied by the ancient inhabitants. It was much the same at Seetzen's visit. That Mkês was formerly a rich and important city, is proved by its many ruined tombs and monuments. Seetzen identified it with Gadara, one of the minor towns of the Decapolis. Some leagues beyond are the ruins of Abil or Abila. Seetzen's guide, Aoser, refused to go there, being afraid of the Arabs. The traveller was, therefore, obliged to go alone.

"This town," he says, "is entirely in ruins and abandoned. Not a single building remains; but its ancient splendour is sufficiently proved by ruins. Traces of the old fortifications remain, and also many pillars and arches of marble, basalt, and granite. Beyond the walls, I found a great number of pillars; two of them were of an extraordinary size. Hence I concluded that a large temple had formerly existed there."

On leaving El-Botthin, Seetzen entered the district of Edschlun, and speedily discovered the important ruins of Dscherrasch, which may be compared with those of Palmyra and Baalbek.

"It is difficult to conjecture," says Seetzen, "how this town, which was formerly so celebrated, has hitherto escaped the attention of antiquarians. It is situated in an open plain, which is fertile, and watered by a river. Several tombs, with fine bas-reliefs arrested my attention before I entered it; upon one of them, I remarked a Greek inscription. The walls, which were of cut marble, are entirely crumbled away, but their length over three quarters of a league, is still discernible. No private house has been preserved, but I remarked several public buildings of fine architectural design. I found two magnificent amphitheatres constructed of solid marble, the columns, niches, &c., in good condition, a few palaces, and three temples; one of the latter having a peristyle of twelve large Corinthian pillars, of which eleven were still erect. In one of these temples I found a fallen column of the finest polished Egyptian granite. Beside these, I found one of the city gates, formed of three arches, and ornamented with pilasters, in good preservation. The finest of the remains is a street adorned throughout its length with Corinthian columns on either side, and terminating in a semicircle, which was surrounded by sixty Ionic columns, all of the choicest marble. This street was crossed by another, and at the junction of the two, large pedestals of wrought stone occupied each angle, probably in former times these bore statues. Much of the pavement was constructed of hewn stone. Altogether I counted nearly two hundred columns, still in a fair state of preservation; but the number of these is far exceeded by those which have fallen into decay, for I saw only half the extent of the town, and in all probability the other half beyond this was also rich in remarkable relics."

From Seetzen's description, Dscherrasch would appear to be identical with the ancient Gerasa, a town which up to that time had been erroneously placed on the maps.

The traveller crossed Gerka—the Jabok of Jewish history—which forms the northern boundary of the country of the Ammonites, and penetrated into the district of El-Belka, formerly a flourishing country, but which he found uncultivated and barren, with but one small town, Szalt, formerly known as Amathus. Afterwards Seetzen visited Amman, a town which, under the name of Philadelphia, is renowned among the decapolitan cities, and where many antiquities are to be found, Eleal, an ancient city of the Amorites, Madaba, called Madba in the time of Moses, Mount Nebo, Diban, Karrak, the country of the Moabites, and the ruins of Robba, (Rabbath) anciently the royal residence. After much fatigue, he reached the region situated at the southern extremity of the Dead Sea, named Gor-es-Sophia.

The heat was extreme, and great salt-plains, where no watercourses exist, had to be crossed. Upon the 6th of April, Seetzen arrived in Bethlehem, and soon afterwards at Jerusalem, having suffered greatly from thirst, but having passed through most interesting countries, hitherto unvisited by any modern traveller.

Jerusalem.

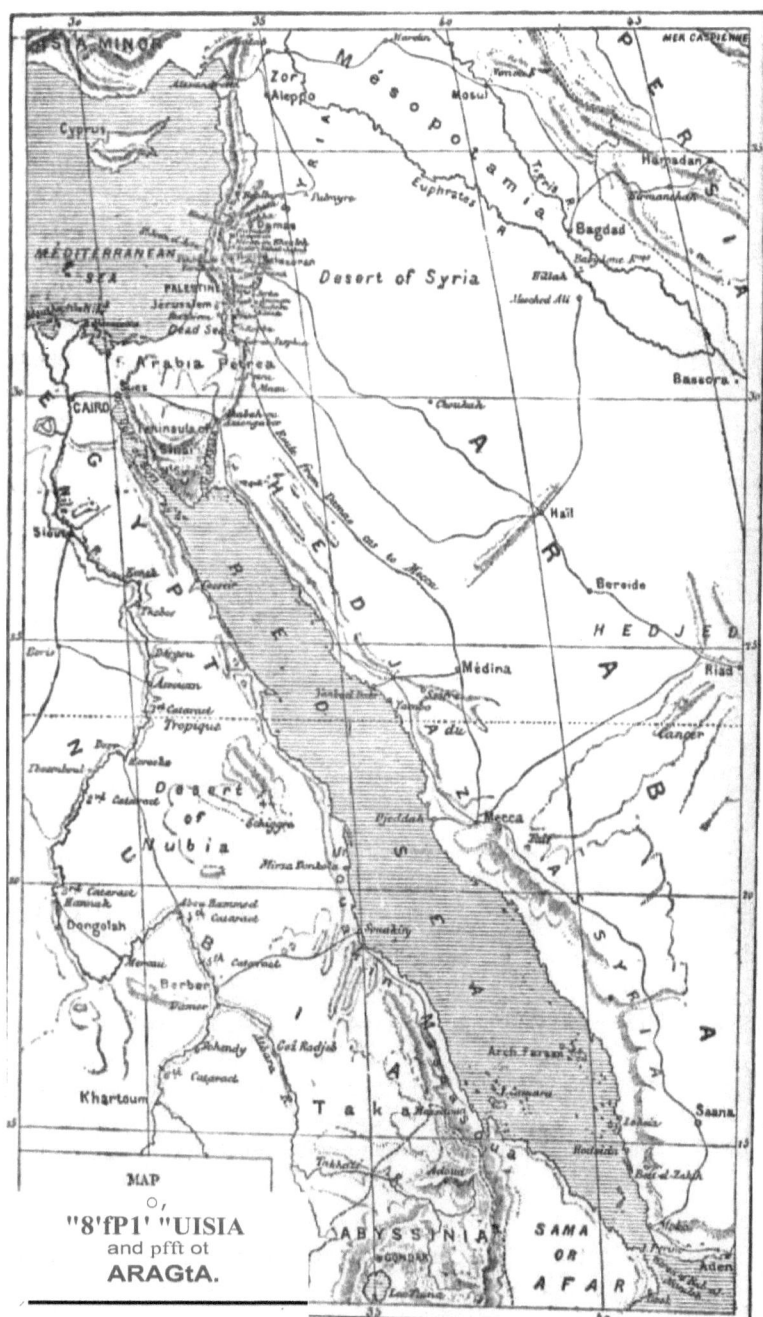

MAP
o,
"8'fP1' "UISIA
and pfft ot
ARAGtA.

21

He had also collected much valuable information respecting the nature of the waters of the Dead Sea, refuted many false notions, corrected mistakes upon the most carefully constructed maps, identified several sites of the ancient Peræa, and established the existence of numberless ruins, which bore witness to the prosperity of all this region under the sway of the Roman Empire. Upon the 25th of June, 1806, Seetzen left Jerusalem, and returned to St. Jean d'Acre by sea.

In an article in the *Revùe Germanique* for 1858, M. Vinen speaks of his expedition as a veritable journey of discovery. Seetzen, however, was unwilling to leave his discoveries incomplete. Ten months later, he again visited the Dead Sea, and added largely to his observations. From thence he proceeded to Cairo, where he remained for two years, and bought a large portion of the oriental manuscripts which now enrich the library of Gotha. He collected many facts about the interior of the country, choosing instinctively those only which could be amply substantiated.

Seetzen, with his insatiable thirst for discovery, could not remain long in repose, far removed from idleness though it was. In April, 1809, he finally left the capital of Egypt, and directed his course towards Suez and the peninsula of Sinai, which he resolved to explore before proceeding to Arabia. At this time Arabia was a little-known country, frequented only by merchants trading in Mocha coffee-beans. Before Niebuhr's time no scientific expedition for the study of the geography of the country or the manners and customs of the inhabitants had been organized.

This expedition owed its formation to Professor Michälis, who was anxious to obtain information which would throw light on certain passages in the Bible, and its expenses were defrayed by the generosity of King Frederick V. of Denmark. It comprised Von Hannen, the mathematician, Forskaal, the naturalist, a physician named Cramer, Braurenfeind, the painter, and Niebuhr, the engineer, a company of learned and scientific men, who thoroughly fulfilled all expectations founded upon their reputations.

In the course of two years, from 1762 to 1764, they visited Egypt, Mount Sinai, Jeddah, landed at Loheia, and advancing into Arabia Felix, explored the country in accordance with the speciality of each man. But the enterprising travellers succumbed to illness and fatigue, and Niebuhr alone survived to utilize the observations made by himself and his companions. His work on the subject is an inexhaustible treasury, which may be drawn upon in our own day with advantage.

Seetzen, therefore, had much to achieve to eclipse the fame of his predecessor. He omitted no means of doing so. After publicly professing the faith of Islam, he embarked at Suez for Mecca, and hoped to enter that city disguised as a pilgrim. Tor and Jeddah were the places visited by him before he travelled to the holy city of Mecca. He was much impressed by the wealth of the faithful and the peculiar characteristics of that city, which lives for and by the Mahometan cultus. "I was seized," says the traveller, "with an emotion which I have never experienced elsewhere."

It is alike unnecessary to dwell upon this portion of the voyage and upon that relating to the excursion to Medina. Burckhardt's narrative gives a precise and trustworthy account of those holy places, and besides, there remain of Seetzen's works only the extracts published in "Les Annales des Voyages," and in the Correspondence of the Baron de Zach. The Journal of Seetzen's travels was published in German, and in a very incomplete manner, only in 1858.

The traveller returned from Medina to Mecca, and devoted himself to a secret study of the town, with its religious ceremonies, and to taking astronomical observations, which determined the position of the capital of Islam.

Seetzen returned to Jeddah on the 23rd March, 1810. He then re-embarked, with the Arab who had been his guide to Mecca, for Hodeidah, which is one of the principal ports of Yemen. Passing the mountainous district of Beith-el-Fakih, where coffee is cultivated, after a month's delay at Doran on account of illness, Seetzen entered Sana, the capital of Yemen, which he calls the most beautiful city of the East, on the 2nd of June. Upon the 22nd of July he reached Aden, and in November he was at Mecca, whence the last letters received from him are dated. Upon re-entering Yemen, he, like Niebuhr, was robbed of his collections and baggage, upon the pretext that he collected animals, in order to compose a philtre, with the intention of poisoning the springs.

Seetzen, however, would not quietly submit to be robbed. He started at once for Sana, intending to lay a complaint before the Iman. This was in December, 1811. A few days later news of his sudden death arrived at Taes, and the tidings soon reached the ears of the Europeans who frequented the Arabian ports.

It is little to the purpose now to inquire upon whom the responsibility of this death rests—whether upon the Iman or upon those who had plundered the traveller—but we may well regret that so thorough an explorer, already familiar with the habits and customs of the Arabs, was unable to continue his explorations, and that the greater portion of his diaries and observations have been entirely lost.

"Seetzen," says M. Vivien de Saint Martin, "was the first traveller since

Ludovico Barthema (1503) who visited Mecca, and before his time no European had even seen the holy city of Medina, consecrated by the tomb of the Prophet."

From these remarks we gather how invaluable the trustworthy narrative of this disinterested and well-informed traveller would have been.

Just as an untimely death ended Seetzen's self-imposed mission, Burckhardt set out upon a similar enterprise, and like him commenced his long and minute exploration of Arabia by preliminary travel through Syria.

"It is seldom in the history of science," says M. Vivien de Saint Martin, "that we see two men of such merit succeed each other in the same career or rather continue it; for in reality Burckhardt followed up the traces Seetzen had opened out, and, seconded for a considerable time by favourable circumstances which enabled him to prosecute his explorations, he was enabled to add very considerably to the known discoveries of his predecessor."

Although John Lewis Burckhardt was not English, for he was a native of Lausanne, he must none the less be classed among the travellers of Great Britain. It was owing to his relations with Sir Joseph Banks, the naturalist who had accompanied Cook, and Hamilton, the secretary of the African Association, who gave him ready and valuable support, that Burckhardt was enabled to accomplish what he did.

Burckhardt was a deeply learned man. He had passed through the universities of Leipzic, and Göttingen, where he attended Blumenbach's lectures, and afterwards through Cambridge, where he studied Arabic. He started for the East in 1809. To inure himself to the hardships of a traveller's life, he imposed long fasts upon himself, accustomed himself to endure thirst, and chose the pavements of London or dusty roads for a resting-place. But how trifling were these experiences in comparison with those involved in an apostolate of science!

Leaving London for Syria, where he hoped to perfect his knowledge of Arabic, Burckhardt intended to proceed to Cairo and to reach Fezzan by the route formerly opened up by Hornemann. Once arrived in that country, circumstances must determine his future course.

Burckhardt, having taken the name of Ibrahim-Ibn-Abdallah, intended to pass as an Indian Mussulman. In order to carry out this disguise, he had recourse to many expedients. In an obituary notice of him in the "Annales des Voyages," it is related that when unexpectedly called upon to speak the Indian language, he immediately had recourse to German. An Italian dragoman, suspecting him of being a giaour, pulled him by his beard, thereby offering him the greatest insult possible in his character of Mussulman. But Burckhardt had so thoroughly entered into the spirit of his rôle, that he responded by a vigorous blow, which sending the unfortunate dragoman spinning to a distance, turned the laugh against him, and thoroughly convinced the bystanders of the sincerity of the traveller.

Portrait of Burckhardt.
(Fac-simile of early engraving.)

Burckhardt remained at Aleppo from September, 1809, to February, 1812, pursuing his studies of Syrian manners and customs, and of the language of the country, with but one interruption, a six months' excursion to Damascus, Palmyra, and the Hauran, a country which had hitherto been visited by Seetzen only.

It is related that, during an excursion into Gor, a district north of Aleppo, upon the shores of the Euphrates, the traveller was robbed of his baggage and stripped of his clothes by a band of robbers. When nothing remained to him but his trousers, the wife of a chief, who had not received her share of the spoil, wished to relieve him even of those indispensable garments!

The *Revue Germanique* says:—"We owe a great deal of information to these excursions, respecting a country of which we had only crude notions, gained from Seetzen's incomplete communications. Burckhardt's power of close observation detected a number of interesting facts, even in well-known districts, which had escaped the notice of other travellers. These materials were published by Colonel Martin William Leake, himself a geographer, a man of learning, and a distinguished traveller."

Burckhardt had seen Palmyra and Baalbek, the slopes of Lebanon and the valley of the Orontes, Lake Huleh, and the sources of the Jordan; he had discovered many ancient sites; and his observations had led especially to the discovery of the site of the far-famed Apamoea, although both he and his publisher were mistaken in their application of the data obtained. His excursions in the Auranitis were equally rich, even though coming after Seetzen's, in those geographical and archæological details which represent the actual condition of a country, and throw a light upon the comparative geography of every age.

Leaving Damascus in 1813, Burckhardt visited the Dead Sea, the valley of Akâba, and the ancient port of Azcongater, districts which in our own day are traversed by parties of English, with their *Murray*, *Cook*, or *Bædeker* in their hands; but which then were only to be visited at the risk of life. In a lateral valley, the traveller came upon the ruins of Petra, the ancient capital of Arabia Petræa.

At the end of the year Burckhardt was at Cairo. Judging it best not to join the caravan which was just starting for Fezzan, he felt a great inclination to visit Nubia, a country rich in attractions for the historian, geographer, and archæologist. Nubia, the cradle of Egyptian civilization, had only been visited, since the days of the Portuguese Alvares, by Poncet and Lenoir Duroule, both Frenchmen, at the close of the seventeenth century, at the opening of the eighteenth by Bruce, whose narrative had so often been doubted, and by Norden, who had not penetrated beyond Derr.

In 1813 Burckhardt explored Nubia proper, including Mahass and Kemijour.

This expedition cost him only forty-two francs, a very paltry sum in comparison with the price involved in the smallest attempt at an African journey in our own day; but we must not forget that Burckhardt was content to live upon millet-seed, and that his entire *cortége* consisted of two dromedaries.

Two Englishmen, Mr. Legh and Mr. Smelt, were travelling in the country at the same time, scattering gold and presents as they passed, and thus rendering the visits of their successors costly.

Burckhardt crossed the cataracts of the Nile. "A little farther on," says the narrative, "near a place called Djebel-Lamoule, the Arab guides practise a curious extortion." This is their plan of proceeding. They halt, descend from their camels, and arrange a little heap of sand and pebbles, in imitation of a Nubian tomb. This they, call *"preparing the grave for the traveller"* and follow up the demonstration by an imperious demand for money. Burckhardt having watched his guide commence this operation, began quietly to imitate him, and then said, "Here is thy grave; as we are brothers, it is but fair that we should be buried together." The Arab could not help laughing, both graves were simultaneously destroyed, and remounting the camels, the cavalcade proceeded, better friends than before. The Arab quoted a saying from the Koran: "No human being knows in what spot of the earth he will find his grave."

"Here is thy grave."

Burckhardt had hoped to get as far as Dingola, but was obliged to rest satisfied with collecting information about the country and the Mamelukes, who had taken refuge there after the massacre of their army by order of the viceroy of Egypt.

The attention of the traveller was frequently directed to the ruins of temples and ancient cities, than which none are more curious than those of Isambul.

"The temple on the banks of the Nile is approached by an avenue flanked by six colossal figures, which measure six feet and a half from the ground to the knees. They are representations of Isis and Osiris, in various attitudes. The sides and capitals of the pillars are covered with paintings or hieroglyphic carvings, in which Burckhardt thought a very ancient style was to be traced. All these are hewn out of the rock, and the faces appear to have been painted yellow, with black hair. Two hundred yards from this temple are the ruins of a still larger monument, consisting of four enormous figures, so deeply buried in the sand that it is impossible to say whether they are in a standing or sitting posture."

These descriptions of antiquities, which in our own day are accurately known by drawings and photographs, have, however, little value for us; and are merely interesting as indicating the state of the ruins when Burckhardt visited them, and enabling us to judge how far the depredations of the Arabs have since changed them.

Burckhardt's first excursion was limited to the borders of the Nile, a narrow space made up of little valleys, which debouched into the river. The traveller estimated the population of the country at 100,000, distributed over a surface of fertile land 450 miles in length, by a quarter of a mile in width.

"The men," says the narrative, "are, as a rule, muscular, rather shorter than the Egyptians, having little beard or moustache, usually merely a pointed beard under the chin. They have a pleasant expression, are superior to the Egyptians in courage and intelligence, and naturally inquisitive. They are not thieves. They occasionally pick up a fortune by dint of hard work, but they have little enterprise. Women share the same physical advantages, are pretty as a rule, and well made; their appearance is gentle and pleasing, and they are modest in behaviour. M. Denon has underrated the Nubians, but it must not be forgotten that their physique varies in different districts. Where there is much land to cultivate, they are well developed; but in districts where arable land is a mere strip, the people diminish in vigour, and are sometimes walking skeletons."

The whole country groaned under the yoke of the Kashefs, who were descendants of the commander of the Bosniacs, and paid only a small annual tribute to Egypt, which, however, was sufficient to serve as a pretext for oppressing the unfortunate fellaheen. Burckhardt cites a curious example of the insolence with which the Kashefs behaved.

"Hassan Kashef," he says, was in need of barley for his horses. Accompanied by his slaves, he walked into the fields, and there met the owner of a fine plot of barley. "How badly you cultivate your land," said he. "Here you plant barley in a field where you might have reaped an excellent crop of water- melons of double the value. See, here are some melon-seeds (offering a handful to the peasant proprietor); sow your field with these; and you, slaves, tear up this bad barley and bring it to me."

In March, 1814, after a short rest, Burckhardt undertook a fresh exploration, not this time of the banks of the Nile, but of the Nubian desert. Justly conceiving poverty to be his surest safe guard, he dismissed his servant, sold his camel, and contenting himself with one ass, joined a caravan of poor traders. The caravan started from Daraou, a village inhabited partly by fellahs and partly by Ababdéh Arabs. The traveller had good reason to complain of the former, not because they recognized him as a European, but because they imagined him to be a Syrian Turk, come to share the commerce in slaves of which they had the monopoly.

It would be useless to enumerate the names of the bridges, hills, and valleys in this desert. We will rather summarize the traveller's report of the physical aspect of the country.

Bruce, who had explored it, paints it in too gloomy colours, and exaggerates the difficulties of the route. If Burckhardt is to be credited, the country is less barren than that between Aleppo and Bagdad, or Damascus and Medina. The Nubian desert is not merely a plain of sand, where nothing interrupts the dreary monotony. It is interspersed with rocks, some not less than 300 feet in height, and shaded by thickets of acacias or date-trees. The shelter of these trees is, however, unavailing against the vertical rays of the sun, which explains an Arabic proverb, "Rely upon the favour of the great and the shade of an acacia."

At Ankheyre, or Wady-Berber, the caravan reached the Nile, after passing Shigre, one of the best mountain springs. One danger only is to be feared in crossing the desert; that of finding the wells at Nedjeym dry; and, unless the traveller should lose his way, which, however, with trustworthy guides, is little likely to happen, no serious obstacle arises.

It would appear, therefore, that the sufferings experienced by Bruce must have been greatly exaggerated, although the narrative of the Scotch traveller is generally trustworthy. The natives of the province of Berber appear to be identical with the Barbarins of Bruce, the Barabas mentioned by D'Anville, and the Barauras spoken of by Poncet. They are a well-made race, and different in feature from the negroes. They maintain their purity of descent by marrying only with the women of their own or of kindred tribes. Curious as is the picture Burckhardt draws of the character and manners of this tribe, it is not at all edifying. It would be difficult to convey an idea of the corruption and degradation of the Berbers. The little town of Wady-Berber, a commercial centre, the rendezvous for caravans, and a depôt for slaves, is a regular resort of banditti.

Burckhardt, who had trusted to the protection of the merchants of Daraou, found that he had made a great mistake in so doing. They sought every means of plundering him, chased him out of their company, and forced him to seek refuge with the guides and donkey-drivers, who cordially welcomed him.

Upon the 10th of April a fine was levied upon the caravan by the Mek of Damer, which lies a little south of the tributary Mogren (called Mareb by Bruce). This is a well-kept and cleanly Fakir village, which contrasts agreeably with the ruins and filth of Berber. The Fakirs give themselves up to the practices of sorcery, magic, and charlatanism. One of them, it is said, could even make a lamb bleat in the stomach of the man who had stolen and eaten it! These ignorant people have entire faith in such fables, and it must be reluctantly admitted that the fact contributes not a little to the peace of the town and the prosperity of the country.

From Damer, Burckhardt proceeded to Shendy, where he passed a month, during which time no one suspected him to be an infidel. Shendy had grown in importance since Bruce's visit, and now consisted of about a thousand houses. Considerable trade was carried on—grass, slaves, and cattle taking the place of specie. The principal marketable commodities were gum, ivory, gold, and ostrich feathers.

According to Burckhardt, the number of slaves sold yearly at Shendy amounts to 5000; 2500 of these are for Arabia, 400 for Egypt, 1000 for Dongola and the districts of the Red Sea.

The traveller employed his time during his stay at Sennaar in collecting information about that kingdom. Amongst other curious things, he was told that the king having one day invited the ambassador of Mehemet Ali to a cavalry review, which he considered rather formidable, the envoy in his turn begged the king to witness part of the Turkish artillery exercises. But at the outset of the performance—at the discharge of two small mounted guns—cavalry, infantry, spectators, courtiers, and the king himself, fled in terror.

Burckhardt sold his wares, and then, worn out by the persecutions of the Egyptian merchants who were his companions, he joined the caravan at Suakin, intending to traverse the unknown district between that town and Shendy. From Suakin he meant to set out for Mecca, hoping to find the Hadji useful to him in the realization of his projects.

"The Hadji," he says, "form one powerful body, and every member is protected, because if one is attacked the whole number take up arms." The caravan which Burckhardt now joined consisted of 150 merchants and 300 slaves. Two hundred camels were employed to convey heavy bales of "danmour," a stuff manufactured in Sennaar, and cargoes of tobacco.

The first object of interest to the travellers was the Atbara, a tributary of the Nile, whose banks, with their verdant trees, were grateful to the eye after the sandy desert. The course of the river was followed as far as the fertile district of Taka. During the journey the white skin of the pretended sheik Ibrahim (it will be remembered that this was the name assumed by Burckhardt) attracted much attention from the female population, who were little accustomed to the sight of Arabs.

"One day," relates the traveller, "a girl of the country, of whom I had been buying onions, offered to give me an extra quantity if I would remove my turban, and show her my head. I demanded eight more onions, which she immediately produced. As I removed my turban, and exposed my white and close-shaven head to view, she sprang back in horror and dismay. I asked her jokingly if she would not like a husband with a similar head, to which she replied with much energy, and many expressions of disgust, that she would prefer the ugliest slave ever brought from Darfur."

Just before Goz Radjeh was reached, Burckhardt's attention was attracted to a building, which he was told was either a church or temple, the same word having the two meanings. He at once proceeded in that direction, hoping to examine it, but his companions stopped him, saying, "It is surrounded by bands of robbers; you cannot go a hundred steps without danger of attack."

Burckhardt was unable to decide whether it was an Egyptian temple, or a monument of the empire of Axum.

At last the caravan entered the fertile district of Tak or El Gasch, a wide watered plain, whose soil is wonderfully fertile, but which for two months in the year is uninhabited. Grain is plentiful and is sold in Jeddah for twenty per cent. more than the best Egyptian millet.

The inhabitants, who are called Hadendoa, are treacherous, dishonest, and bloodthirsty; and their women are almost as degraded as those of Shendy and Berber.

Upon leaving Taka, the road to Suakin and the shores of the Red Sea lay over a chain of chalk hills. At Schenterab granite is found. The hills presented few difficulties, and the caravan reached Suakin in safety upon the 26th May. But Burckhardt's troubles were not yet at an end. The Emir and Aga combined to plunder him, and treated him as the lowest of slaves, until he produced the firman which he had received from Mehemet Ali and Ibrahim Pasha. This changed the face of affairs. Instead of being thrown into prison the traveller was invited to the Aga's, who offered him a present of a young slave. M. Vivien de Saint Martin writes of this expedition, "This journey of from twenty to twenty-five days, between the Nile and the Red Sea, was the first ever undertaken by a European. The observations collected, as to the settled or nomad tribes of these districts are invaluable for Europe. Burckhardt's narrative is of increasing interest, and few can compare with it for instruction and interest."

Upon the 7th of July Burckhardt succeeded in embarking in a boat, and eleven days later he reached Jeddah, which serves as a harbour to Mecca. Jeddah is built upon the sea-shore, and is surrounded by a wall, which, insufficient as it would be against artillery, protects it perfectly from the attacks of the Wahabees, who have been nicknamed the "Puritans of Islamism." These people are a distinct sect, who claim to restore Mahomedanism to its primitive simplicity.

"The entrance to the town, upon the side nearest the sea," says Burckhardt, "is protected by a battery which overlooks the entire fort, and is surmounted by one enormous piece of artillery capable of discharging a five-hundred pound shot, which is so renowned throughout the Arabian Gulf, that its reputation alone is enough to protect Jeddah."

The greatest drawback to this city is its want of fresh water, which is brought from small wells two miles distant. Without gardens, vegetables, or date-trees, Jeddah, in spite of its population of twelve or fifteen thousand (a number which is doubled in the pilgrimage season) presents a strange appearance. The population is the reverse of autochthonous; it is composed of natives of Hadramaut and Yemen, Indians from Surat and Bombay, and Malays who come as pilgrims and settle in the town. Burckhardt introduces many anecdotes of interest into his account of the manners, mode of living, price of commodities, and number of traders in the place.

Merchant of Jeddah.
(Fac-simile of early engraving.)

Speaking of the singular customs of the natives of Jeddah, he says:—"It is the almost universal custom for everybody to swallow a cup full of ghee or melted butter in the morning. After this they take coffee, which they regard as a strong tonic; and they are so accustomed to this habit from their earliest years, that they feel greatly inconvenienced if they discontinue it. The higher classes are satisfied with drinking the cup of butter, but the lower classes add another half cup, which they draw up through the nostrils, imagining that they thus prevent bad air entering the body by those apertures."

The traveller left Jeddah for Tayf on the 24th of August. The road winds over mountains and across valleys of romantic beauty and luxuriant verdure. Burckhardt was taken for an English spy at Tayf, and, although he was well received by the Pasha, he had no liberty, and could not carry on his observations.

Tayf, it appears, is famous for the beauty of its gardens; roses and grapes are sent from it into all the districts of Hedjaz. This town had a considerable trade, and was very prosperous before it was plundered by the Wahabees.

Shores and boats of the Red Sea.

The surveillance to which he was subjected hastened Burckhardt's departure, and upon the 7th of September he started for Mecca. Well versed in the study of the Koran, and acquainted with all the practices of Islamism, he was prepared to act the part of a pilgrim. His first care was to dress himself in accordance with the law prescribed for the faithful who enter Mecca—in the "ihram," or pieces of cloth without seam, one covering the loins, the other thrown over the neck and shoulders. The pilgrim's first duty is to proceed to the temple, without waiting even to procure a lodging. This Burckhardt did not fail to do, observing at the same time the rites and ceremonies prescribed in such cases, of which he gives many interesting particulars; we cannot, however, dwell upon them here.

"Mecca," says Burckhardt, "may be called a pretty town. As a rule, the streets are wider than in most Eastern cities. The houses are lofty and built of stone; and its numerous windows, opening upon the street, give it a more cheerful and European aspect than the cities of Egypt or Syria, whose dwellings generally have few windows on the outside. Every house has a terrace built of stone, and sloping in such a way as to allow water to run down the gutters into the street. Low walls with parapets conceal these terraces; for, as everywhere else in the East, it is not thought right for a man to appear there; he would be accused of spying upon the women, who spend much of their time upon the terrace of the house, engaged in domestic work, drying corn, hanging out linen, &c."

The only public place in the city is the large court of the Grand Mosque. Trees are rare; not a garden enlivens the view, and the scene depends for animation upon the well-stocked shops which abound during the pilgrimage. With the exception of four or five large houses belonging to the administration, two colleges, which have since been converted into warehouses for corn, and the mosque with the few buildings and colleges connected with it, Mecca can boast of no public buildings, and cannot compete in this respect with other cities in the East of the same size.

The streets are unpaved; and as drains are unknown, water collects in puddles, and the accumulation of mud is inconceivable. For a water supply the natives trust to heaven, catching the rain in cisterns, for that obtained from the wells is so foul that it is impossible to drink it.

In the centre of the town, where the valley widens a little, the mosque known as Beithóu'llah, or El Haram, is situated. This edifice owes its fame to the Kaaba which is enclosed in it, for other Eastern towns can boast of mosques equally large and more beautiful. El Haram is situated in an oblong space, surrounded on the eastern side by a quadruple colonnade, and by a triple one on the other. The columns are connected by pointed arches, upon each four stand little domes constructed of mortar and whitened outside. Some of these columns are of white marble, granite, or porphyry, but the greater part are of the common stone found among the mountains of Mecca.

The Kaaba has been so often ruined and restored that no trace of a remote antiquity remains. It was in existence before this mosque was built.

The traveller says, "The Kaaba is placed upon an inclined base some two feet high, and its roof being flat, it presents the appearance at a little distance of a perfect cube. The only door by which it can be entered, and which is opened two or three times a year, is on the north side, about seven feet above the ground, for which reason one cannot enter except by means of a wooden staircase. The famous 'black stone' is enshrined at the north-eastern corner of the Kaaba, near the door, and forms one of the angles of the building four or five feet above the floor of the court. It is difficult to ascertain the exact nature of this stone, as its surface has been completely worn and reduced to its present condition by the kisses and worshipping touches bestowed upon it by countless millions of pilgrims. The Kaaba is entirely covered with black silk, which envelopes its sides, leaving the roof exposed. This veil or curtain is called 'the Kesoua,' and is renewed yearly during the pilgrimage. It is brought from Cairo, where it is manufactured at the expense of the Viceroy."

Up to the time of Burckhardt no such detailed account of Mecca and her sanctuary had been given to the world. For this reason we shall insert extracts from the original narrative; extracts which might indeed be multiplied, for they include circumstantial accounts of the sacred well, called Zemzem, water from which is considered as an infallible remedy for every complaint. The traveller speaks also of the "Gate of Salvation," of the Makam Ibrahim, a monument containing the stone upon which Abraham sat when he was engaged in building the Kaaba, and where the marks of his knees may still be seen, and of all the buildings enclosed within the temple precincts.

Judging from Burckhardt's minute and complete description, these spots still retain their former physiognomy. The same number of pilgrims chant the same songs; the men only are no longer the same. His accounts of the feast of the pilgrimage and the holy enthusiasm of the faithful, are followed by a picture which brings before us, in the most sombre colours, the effects of this great gathering of men, attracted from every part of the world.

"The termination of the pilgrimage," he says, "lends a very different aspect to the mosque. Illness and death, consequent upon the great fatigues undergone during the voyage, are accelerated by the scanty covering afforded by the Ihram, the unhealthy dwellings of Mecca, the bad food, and frequent absolute dearth of provisions. The temple is filled with corpses brought thither to receive the prayers of the Iman, or with sick persons who insist upon being carried, as their last hours approach, to the colonnade, hoping to be saved by the sight of the Kaaba, or in any case to have the consolation of expiring within the sacred precincts. One sees poor pilgrims, sinking under illness and hunger, dragging their weary bodies along the colonnade; and when they no longer have the strength to stretch out a hand to the passer-by, they place a little jar beside the mat upon which they are laid, to receive what charity may bestow upon them. As they feel the last moment approach, they cover themselves with their ragged clothes, and very often a day passes before it is ascertained that they are dead."

We will conclude our extracts from Burckhardt's account of Mecca with his opinion of the inhabitants.

"Although the natives of Mecca possess grand qualities, although they are pleasant, hospitable, cheerful and proud, they openly transgress the Koran by drinking, gambling, and smoking. Deceit and perjury are no longer looked upon as crimes by them; they do not ignore the scandal such vices bring upon them; but while each individually exclaims against the corruption of manners, none reform themselves."

Upon the 15th of January, 1815, Burckhardt left Mecca with a caravan of pilgrims on their way to visit the tomb of the prophet. The journey to Medina, like that between Mecca and Jeddah, was accomplished at night, and afforded little opportunity for observation. In the winter night-travelling is less comfortable than travelling by day. A valley called Wady-Fatme, but generally known as El-Wadi, was crossed; it abounded in shrubs and date-trees, and was well cultivated in the eastern portion. A little beyond it lies the valley of Es-Ssafra, the market of the neighbouring tribes and celebrated for its plantations of dates.

The traveller relates that "The groves of date-trees extend for nearly four miles, and belong to the natives of Ssafra as well as to the Bedouins of the neighbourhood, who employ labourers to water the ground, and come themselves to reap the harvest. The date-trees pass from one person to another in the course of trade; they are sold separately. A father often receives three date-trees as the price of the daughter he gives in marriage. They are all planted in deep sand brought from the middle of the valley, and piled up over their roots; they ought to be renewed every year, and they are generally swept away by the torrents. Each little plot is surrounded by a wall of mud or stone, and the cultivators live in hamlets or isolated cabins among the trees. The principal stream flows through a grove near the market; beside it rises a little mosque, shaded by large chestnuts. I had seen none before in the Hedjaz."

Burckhardt was thirteen days in reaching Medina. But this rather long journey was not lost time to him; he collected much information about the Arabs and the Wahabees. At Medina, as at Mecca, the pilgrim's first duty is to visit the tomb and mosque of Mahomet; but the ceremonies attending the visit are much easier and shorter, and the traveller performed them in a quarter of an hour.

Burckhardt's stay at Mecca had already been prejudicial to him. At Medina he was attacked by intermittent fever, which increased in violence, and was accompanied by violent sickness. This soon so reduced him, that he could no longer rise from his carpet without the assistance of his slave, "a poor fellow who by nature and habit was more fit to tend camels than to take care of his worn-out and enfeebled master."

Burckhardt being detained at Medina for more than three months by a fever, due to bad climate, the detestable quality of the water, and the prevalence of infectious illnesses, was forced to relinquish his project of crossing the desert to Akabah, in order to reach Yanibo as quickly as possible, and from thence embark for Egypt.

"Next to Aleppo," he says, "Medina is the best-built town I have seen in the East. It is entirely of stone, the houses being generally three stories high, with flat tops. As they are not whitewashed, and the stone is brown in colour, the streets, which are very narrow, have usually a sombre appearance. They are often only two or three paces wide. At the present time Medina looks desolate enough; the houses are falling into ruins. Their owners, who formerly derived a considerable profit from the inroad of pilgrims, find their revenues diminishing, as the Wahabees forbid visitors to the tomb of the prophet, alleging that he was but a mere mortal. The possession which places Medina on a par with Mecca is the Grand Mosque, containing the tomb of Mahomet. This is smaller than that at Mecca, but is built upon the same plan, in a large square courtyard, surrounded on all sides by covered galleries, and having a small building in the centre. The famous tomb, surrounded by an iron railing painted green, is near the eastern corner. It is of good workmanship, in imitation of filagree, and interlaced with inscriptions in copper. Four doors, of which three lead into this enclosure, are kept constantly shut. Permission to enter is freely accorded to persons of rank, and others can purchase permission of the principal eunuchs for about fifteen piasters. In the interior are hangings which surround the tomb, and are only a few feet from it." According to the historian of Medina, these hangings cover a square edifice, built of black stones, and supported upon two columns, in the interior of which are the sepulchres of Mahomet and his two eldest disciples, Abou-Bekr and Omar. He also states that these sepulchres are deep holes, and that the coffin which contains the ashes of Mahomet is covered with silver, and surmounted by a marble slab with the inscription, "In the name of God, give him thy pity." The fables which were spread throughout Europe as to the tomb of the prophet being suspended in mid air, are unknown in the Hedjaz. The mosque was robbed of a great part of its treasures by the Wahabees, but there is some ground for believing that they had been forestalled by the successive guardians of the tomb.

Many other interesting details of Medina, and its inhabitants, surroundings, and the haunts of pilgrims, are to be found in Burckhardt's narrative. But we have given sufficient extracts to induce the reader who desires further information respecting the manners and customs of the Arabs, which have not changed, to refer to the book itself.

Upon the 21st of April, 1815, Burckhardt joined a caravan which conducted him to Yembo, where the plague was raging. The traveller at once fell ill and became so weak that it was impossible for him to resort to a country place. To embark was equally impossible; all the vessels which were ready to start were crowded with soldiers. He was compelled to remain eighteen days in the unhealthy little town, before he could obtain a passage in a small vessel which took him to Cosseir, and thence to Egypt.

Upon his return to Cairo Burckhardt heard of his father's death. The traveller's constitution had been sorely tried by illness, and he was unable to attempt the ascent of Mount Sinai until 1816. The study of natural history, the publication of his diary, and his correspondence, occupied him until 1817, at which time he expected to go with a caravan to Fezzan. Unfortunately he succumbed to a sudden attack of fever, his last words being, "Write and tell my mother that my last thought was of her."

Burckhardt was an accomplished traveller; well-informed, exact to minuteness, patient, courageous, and endowed with an upright and energetic character. His writings are of great value; the narrative of his voyage in Arabia—of which he unfortunately could not explore the interior—is so complete and precise, that owing to it that country was then better known than many in Europe.

In writing to his father from Cairo on the 13th of March, 1817, he says, "I have never said a word about what I have seen and met with that my conscience did not entirely justify; I did not expose myself to so much danger in order to write a romance!"

The explorers who have succeeded him in the same countries unanimously testify to his exactness, and agree in praising his fidelity, knowledge, and sagacity.

"Few travellers," says the *Revue Germanique*, "have enjoyed in a like degree the faculty of observation. That is a rare gift of nature, like all eminent qualities. He possessed a sort of intuition which discerned the truth, apart from his own observations, and thus information given by him from hearsay has a value that seldom attaches to statements of that nature. His mind, early ripened by reflection and study (he was but in his thirty-third year at the time of his death), invariably went straight to the point. His narrative, always sober, is filled—one may say—rather with things than words; yet his narratives possess infinite charm; one admires the man in them as much as the savant and observer."

While the Biblical countries occupied the attention of Seetzen and Burckhardt, India, the birthplace of most of the European languages, was about to command the attention of students of language, literature, and religion, as well as of geography. For the present our concern is with those problems of physical geography, which the conquests and studies of the India Company were about to solve by degrees.

In a preceding volume we have related how the Portuguese rule was established in India. The union of Portugal with Spain, in 1599, led to the fall of the Portuguese colonies, which came into the possession of the English and Dutch. England soon afterwards granted a monopoly of the commerce of India to a Company which was destined to play an important part in history.

At this time Akbar, the great Mogul emperor, the seventh descendant of Timour Leng, had established a vast empire in Hindustan and Bengal, upon the ruins of the Rajpoot kingdoms. Owing to the personal qualities of Akbar, which had gained for him the surname of the Benefactor of Man, that empire was at the height of its glory. The same brilliant course was pursued by Shah Jehan; but Akbar's grandson, Aurung Zeb, inspired by an insatiable ambition, assassinated his brothers, imprisoned his father, and seized the reins of government. While the Mogul Empire was in the enjoyment of profound peace, a clever adventurer laid the foundations of the Mahratta Empire. The religious intolerance of Aurung Zeb, and his crafty policy, led to the insurrection of the Rajpoots, and a struggle, which by draining the resources of the empire, shook his power. The death of the great usurper was followed by the decadence of the empire.

Up to this period the India Company had been unable to add to the narrow strip of territory which they possessed at the ports, but it was now to benefit by the conflict between the nabobs and rajahs of Hindustan. It was not, however, until after the taking of Madras, in 1746, by La Bourdonnais, and the struggle against Dupleix, that the influence and dominion of the English Company was materially increased.

The crafty policy of Clive and Hastings, the English Governors, who successively employed force, stratagem, and bribery, to attain their ends, laid the foundation of British greatness in India, and, at the close of the last century, the Company were possessors of an immense extent of country, with no less than sixty millions of inhabitants. Their territory included Bengal, Behar, the provinces of Benares, Madras, and the Sircars. Tippoo Saib alone, the Sultan of Mysore, struggled against the English encroachments, but he was unable to hold out against the coalition formed against him by the skill of Colonel Wellesley. When rid of their formidable enemies, the Company overcame such opposition as remained by pensions; and, under the pretext of protection, imposed upon the rajahs an English garrison which was maintained at their expense.

One would imagine from all this that the English rule was detested; but that is not the case. The Company, recognizing the rights of individuals, did not attempt to change the religion, laws, or customs of their subjects. Neither is it surprising that travellers, even when they ventured into districts which, properly speaking, did not belong to Great Britain, incurred but little danger. In fact, so soon as the East India Company was free from political embarrassments, it encouraged explorers throughout its vast domains. At the same time travellers were despatched to the neighbouring territories to collect observations, and we propose rapidly to review those expeditions.

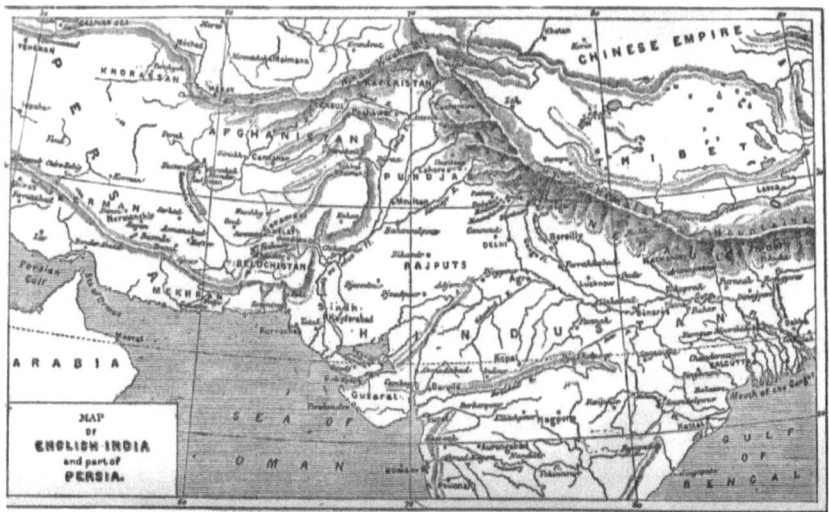

Gravé par E. Morieu.

One of the first and most curious was that of Webb to the sources of the Ganges, a river concerning which uncertain and contradictory opinions prevailed. The Government of Bengal, recognizing the great importance of the Ganges in the interests of commerce, organized an expedition, of which Messrs. Webb, Roper, and Hearsay, formed part. They were to be accompanied by Sepoys, native servants, and interpreters.

The expedition reached Herdouar, a small village on the left of the river, upon the 1st of April, 1808. The situation of this village, at the entrance of the fertile plains of Hindustan, had caused it to be much frequented by pilgrims, and it was at this spot that purifications in the waters of the holy river took place during the hot season.

As every pilgrimage implies the sale of relics, Herdouar was the centre of an important market, where horses, camels, antimony, asafoetida, dried fruits, shawls, arrows, muslins, cotton and woollen goods from the Punjab, Cabulistan, and Cashmere, were to be had. Slaves, too, were to be bought there from three to thirty years of age, at prices varying from 10 to 150 rupees. This fair, where such different races, languages, and costumes were to be met with, presented a curious spectacle.

Upon the 12th of April the English expedition set out for Gangautri, following a road planted with white mulberries and figs, as far as Gourondar. A little farther on water-mills of simple construction were at work, upon the banks of streams shaded with willows and raspberry-trees. The soil was fertile, but the tyranny of the Government prevented the natives from making the best of it.

The route soon became mountainous, but peach, apricot, nut, and other European trees abounded, and at length the expedition found themselves in the midst of a chain of mountains, which appeared to belong to the Himalaya range.

The Baghirati, which is known further on as the Ganges, was met with at the end of a pass. To the left, the river is bounded by high, almost barren mountains; to the right stretches a fertile valley. At the village of Tchiavli, the poppy is largely cultivated for the preparation of opium; here, owing probably, to the bad quality of the water, all the peasants suffer from wens.

At Djosvara the travellers had to cross a bridge of rope, called a "djorila." This was a strange and perilous structure.

"On either side of the river," says Webb, "two strong poles are driven in, at a distance of two feet from each other, and across them is placed another piece of wood. To this is attached a dozen or more thick ropes, which are held down upon the ground by large heaps of wood. They are divided into two packets, about a foot apart; Blow hangs a ladder of rope knotted to one of these, which answers instead of a parapet. The flooring of the bridge is composed of small branches of trees, placed at intervals of two and a half, or three feet from each other. As these are generally slender, they seem as if they were on the point of breaking every moment, which naturally induces the traveller to depend upon the support of the ropes which form the parapet, and to keep them constantly under their arms. The first step taken upon so shaky a structure is sufficient to cause giddiness, for the action of walking makes it swing to either side, and the noise of the torrent over which it is suspended is not reassuring. Moreover the bridge is so narrow, that if two persons meet upon it, one must draw completely to the side to make room for the other."

Bridge of rope.

The expedition afterwards passed through the town of Baharat, where but few of the houses have been rebuilt since the earthquake of 1803. This locality has always enjoyed a certain importance from the fact that a market is held there, and also on account of the difficulty of obtaining provisions in the towns higher up, as well as from its central position. The routes to Jemauhi, Kedar, Nath, and Sirinagur all meet there.

Beyond Batheri the road became so bad that the travellers were obliged to abandon their baggage. There was a mere path-track by the edge of precipices, amid débris of stones and rocks; and the attempt to proceed was soon relinquished.

Devaprayaga is situated at the junction of the Baghirati, and the Aluknanda. The first, coming from the north, hurries along with noise and impetuosity; the second, broader, deeper, and more tranquil, rises no less than forty-six feet above its ordinary level in the rainy season. The junction of these two rivers forms the Ganges, and is a sacred spot from which the Brahmins draw considerable profit, as they have arranged pools there, where for a certain price pilgrims can perform their ablutions without danger of being carried away by the current.

The Aluknanda was crossed by means of a running bridge, or "Dindla," which is thus described:—

"This bridge consists of three or four large ropes fixed upon either bank, and upon these a small seat some eighteen inches square is slung by means of hoops at either end. Upon this seat the traveller takes his place, and is drawn from one side of the river to the other by a rope pulled by the man upon the opposite bank."

The expedition reached Sirinagur upon the 13th of May. The curiosity of the inhabitants had been so much excited that the magistrates sent a message to the English begging them to march through the town.

Sirinagur, which had been visited by Colonel Hardwick in 1796, had been almost completely destroyed by the earthquake of 1803, and had in the same year been conquered by the Gorkhalis. Here Webb was joined by the emissaries whom he had sent to Gangautri by the route which he himself had been unable to follow, and who had visited the source of the Ganges.

"A large rock," he says, "on either side of which water flows, and which is very shallow, roughly resembles the body and mouth of a cow. A cavity at one end of its surface gave rise to its name of Gaoumokhi, the mouth of the cow, who, by its fancied resemblance, is popularly supposed to vomit the water of the sacred river. A little farther on, advance is impossible, a mountain as steep as a wall rises in front; the Ganges appeared to issue from the snow, which lay at its feet; the valley terminated here. No one has ever gone any farther."

The expedition returned by a different route. It met with the tributaries of the Ganges, and of the Keli Ganga, or Mandacni, rivers rising in the Mountains of Kerdar. Immense flocks of goats and sheep laden with grain were met with, numbers of defiles crossed, and after passing the towns of Badrinath and Manah the expedition finally reached the cascade of Barson, in the midst of heavy snow and intense cold.

"This," says Webb's narrative, "is the goal of the devotions of the pilgrims. Some of them come here to be sprinkled by the sacred spray of the cascade. At this spot the course of the Aluknanda may be traced as far as the south-western extremity of the valley, but its source is hidden under heaps of snow, which have probably been accumulating for centuries."

Webb furnishes some details respecting the women of Manah. They wore necklaces, earrings, and gold and silver ornaments, which were scarcely in keeping with their coarse attire. Some of the children wore necklaces and bracelets of silver to the value of six hundred rupees.

In winter, this town, which does a great trade with Thibet, is completely buried in snow, and the natives take refuge in neighbouring towns.

The expedition visited the temple at Badrinath, which is far-famed for its sanctity. Neither its internal nor external structure or appearance give any idea of the immense sums which are expended upon it. It is one of the oldest and most venerated sanctuaries of India. Ablutions are performed there in reservoirs fed with very warm sulphureous water.

"There are," says the narrative, "a great number of hot springs, each having their special name and virtue, and from all of them doubtless the Brahmins derive profit. For this reason, the poor pilgrim, as he gets through the requisite ablutions, finds his purse diminish with the number of his sins, and the many tolls exacted from him upon the road to paradise might induce him to consider the narrow way by no means the least expensive one. This temple possesses seven hundred villages, which have either been ceded to it by government, given as security for loans, or bought by private individuals and given as offerings."

The expedition reached Djosimah on the 1st of June. There the Brahmin who acted as guide received orders from the government of Nepaul, to conduct the travellers back immediately to the territories of the Company. The government had discovered, a little late it must be admitted, that the English explorations had a political as well as a geographical significance. A month afterwards, Webb and his companions entered Delhi, having definitely settled the course of the Ganges, and ascertained the sources of the Baghirati and Aluknanda; in fact, having attained the object which the Company had had in view.

In 1808, the English government decided upon sending a new mission to the Punjab, then under the dominion of Runjeet Sing. The anonymous narrative of this expedition published in the "Annales des Voyages" offers some particulars of interest, from which we will extract a few.

Upon the 6th of April, 1808, an English officer, in charge of the expedition, reached Herdonai, which he represents as the rendezvous of a million individuals at the time of the yearly fair. At Boria, which is situated between the Jumna and the Sutlej, the traveller was an object of much curiosity to the women, who begged permission to come and see him.

"Their looks and gestures," says the narrative, "sufficiently expressed their surprise. They approached me laughing heartily, the colour of my face amused them extremely. They addressed many questions to me, asking me whether I never wore a hat, whether I exposed my face to the sun, whether I remained continually shut up, or only walked out under shelter, and whether I slept upon the table placed in my tent, although my bed occupied one side of it; the curtains were, however, closed. They then examined it in detail, together with the lining of my tent and everything belonging to it. These women were all good-looking, with mild and regular features, their complexion was olive, and contrasted agreeably with their white and even teeth, which are a distinguishing feature of all the inhabitants of the Punjab."

Mustafabad, Mulana, and Umballa were visited in succession by the British officer. The country through which he passed was inhabited by Sikhs, a race remarkable for benevolence, hospitality, and truthfulness. The author of the narrative is of opinion that they are the finest race of men in India. Puttiala, Makeonara, Fegonara, Oudamitta, which Lord Lake entered in 1805 in his pursuit of a Mahratta chief, and finally Amritsur were stages easily passed.

Amritsur is better built than the generality of towns in Hindustan. It is the largest depôt of shawls and saffron as well as other articles of Deccan merchandise. The traveller says:—

"Upon the 14th, having put white shoes on my feet, I paid a visit to the Amritsur or reservoir of the elixir of immortality from whence the city derives its name. It is a reservoir of about 135 feet square, built of brick, and in the centre is a pretty temple dedicated to Gourogovind Sing. A footpath leads to it; it is decorated both within and without, and the rajah often adds to its stores by gifts of ornaments. In this sacred receptacle, the book of the laws, written by Gouron in the 'gourou moukhtis' character, is placed. This temple is called Hermendel, or the Dwelling of God. Some 600 priests are attached to its service, and comfortable dwellings are provided for them out of the voluntary contributions of the devotees who visit the temple. Although the priests are regarded with infinite respect, they are not absolutely free from vice. When they have money, they spend it as freely as they have gained it. The number of pretty women who daily repair to the temple is very great. They far excel the women of the inferior classes in Hindustan in the elegance of their manners, their fine proportions, and handsome features."

Lahore was next visited by the officer. It is interesting to know what remained of that fine city at the commencement of the present century. The narrative says:—

"Its very high walls are ornamented externally with all the profusion of Eastern taste, but they are falling into ruins, as are also the mosques and houses inside the town. Time has laid its destructive hand upon this city, as upon Delhi and Agra. The ruins of Lahore are already as extensive as those of that ancient capital."

Three days after his arrival the traveller was received with great politeness by Runjeet Sing, who conversed with him, principally upon military topics. The rajah was then twenty-seven years of age. His countenance would have been pleasant, had not the small-pox deprived him of one eye; his manners were simple, affable, and yet kingly. After paying visits to the tomb of Shah Jehan, to the Schalamar, and other monuments at Lahore, the officer returned to Delhi and the possessions of the Company. To his visit was due that better knowledge of the country which could not fail to tempt the ambition of the English Government.

The following year (1809), an embassy, consisting of Messrs. Nicholas Hankey Smith, Henry Ellis, Robert Taylor, and Henry Pottinger, was sent to the Emirs of Scinde. The escort was commanded by Captain Charles Christie.

The mission was transported to Keratchy by boat. The governor of that fort refused to allow the embassy to disembark, without instructions from the emirs. An interchange of correspondence ensued, as a result of which the envoy, Smith, drew attention to certain improprieties relating to the title and respective rank of the Governor-General and the emirs. The governor excused himself upon the ground of his ignorance of the Persian language, and said, that not wishing a cause of misunderstanding to exist, he was quite ready to kill or put out the eyes (as the envoy pleased) of the person who had written the letter. This declaration appeared sufficient to the English, who deprecated the execution of the guilty person.

In their letters the emirs affected a tone of contemptuous superiority; at the same time they brought a body of 8000 men within reach, and put every possible difficulty in the way of the English efforts to procure information.

After tedious negotiations, in the course of which British pride was humbled more than once, the embassy received permission to start for Hyderabad.

Above Keratchy, which is the principal export harbour of Scinde, a vast plain without trees or vegetation extends along the coast. Five days are necessary to cross this, and reach Tatah, the ancient capital of Scinde, then ruined and deserted. Formerly it was brought into communication by means of canals, with the Sind, an immense river, which is, at its mouth, in reality an arm of the sea. Pottinger collected the most precise, complete, and useful details respecting the Sind, which were then known.

It had been arranged beforehand that the embassy should find a plausible excuse for separating and reaching Hyderabad by two different routes, in order to obtain geographical information on the country. The city was soon reached, and the same difficult negotiations about the reception of the embassy, who refused to submit to the humiliating exactions of the emirs, had to be gone through. Pottinger thus describes the arrival at Hyderabad. "The precipice upon which the eastern façade of the fortress of Hyderabad is situated, the roofs of the houses, and even the fortifications, were thronged by a multitude of both sexes, who testified friendly feeling towards us by acclamation and applause. Upon reaching the palace, where they were to dismount, the English were met by Ouli Mahommed Khan and other eminent officers, who walked before us towards a covered platform, at the extremity of which the emirs were seated. This platform being covered with the richest Persian carpet, we took off our shoes. From the moment the envoy took the first step towards the princes, they all three rose, and remained standing until he reached the place pointed out to him—an embroidered cloth, which distinguished him from the rest of the embassy. The princes addressed to each of us polite questions respecting our health. As it was a purely ceremonial reception, everything went off well, with compliments and polite expressions.

"The emirs wore a great number of precious stones, in addition to those which ornamented the hilts and scabbards of their swords and daggers, and emeralds and rubies of extraordinary size shone at their girdles. They were seated according to age, the eldest in the centre, the second to his right, the youngest on the left. A carpet of light felt covered the entire circle, and over this was a mattress of silk about an inch thick, exactly large enough to accommodate the three princes."

"They were seated according to age."

The narrative concludes with a description of Hyderabad, a fortress which would have scarcely been able to offer any resistance to a European enemy, and with various reflections upon the nature of the embassy, which had amongst other aims the closing of the entrance of Scinde against the French.

The treaty concluded, the English returned to Bombay.

By this expedition the East India Company gained a better knowledge of one of the neighbouring kingdoms, and collected precious documents relating to the resources and productions of a country traversed by an immense river, the Indus of the ancients, which rises in the Himalayas, and might readily serve to transport the products of an immense territory. The end gained was perhaps rather political than geographical; but science profited, once more, by political needs.

Hitherto the little knowledge that had been gained of the regions lying between Cabulistan, India, and Persia, had been as incomplete as it was defective.

The Company, thoroughly satisfied with the manner in which Captain Christie and Lieutenant Pottinger had accomplished their embassy, resolved to confide to them a delicate and difficult mission. They were to rejoin General Malcolm, ambassador to Persia, by crossing Beluchistan, and in so doing to collect more accurate and precise details of that vast extent of country than had hitherto been acquired.

It was useless to think of crossing Beluchistan, with its fanatic population, in European dress. Christie and Pottinger, therefore, had recourse to a Hindu merchant, who provided horses on behalf of the Governments of Madras and Bombay, and accredited them as his agents to Kelat, the capital of Beluchistan.

Upon the 2nd of January, 1810, the two officers embarked at Bombay for Someany, the sole sea-port of the province of Lhossa, which they reached after a stay at Poorbunder, on the coast of Guzerat.

The entire country traversed by the travellers before they arrived at Bela was a morass, interspersed with jungle. The "Djam," or governor of that town, was an intelligent man. He put numerous questions to the English, by which he showed a desire to learn, and then confided the task of conducting the travellers to Kelat, to the chief of the tribe of Bezendjos, who are Belutchis.

Beluchistan warriors.
(Fac-simile of early engraving.)

The climate had changed since they left Bombay, and in the mountains,
Pottinger and Christie experienced cold sufficiently keen to freeze the water

in the leather bottles.

"Kelat," says Pottinger, "the capital of the whole of Beluchistan, whence it derives its name, Kelat, or *the city*, is situated upon a height to the west of a well-cultivated plain or valley, eight miles long and three wide. The greater portion of this is laid out in gardens. The town forms a square. It is surrounded on three sides by a mud wall about twenty feet high, flanked, at distances of 250 feet, by bastions, which, like the walls, are pierced with a large number of barbicans for musketry. I had no opportunity of visiting the interior of the palace, but it consists merely of a confused mass of mud buildings with flat roofs like terraces; the whole is defended by low walls, furnished with parapets and pierced with barbicans. There are about 2500 houses in the town, and nearly half as many in the suburbs. They are built of half-baked bricks and wood, the whole smeared over with mud. The streets, as a rule, are larger than those in towns inhabited by Asiatics. They usually have a raised footway on either side for pedestrians, in the centre an open stream, which is rendered very unpleasant by the filth and rubbish thrown into it, and by the stagnant rainwater which collects, for there is no regulation insisting upon it being cleaned. Another obstacle to the cleanliness and comfort of the town exists in the projection of the upper stories of the houses, which makes the under buildings damp and dark. The bazaar of Kelat is very large, and well stocked with every kind of merchandize. Every day it is supplied with provisions, vegetables, and all kinds of food, which are cheap."

According to Pottinger's account, the population is divided into two distinct classes—the Belutchis and the Brahouis, and each of these is subdivided into a number of tribes. The first is related to the modern Persian, both in appearance and speech; the Brahoui, on the contrary, retains a great number of Hindu words. Intermarriage between the two has given rise to a third.

The Belutchis, coming from the mountains of Mekram, are "Tunnites," that is to say, they consider the first four Imans as the legitimate successors of Mahomet.

They are a pastoral people, and have the faults and virtues of their class. If they are hospitable, they are also indolent, and pass their time in gambling and smoking. As a rule, they content themselves with one or two wives, and are less jealous of their being seen by strangers than are other Mussulmen. They have a large number of slaves of both sexes, whom they treat humanely. They are excellent marksmen, and passionately fond of hunting. Brave under all circumstances, they take pleasure in "razzias," which they call "tchépaos." As a rule, these expeditions are undertaken by the Nherouis, the wildest and most thievish of the Belutchis.

The Brahouis carry their wandering habits still farther. Few men are more active and strong; they endure the glacial cold of the mountains equally with the burning heat of the plains. They are of small stature, but as brave, as skilful in shooting, as faithful to their promises, as the Belutchis, and have not so pronounced a taste for plunder.

Pottinger says, "I have seen no Asiatic people whom they resemble, for a large number have brown hair and beards."

After a short stay at Kelat, the two travellers, who still passed as horse- dealers, resolved to continue their journey, but instead of following the high road to Kandahar, they crossed a dreary and barren country, ill-populated, watered by the Caisser, a river which dries up during the summer; and they reached a little town, called Noschky or Nouchky, on the frontier of Afghanistan.

At this place, the Belutchis, who appeared friendly, represented to them the great difficulty of reaching Khorassan and its capital, Herat, by way of Sedjistan. They advised the travellers to try to reach Kerman by way of Kedje and Benpor, or by Serhed, a village on the western frontier of Beluchistan, and from thence to enter Nermanchir. At the same moment the idea of following two distinct routes presented itself to both Christie and Pottinger. This course was contrary to their instructions; "but," said Pottinger, "we found a ready excuse in the unquestionable advantage which would result from our procuring more extensive geographical and statistical knowledge of the country we were sent to explore than we could hope to do by travelling together."

Christie set out first, by way of Douchak. We shall follow his fortunes hereafter.

A few days later, while still at Noutch, Pottinger received letters from his correspondent at Kelat, telling him that the emirs of Scinde were searching for them, as they had been recognized, and that his best plan for safety was to set out immediately.

Upon the 25th of March Pottinger started for Serawan, a very small town near the Afghan frontier. Upon his way thither Pottinger met with some singular altars, or tombs, the construction of which was attributed to the Ghebers, or fire-worshippers, who are known in our day as Parsees.

Serawan is six miles from the Serawani mountains, in a sterile and bare district. This town owes its existence to the constant supply of water it derives from the Beli, an inestimable advantage in a country constantly exposed to drought, scarcity, and famine.

Pottinger afterwards visited the Kharan, celebrated for the strength and activity of its camels, and crossed the desert which forms the southern extremity of Afghanistan. The sand of this desert is so fine that its particles are almost impalpable, and the action of the wind causes it to accumulate into heaps ten or twenty feet high, divided by deep valleys. Even in calm weather a great number of particles float in the air, giving rise to a mirage of a peculiar kind, and getting into the traveller's eyes, mouth, and nostrils, cause an excessive irritation, with an insatiable thirst.

In all this territory, Pottinger personated a "pyrzadeh," or holy man, for the natives are of a very thievish disposition, and in the character of a merchant he might have been involved in unpleasant adventures. After leaving the village of Goul, in the district of Daizouk, the traveller passed through the ruined towns of Asmanabad, Hefter, and Pourah, where Pottinger was forced to admit that he was a "Feringhi," to the great scandal of the guide, who during the two months they had been together had never doubted him, and to whom he had given many proofs of sanctity.

At last, worn out by fatigue, and at the end of his resources, Pottinger reached Benpor, a locality which had been visited in 1808 by Mr. Grant, a captain in the Bengal Sepoy Infantry. Encouraged by the excellent account given by that officer, Pottinger presented himself to the Serdar. But instead of affording him the necessary help for the prosecution of his journey, that functionary, discontented with the small present Pottinger offered him, found means to extort from him a pair of pistols, which would have been of great use to him.

Basman is the last inhabited town of Beluchistan. At this spot there is a hot sulphureous spring, which the Belutchis consider a certain cure for cutaneous diseases.

The frontiers of Persia are far from "scientific," hence a large tract of country remains not neutral, but a subject of dispute, and is the scene of sanguinary contests.

The little town of Regan, in Nermanchir, is very pretty. It is a fort, or rather a fortified village, surrounded by high walls, in good repair, and furnished with bastions.

Further on, in Persia proper, lies Benn, a town which was formerly of importance, as the ruins which surround it sufficiently prove. Here Pottinger was cordially received by the governor.

"On approaching," says Pottinger, "he turned to one of his suite and asked where the 'Feringhi' was. I was pointed out to him. Making me a sign to follow him, his fixed look at me, which took me in from head to foot, proclaimed his astonishment at my costume, which in truth was strange enough to serve as an excuse for the impoliteness of his staring. I was wearing the long shirt of a Belutchi, and a pair of trousers which had once been white, but which in the six weeks I had worn them had become brown, and were all but in rags; in addition to this I had on a blue turban, a piece of rope served me as a girdle, and I carried in my hand a thick stick, which had assisted me greatly in my walking, and protected me from dogs."

In spite of the dilapidated appearance of the tatterdemalion who thus presented himself before him, the governor received Pottinger with as much cordiality as was to be expected from a Mussulman, and provided him with a guide to Kerman. The traveller reached that town upon the 3rd of May, feeling that he had accomplished the most difficult portion of his journey, and was almost in safety.

Kerman is the capital of ancient Karamania. Under the Afghan rule it was a flourishing town, and manufactured shawls which rivalled those of Cashmere.

Here Pottinger witnessed one of those spectacles which, common enough to countries where human life is of little value, always fill Europeans with horror and disgust. The governor of this town was both son-in-law and nephew of the shah, and also the son of the Shah's wife. "Upon the 15th of May," says Pottinger, "the prince himself judged certain persons who were accused of killing one of their servants. It is difficult to estimate the state of restlessness and alarm which prevailed in the village during the entire day. The gates of the town were shut, that no one might pass out. The government officials did not transact any business. People were cited as witnesses, without previous notice. I saw two or three taken to the palace in a state of agitation which could scarcely have been greater had they been going to the scaffold. About three in the afternoon the prince passed sentence upon those who had been convicted. Some had their eyes put out, some the tongue split. Some had the ears, nose, and lips cut off; others were deprived of their hands, fingers, or toes. I learned that whilst these horrible punishments were inflicted, the prince remained seated at the window where I had seen him, and gave his orders without the least sign of compassion or of horror at the scene which took place before him."

Leaving Kerman, Pottinger reached Cheré Bebig, which is equally distant from Yezd, Shiraz, and Kerman, and thence proceeded to Ispahan, where he had the pleasure of finding his companion Christie. At Meragha he met General Malcolm. It was now seven months since they had left Bombay. Christie had traversed 2250 miles, and Pottinger 2412. Meanwhile Christie had accomplished his perilous journey much better than he had anticipated.

Leaving Noutch upon the 22nd of March, he crossed the Vachouty mountains and some uncultivated country, to the banks of the Helmend, a river which flows into Lake Hamoun.

Christie in his report to the Company says:—

"The Helmend, after passing near Kandahar, flows south-west and west, and enters Sedjestan some four days march from Douchak; making a détour around the mountains, it finally forms a lake. At Peldalek, which we visited, it is about 1200 feet in width, and very deep; the water is very good. The country is cultivated by irrigation for half a mile on either side; then the desert begins, and rises in perpendicular cliffs. The banks of the river abound in tamarind-trees and provide pasturage for cattle."

Sedjestan, which is watered by this river, comprises only 500 square miles. The portions of this district which are inhabited are those upon the river Helmend, whose bed deepens every year.

At Elemdar Christie sent for a Hindu, to whom he had an introduction. This man advised him to dismiss his Belutchi attendants and to personate a pilgrim. A few days later he penetrated to Douchak, now known as Jellalabad. He says:—

"The ruins of the ancient city cover quite as large a space of ground as Ispahan. It was built, like all the towns of Sedjistan, of half-burned bricks, the houses being two stories high, with vaulted roofs. The modern town of Jellalabad is clean, pretty, and growing; it contains nearly 2000 houses and a fair bazaar." The road from Douchak to Herat was easy. Christie's sole difficulty was in carrying out his personation of a pilgrim. Herat lies in a valley, surrounded by high mountains and watered by a river, to which it is due that gardens and orchards abound. The town covers an area of about four square miles; it is surrounded by a wall flanked with towers, and a moat full of water. Large bazaars, containing numerous shops, and the Mechedé Djouna, or Mosque of Friday, are its chief ornaments.

No town has less waste land or a denser population. Christie estimates it at 100,000. Herat is the most commercial of all Asiatic towns under the dominion of native princes. It is the depôt for all the traffic between Cabul, Candahar, Hindustan, Cashmere, and Persia, and itself produces choice merchandize, silks, saffron, horses, and asafoetida.

"This plant," says Christie, "grows to a height of two or three feet, the stalk is two inches thick; it finishes off in an umbel which at maturity is yellow, and not unlike a cauliflower. It is much relished by Hindus and Belutchis. They prepare it for eating by cooking the stalks in ashes, and boiling the head like other vegetables; but it always retains its pungent smell and taste." Herat, like so many other Eastern towns, possesses beautiful public gardens, but they are only cultivated for the sake of the produce, which is sold in the bazaar. After a stay of a month at Herat, disguised as a horse-dealer, Christie, announcing that he would return after a pilgrimage to Meshid, which he contemplated, left the town. He directed his course to Yezd, across a country ravaged by the Osbeks, who had destroyed the tanks intended to receive the rain-water.

Yezd is a large and populous town on the skirts of a desert of sand. It is called "Dar-oul-Ehabet" or "The Seat of Adoration." It is celebrated for the security to be enjoyed there, which contributes largely to the development of its trade with Hindustan, Khorassan, Persia, and Bagdad. Christie describes the bazaar as large and well stocked. The town contains 20,000 houses, apart from those belonging to the Ghebers, who are estimated at 4000. They are an active and laborious people, although cruelly oppressed. From Yezd to Ispahan, where he alighted at the palace of the Emir Oud-Daoulé, Christie had travelled a distance of 170 miles upon a good road.

At Yezd, as we have seen, he met his companion, Pottinger. The two friends could but exchange mutual congratulations at the accomplishment of their mission, and their escape from the dangers of a fanatical country.

Pottinger's narrative, as may perhaps be gathered from the sketch we have given, was very curious. More exact than most of his predecessors, he had collected and offered to the public a mass of most interesting historical facts, anecdotes, and geographical descriptions.

Cabulistan had been, from the middle of the eighteenth century, the scene of a succession of ruinous civil wars. Competitors, with more or less right to the throne, had carried fire and sword everywhere, and converted that rich and fertile province into a desert, where the remains of ruined cities alone bore witness to former prosperity.

About the year 1808 the throne of Cabul was occupied by Soojah-Oul-Moulk. England, uneasy at the projects formed by Napoleon with a view of attacking her possessions in India, and at the offers of alliance made by him through General Gardane to the Shah of Persia, resolved to send an embassy to the court of Cabul, hoping to gain the king over to the interests of the East India Company.

Mountstuart Elphinstone was selected as envoy, and has left an interesting account of his mission. He collected much novel information concerning this region and the tribes by which it is peopled. His book acquires a new interest in our own day, and we turn with pleasure to pages devoted to the Khyberis and other mountain tribes, amid the events which are now taking place.

Leaving Delhi in October, 1808, Elphinstone reached Kanun, where the desert commences, and then the Shekhawuttée, a district inhabited by Rajpoots. At the end of October the embassy arrived at Singuana, a pretty town, the rajah of which was an inveterate opium-smoker. He is described as a small man, with large eyes, much inflamed by the use of opium. His beard, which was curled up to his ears on each side, gave him a ferocious appearance.

Djounjounka, whose gardens give freshness in the midst of these desert regions, is not now a dependency of the Rajah of Bekaneer, whose revenues do not exceed 1,250,000 francs. How is it possible for that prince to collect such revenues from a desert and uncultivated territory, overrun by myriads of rats, flocks of gazelles, and herds of wild asses?

The path across the sand-hills was so narrow that two camels abreast could scarcely pass it. At the least deviation from the path those animals would sink in the sand as if it had been snow, so that the smallest difficulty with the head of the column delayed the entire caravan. Those in front could not advance if those in the rear were delayed; and lest they should lose sight of the guides, trumpets and drums were employed as signals to prevent separation.

One could almost fancy it the march of an army. The warlike sounds, the brilliant uniforms and arms, were scarcely calculated to convey the idea of a peaceful embassy. The envoy speaks of the want of water, and the bad quality of that which was procurable was unbearable to the soldiers and servants. Although they quenched their thirst with the abundant water-melons, they could not do so without ill results to their health. Most of the natives of India who accompanied the embassy suffered from low fever and dysentery. Forty persons died during the first week's stay at Bekaneer. La Fontaine's description of the floating sticks might be aptly applied to Bekaneer. "From afar off it is something, near at hand it is nought." The external appearance of the town is pleasant, but it is a mere disorderly collection of cabins enclosed by mud walls.

At that time the country was invaded by five armies, and the belligerents sent a succession of envoys to the English ambassador, hoping to obtain, if not substantial assistance, at least moral support. Elphinstone was received by the Rajah of Bekaneer. "This court," he says, "was different from all I had seen elsewhere in India. The men were whiter than the Hindus, resembled Jews in feature, and wore magnificent turbans. The rajah and his relatives wore caps of various colours, adorned with precious stones.

"The rajah leant upon a steel buckler, the centre of which was raised, and the border encrusted with diamonds and rubies. Shortly after our entrance the rajah proposed that we should retire from the heat and importunity of the crowd. We took our seats on the ground, according to Indian custom, and the rajah delivered a discourse, in which he said he was the vassal of the sovereign of Delhi, and that as Delhi was in the possession of the British, he honoured the sovereignty of my government in my person.

"He caused the keys of the fort to be brought to him and handed them to me, but having received no instructions regarding such an event, I refused them. After much persuasion the rajah consented to keep his keys. Shortly afterwards a troop of bayadères came in, and dancing and singing continued until we took our leave."

Upon leaving Bekaneer the travellers entered a desert, in the middle of which stand the cities of Monyghur and Bahawulpore, where a compact crowd awaited the embassy. The Hyphases, upon which Alexander's fleet sailed, scarcely answered to the idea such a reminiscence inspires. Upon the morrow Bahaweel-Khan, governor of one of the eastern provinces of Cabul, arrived, bringing magnificent presents for the English ambassador, whom he conducted by the river Hyphases as far as Moultan, a town famous for its silk manufactures. The governor of the town had been terror-struck at hearing of the approach of the English, and there had been a discussion as to the attitude it was to assume, and whether the latter intended to take the town by stratagem, or to demand its surrender. When these fears were allayed, a cordial welcome followed.

Elphinstone's description, if somewhat exaggerated, is not the less curious. After describing how the governor saluted Mr. Strachey, the secretary to the embassy, after the Persian custom, he adds,—"They took their way together towards the tent, and the disorder increased. Some were wrestling, others on horseback mixed with the pedestrians. Mr. Strachey's horse was nearly thrown to the ground, and the secretary regained his equilibrium with difficulty. The khan and his suite mistook the road in approaching the tent, and threw themselves upon the cavalry with such impetuosity that the latter had scarcely time to face about and let them pass. The disordered troops fell back upon the tent, the servants of the khan fled, the barriers were torn up and trampled under foot; even the ropes of the tent broke, and the cloth covering very nearly fell on our heads. The tents were crowded immediately, and all was in darkness. The governor and six of his suite seated themselves, the others stood at arms. The visit was of short duration; the governor took refuge in repeating his rosary with great fervour, and in saying to me, in agitated tones, 'You are welcome! you are welcome!' Then on the pretext that the crowd inconvenienced me, he retired."

The account is amusing, but are all its details accurate? That, however, is of little moment. On the 31st December the embassy passed the Indus, and entered a country cultivated with a care and method unlike anything to be seen in Hindustan. The natives of this country had never heard of the English, and took them for Moguls, Afghans, or Hindus. The strangest reports were current among these lovers of the marvellous.

It was necessary to remain a month at Déra, to await the arrival of a "Mehnandar," a functionary whose duty it was to introduce ambassadors. Two persons attached to the embassy availed themselves of that opportunity to ascend the peak of Tukhte Soleiman, or the Crown of Solomon, upon which, according to the legend, the ark of Noah rested after the deluge.

The departure from Déra took place upon the 7th of February, and after travelling through delightful countries, the embassy arrived at Peshawur. The king had come to meet them, for Peshawur was not the usual residence of the court. The narrative says,—"Upon the day of our arrival our dinner was furnished from the royal kitchen. The dishes were excellent. Afterwards we had the meat prepared in our own way; but the king continued to provide us with breakfast, dinner, and supper, more than sufficient for 2000 persons, 200 horses, and a large number of elephants. Our suite was large, and much of this was needed; still I had great trouble at the end of a month in persuading his majesty to allow some retrenchment of this useless profusion."

As might have been expected, the negotiations preceding presentation at court were long and difficult. Finally, however, all was arranged, and the reception was as cordial as diplomatic customs permitted. The king was loaded with diamonds and precious stones; he wore a magnificent crown, and the Koh-i-noor sparkled upon one of his bracelets. This is the largest diamond in existence; a drawing of it may be seen in Tavernier's Travels.[1]

[1] The Koh-i-noor is now in the possession of the Queen of England.

Elphinstone, after describing the ceremonies, says,—"I must admit that if certain things, especially the extraordinary richness of the royal costume, excited my astonishment, there was also much that fell below my expectations. Taking it as a whole, one saw less indication of the prosperity of a powerful state than symptoms of the decay of a monarchy which had formerly been flourishing."

The ambassador goes on to speak of the rapacity with which the king's suite quarrelled about the presents offered by the English, and gives other details which struck him unpleasantly.

Elphinstone was more agreeably impressed with the king at his second interview. He says,—"It is difficult to believe that an Eastern monarch can possess such a good manner, and so perfectly preserve his dignity while trying to please."

The plain of Peshawur, which is surrounded on all but the eastern side by high mountains, is watered by three branches of the Cabul river, which meet here, and by many smaller rivers. Hence it is singularly fertile. Plums, peaches, pears, quinces, pomegranates, dates, grow in profusion. The population, so sparsely sprinkled throughout the arid countries which the ambassador had come through, were collected here, and Lieut. Macartney counted no less than thirty-two villages.

At Peshawur there are 100,000 inhabitants, living in brick houses three stories high. Various mosques, not in any way remarkable for architecture, a fine caravanserai, and the fortified castle in which the king received the embassy, are the only buildings of importance. The varieties of races, with different costumes, present a constantly changing picture, a human kaleidoscope, which appears made especially for the astonishment of a stranger. Persians, Afghans, Kyberis, Hazaurehs, Douranis, &c., with horses, dromedaries, and Bactrian camels, afford the naturalist much both to observe and to describe respecting bipeds and quadrupeds. But the charm of this town, as of every other throughout India, is to be found in its gardens, with their abundant and fragrant flowers, especially roses.

Afghan costumes.
(Fac-simile of early engraving.)

The king's situation at this time was far from pleasant. His brother, whom he had dethroned after a popular insurrection, had now taken arms and just seized Cabul. A longer stay was impossible for the embassy. They had to return to India by way of Attock and the valley of Hussoun Abdoul, which is celebrated for its beauty. There Elphinstone was to await the result of the struggle between the brothers, which would decide the fate of the throne of Cabul, but he had received letters of recall. Moreover, fate was against Soojah, who, after being completely worsted, had been forced to seek safety in flight.

The embassy proceeded on its way, and crossed the country of the Sikhs—a rude mountain race, half-naked and semi-barbarous.

"The Sikhs, who a few years later were to make themselves terribly famous," says Elphinstone, "are tall, thin men, and very strong. Their garments consist of trousers which reach only half way down the thigh. They wear cloaks of skins which hang negligently from the shoulder. Their turbans are not large, but are very high and flattened in front. No scissors ever touch either hair or beard. Their arms are bows and arrows or muskets. Men of rank have very handsome bows, and never pay a visit without being armed with them. Almost the whole Punjab belongs to Runjeet Sing, who in 1805 was only one among many chiefs in the country. At the time of our expedition, he had acquired the sovereignty of the whole country occupied by the Sikhs, and had taken the title of king."

No incident of any moment marked the return of the embassy to Delhi. In addition to the narrative of events which had taken place before their eyes, its members brought back invaluable documents concerning the geography of Afghanistan and Cabulistan, the climate, animals, and vegetable and mineral productions of that vast country.

Elphinstone devotes several chapters of his narrative to the origin, history, government, legislation, condition of the women, language, and commerce of these countries; facts that were largely appropriated by the best informed newspapers when the recent English expedition to Afghanistan was undertaken.

His work ends with an exhaustive treatise upon the tribes who form the population of Afghanistan, and a summary of invaluable information respecting the neighbouring countries.

Elphinstone's narrative is curious, interesting, and valuable for many reasons, and may be consulted in our own day with advantage.

Persian costumes.
(Fac-simile of early engraving.)

The zeal of the East India Company was indefatigable. One expedition had no sooner returned than another was started, with different instructions. It was highly important to be thoroughly *au fait* of the ever-changing Asiatic policy, and to prevent coalition between the various native tribes against the conquerors of the soil. In 1812, a new idea, and a more peaceful one, gave rise to the journey of Moorcroft and Captain Hearsay to Lake Manasarowar, in the province of the Un-dés, which is a portion of Little Thibet.

This time the object was to bring back a flock of Cashmere goats, whose long silk hair is used in the manufacture of the world-famed shawls. In addition, it was proposed to disprove the assertion of the Hindus that the source of the Ganges is beyond the Himalayas, in Lake Manasarowar. A difficult and perilous task! It was first of all necessary to penetrate into Nepaul, whilst the government of that country made such an attempt very difficult, and thence to enter a region from which the natives of Nepaul are excluded, and with still greater reason the English.

The explorers disguised themselves as Hindu pilgrims. Their suite consisted of twenty-five persons, one of whom pledged himself to walk in strides of four feet! This was certainly a rough method of ascertaining the distance traversed!

Messrs. Moorcroft and Hearsay passed through Bareilly, and followed Webb's route as far as Djosimath, which place they left on the 26th of May, 1812. They soon had to cross the last chain of the Himalayas, with increasing difficulties, owing to the rarity of the villages, which caused a scarcity of provisions and service, and the bad roads, at so great a height above the level of the sea.

Nevertheless they saw Daba, where there is an important lamasery, Gortope, Maisar; and, a quarter of a mile from Tirthapuri, curious hot springs.

The original narrative, which appeared in the "Annales des Voyages," speaks of this water as flowing from two openings six inches in diameter in a calcareous plain some three miles in extent, and which is raised in almost every direction from ten to twelve feet above the surrounding country. It is formed of the earthy deposits left by the water in cooling. The water rises four inches above the level of the plain. It is clear, and so warm that one cannot keep a hand in it longer than a few minutes. It is surrounded by a thick cloud of smoke. The water, flowing over a horizontal surface, hollows out basins of various shapes, which as they receive the earthy deposits contract again. When they are filled up, the flow of the water again hollows out a new reservoir, which in its turn becomes full. Flowing thus from one to the other, it finally reaches the plain below. The deposit left by the water is as white as the purest stucco close to the opening, a little further it becomes pale yellow, and further still saffron-coloured. At the other spring it is first rose-coloured, and then dark red. These different colours are to be found in the calcareous plain, and are no doubt the work of centuries.

Tirthapuri, the residence of a lama, is of great antiquity, and is a favourite rendezvous for the faithful, as a wall more than 400 feet long and four wide, formed of stones upon which prayers are inscribed, sufficiently testifies.

Upon the 1st of August the travellers left this place, hoping to reach Lake Manasarowar, and leaving on the right Lake Rawan-rhad, which is supposed to be the source of the largest branch of the Sutlej.

Lake Manasarowar lies at the foot of immense sloping prairies, to the south of the gigantic mountains. This is the most venerated of all the sacred places of the Hindus, which is no doubt owing to its distance from Hindustan, the dangers and fatigues of the journey, and the necessity of pilgrims providing themselves with money and provisions. Hindu geographers regard this lake as the source of the Ganges, the Sutlej, and the Kali rivers. Moorcroft had no doubt as to the error of this assertion as regards the Ganges. Desiring to ascertain the truth as to the other rivers, he explored the steep banks of the lake, and found a number of streams which flowed into it, but none flowing out of it. It is possible that before the earthquake which destroyed Srinagar, the lake had an outlet, but Moorcroft found no trace of it. The lake is situated between the Himalayas and the Cailas chain, and is of irregular oblong shape, five leagues long by four wide.

The end of the expedition was attained. Moorcroft and Hearsay returned towards India, passed by Kangri, and saw Rawan-rhad; but Moorcroft was too weak, and could not continue the tour; he regained Tirthapuri and Daba, and suffered a great deal in crossing the ghat which separates Hindustan from Thibet.

The narrative describes the wind which comes from the snow-covered mountains of Bhutan as cold and piercing, and the ascent of the mountain as long and painful, its descent slippery and steep, making precautions necessary. "We suffered greatly," says the writer; "our goats escaped by the negligence of their drivers, and climbed up to the edge of a precipice some hundred feet in height. A mountaineer disturbing them from their perilous position, they began the descent, running down a very steep incline. The hinder ones kicked up the stones, which, falling with violence, threatened to strike the foremost. It was curious to note how cleverly they managed to run, and avoid the falling stones."

Very soon the Gorkhalis, who had hitherto been content to place obstacles in the way of the travellers, approached them with intent to stop them. For some time the firmness displayed by the English kept them at bay; but at last, gaining courage from their numbers, they began an attack.

"Twenty men," says Moorcroft, "threw themselves upon me. One seized me by my neck, and, pressing his knees against me, tried to strangle me by tightening my cravat; another passed a cord round my legs and pulled me from behind. I was on the point of fainting. My gun, upon which I was leaning, escaped my hold; I fell; they dragged me up by my feet until I was nearly garotted. When at last I rose, nothing could exceed the expression of fierce delight on the faces of my conquerors. Fearing that I should attempt to escape, two soldiers held me by a rope and gave me a blow from time to time, no doubt to remind me of my position. Mr. Hearsay had not supposed that he should be attacked so soon; he was rinsing out his mouth when the hubbub began, and did not hear my cries for help. Our men could not find the few arms we possessed; some escaped, I know not how; the others were seized, amongst them Mr. Hearsay. He was not bound as I was; they contented themselves with holding his arms."

"Two soldiers held me."

The chief of this band of savages informed the two Englishmen that they had been recognized, and were arrested for having travelled in the country in the disguise of Hindu pilgrims. A fakir, whom Moorcroft had engaged as a goatherd, succeeded in escaping, and took two letters to the English authorities.

Aid was sent, and on the 1st of November the prisoners were released. Not only were excuses offered for their treatment, but what had been taken from them was returned, and the Rajah of Nepaul gave them permission to leave his dominions. All's well that ends well!

To complete our sketch, we must give an account of Mr. Fraser's expedition to the Himalayas, and Hodgson's exploration to the source of the Ganges, in 1817.

Captain Webb, as we have seen, had traced the course of that river past the valley of Dhoun, to Cadjani, near Reital. Leaving this spot upon the 28th of May, 1817, Captain Hodgson reached the source of the Ganges in three days, and proceeded to Gangautri. He found that the river issues from a low arch in the midst of an enormous mass of frozen snow, more than 300 feet high. The stream was already of considerable size, being no less than twenty-seven feet wide and eighteen inches deep. In all probability the Ganges first emerged into the light at this spot.

Captain Hodgson wished to solve various questions; for example:—What was the length of the river under the frozen snow? Is it the product of the melting of these snows? or did it spring from the ground? But, wishing to explore further upwards than his guides advised, the traveller sank into the snow up to his neck, and had to retrace his steps with great difficulty. The spot from which the Ganges issues is situated 12,914 feet above the level of the sea, in the Himalayas.

Hodgson also explored the source of the Jumna. At Djemautri the mass of snow from which the river makes its escape is no less than 180 feet wide and more than forty feet deep, between two perpendicular walls of granite. This source is situated on the south-east slope of the Himalayas.

The extension of the British power in India was necessarily attended by considerable danger. The various native States, many of which could boast of a glorious past, had only yielded in obedience to the well-known political principle "divide and govern," ascribed to Machiavelli. But the day might come when they would merge their rivalries and enmities, to make common cause against the invader.

This was anything but a cheering prospect for the Company, whose policy it was to maintain the system that had hitherto worked so well. Certain neighbouring States, still powerful enough to regard the growth of the British power with jealousy, might serve as harbours of refuge to the discontented, and become the centres of dangerous intrigues. Of all these neighbouring States that which demanded the strictest surveillance was Persia, not only on account of its contiguity to Russia, but because Napoleon was known to have designs in connexion with it which nothing but his European wars prevented him from putting into execution.

In February, 1807, General Gardane, who had gained his promotion in the wars of the Republic, and had distinguished himself at Austerlitz, Jena, and Eylau, was appointed Minister Plenipotentiary to Persia, with instructions to ally himself with Shah Feth-Ali against England and Russia. The selection was fortunate, for the grandfather of General Gardane had held a similar post at the court of the shah. Gardane crossed Hungary, and reached Constantinople and Asia Minor; but when he entered Persia, Abbas Mirza had succeeded his father Feth-Ali.

The new shah received the French ambassador with respect, loaded him with presents, and granted certain privileges to Catholics and French merchants. These were, however, the only results of the mission, which was thwarted by the English General Malcolm, whose influence was then paramount; and Gardane, disheartened by finding all his efforts frustrated, and recognizing that success was hopeless, returned to France the following year.

His brother Ange de Gardane, who had acted as his secretary, published a brief narrative of the journey, containing several curious details respecting the antiquities of Persia, which have been, however, largely supplemented by works brought out by Englishmen.

The French Consul, Adrien Dupré, attached to Gardane's mission, also published a work, under the title of "Voyage en Perse, fait dans les années 1807 à 1809, en traversant l'Anatolie, la Mésopotamie, depuis Constantinople jusqu'à l'extremité du golfe Persique et de là à Irwan, suivi de détails sur les moeurs, les usages et le commerce des Persans, sur la cour de Téhéran et d'une notice des tribus de la Perse." The book bears out the assertions of its title, and is a valuable contribution to the geography and ethnography of Persia.

The English, who made a much longer stay in the country than the French, were better able to collect the abundant materials at hand, and to make a judicious selection from them.

Two works were long held to be the chief authorities on the subject. One of these was by James Morier, who availed himself of the leisure he enjoyed as secretary to the embassy to acquaint himself with every detail of Persian manners, and on his return to England published several Oriental romances, which obtained a signal success, owing to the variety and novelty of the scenes described, and the fidelity to nature of every feature, however minute.

The second of the two volumes alluded to above was the large quarto work by John Macdonald Kinneir, on the geography of Persia. This book, which made its mark, and left far behind it everything previously published on the subject, not only gives, as its title implies, very valuable information on the boundaries of the country, its mountains, rivers, and climate, but also contains interesting and trustworthy details respecting its government, constitution, army, commerce, animal, vegetable, and mineral productions, population, and revenue.

After giving an exhaustive and brilliant picture of the material and moral resources of the Persian Empire, Kinneir goes on to describe its different provinces, quoting from the mass of valuable documents accumulated by himself, thus making his work the most complete and impartial yet issued.

Kinneir passed the years 1808 to 1814 in travelling about Asia Minor, Armenia, and Kurdistan; and the different posts held by him during that period were such as to give him exceptional opportunities for making observations and comparing their results. In his several capacities as captain in the service of the Company, political agent to the Nawab of the Carnatic, or private traveller, his critical acumen was never at fault; and his wide knowledge of Oriental character and Oriental manners, enabled him to recognize the true significance of many an event and many a revolution which would have escaped the notice of less experienced observers.

At the same time, William Price, also a captain in the East India Company's service, who had been attached as interpreter and secretary to Sir William Gore Ouseley's embassy to Persia in 1810, devoted himself to the study of the cuneiform character. Many had previously attempted to decipher it, with results as various as they were ridiculous; and, like those of his predecessors and contemporaries, Price's opinions were mere guess-work; but he succeeded in interesting a certain class of students in this obscure branch of research, and may be said to have perpetuated the theories of Niebuhr and other Orientalists.

To Price we owe an account of the journey of the English embassy to the Persian court, after which he published two essays on the antiquities of Persepolis and Babylon.

Mr. Ouseley, who had accompanied his brother Sir William as secretary, availed himself of his sojourn at the Court of Teheran to study Persian. His works do not, however, bear upon geography or political economy, but treat only of inscriptions, coins, manuscripts, and literature—in a word, of everything connected with the intellectual and material history of the country. To him we owe an edition of Firdusi, and many other volumes, which came out at just the right time to supplement the knowledge already acquired of the country of the Shah.

Another semi-Asiatic semi-European country was also now becoming known. This was the mountainous district of the Caucasus. As early as the second half of the eighteenth century, John Anthony Guldenstædt, a Russian doctor, had visited Astrakhan, and Kisliar on the Terek, at the most remote boundary of the Russian possessions, entered Georgia, where the Czar Heraclius received him with great respect, and penetrated to Tiflis and the country of the Truchmenes, finally arriving at Imeritia. The next year, 1773, he visited the great Kabardia, the Oriental Kumania, examined the ruins of Madjary, visited Tscherkask and Asov, discovered the mouth of the Don, and was about to extend his researches to the Crimea when he was recalled to St. Petersburg.

Guldenstædt's travels have not been translated into French. Their author's career was cut short by death before he had completed their revision for the press, and they were edited at St. Petersburg by Henry Julius von Klaproth, a young Prussian, who afterwards explored the same countries.

Klaproth, who was born at Berlin on the 11th October, 1783, gave proof at a very early age of a special aptitude for the study of Oriental languages. At fifteen years old he taught himself Chinese; and he had scarcely finished his studies at the Universities of Halle and Dresden, when he began the publication of his "Asiatic Magazine." Invited to Russia by Count Potoki, he was at once named Professor of Oriental Languages at the Academy of St. Petersburg.

Klaproth did not belong to the worthy race of book-worms who shut themselves up in their own studies. He took a wider view of the nature of true knowledge, feeling that the surest way to attain a thorough acquaintance with the languages of Asia and of Oriental manners and customs was to study them on the spot. He therefore asked permission to accompany the ambassador Golowkin, who was going to China overland; and the necessary credentials obtained, he started alone for Siberia, making acquaintance with the Samoyèdes, the Tongouses, Bashkirs, Yakontes, Kirghizes, and other of the Finnic and Tartar hordes which frequent these vast steppes, finally arriving at Yakutsk, where he was soon joined by Golowkin. After a halt at Kiakta, the embassy crossed the Chinese frontier on the 1st January, 1806.

The Viceroy of Mongolia, however, insisted upon the observance by the ambassador of certain ceremonies which were considered by the latter degrading to his dignity; and neither being disposed to yield, Golowkin set out with his suite to return to St. Petersburg. Klaproth, not caring to retrace his steps, preferred to visit hordes still unknown to him, and he therefore crossed the southern districts of Siberia, and collected during a journey extending over twenty months, a large number of Chinese, Mandchoorian, Thibetan, and Mongolian books, which were of service to him in his great work "Asia Polyglotta."

On his return to St. Petersburg he was invested with all the honours of the Academy; and a little later, at the suggestion of Count Potoki, he was appointed to the command of an historical, archæological, and geographical expedition to the Caucasus. Klaproth now passed a whole year in journeys, often full of peril, amongst thievish tribes, through rugged districts, and penetrated to the country traversed by Guldenstædt at the end of the previous century.

Klaproth's description of Tiflis is curious as compared with that of contemporary authors. "Tiflis," he says, "so called on account of its mineral springs, is divided into three parts: Tiflis properly so called, or the ancient town; Kala, or the citadel; and the suburb of Issni. This town is built on the Kur, and the greater part of its outer walls is now in ruins. Its streets are so narrow, that 'arbas,' as the lofty carriages so characteristic of Oriental places are called, could only pass with difficulty down the widest, whilst in the others a horseman would barely find room to ride. The houses, badly built of flints and bricks cemented with mud, never last longer than about fifteen years." In Klaproth's time Tiflis boasted of two markets, but everything was extremely dear, shawls and silk scarves manufactured in the neighbouring Asiatic countries bringing higher prices than in St. Petersburg.

Tiflis must not be dismissed without a few words concerning its hot springs. Klaproth tells us that the famous hot baths were formerly magnificent, but they are falling into ruins, although some few remain; the floors of which are cased in marble. The waters contain very little sulphur and are most salutary in their effects. The natives, especially the women, use them to excess, the latter remaining in them several days, and even taking their meals in the bath.

The chief food of the people of Tiflis, at least in the mountainous districts, is the bhouri, a kind of hard bread with a very disagreeable taste, prepared in a way repugnant to our sybarite notions.

When the dough is sufficiently kneaded a bright clear fire of dry wood is made, in earthen vessels four feet high by two wide, which are sunk in the ground. When the fire is burning fiercely, the Georgians shake into it the vermin by which their shirts and red-silk breeches are infested. Not until this ceremony has been performed do they throw the dough, which is divided into pieces of the size of two clenched fists, into the pots. The dough once in, the vessels are covered with lids, over which rags are placed, to make sure of all the heat being kept in and the bread being thoroughly baked. It is, however, always badly done, and very difficult of digestion.

Having thus assisted at the preparation of the food of the poor mountaineer, let us join Klaproth at the table of a prince. A long striped cloth, about a yard and a half wide and very dirty, was spread for his party; on this was placed for each guest an oval-shaped wheaten cake, three spans long by two wide, and scarcely as thick as a finger. A number of little brass bowls, filled with mutton and boiled rice, roast fowls, and cheese cut in slices, were then brought in. As it was a fast day, smoked salmon with uncooked green vegetables was served to the prince and his subjects. Spoons, forks, and knives are unknown in Georgia; soup is eaten from the bowl, meat is taken in the hands, and torn with the fingers into pieces the size of a mouthful. To throw a tid-bit to another guest is a mark of great friendship. The repast over, grapes and dried fruits are eaten. During the meal a good red native wine, called traktir by the Tartars, and ghwino by the Georgians, is very freely circulated. It is drunk from flat silver bowls greatly resembling saucers.

Klaproth's account of the different incidents of his journey is no less interesting and vivid than this description of the manners of the people. Take, for instance, what he says of his trip to the sources of the Terek, the site of which had been pretty accurately indicated by Guldenstædt, although he had not visited them.

"I left the village of Utzfars-Kan on the 17th March, on a bright but cold morning. Fifteen Ossetes accompanied me. After half an hour's march, we began to climb the steep and rugged ascent leading to the junction of the Utzfars-Don with the Terek. This was succeeded by a still worse road, running for a league alongside of the river, which is scarcely ten paces wide here, although it was then swollen by the melting of the snow. This part of the river banks is inhabited. We continued to ascend, and reached the foot of the Khoki, also called Istir-Khoki, finally arriving at a spot where an accumulation of large stones in the bed of the river rendered it possible to cross over to the village of Tsiwratté-Kan, where we breakfasted. Here the small streams forming the Terek meet. I was so glad to have reached the end of my journey, that I poured a glass of Hungarian wine into the river, and made a second libation to the genius of the mountain in which the Terek rises. The Ossetes, who thought I was performing a religious ceremony, observed me gravely. On the smooth sides of an enormous block of schist I engraved in red the date of my journey, together with my name and those of my companions, after which I climbed up to the village of Ressi."

"Fifteen Ossetes accompanied me."

After this account of his journey, from which we might multiply extracts, Klaproth sums up all the information he has collected on the tribes of the Caucasus, dwelling specially on the marked resemblances which exist between the different Georgian dialects and those of the Finns and Lapps. This was a new and useful suggestion.

Speaking of the Lesghians, who occupy the eastern Caucasus, known as Daghestan, or Lezghistan, Klaproth says their name is a misnomer, just as Scythian or Tartar was used to indicate the natives of Northern Asia; adding, that they do not form one nation, as is proved by the number of dialects in use, which, however, would seem to have been derived from a common source, though time has greatly modified them. This is a contradiction in terms, implying either that the Lesghians, speaking one language, form one nation, or that forming one nation the Lesghians speak various dialects derived from the same source.

According to Klaproth, Lesghian words have a considerable affinity with the other languages of the Caucasus, and with those of Western Asia, especially the dialects of the Samoyedes and Siberian Finns.

West and north-west of the Lesghians dwell the Metzdjeghis, or Tchetchentses, who are probably the most ancient inhabitants of the Caucasus. This is not, however, the opinion of Pallas, who looks upon them as a separate tribe of the Alain family. The Tchetchentse language greatly resembles the Samoyede and other Siberian dialects, as well as those of the Slavs.

The Tcherkesses, or Circassians, are the Sykhes of the Greeks. They formerly inhabited the eastern Caucasus and the Crimea. Their language differs much from other Caucasian idioms, although the Tcherkesses proceed, with the Wogouls and the Ostiakes—we have just seen that the Lesghian and Tchetchentse dialects resemble the Siberian—from one common stock, which at some remote date separated into several branches, of which the Huns probably formed one. The Tcherkesse dialect is one of the most difficult to pronounce, some of the consonants being produced in a manner so loud and guttural that no European has yet been able to acquire it.

In the Caucasus also dwell the Abazes—who have never left the shores of the Black Sea, where they have been settled from time immemorial—and the Ossetes, or As, who belong to the Indo-Germanic stock. They call their country Ironistan, and themselves the Irons. Klaproth takes them to be Sarmatic Medes, not only on account of their name, which resembles Iran, but because of the structure of their language, which proves more satisfactorily than historical documents, and in a most conclusive manner, that they spring from the same stock as the Medes and Persians. This opinion, however, appears to us mere conjecture, as in the time of Klaproth the interpretation of cuneiform inscriptions had not been accomplished, and too little was known of the language of the Medes for any one to judge of its resemblance to the

Ossete idiom.

"However," continues Klaproth, "after meeting again the Sarmatic Medes of the ancients in this people, it is still more surprising also to recognize the Alains, who occupied the districts north of the Caucasus."

He adds: "It follows from all we have said, that the Ossetes, who call themselves Irons, are the Medes, who assumed the name of Irans, and whom Herodotus styles the Arioi. They are, moreover, the Sarmatic Medes of the ancients, and belong to the Median colony founded in the Caucasus by the Scythians. They are the As or Alains of the middle ages. And lastly, they are the Iasses of Russian chronicles, from whom some of the Caucasus range took their name of the Iassic Mountains." This is not the place to discuss identifications belonging to the realm of criticism. We will content ourselves with adding to these remarks of Klaproth on the Ossete language, that its pronunciation resembles that of the Low-German and Slavonic dialects.

The Georgians differ essentially from the neighbouring nations, alike in their language and in their physical and moral qualities. They are divided into four principal tribes—the Karthalinians, Mingrelians, and Shvans (or Swanians), inhabiting the southern range of the Caucasus, and the Lazes, a wild robber tribe.

As we have seen, the facts collected by Klaproth are very curious, and throw an unexpected light on the migration of ancient races. The penetration and sagacity of the traveller were marvellous, and his memory was extraordinary. The scholar of Berlin rendered signal services to the science of philology. It is to be regretted that his qualities as a man, his principles, and his temper, were not on a level with his knowledge and acumen as a professor.

We must now leave the Old World for the New, and give an account of the explorations of the young republic of the United States. So soon as the Federal Government was free from the anxieties of war, and its position was alike established and recognized, public attention was directed to the "fur country," which had in turn attracted the English, the Spanish, and the French. Nootka Sound and the neighbouring coasts, discovered by the great Cook and the talented Quadra, Vancouver, and Marchand, were American. Moreover, the Monroe doctrine, destined later to excite so much discussion, already existed in embryo in the minds of the statesmen of the day.

In accordance with an Act of Congress, Captain Merryweather Lewis and Lieutenant William Clarke, were commissioned to trace the Missouri, from its junction with the Mississippi to its source, and to cross the Rocky Mountains by the easiest and shortest route, thus opening up communication between the Gulf of Mexico and the Pacific Ocean. The officers were also to trade with any Indian tribes they might meet.

The expedition was composed of regular troops and volunteers, numbering altogether, including the leaders, forty-three men; one boat and two canoes completed the equipment.

On the 14th May, 1804, the Americans left Wood River, which flows into the Mississippi, and embarked on the Missouri. From what Cass had said in his journal, the explorers expected to have to contend with natural dangers of a very formidable description, and also to fight their way amongst natives of gigantic stature, whose hostility to the white man was invincible.

During the first days of this long canoe voyage, only to be compared to those of Orellana and Condamine on the Amazon, the Americans were fortunate enough to meet with some Sioux Indians, an old Frenchman, a Canadian *coureur des bois*, or trapper, who spoke the languages of most of the Missouri tribes, and consented to accompany the expedition as interpreter.

They passed the mouths of the Osage, Kansas, Platte or Nebraska, and White River, all tributaries of the Missouri, successively, and met various parties of Osage and Sioux, or Maha Indians, who all appeared to be in a state of utter degradation. One tribe of Sioux had suffered so much from smallpox, that the male survivors, in a fit of rage and misery, had killed the women and children spared by the terrible malady, and fled from the infected neighbourhood.

A little farther north dwelt the Ricaris, or Recs, at first supposed to be the cleanest, most polite, and most industrious of the tribes the expedition met with; but a few thefts soon modified that favourable judgment. It is curious that these people do not depend entirely on hunting, but cultivate corn, peas, and tobacco.

This is not, however, the case with the Mandans, who are a more robust race. A custom obtains among them, also characteristic of Polynesia—they do not bury their dead, but expose them on a scaffold.

Clarke's narrative gives us a few details relating to this strange tribe. The Mandans look upon the Supreme Being only as an embodiment of the power of healing. As a result they worship two gods, whom they call the Great Medicine or the Physician, and the Great Spirit. It would seem that life is so precious to them that they are impelled to worship all that can prolong it!

Their origin is strange. They originally lived in a large subterranean village hollowed out under the ground on the borders of a lake. A vine, however, struck its roots so deeply in the earth as to reach their habitations, and some of them ascended to the surface by the aid of this impromptu ladder. The descriptions given by them on their return of the vast hunting-grounds, rich in game and fruit, which they had seen, led the rest of the tribe to resolve to reach so favoured a land. Half of them had gained the surface, when the vine, bending beneath the weight of a fat woman, gave way, and rendered the ascent of the rest impossible. After death the Mandans expect to return to their subterranean home, but only those who die with a clear conscience can reach it; the guilty will be flung into a lake.

The explorers took up their quarters for the winter amongst the Mandans, on the 1st of November. They built huts, as comfortable as possible with the materials at their command; and in spite of the extreme cold, gave themselves up to the pleasures of hunting, which soon became a positive necessity of their existence.

When the ice should break up on the Missouri, the explorers hoped to continue their voyage; but on their sending the boat down to St. Louis, laden with the skins and furs already obtained, only thirty men were found willing to carry the expedition through to the end.

The travellers soon passed the mouth of the Yellowstone River, with a current nearly as strong as that of the Missouri, flowing through districts abounding in game.

Cruel was their perplexity when they arrived at a fork where the Missouri divided into two rivers of nearly equal volume, for which was the main stream? Captain Lewis with a party of scouts ascended the southern branch, and soon came in sight of the Rocky Mountains, completely covered with snow. Guided to the spot by a terrific uproar, he beheld the Missouri fling itself in one broad sheet of water over a rocky precipice, beyond which it formed a broken series of rapids, extending for several miles.

"He beheld the Missouri."

The detachment now followed this branch, which led them into the heart of the mountains, and for three or four miles dashed along between two perpendicular walls of rock, finally dividing itself into three parts, to which were given the names of Jefferson, Madison, and Galatin, after celebrated

American statesmen.

The last heights were soon crossed, and then the expedition descended the slopes overlooking the Pacific. The Americans had brought with them a Soshone woman, who had been protected as a girl by the Indians of the east, and not only did she serve the explorers faithfully as an interpreter, but also, through her recognition of a brother in the chief of a tribe disposed to be hostile, she from that moment secured cordial treatment for the white men. Unfortunately the country was poor, the people living entirely on wild berries, bark, and the little game they were able to obtain.

The Americans, little accustomed to this frugal fare, had to eke it out by eating their horses, which had grown very thin, and buying all the dogs the natives would consent to sell. Hence they obtained the nickname of Dog- eaters.

As the temperature became milder, so did the character of the natives, whilst food grew more abundant; and as they came down the Oregon, also known as the Columbia, the salmon formed a seasonable addition to the bill of fare. When the Columbia, which is dangerous for navigation, approaches the sea, it forms a vast estuary, where the waves from the offing meet the current of the river. The Americans more than once incurred considerable risk of being swallowed up, with their frail canoe, before they reached the shores of the ocean.

Glad to have accomplished the aim of their expedition, the explorers wintered at the mouth of the river, and when the fine weather set in they made their way back to St. Louis, arriving there in May, 1806, after an absence of two years, four months, and ten days. They had in that time, according to their own estimate, traversed less than 1378 leagues.

The impulse was now given, and reconnoitring expeditions in the interior of the new continent rapidly succeeded each other, assuming, a little later, a scientific character which gives them a position of their own in the history of discovery.

A few years later, one of the greatest colonizers of whom England can boast, Sir Stamford Raffles, organizer of the expedition which took possession of the Dutch colonies, was appointed Military Governor of Java. During an administration extending over five years, Raffles brought about numerous reforms, and abolished slavery. Absorbing as was this work, however, it did not prevent him from publishing two huge quarto volumes, which are as interesting as they are curious. They contain, in addition to the history of Java, a vast number of details about the natives of the interior, until then little known, together with much circumstantial information respecting the geology and natural history of the country. It is no wonder, therefore, that in honour of the man who did so much to make Java known, the name of Rafflesia should have been given to an immense flower native to it, and of which some specimens measure over three feet in diameter, and weigh some ten pounds.

Raffles was also the first to penetrate to the interior of Sumatra, of which the coast only was previously known. He visited the districts occupied by the Passoumahs, sturdy tillers of the soil, the northern provinces, with Memang-Kabou, the celebrated Malayan capital, and crossed the southern half of the island, from Bencoulen to Palimbang.

Sir Stamford Raffles' fame, however rests principally upon his having drawn the attention of the Indian Government to the exceptionally favourable position of Singapore, which was converted by him into an open port, and grew rapidly into a prosperous settlement.

CHAPTER II.

THE EXPLORATION AND COLONIZATION OF AFRICA.

I.

Peddie and Campbell in the Soudan—Ritchie and Lyon in Fezzan—Denham, Oudney, and Clapperton in Fezzan, and in the Tibboo country—Lake Tchad and its tributaries—Kouka and the chief villages of Bornou—Mandara—A razzia, or raid, in the Fellatah country—Defeat of the Arabs and death of Boo-Khaloum—Loggan—Death of Toole—En route for Kano—Death of Oudney—Kano—Sackatoo—Sultan Bello—Return to Europe.

The power of Napoleon, and with it the supremacy of France, was scarcely overthrown—the Titanic contests, to gratify the ambition of one man at the expense of the intellectual progress of humanity, were scarcely at an end, before an honourable rivalry awoke once more, and new scientific and commercial expeditions were set on foot. A new era had commenced.

Foremost in the ranks of the governments which organized and encouraged exploring expeditions we find as usual that of England. It was in Central Africa, the vast riches of which had been hinted at in the accounts given of their travels by Hornemann and Burckhardt, that the attention of the English was now concentrated.

As early as 1816 Major Peddie, starting from Senegal, reached Kakondy, on the River Nuñez, succumbing, however, to the fatigue of the journey and unhealthiness of the climate soon after his arrival in that town. Major Campbell succeeded him in the command of the expedition, and crossed the lofty mountains of Foota-Djalion, losing in a few days several men and part of the baggage animals.

Arrived at the headquarters of the Almamy, as most of the kings of this part of Africa are called, the expedition was detained for a long time, and only obtained permission to depart on payment of a large sum.

Most disastrous was the return journey, for the explorers had not only to recross the streams they had before forded with such difficulty, but they were subjected to so many insults, annoyances, and exactions, that to put an end to them Campbell was obliged to burn his merchandize, break his guns, and sink his powder.

Against so much fatigue and mortification, added to the complete failure of his expedition, Major Campbell failed to bear up, and he died, with several of his officers, in the very place where Major Peddie had closed his career. The few survivors of the party reached Sierra Leone after an arduous march.

A little later, Ritchie and Captain George Francis Lyon, availing themselves of the prestige which the siege of Algiers had brought to the British flag, and of the cordial relations which the English consul at Tripoli had succeeded in establishing with the principal Moorish authorities, determined to follow Hornemann's route, and penetrate to the very heart of Africa.

On the 25th March, 1819, the travellers left Tripoli with Mahommed el Moukni, Bey of Fezzan, who is called sultan by his subjects. Protected by this escort, Ritchie and Lyon reached Murzuk without molestation, but there the former died on the 2nd November, worn out by the fatigue and privations of the journey across the desert. Lyon, who was ill for some time from the same causes, recovered soon enough to foil the designs of the sultan, who counting on his death, had already begun to take possession of his property, and also of Ritchie's. The captain could not penetrate beyond the southern boundaries of Fezzan, but he had time to collect a good deal of valuable information about the chief towns of that province and the language of its inhabitants. To him we likewise owe the first authentic details of the religion, customs, language, and extraordinary costumes of the Tuarick Arabs, a wild tribe inhabiting the Great Sahara desert.

Captain Lyon's narrative also contains a good deal of interesting information collected by himself on Bornou, Wadai, and the Soudan, although he was unable to visit those places in person.

The results obtained did not by any means satisfy the English Government, which was most eager to open up the riches of the interior to its merchants. Consequently the authorities received favourably the proposals made by Dr. Walter Oudney, a Scotchman, whose enthusiasm had been aroused by the travels of Mungo Park. This Dr. Oudney was a friend of Hugh Clapperton, a lieutenant in the Navy, three years his senior, who had distinguished himself in Canada and elsewhere, but had been thrown out of employment and reduced to half-pay by the peace of 1815.

Hearing of Oudney's scheme, Clapperton at once determined to join him in it, and Oudney begged the minister to allow him the aid of that enterprising officer, whose special knowledge would be of great assistance. Lord Bathurst made no objection, and the two friends, after receiving minute instructions, embarked for Tripoli, where they ascertained that Major Denham was to take the command of their expedition.

Denham was born in London on the 31st December, 1783, and began life as an articled pupil to a country lawyer. As an attorney's clerk he found his duties so irksome and so little suited to his daring spirit that his longing for adventure soon led him to enlist in a regiment bound for Spain. Until 1815 he remained with the army, but after the peace he employed his leisure in visiting France and Italy.

Denham, eager to obtain distinction, had chosen the career which would best enable him to achieve it, even at the risk of his life, and he now resolved to become an explorer. With him to think was to act. He had asked the minister to commission him to go to Timbuctoo by the route Laing afterwards took when he heard of the expedition under Clapperton and Oudney; and he now begged to be allowed to join them.

Without any delay Denham obtained the necessary equipment, and accompanied by a carpenter named William Hillman, he embarked for Malta, joining his future travelling companions at Tripoli on the 21st November, 1821. The English at this time enjoyed very great prestige, not only in the States of Barbary, on account of the bombardment of Algiers, but also because the British consul at Tripoli had by his clever diplomacy established friendly relations with the government to which he was accredited.

This prestige extended beyond the narrow range of the northern states. The nationality of certain travellers, the protection accorded by England to the Porte, the British victories in India had all been vaguely rumoured even in the heart of Africa, and the name of Englishman, was familiar without any particular meaning being attached to it. According to the English consul, the route from Tripoli to Bornou was as safe as that from London to Edinburgh. This was, therefore, the moment to seize opportunities which might not occur again.

The three travellers, after a cordial reception from the bey, who placed all his resources at their disposal, lost no time in leaving Tripoli, and with an escort provided by the Moorish governor, they reached Murzuk, the capital of Fezzan, on the 8th April, 1822, without difficulty, having indeed been received with great enthusiasm in some of the places through which they passed.

At Sockna, Denham tells us, the governor came out to meet them, accompanied by the principal inhabitants and hundreds of the country people, who crowded round their horses, kissing their hands with every appearance of cordiality and delight, and shouting *Inglesi*, *Inglesi*, as the visitors entered the town. This welcome was the more gratifying from the fact that the travellers were the first Europeans to penetrate into Africa without wearing a disguise. Denham adds that he feels sure their reception would have been far less cordial had they stooped to play the part of impostors by attempting to pass for Mahommedans.

At Murzuk they were harassed by annoyances similar to those which had paralyzed Hornemann; in their case, however, circumstances and character were alike different, and without allowing themselves to be blinded by the compliments paid them by the sultan, the English, who were thoroughly in earnest, demanded the necessary escort for the journey to Bornou.

It was impossible, they were told, to start before the following spring, on account of the difficulty of collecting a kafila or caravan, and the troops necessary for its escort across the desert.

A rich merchant, however, Boo-Bucker-Boo-Khaloum by name, a great friend of the pacha, gave the explorers a hint that if he received certain presents he would smooth away all difficulties. He even offered to escort them himself to Bornou, for which province he was bound if he could obtain the necessary permission from the Pacha of Tripoli.

Denham, believing Boo-Khaloum to be acting honestly, went off to Tripoli to obtain the governor's sanction, but on his arrival there he obtained only evasive answers, and finally threatened to embark for England, where he said he would report the obstacles thrown in his way by the pacha, in the carrying out of the objects of the exploring expedition.

These menaces produced no effect, and Denham actually set sail, and was about to land at Marseilles when he received a satisfactory message from the bey, begging him to return, and authorizing Boo-Khaloum to accompany him and his companions.

On the 30th October Denham rejoined Oudney and Clapperton at Murzuk, finding them considerably weakened by fever and the effects of the climate.

Denham, convinced that change of air would restore them to health, persuaded them to start and begin the journey by easy stages. He himself set out on the 20th of November with a caravan of merchants from Mesurata, Tripoli, Sockna, and Murzuk, escorted by 210 Arab warriors chosen from the most intelligent and docile of the tribes, and commanded by Boo-Khaloum.

The expedition took the route followed by Lyon and soon reached Tegerry, which is the most southerly town of Fezzan, and the last before the traveller enters the desert of Bilma.

Denham made a sketch of the castle of Tegerry from the southern bank of a salt lake near the town. Tegerry is entered by a low narrow vaulted passage leading to a gate in a second rampart. The wall is pierced with apertures which render the entrance by the narrow passage very difficult. Above the second gate there is also an aperture through which darts, and fire-brands may be hurled upon the besiegers, a mode of warfare once largely indulged in by the Arabs. Inside the town there are wells of fairly good water. Denham is of opinion that Tegerry restored, well-garrisoned and provisioned, could sustain a long siege. Its situation is delightful. It is surrounded by date-trees, and the water in the neighbourhood is excellent. A chain of low hills stretches away to the east. Snipes, ducks, and wild geese frequent the salt lakes near the town.

Leaving Tegerry, the travellers entered a sandy desert, across which it would not have been easy to find the way, had it not been marked out by the skeletons of men and animals strewn along it, especially about the wells.

"One of the skeletons we saw to-day," says Denham, "still looked quite fresh. The beard was on the chin, the features could be recognized. 'It is my slave,' exclaimed one of the merchants of the kafila. 'I left him near here four months ago.' 'Make haste and take him to the market!' cried a facetious slave merchant, 'lest some one else should claim him.'"

A kafila of slaves.
(Fac-simile of early engraving.)

Here and there in the desert are oases containing towns of greater or less importance, at which the caravans halt. Kishi is one of the most frequented of these places, and there the money for the right of crossing the desert is paid. The Sultan of Kishi, the ruler of a good many of these petty principalities, and who takes the title of Commander of the Faithful, was remarkable for a complete disregard of cleanliness, a peculiarity in which, according to Denham, his court fully equalled him.

This sultan paid Boo-Khaloum a visit in his tent, accompanied by half a dozen Tibboos, some of whom were positively hideous. Their teeth were of a dark yellow colour, the result of chewing tobacco, of which they are so fond that they use it as snuff as well as to chew. Their noses looked like little round bits of flesh stuck on to their faces with nostrils so wide that they could push their fingers right up them. Denham's watch, compass, and musical snuffbox astonished them not a little. He defines these people as brutes with human faces.

A little further on the travellers reached the town of Kirby, situated in a wâdy near a low range of hills of which the highest are not more than 400 feet above the sea level, and between two salt lakes, produced by the excavations made for building. From the centre of these lakes rise islets consisting of masses of muriate and carbonate of soda. The salt produced by these wâdys, or depressions of the soil, form an important article of commerce with Bornou and the whole of the Soudan.

It would be impossible to imagine a more wretched place than Kirby. Its houses are empty, containing not so much as a mat. How could it be otherwise with a place liable to incessant raids from the Tuaricks?

The caravan now crossed the Tibboo country, inhabited by a peaceful, hospitable people to whom, as keepers of the wells and reservoirs of the desert, the leaders of caravans pay passage-money. The Tibboos are a strong, active race, and when mounted on their nimble steeds they display marvellous skill in throwing the lance, which the most vigorous of their warriors can hurl to a distance of 145 yards. Bilma is their chief city, and the residence of their sultan.

On the arrival of the travellers at Bilma, the sultan, escorted by a number of men and women, came out to meet the strangers. The women were much better-looking than those in the smaller towns; some of them had indeed very pleasant faces, their white, regular teeth contrasting admirably with their shining black skins, and the three "triangular flaps of hair, streaming with oil." Coral ornaments in their noses, and large amber necklaces round their throats, gave them what Denham calls a "seductive appearance." Some of them carried fans made of grass or hair, with which to keep off the flies; others were provided with branches of trees; all, in fact, carried something in their hands, which they waved above their heads. Their costume consisted of a loose piece of Soudan cloth, fastened on the left shoulder, and leaving the right uncovered, with a smaller piece wound about the head, and falling on the shoulders or flung back. In spite of this paucity of clothing, there was not the least immodesty in their bearing.

A mile from Bilma, and beyond a limpid spring, which appears to have been placed there by nature to afford a supply of water to travellers, lies a desert, which it takes no less than ten days to cross. This was probably once a huge salt lake.

On the 4th February, 1823, the caravan reached Lari, a town on the northern boundary of Bornou, in lat. 14° 40' N. The inhabitants, astonished at the size of the "kafila," fled in terror at its approach.

"Beyond, however," says Denham, "was an object full of interest to us, and the sight of it produced a sensation so gratifying and inspiring, that it would be difficult for language to convey an idea of its force or pleasure. The great Lake Tchad, glowing with the golden rays of the sun in its strength, appeared to be within a mile of the spot on which we stood."

On leaving Lari, the appearance of the country changed completely. The sandy desert was succeeded by a clay soil, clothed with grass and dotted with acacias and other trees of various species, amongst which grazed herds of antelopes, whilst Guinea fowls and the turtle-doves of Barbary flew hither and thither above them. Towns took the place of villages, with huts of the shape of bells, thatched with durra straw.

The travellers continued their journey southwards, rounding Lake Tchad, which they had first touched at its most northerly point.

The districts bordering on this sheet of water were of a black, firm, but muddy soil. The waters rise to a considerable height in winter, and sink in proportion in the summer. The lake is of fresh water, rich in fish, and frequented by hippopotami and aquatic birds. Near its centre, on the south-east, are the islands inhabited by the Biddomahs, a race who live by pillaging the people of the mainland.

The explorers had sent a messenger to Sheikh El Khanemy, to ask permission to enter his capital, and an envoy speedily arrived to invite Boo-Khaloum and his companions to Kouka.

On their way thither, the travellers passed through Burwha, a fortified town which had thus far resisted the inroads of the Tuaricks, and crossed the Yeou, a large river, in some parts more than 500 feet in width, which, rising in the Soudan, flows into Lake Tchad.

On the southern shores of this river rises a little town of the same name, about half the size of Burwha.

The caravan soon reached the gates of Kouka, where, after a journey extending over two months and a half, they were received by a body of cavalry 4000 strong, under perfect discipline. Amongst these troops was a corps of blacks forming the body-guard of the sheikh, whose equipments resembled those of ancient chivalry.

Member of the body-guard of the Sheikh of Bornou.
(Fac-simile of early engraving.)

They wore, Denham tells us, suits of chain armour covering the neck and shoulders. These were fastened above the head, and fell in two portions, one in front and one behind, so as to protect the flanks of the horse and the thighs of the rider. A sort of casque or iron coif, kept in its place by red, white or yellow turbans, tied under the chin, completed the costume. The horses' heads were also guarded by iron plates. Their saddles were small and light, and their steel stirrups held only the point of the feet, which were clad in leather shoes, ornamented with crocodile skin. The horsemen managed their steeds admirably, as, advancing at full gallop, brandishing their spears, they wheeled right and left of their guests, shouting "Barca! Barca!" (Blessing! Blessing!).

Surrounded by this brilliant and fantastic escort, the English and Arabs entered the town, where a similar military display had been prepared in their honour.

They were presently admitted to the presence of Sheikh El-Khanemy, who appeared to be about forty-five years old, and whose face was prepossessing, with a happy, intelligent, and benevolent expression.

The English presented the letters of the pacha, and when the sheikh had read them, he asked Denham what had brought him and his companions to Bornou.

"We came merely to see the country," replied Denham, "to study the character of its people, its scenery, and its productions."

"You are welcome," was the reply; "it will be a pleasure to me to show you everything. I have ordered huts to be built for you in the town; you may go and see them, accompanied by one of my people, and when you are recovered from the fatigue of your long journey, I shall be happy to see you."

Reception of the Mission.
(Fac-simile of early engraving.)

The travellers soon afterwards obtained permission to make collections of
such animals and plants as appeared to them curious, and to make notes of all

their observations. They were thus enabled to collect a good deal of information about the towns near Kouka.

Kouka, then the capital of Bornou, boasted of a market for the sale of slaves, sheep, oxen, cheese, rice, earth-nuts, beans, indigo, and other productions of the country. There 100,000 people might sometimes be seen haggling about the price of fish, poultry, meat—the last sold both raw and cooked—or that of brass, copper, amber and coral. Linen was so cheap in these parts, that some of the men wore shirts and trousers made of it.

Beggars have a peculiar mode of exciting compassion; they station themselves at the entrance to the market, and, holding up the rags of an old pair of trousers, they whine out to the passers-by, "See! I have no pantaloons!" The novelty of this mode of proceeding, and the request for a garment, which seemed to them even more necessary than food, made our travellers laugh heartily until they became accustomed to it.

Hitherto the English had had nothing to do with any one but the sheikh, who, content with wielding all real power, left the nominal sovereignty to the sultan, an eccentric monarch, who never showed himself except through the bars of a wicker cage near the gate of his garden, as if he were some rare wild beast. Curious indeed were some of the customs of this court, not the least so the fancy for obesity: no one was considered elegant unless he had attained to a bulk generally looked upon as very inconvenient.

Some exquisites had stomachs so distended and prominent that they seemed literally to hang over the pommel of the saddle; and in addition to this, fashion prescribed a turban of such length and weight that its wearer had to carry his head on one side.

These uncouth peculiarities rivalled those of the Turks of a masked ball, and the travellers had often hard work to preserve their gravity. To compensate, however, for the grotesque solemnity of the various receptions, a new field for observation was open, and much valuable information might now be acquired.

Denham wished to proceed to the south at once, but the sheikh was unwilling to risk the lives of the travellers entrusted to him by the Bey of Tripoli. On their entry into Bornou, the responsibility of Boo-Khaloum for their safety was transferred to him.

So earnest, however, were the entreaties of Denham, that El-Khanemy at last sanctioned his accompanying Boo-Khaloum in a "ghrazzie," or plundering expedition against the Kaffirs or infidels.

The sheikh's army and the Arab troops passed in succession Yeddie, a large walled city twenty miles from Angoumou, Badagry, and several other towns built on an alluvial soil which has a dark clay-like appearance.

They entered Mandara, at the frontier town of Delow, beyond which the sultan of the province, with five hundred horsemen, met his guests.

Denham describes Mahommed Becker as a man of short stature, about fifty years old, wearing a beard, painted of a most delicate azure blue. The presentations over, the sultan at once turned to Denham, and asked who he was, whence he came, what he wanted, and lastly if he were a Mahommedan. On Boo-Khaloum's hesitating to reply, the sultan turned away his head, with the words, "So the pacha numbers infidels amongst his friends!"

This incident had a very bad effect, and Denham was not again admitted to the presence of the sultan.

Lancer of the army of the Sultan of Begharmi.
(Fac-simile of early engraving.)

The enemies of the Pacha of Bornou and the Sultan of Mandara, were called
Fellatahs. Their vast settlements extended far beyond Timbuctoo. They are a

handsome set of men, with skins of a dark bronze colour, which shows them to be of a race quite distinct from the negroes. They are professors of Mahommedanism, and mix but little with the blacks. We shall presently have to speak more particularly of the Fellatahs, Foulahs, or Fans, as they are called throughout the Soudan.

South of the town of Mora rises a chain of mountains, of which the loftiest peaks are not more than 2500 feet high, but which, according to the natives, extend for more than "two months' journey."

The most salient point noticed by Denham in his description of the country, is a vast and apparently interminable chain of mountains, shutting in the view on every side; this, though in his opinion, inferior to the Alps, Apennines, Jura, and Sierra Morena in rugged magnificence and gigantic grandeur, are yet equal to them in picturesque effect. The lofty peaks of Valhmy, Savah, Djoggiday, Munday, &c., with clustering villages on their stony sides, rise on the east and west, while Horza, exceeding any of them in height and beauty, rises on the south with its ravines and precipices.

Derkulla, one of the chief Fellatah towns, was reduced to ashes by the invaders, who lost no time in pressing on to Musfeia, a position which, naturally very strong, was further defended by palisades manned by a numerous body of archers. The English traveller had to take part in the assault. The first onslaught of the Arabs appeared to carry all before it; the noise of the fire-arms, with the reputation for bravery and cruelty enjoyed by Boo-Khaloum and his men, threw the Fellatahs into momentary confusion, and if the men of Mandara and Bornou had followed up their advantage and stormed the hill, the town would probably have fallen.

The besieged, however, noticing the hesitation of their assailants, in their turn assumed the defensive, and rallying their archers discharged a shower of poisoned arrows, to which many an Arab fell a victim, and before which the forces of Bornou and Mandara gave way.

Barca, the Bornou general, had three horses killed under him. Boo-Khaloum and his steed were both wounded, and Denham was in a similar plight, with the skin of his face grazed by one arrow and two others lodged in his burnoos.

The retreat soon became a rout. Denham's horse fell under him, and the major had hardly regained his feet when he was surrounded by Fellatahs. Two fled on the presentation of the Englishman's pistols, a third received the charge in his shoulder.

Denham thought he was safe, when his horse fell a second time, flinging his master violently against a tree. This time when the major rose he found himself with neither horse nor weapons; and the next moment he was surrounded by enemies, who stripped him and wounded him in both hands and the right side, leaving him half dead at last to fight over his clothes, which seemed to them of great value.

Availing himself of this lucky quarrel, Denham slipped under a horse standing by, and disappeared in the thicket. Naked, bleeding, wild with pain, he reached the edge of a ravine with a mountain stream flowing through it. His strength was all but gone, and he was clutching at a bough of a tree overhanging the water with a view to dropping himself into it as the banks were very steep, and the branches were actually bending beneath his weight, when from beneath his hand a gigantic liffa, the most venomous kind of serpent in the country, rose from its coil in the very act of striking. Horror- struck, Denham let slip the branch, and tumbled headlong into the water, but fortunately the shock revived him, he struck out almost unconsciously, swam to the opposite bank, and climbing it, found himself safe from his pursuers.

Fortunately the fugitive soon saw a group of horsemen amongst the trees, and in spite of the noise of the pursuit, he managed to shout loud enough to make them hear him. They turned out to be Barca Gana and Boo-Khaloum, with some Arabs. Mounted on a sorry steed, with no other clothing than an old blanket swarming with vermin, Denham travelled thirty-seven miles. The pain of his wounds was greatly aggravated by the heat, the thermometer being at 32°.

The only results of the expedition, which was to have brought in such quantities of booty and numerous slaves, were the deaths of Boo-Khaloum and thirty-six of his Arabs, the wounding of nearly all the rest, and the loss or destruction of all the horses.

The eighty miles between Mora and Kouka were traversed in six days. Denham was kindly received in the latter town by the sultan, who sent him a native garment to replace his lost wardrobe. The major had hardly recovered from his wounds and fatigue, before he took part in a new expedition, sent to Munga, a province on the west of Bornou, by the sheikh, whose authority had never been fully recognized there, and whose claim for tribute had been refused by the inhabitants.

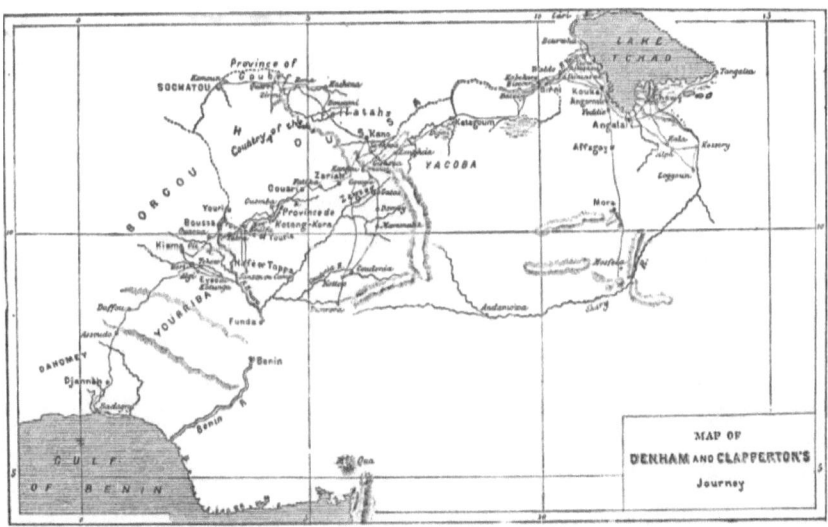

Gravé par E. Morieu.

Denham and Oudney left Kouka on the 22nd May, and crossed the Yeou, then nearly dried up, but an important stream in the rainy season, and visited Birnie, with the ruins of the capital of the same name, which was capable of containing two hundred thousand inhabitants. The travellers also passed through the ruins of Gambarou with its magnificent buildings, the favourite residence of the former sultan, destroyed by the Fellatahs, Kabshary, Bassecour, Bately, and many other towns or villages, whose numerous populations submitted without a struggle to the Sultan of Bornou.

The rainy season was disastrous to the members of the expedition, Clapperton fell dangerously ill of fever, and Oudney, whose chest was delicate even before he left England, grew weaker every day. Denham alone kept up. On the 14th of December, when the rainy season was drawing to a close, Clapperton and Oudney started for Kano. We shall presently relate the particulars of this interesting part of their expedition.

Seven days later, an ensign, named Toole, arrived at Kouka, after a journey from Tripoli, which had occupied only three months and fourteen days.

In February, 1824, Denham and Toole made a trip into Luggun, on the south of Lake Tchad. All the districts near the lake and its tributary, the Shari, are marshy, and flooded during the rainy season. The unhealthiness of the climate was fatal to young Toole, who died at Angala, on the 26th of February, at the early age of twenty-two. Persevering, enterprising, bright and obliging, with plenty of pluck and prudence, Toole was a model explorer.

Luggun was then very little known, its capital Kernok, contained no less than 15,000 inhabitants. The people of Luggun, especially the women—who are very industrious, and manufacture the finest linens, and fabrics of the closest texture—are handsomer and more intelligent than those of Bornou.

The necessary interview with the sultan ended, after an exchange of complimentary speeches and handsome presents, in this strange proposal from his majesty to the travellers: "If you have come to buy female slaves, you need not be at the trouble to go further, as I will sell them to you as cheap as possible." Denham had great trouble in convincing the merchant prince that such traffic was not the aim of his journey, but that the love of science alone had brought him to Luggun.

On the 2nd of March, Denham returned to Kouka, and on the 20th of May, he was witness to the arrival of Lieutenant Tyrwhitt, who had come to take up his residence as consul at the court of Bornou, bearing costly presents for the sultan.

Portrait of Clapperton.
(Fac-simile of early engraving.)

After a final excursion in the direction of Manou, the capital of Kanem, and a
visit to the Dogganah, who formerly occupied all the districts about Lake

Fitri, the major joined Clapperton in his return journey to Tripoli, starting on the 16th of April, and arriving there in safety at the close of a long and arduous journey, whose geographical results, important in any case, had been greatly enhanced by the labours of Clapperton. To the adventures and discoveries of the latter we must now turn. Clapperton and Oudney started for Kano, a large Fellatah town on the west of Lake Tchad, on the 14th of December, 1823, followed the Yeou as far as Damasak, and visited the ruins of Birnie, and those of Bera, on the shores of a lake formed by the overflowing of the Yeou, Dogamou and Bekidarfi, all towns of Houssa. The people of this province, who were very numerous before the invasion of the Fellatahs, are armed with bows and arrows, and trade in tobacco, nuts, gouro, antimony, tanned hares' skins, and cotton stuffs in the piece and made into clothes.

The caravan soon left the banks of the Yeou or Gambarou, and entered a wooded country, which was evidently under water in the rainy season.

The travellers then entered the province of Katagoum, where the governor received them with great cordiality, assuring them that their arrival was quite an event to him, as it would be to the Sultan of the Fellatahs, who, like himself, had never before seen an Englishman. He also assured them that they would find all they required in his district, just as at Kouka.

The only thing which seemed to surprise him much, was the fact that his visitors wanted neither slaves, horses, nor silver, and that the sole proof of his friendship they required was permission to collect flowers and plants, and to travel in his country.

According to Clapperton's observations, Katagoum is situated in lat. 12° 17′ 11″ N., and about 12° E. long. Before the Fellatahs were conquered, it was on the borders of the province of Bornou. It can send into the field 4000 cavalry, and 2000 foot soldiers, armed with bows and arrows, swords and lances. Wheat, and oxen, with slaves, are its chief articles of commerce. The citadel is the strongest the English had seen, except that of Tripoli. Entered by gates which are shut at night, it is defended by two parallel walls, and three dry moats, one inside, one out, and the third between the two walls which are twenty feet high, and ten feet wide at the base. A ruined mosque is the only other object of interest in the town, which consists of mud houses, and contains some seven or eight hundred inhabitants.

There the English for the first time saw cowries used as money. Hitherto native cloth had been the sole medium of exchange.

South of Katagoum is the Yacoba country, called Mouchy by the Mahommedans. According to accounts received by Clapperton, the people of

Yacoba, which is shut in by limestone mountains, are cannibals. The Mahommedans, however, who have an intense horror of the "Kaffirs," give no other proof of this accusation than the statement that they have seen human heads and limbs hanging against the walls of the houses.

In Yacoba rises the Yeou, a river which dries up completely in the summer; but, according to the people who live on its banks, rises and falls regularly every week throughout the rainy season.

On the 11th of January, the journey was resumed; but a halt had to be made at Murmur at noon of the same day, as Oudney showed signs of such extreme weakness and exhaustion, that Clapperton feared he could not last through another day. He had been gradually failing ever since they left the mountains of Obarri in Fezzan, where he had inflammation of the throat from sitting in a draught when over-heated.

On the 12th of January, Oudney took a cup of coffee at daybreak, and at his request Clapperton changed camels with him. He then helped him to dress, and leaning on his servant, the doctor left the tent. He was about to attempt to mount his camel, when Clapperton saw death in his face. He supported him back to the tent, where to his intense grief, he expired at once, without a groan or any sign of suffering. Clapperton lost no time in asking the governor's permission to bury his comrade; and this being obtained, he dug a grave for him himself under an old mimosa-tree near one of the gates of the town. After the body had been washed according to the custom of the country, it was wrapped in some of the turban shawls which were to have served as presents on the further journey; the servants carried it to its last resting-place, and Clapperton read the English burial service at the grave. When the ceremony was over, he surrounded the modest resting-place with a wall of earth, to keep off beasts of prey, and had two sheep killed, which he divided amongst the poor.

Thus closed the career of the young naturalist and ship's doctor, Oudney. His terrible malady, whose germs he had brought with him from England, had prevented him from rendering so much service to the expedition as the Government had expected from him, although he never spared himself, declaring that he felt better on the march, than when resting. Knowing that his weakened constitution would not admit of any sustained exertion on his part, he would never damp the ardour of his companions.

After this sad event, Clapperton resumed his journey to Kano, halting successively at Digou, situated in a well-cultivated district, rich in flocks; Katoungora, beyond the province of Katagoum; Zangeia, once—judging from its extent and the ruined walls still standing—an important place, near the end of the Douchi chain of hills; Girkoua, with a finer market-place than that of

Tripoli; and Souchwa, surrounded by an imposing earthwork.

Kano, the Chana of Edrisi and other Arab geographers, and the great emporium of the kingdom of Houssa, was reached on the 20th January.

Clapperton tells us that he had hardly entered the gates before his expectations were disappointed; after the brilliant description of the Arabs, he had expected to see a town of vast extent. The houses were a quarter of a mile from the walls, and stood here and there in little groups, separated by large pools of stagnant water. "I might have dispensed with the care I had bestowed on my dress," (he had donned his naval uniform), "for the inhabitants, absorbed in their own affairs, let me pass without remark and never so much as looked at me."

Kano, the capital of the province of that name and one of the chief towns of the Soudan, is situated in N. lat. 12° 0' 19", and E. long. 9° 20'. It contains between thirty and forty thousand inhabitants, of whom the greater number are slaves.

The market, bounded on the east and west by vast reedy swamps, is the haunt of numerous flocks of ducks, storks, and vultures, which act as scavengers to the town. In this market, stocked with all the provisions in use in Africa, beef, mutton, goats' and sometimes even camels' flesh, are sold.

Writing paper of French manufacture, scissors and knives, antimony, tin, red silk, copper bracelets, glass beads, coral, amber, steel rings, silver ornaments, turban shawls, cotton cloths, calico, Moorish habiliments, and many other articles, are exposed for sale in large quantities in the market-place of Kano.

There Clapperton bought for three piastres, an English cotton umbrella from Ghadames. He also visited the slave-market, where the unfortunate human chattels are as carefully examined as volunteers for the navy are by our own inspectors.

The town is very unhealthy, the swamps cutting it in two, and the holes produced by the removal of the earth for building, produce permanent malaria.

It is the fashion at Kano to stain the teeth and limbs with the juice of a plant called *gourgi*, and with tobacco, which produces a bright red colour. Gouro nuts are chewed, and sometimes even swallowed when mixed with *trona*, a habit not peculiar to Houssa, for it extends to Bornou, where it is strictly forbidden to women. The people of Houssa smoke a native tobacco.

On the 23rd of February, Clapperton started for Sackatoo. He crossed a picturesque well-cultivated country, whose wooded hills gave it the appearance of an English park. Herds of beautiful white or dun-coloured oxen gave animation to the scenery.

The most important places passed en route by Clapperton were Gadania, a densely populated town, the inhabitants of which had been sold as slaves by the Fellatahs, Doncami, Zirmia, the capital of Gambra, Kagaria, Kouari, and the wells of Kamoun, where he met an escort sent by the sultan.

Sackatoo was the most thickly populated city that the explorer had seen in Africa. Its well-built houses form regular streets, instead of clustering in groups as in the other towns of Houssa. It is surrounded by a wall between twenty and thirty feet high, pierced by twelve gates, which are closed every evening at sunset, and it boasts of two mosques, with a market and a large square opposite to the sultan's residence.

The inhabitants, most of whom are Fellatahs, own many slaves; and the latter, those at least who are not in domestic service, work at some trade for their masters' profit. They are weavers, masons, blacksmiths, shoemakers, or husbandmen.

To do honour to his host, and also to give him an exalted notion of the power and wealth of England, Clapperton assumed a dazzling costume when he paid his first visit to Sultan Bello. He covered his uniform with gold lace, donned white trousers and silk stockings, and completed this holiday attire by a Turkish turban and slippers. Bello received him, seated on a cushion in a thatched hut like an English cottage. The sultan, a handsome man, about forty-five years old, wore a blue cotton *tobe* and a white cotton turban, one end of which fell over his nose and mouth in Turkish fashion.

Bello accepted the traveller's presents with childish glee. The watch, telescope, and thermometer, which he naively called a "heat watch," especially delighted him; but he wondered more at his visitor than at any of his gifts. He was unwearied in his questions as to the manners, customs, and trade of England; and after receiving several replies, he expressed a wish to open commercial relations with that power. He would like an English consul and a doctor to reside in a port he called Raka, and finally he requested that certain articles of English manufacture should be sent to Funda, a very thriving sea-port of his. After a good many talks on the different religions of Europe, Bello gave back to Clapperton the books, journals, and clothes which had been taken from Denham, at the time of the unfortunate excursion in which Boo-Khaloum lost his life.

On the 3rd May, Clapperton took leave of the sultan. This time there was a good deal of delay before he was admitted to an audience. Bello was alone, and gave the traveller a letter for the King of England, with many expressions of friendship towards the country of his visitor, reiterating his wish to open commercial relations with it and begging him to let him have a letter to say when the English expedition promised by Clapperton would arrive on the coast of Africa.

Clapperton returned by the route by which he had come, arriving on the 8th of July at Kouka, where he rejoined Denham. He had brought with him an Arab manuscript containing a geographical and historical picture of the kingdom of Takrour, governed by Mahommed Bello of Houssa, author of the manuscript. He himself had not only collected much valuable information on the geology and botany of Bornou and Houssa, but also drawn up a vocabulary of the languages of Begharmi, Mandara, Bornou, Houssa, and Timbuctoo.

The results of the expedition were therefore considerable. The Fellatahs had been heard of for the first time, and their identity with the Fans had been ascertained by Clapperton in his second journey. It had been proved that these Fellatahs had created a vast empire in the north and west of Africa, and also that beyond a doubt they did not belong to the negro race. The study of their language, and its resemblance to certain idioms not of African origin, will some day throw a light on the migration of races. Lastly, Lake Tchad had been discovered, and though not entirely examined, the greater part of its shores had been explored. It had been ascertained to have two tributaries: the Yeou, part of whose course had been traced, whilst its source had been pointed out by the natives, and the Shari, the mouth and lower portion of which had been carefully examined by Denham. With regard to the Niger, the information collected by Clapperton from the natives was still very contradictory, but the balance of evidence was in favour of its flowing into the Gulf of Benin. However, Clapperton intended, after a short rest in England, to return to Africa, and landing on the western coast make his way up the Kouara or Djoliba as the natives call the Niger; to set at rest once for all the dispute as to whether that river was or was not identical with the Nile; to connect his new discoveries with those of Denham, and lastly to cross Africa, taking a diagonal course from Tripoli to the Gulf of Benin.

II.

Clapperton's second journey—Arrival at Badagry—Yariba and its capital Katunga—Boussa—Attempts to get at the truth about Mungo Park's fate—"Nyffé," Yaourie, and Zegzeg—Arrival at Kano— Disappointments—Death of Clapperton—Return of Lander to the coast

—Tuckey on the Congo—Bowditch in Ashantee—Mollien at the sources of the Senegal and Gambia—Major Grey—Caillié at Timbuctoo—Laing at the sources of the Niger—Richard and John Lander at the mouth of the Niger—Cailliaud and Letorzec in Egypt, Nubia, and the oasis of Siwâh.

So soon as Clapperton arrived in England, he submitted to Lord Bathurst his scheme for going to Kouka *viâ* the Bight of Benin—in other words by the shortest way, a route not attempted by his predecessors—and ascending the Niger from its mouth to Timbuctoo.

In this expedition three others were associated with Clapperton, who took the command. These three were a surgeon named Dickson, Pearce, a ship's captain, and Dr. Morrison, also in the merchant service; the last-named well up in every branch of natural history.

On the 26th November, 1825, the expedition arrived in the Bight of Benin. For some reason unexplained, Dickson had asked permission to make his way to Sockatoo alone and he landed for that purpose at Whydah. A Portuguese named Songa, and Colombus, Denham's servant, accompanied him as far as Dahomey. Seventeen days after he left that town, Dickson reached Char, and a little later Yaourie, beyond which place he was never traced.[1]

[1] Dickson quarrelled with a native chief, and was murdered by his followers. See Clapperton's "Last Journey in Africa."—*Trans.*

The other explorers sailed up the Bight of Benin, and were warned by an English merchant named Houtson, not to attempt the ascent of the Quorra, as the king of the districts watered by it had conceived an intense hatred of the English, on account of their interference with the slave-trade, the most remunerative branch of his commerce.

It would be much better, urged Houtson, to go to Badagry, no great distance from Sackatoo, the chief of which, well-disposed as he was to travellers, would doubtless give them an escort as far as the frontiers of Yariba. Houtson had lived in the country many years, and was well acquainted with the language and habits of its people. Clapperton, therefore, thought it desirable to attach him to the expedition as far as Katunga, the capital of Yariba.

The expedition disembarked at Badagry, on the 29th November, 1825, ascended an arm of the Lagos, and then, for a distance of two miles, the Gazie creek, which traverses part of Dahomey. Descending the left bank, the explorers began their march into the interior of the country, through districts consisting partly of swamps and partly of yam plantations. Everything indicated fertility. The negroes were very averse to work, and it would be impossible to relate the numerous "palavers" and negotiations which had to be gone through, and the exactions which were submitted to, before porters could be obtained.

The explorers succeeded, in spite of these difficulties, in reaching Jenneh, sixty miles from the coast. Here Clapperton tells us he saw several looms at work, as many as eight or nine in one house, a regular manufactory in fact. The people of Jenneh also make earthenware, but they prefer that which they get from Europe, often putting the foreign produce to uses for which it was never intended.

At Jenneh the travellers were all attacked with fever, the result of the great heat and the unhealthiness of the climate. Pearce and Morrison both died on the 27th December, the former soon after he left Jenneh with Clapperton, the latter at that town, to which he had returned to rest.

At Assondo, a town of no less than 10,000 inhabitants; Daffou, containing some 5000, and other places visited by Clapperton on his way through the country, he found that an extraordinary rumour had preceded him, to the effect that he had come to restore peace to the districts distracted by war, and to do good to the lands he explored.

At Tchow the caravan met a messenger with a numerous escort, sent by the King of Yariba to meet the explorers, and shortly afterwards Katunga was entered. This town is built round the base of a rugged granite mountain. It is about three miles in extent, and is both framed in and planted with bushy trees presenting a most picturesque appearance.

"The caravan met a messenger."

Clapperton remained at Katunga from the 24th January to the 7th March, 1826. He was entertained there with great hospitality by the sultan, who, however, refused to give him permission to go to Houssa and Bornou by way of Nyffé or Toppa, urging as reasons that Nyffé was distracted by civil war, and one of the pretenders to the throne had called in the aid of the Fellatahs. It would be more prudent to go through Yaourie. Whether these excuses were true or not, Clapperton had to submit.

The explorer availed himself of his detention at Katunga to make several interesting observations. This town contains no less than seven markets, in which are exposed for sale yams, cereals, bananas, figs, the seeds of gourds, hares, poultry, sheep, lambs, linen cloth, and various implements of husbandry.

The houses of the king and those of his wives are situated in two large parks. The doors and the pillars of the verandahs are adorned with fairly well executed carvings, representing such scenes as a boa killing an antelope, or a pig, or a group of warriors and drummers.

According to Clapperton the people of Yariba have fewer of the characteristics of the negro race than any natives of Africa with whom he was brought in contact. Their lips are not so thick and their noses are of a more aquiline shape. The men are well made, and carry themselves with an ease which cannot fail to be remarked. The women are less refined-looking than the men, the result, probably, of exposure to the sun and the fatigue they endure, compelled as they are to do all the work of the fields.

Soon after leaving Katunga, Clapperton crossed the Mousa, a tributary of the Quorra and entered Kiama, one of the halting-places of the caravans trading between Houssa and Borghoo, and Gandja, on the frontiers of Ashantee. Kiama contains no less than 13,000 inhabitants, who are considered the greatest thieves in Africa. To say a man is from Borghoo is to brand him as a blackguard at once.

Outside Kiama the traveller met the Houssa caravan. Some thousands of men and women, oxen, asses, and horses, marching in single file, formed an interminable line presenting a singular and grotesque appearance. A motley assemblage truly: naked girls alternating with men bending beneath their loads, or with Gandja merchants in the most outlandish and ridiculous costumes, mounted on bony steeds which stumbled at every step.

Clapperton now made for Boussa on the Niger, where Mungo Park was drowned. Before reaching it he had to cross the Oli, a tributary of the Quorra, and to pass through Wow-wow, a district of Borghoo, the capital of which, also called Wow-wow, contained some 18,000 inhabitants. It was one of the cleanest and best built towns the traveller had entered since he left Badagry. The streets are wide and well kept, and the houses are round, with conical thatched roofs. Drunkenness is a prevalent vice in Wow-wow: governor, priests, laymen, men and women, indulge to excess in palm wine, in rum brought from the coast, and in "bouza." The latter beverage is a mixture made of dhurra, honey, cayenne pepper, and the root of a coarse grass eaten by cattle, with the addition of a certain quantity of water.

Clapperton tells us that the people of Wow-wow are famous for their cleanliness; they are cheerful, benevolent, and hospitable. No other people whom he had met with had been so ready to give him information about their country; and, more extraordinary still, did not meet with a single beggar. The natives say they are not aborigines of Borghoo, but that they are descendants of the natives of Houssa and Nyffé. They speak a Yariba dialect, but the Wow-wow women are pretty, which those of Yariba are not. The men are muscular and well-made, but have a dissipated look. Their religion is a lax kind of Mahommedanism tinctured with paganism.

Since leaving the coast Clapperton had met tribes of unconverted Fellatahs speaking the same language, and resembling in feature and complexion others who had adopted Mahommedanism. A significant fact which points to their belonging to one race.

Boussa, which the traveller reached at last, is not a regular town, but consists of groups of scattered houses on an island of the Quorra, situated in lat. 10° 14' N., and long. 6° 11' E. The province of which it is the capital is the most densely populated of Borghoo. The inhabitants are all Pagans, even the sultan, although his name is Mahommed. They live upon monkeys, dogs, cats, rats, beef, and mutton.

Breakfast was served to the sultan whilst he was giving audience to Clapperton, whom he invited to join him. The meal consisted of a large water-rat grilled without skinning, a dish of fine boiled rice, some dried fish stewed in palm oil, fried alligators' eggs, washed down with fresh water from the Quorra. Clapperton took some stewed fish and rice, but was much laughed at because he would eat neither the rat nor the alligators' eggs.

The sultan received him very courteously, and told him that the Sultan of Yaourie had had boats ready to take him to that town for the last seven days. Clapperton replied that as the war had prevented all exit from Bornou and Yaourie, he should prefer going by way of Coulfo and Nyffé. "You are right," answered the sultan; "you did well to come and see me, and you can take which ever route you prefer."

At a later audience Clapperton made inquiries about the Englishmen who had perished in the Quorra twenty years before. This subject evidently made the sultan feel very ill at ease, and he evaded the questions put to him, by saying he was too young at the time to remember what happened.

Clapperton explained that he only wanted to recover their books and papers, and to visit the scene of their death; and the sultan in reply denied having anything belonging to them, adding a warning against his guest's going to the place where they died, for it was a "very bad place."

"But I understood," urged Clapperton, "that part of the boat they were in could still be seen."

"No, it was a false report," replied the sultan, "the boat had long since been carried down by the stream; it was somewhere amongst the rocks, he didn't know where."

To a fresh demand for Park's papers and journals the sultan replied that he had none of them; they were in the hands of some learned men; but as Clapperton seemed to set such store by them, he would have them looked for. Thanking him for this promise, Clapperton begged permission to question the old men of the place, some of whom must have witnessed the catastrophe. No answer whatever was returned to this appeal, by which the sultan was evidently much embarrassed. It was useless to press him further.

This was a check to Clapperton's further inquiries. On every side he was met with embarrassed silence or such replies as, "The affair happened so long ago, I can't remember it," or, "I was not witness to it." The place where the boat had been stopped and its crew drowned was pointed out to him, but even that was done cautiously. A few days later, Clapperton found out that the former Imaun, who was a Fellatah, had had Mungo Park's books and papers in his possession. Unfortunately, however, this Imaun had long since left Boussa. Finally, when at Coulfo, the explorer ascertained beyond a doubt that Mungo Park had been murdered.

Before leaving Borghoo, Clapperton recorded his conviction of the baselessness of the bad reputation of the inhabitants, who had been branded everywhere as thieves and robbers. He had completely explored their country, travelled and hunted amongst them alone, and never had the slightest reason to complain.

The traveller now endeavoured to reach Kano by way of Zouari and Zegzeg, first crossing the Quorra. He soon arrived at Fabra, on the Mayarrow, the residence of the queen-mother of Nyffé, and then went to visit the king, in camp at a short distance from the town. This king, Clapperton tells us, was the most insolent rogue imaginable, asking for everything he saw, and quite unabashed by any refusal. His ambition and his calling in of the Fellatahs, who would throw him over as soon as he had answered their purpose, had been the ruin of his country. Thanks indeed to him, nearly the whole of the industrial population of Nyffé had been killed, sold into slavery, or had fled the country.

Clapperton was detained by illness much longer than he had intended to remain at Coulfo, a commercial town on the northern banks of the Mayarrow containing from twelve to fifteen thousand inhabitants. Exposed for the last twenty years to the raids of the Fellatahs, Coulfo had been burnt twice in six years. Clapperton was witness when there of the Feast of the New Moon. On that festival every one exchanged visits. The women wear their woolly hair plaited and stained with indigo. Their eyebrows are dyed the same colour. Their eyelids are painted with kohl, their lips are stained yellow, their teeth red, and their hands and feet are coloured with henna. On the day of the Feast of the Moon they don their gayest garments, with their glass beads, bracelets, copper, silver, steel, or brass. They also turn the occasion to account by drinking as much bouza as the men, joining in all their songs and dances.

After passing through Katunga, Clapperton entered the province of Gouari, the people of which though conquered with the rest of Houssa by the Fellatahs, had rebelled against them on the death of Bello I., and since then maintained their independence in spite of all the efforts of their invaders. Gouari, capital of the province of the same name, is situated in lat. 10° 54' N., and long. 8° 1' E.

At Fatika Clapperton entered Zegzeg, subject to the Fellatahs, after which he visited Zariyah, a singular-looking town laid out with plantations of millet, woods of bushy trees, vegetable gardens, &c., alternating with marshes, lawns, and houses. The population was very numerous, exceeding even that of Kano, being estimated indeed at some forty or fifty thousand, nearly all Fellatahs.

On the 19th September, after a long and weary journey, Clapperton at last entered Kano. He at once discovered that he would have been more welcome if he had come from the east, for the war with Bornou had broken off all communication with Fezzan and Tripoli. Leaving his luggage under the care of his servant Lander, Clapperton almost immediately started in quest of Sultan Bello, who they said was near Sackatoo. This was an extremely arduous journey, and on it Clapperton lost his camels and horses, and was compelled to put up with a miserable ox; to carry part of his baggage, he and his servants dividing the rest amongst them.

Bello received Clapperton kindly and sent him camels and provisions, but as he was then engaged in subjugating the rebellious province of Gouber, he could not at once give the explorer the personal audience so important to the many interests entrusted by the English Government to Clapperton.

Bello advanced to the attack of Counia, the capital of Gouber, at the head of an army of 60,000 soldiers, nine-tenths of whom were on foot and wore padded armour. The struggle was contemptible in the extreme, and this abortive attempt closed the war. Clapperton, whose health was completely broken up, managed to make his way from Sackatoo to Magaria, where he saw the sultan.

After he had received the presents brought for him, Bello became less friendly. He presently pretended to have received a letter from Sheikh El Khanemy warning him against the traveller, whom his correspondent characterized as a spy, and urging him to defy the English, who meant, after finding out all about the country, to settle in it, raise up sedition and profit by the disturbances they should create to take possession of Houssa, as they had done of India.

The most patent of all the motives of Bello in creating difficulties for Clapperton was his wish to appropriate the presents intended for the Sultan of Bornou. A pretext being necessary, he spread a rumour that the traveller was taking cannons and ammunition to Kouka. It was out of all reason Bello should allow a stranger to cross his dominions with a view to enabling his implacable enemy to make war upon him. Finally, Bello made an effort to induce Clapperton to read to him the letter of Lord Bathurst to the Sultan of Bornou.

Clapperton told him he could take it if he liked, but that he would not give it to him, adding that everything was of course possible to him, as he had force on his side, but that he would bring dishonour upon himself by using it. "To open the letter myself," said Clapperton, "is more than my head is worth." He had come, he urged, bringing Bello a letter and presents from the King of England, relying upon the confidence inspired by the sultan's letter of the previous year, and he hoped his host would not forfeit that confidence by tampering with another person's letter.

On this the sultan made a gesture of dismissal, and Clapperton retired.

This was not, however, the last attempt of a similar kind, and things grew much worse later. A few days afterwards another messenger was sent to demand the presents reserved for El Khanemy, and on Clapperton's refusing to give them up, they were taken from him.

"I told the Gadado," says Clapperton, "that they were acting like robbers towards me, in defiance of all good faith: that no people in the world would act the same, and they had far better have cut my head off than done such an act; but I suppose they would do that also when they had taken everything from me."

An attempt was now made to obtain his arms and ammunition, but this he resisted sturdily. His terrified servants ran away, but soon returned to share the dangers of their master, for whom they entertained the warmest affection.

At this critical moment, the entries in Clapperton's journal ceased. He had now been six months in Sackatoo, without being able to undertake any explorations or to bring to a satisfactory conclusion the mission which had brought him from the coast. Sick at heart, weary, and ill, he could take no rest, and his illness suddenly increased upon him to an alarming degree. His servant, Richard Lander, who had now joined him, tried in vain to be all things at once. On the 12th March, 1827, Clapperton was seized with dysentery. Nothing could check the progress of the malady, and he sank rapidly. It being the time of the feast of the Rhamadan, Lander could get no help, not even servants. Fever soon set in, and after twenty days of great suffering, Clapperton, feeling his end approaching, gave his last instructions to Lander, and died in that faithful servant's arms, on the 11th of April.

"I put a large clean mat," says Lander, "over the whole [the corpse], and sent a messenger to Sultan Bello, to acquaint him with the mournful event, and ask his permission to bury the body after the manner of my own country, and also to know in what particular place his remains were to be interred. The messenger soon returned with the sultan's consent to the former part of my request; and about twelve o'clock at noon of the same day a person came into my hut, accompanied by four slaves, sent by Bello to dig the grave. I was desired to follow them with the corpse. Accordingly I saddled my camel, and putting the body on its back, and throwing a union jack over it, I bade them proceed. Travelling at a slow pace, we halted at Jungavie, a small village, built on a rising ground, about five miles to the south-east of Sackatoo. The body was then taken from the camel's back, and placed in a shed, whilst the slaves were digging the grave; which being quickly done, it was conveyed close to it. I then opened a prayer-book, and, amid showers of tears, read the funeral service over the remains of my valued master. Not a single person listened to this peculiarly distressing ceremony, the slaves being at some distance, quarrelling and making a most indecent noise the whole time it lasted. This being done, the union jack was then taken off, and the body was slowly lowered into the earth, and I wept bitterly as I gazed for the last time upon all that remained of my generous and intrepid master."

"Travelling at a slow pace."

Overcome by heat, fatigue, and grief, poor Lander himself now broke down, and for more than ten days was unable to leave his hut.

Bello sent several times to inquire after the unfortunate servant's health, but he was not deceived by these demonstrations of interest, for he knew they were only dictated by a wish to get possession of the traveller's baggage, which was supposed to be full of gold and silver. The sultan's astonishment may therefore be imagined when it came out that Lander had not even money enough to defray the expenses of his journey to the coast. He never found out that the servant had taken the precaution of hiding his own gold watch and those of Pearce and Clapperton about his person.

Lander saw that he must at any cost get back to the coast as quickly as possible. By dint of the judicious distribution of a few presents he won over some of the sultan's advisers, who represented to their master that should Lander die he would be accused of having murdered him as well as Clapperton. Although Clapperton had advised Lander to join an Arab caravan for Fezzan, the latter, fearing that his papers and journals might be taken from him, resolved to go back to the coast.

On the 3rd May Lander at last left Sackatoo en route for Kano. During the first part of this journey, he nearly died of thirst, but he suffered less in the second half, as the King of Djacoba, who had joined him, was very kind to him, and begged him to visit his country. This king told him that the Niam- Niams were his neighbours; that they had once joined him against the Sultan of Bornou, and that after the battle they had roasted and eaten the corpses of the slain. This, I believe, is the first mention, since the publication of Hornemann's Travels, of this cannibal race, who were to become the subjects of so many absurd fables.

Lander entered Kano on the 25th May, and after a short stay there started for Funda, on the Niger, whose course he proposed following to Benin. This route had much to recommend it, being not only safe but new, so that Lander was enabled to supplement the discoveries of his master.

Kanfoo, Carifo, Gowgie, and Gatas, were visited in turns by Lander, who says that the people of these towns belong to the Houssa race, and pay tribute to the Fellatahs. He also saw Damoy, Drammalik, and Coudonia, passed a wide river flowing towards the Quorra, and visited Kottop, a huge slave and cattle market, Coudgi and Dunrora, with a long chain of lofty mountains running in an easterly direction beyond.

At Dunrora, just as Lander was superintending the loading of his beasts of burden, four horsemen, their steeds covered with foam, dashed up to the chief, and with his aid forced Lander to retrace his steps to visit the King of Zegzeg, who, they said, was very anxious to see him. This was by no means agreeable to Lander, who wanted to get to the Niger, from which he was not very far distant, and down it to the sea; he was, however, obliged to yield to force. His guides did not follow exactly the same route as he had taken on his way to Dunrora, and thus he had an opportunity of seeing the village of Eggebi, governed by one of the chief of the warriors of the sovereign of Zegzeg. He paid his respects as required, excusing the small value of the presents he had to give on the ground of his merchandise having been stolen, and soon obtained permission to leave the place.

Yaourie, Womba, Coulfo, Boussa, and Wow-wow were the halting-places on Lander's return journey to Badagry, where he arrived on the 22nd November, 1827. Two months later he embarked for England.

Although the commercial project, which had been the chief aim of Clapperton's journey, had fallen through, owing to the jealousy of the Arabs, who opposed it in their fear that the opening of a new route might ruin their trade, a good deal of scientific information had rewarded the efforts of the English explorer.

In his "History of Maritime and Inland Discovery," Desborough Cooley thus sums up the results obtained by the travellers whose work we have just described:—

"The additions to our geographical knowledge of the interior of Africa which we owe to Captain Clapperton far exceed in extent and importance those made by any preceding traveller. The limit of Captain Lyon's journey southward across the desert was in lat. 24°, while Major Denham, in his expedition to Mandara, reached lat. 9° 15', thus adding 14¾ degrees, or 900 miles, to the extent explored by Europeans. Hornemann, it is true, had previously crossed the desert, and had proceeded as far southwards as Niffé, in lat. 10° 30'. But no account was ever received of his journey. Park in his first expedition reached Silla, in long. 1° 34' west, a distance of 1100 miles from the mouth of the Gambia. Denham and Clapperton, on the other hand, from the east side of Lake Tchad, in long. 17°, to Sackatoo, in long. 5° 30', explored a distance of 700 miles from east to west in the heart of Africa; a line of only 400 miles remaining unknown between Silla and Sackatoo. The second journey of Captain Clapperton added ten-fold value to these discoveries; for he had the good fortune to detect the shortest and most easy road to the populous countries of the interior; and he could boast of being the first who had completed an itinerary across the continent of Africa from Tripoli to Benin."

We need add but little to so skilful and sensible a summary of the work done. The information given by Arab geographers, especially by Leo Africanus, had been verified, and much had been learnt about a large portion of the Soudan. Although the course of the Niger had not yet been actually traced—that was reserved for the expeditions of which we are now to write—it had been pretty fairly guessed at. It had been finally ascertained that the Quorra, or Djoliba, or

Niger—or whatever else the great river of North-West Africa might be called —and the Nile were totally different rivers, with totally different sources. In a word, a great step had been gained.

In 1816 it was still an open question whether the Congo was not identical with the Niger. To ascertain the truth on this point, an expedition was sent out under Captain Tuckey, an English naval officer who had given proof of intelligence and courage. James Kingston Tuckey was made prisoner in 1805, and was not exchanged until 1814. When he heard that an expedition was to be organized for the exploration of the Zaire, he begged to be allowed to join it, and was appointed to the command. Two able officers and some scientific men were associated with him.

Tuckey left England on the 19th March, 1816, with two vessels, the *Congo* and the *Dorothea*, a transport vessel, under his orders. On the 20th June he cast anchor off Malembé, on the shores of the Congo, in lat. 4° 39' S. The king of that country was much annoyed when he found that the English had not come to buy slaves, and spread all manner of injurious reports against the Europeans who had come to ruin his trade.

On the 18th July, Tuckey entered the vast estuary formed by the mouths of the Zaire, on board the *Congo*; but when the height of the river-banks rendered it impossible to sail farther, he embarked with some of his people in his boats. On the 10th August he decided, on account of the rapidity of the current and the huge rocks bordering the stream, to make his way partly by land and partly by water. Ten days later the boats were brought to a final stand by an impassable fall. The explorers therefore landed, and continued their journey on foot; but the difficulties increased every day, the Europeans falling ill, and the negroes refusing to carry the baggage. At last, when he was some 280 miles from the sea, Tuckey was compelled to retrace his steps. The rainy season had set in, the number of sick increased, and the commander, miserable at the lamentable result of the trip, himself succumbed to fever, and only got back to his vessel to die on the 4th October, 1816.

View on the banks of the Congo.
(Fac-simile of early engraving.)

An exact survey of the mouth of the Congo, and the rectification of the coast-
line, in which there had previously been a considerable error, were the only

results of this unlucky expedition.

In 1807, not far from the scene of Clapperton's landing a few years later, a brave but fierce people appeared on the Gold Coast. The Ashantees, coming none knew exactly whence, flung themselves upon the Fantees, and, after horrible massacres, in 1811 and 1816, established themselves in the whole of the country between the Kong mountains and the sea.

Ashantee warrior.
(Fac-simile of early engraving.)

As a necessary result, this led to a disturbance in the relations between the
Fantees and the English, who owned some factories and counting-houses on

the coast.

In 1816 the Ashantee king ravaged the Fantee territories in which the English had settled, reducing the latter to famine. The Governor of Cape Coast Castle therefore sent a petition home for aid against the fierce and savage conqueror. The bearer of the governor's despatches was Thomas Edward Bowditch, a young man who, actuated by a passion for travelling, had left the parental roof, thrown up his business, and having married against the wishes of his family, had finally accepted a humble post at Cape Coast Castle, where his uncle was second in command.

The English minister at once acceded to the governor's request, and sent Bowditch back in command of an expedition; but the authorities at Cape Coast considered him too young for the post, and superseded him by a man whose long experience and thorough knowledge of the country and its people seemed to fit him for the important task to be accomplished. The result showed that this was an error. Bowditch was attached to the mission as scientific observer, his chief duty being to take the latitude and longitude of the different places visited.

Frederick James and Bowditch left the English settlement on the 22nd August, 1817, and arrived at Coomassie, the Ashantee capital, without meeting with any other obstacle than the insubordination of the bearers. The negotiations with a view to the conclusion of a treaty of commerce, and the opening of a road between Coomassie and the coast, were brought to something of a successful issue by Bowditch, but James proved himself altogether wanting in either the power of making or enforcing suggestions. The wisdom of Bowditch's conduct was fully recognized, and James was recalled.

It would seem that geographical science had little to expect from a diplomatic mission to a country already visited by Bosman, Loyer, Des Marchais, and many others, and on which Meredith and Dalzel had written; but Bowditch turned to account his stay of five months at Coomassie, which is but ten days' march from the Atlantic, to study the country, manners, customs, and institutions of one of the most interesting races of Africa.

We will now briefly describe the pompous entry of the English mission into Coomassie. The whole population turned out on the occasion, and all the troops, whose numbers Bowditch estimated at 30,000 at least, were under arms.

Before they were admitted to the presence of the king, the English witnessed a scene well calculated to impress upon them the cruelty and barbarity of the Ashantees. A man with his hands tied behind him, his cheeks pierced with wire, one ear cut off, the other hanging by a bit of skin, his shoulders bleeding from cuts and slashes, and a knife run through the skin above each shoulder-blade, was dragged, by a cord fastened to his nose, through the town to the music of bamboos. He was on his way to be sacrificed in honour of the white men!

"Our observations *en passant*," says Bowditch, "had taught us to conceive a spectacle far exceeding our original expectations; but they had not prepared us for the extent and display of the scene which here burst upon us. An area of nearly a mile in circumference was crowded with magnificence and novelty. The king, his tributaries and captains, were resplendent in the distance, surrounded by attendants of every description, fronted by a mass of warriors which seemed to make our approach impervious. The sun was reflected, with a glare scarcely more supportable than the heat, from the massive gold ornaments which glistened in every direction. More than a hundred bands burst at once on our arrival, into the peculiar airs of their several chiefs; the horns flourished their defiances, with the beating of innumerable drums and metal instruments, and then yielded for a while to the soft harmonious breathings of their long flutes, with which a pleasing instrument, like a bagpipe without the drone, was happily blended. At least a hundred large umbrellas or canopies, which could shelter thirty persons, were sprung up and down by the bearers with brilliant effect, being made of scarlet, yellow, and the most showy cloths and silks, and crowned on the top with crescents, pelicans, elephants, barrels, and arms, and swords of gold.

"The king's messengers, with gold breastplates, made way for us, and we commenced our round, preceded by the canes and the English flag. We stopped to take the hand of every caboceer, (which, as their household suites occupied several spaces in advance, delayed us long enough to distinguish some of the ornaments in the general blaze of splendour and ostentation). The caboceers, as did their superior captains and attendants, wore Ashantee cloths of extravagant price, from the costly foreign silks which had been unravelled to weave them, in all the varieties of colour as well as pattern; they were of an incredible size and weight, and thrown over the shoulder exactly like the Roman toga; a small silk fillet generally encircled their temples, and massy gold necklaces, intricately wrought, suspended Moorish charms, inclosed in small square cases of gold, silver, and curious embroidery. Some wore necklaces reaching to the navel, entirely of aggry beads; a band of gold and beads encircled the knee, from which several strings of the same depended; small circles of gold, like guineas, rings, and casts of animals, were strung round their ancles; their sandals were of green, red, and delicate white leather; manillas, and rude lumps of rock gold, hung from their left wrists, which were so heavily laden as to be supported on the head of one of their handsomest boys. Gold and silver pipes, and canes, dazzled the eye in every direction. Wolves' and rams' heads, as large as life, cast in gold, were suspended from their gold-handled swords, which were held around them in great numbers; the blades were shaped like round bills, and rusted in blood; the sheaths were of leopard skin, or the shell of a fish like shagreen. The large drums, supported on the head of one man, and beaten by two others, were braced around with the thigh-bones of their enemies, and ornamented with their skulls. The kettle-drums, resting on the ground, were scraped with wet fingers, and covered with leopard skin. The wrists of the drummers were hung with bells and curiously-shaped pieces of iron, which jingled loudly as they were beating. The smaller drums were suspended from the neck by scarves of red cloth; the horns (the teeth of young elephants) were ornamented at the mouth-piece with gold, and the jaw-bones of human victims. The war-caps of eagles' feathers nodded in the rear, and large fans, of the wing feathers of the ostrich, played around the dignitaries; immediately behind their chairs (which were of a black wood, almost covered by inlays of ivory and gold embossment) stood their handsomest youths, with corslets of leopard's skin, covered with gold cockle-shells, and stuck full of small knives, sheathed in gold and silver and the handles of blue agate; cartouch-boxes of elephant's hide hung below, ornamented in the same manner; a large gold-handled sword was fixed behind the left shoulder, and silk scarves and horses' tails (generally white), streamed from the arms and waist cloth; their long Danish muskets had broad rims of gold at small distances, and the stocks were ornamented with shells. Finely-grown girls stood behind the chairs of some, with silver basins. Their stools (of the most laborious carved work, and generally with two large bells attached to them) were conspicuously placed on the heads of favourites; and crowds of small boys were seated around, flourishing elephants' tails curiously mounted. The warriors sat on the ground close to these, and so thickly as not to admit of our passing without treading on their feet, to which they were perfectly indifferent; their caps were of the skin of the pangolin and leopard, the tails hanging down behind; their cartouch-belts (composed of small gourds which hold the charges, and covered with leopard's or pig's skin) were embossed with red shells, and small brass bells thickly hung to them; on their hips and shoulders was a cluster of knives; iron chains and collars dignified the most daring, who were prouder of them than of gold; their muskets had rests affixed of leopard's skin, and the locks a covering of the same; the sides of their faces were curiously painted in long white streaks, and their arms also striped, having the appearance of armour.

"We were suddenly surprised by the sight of Moors, who afforded the first general diversity of dress. There were seventeen superiors, arrayed in large cloaks of white satin, richly trimmed with spangled embroidery; their shirts and trousers were of silk; and a very large turban of white muslin was studded with a border of different coloured stones; their attendants wore red caps and turbans, and long white shirts, which hung over their trousers; those of the inferiors were of dark blue cloth. They slowly raised their eyes from the ground as we passed, and with a most malignant scowl.

"The prolonged flourishes of the horns, a deafening tumult of drums, and the fuller concert at the intervals, announced that we were approaching the king. We were already passing the principal officers of his household. The chamberlain, the gold horn blower, the captain of the messengers, the captain for royal executions, the captain of the market, the keeper of the royal burying-ground, and the master of the bands, sat surrounded by a retinue and splendour which bespoke the dignity and importance of their offices. The cook had a number of small services, covered with leopard's skin, held behind him, and a large quantity of massy silver plate was displayed before him— punch-bowls, waiters, coffee-pots, tankards, and a very large vessel with heavy handles and clawed feet, which seemed to have been made to hold incense. I observed a Portuguese inscription on one piece, and they seemed generally of that manufacture. The executioner, a man of immense size, wore a massy gold hatchet on his breast; and the execution stool was held before him, clotted in blood, and partly covered with a cawl of fat. The king's four linguists were encircled by a splendour inferior to none, and their peculiar insignia, gold canes, were elevated in all directions, tied in bundles like fasces. The keeper of the treasury added to his own magnificence by the ostentatious display of his service; the blow pan, boxes, scales and weights, were of solid gold.

"A delay of some minutes whilst we severally approached to receive the king's hand, afforded us a thorough view of him. His deportment first excited my attention; native dignity in princes we are pleased to call barbarous was a curious spectacle; his manners were majestic, yet courteous, and he did not allow his surprise to beguile him for a moment of the composure of the monarch. He appeared to be about thirty-eight years of age, inclined to corpulence, and of a benevolent countenance."

This account is followed by a description, extending over several pages, of the costume of the king, the filing past of the chiefs and troops, the dispersing of the crowd, and the ceremonies of reception, which lasted far on into the night.

Reading Bowditch's extraordinary narrative, we are tempted to ask if it be not the outcome of the traveller's imagination, for we can scarcely credit what he says of the wonderful luxury of this barbarous court, the sacrifice of thousands of persons at certain seasons of the year, the curious customs of this warlike and cruel people, this mixture of barbarism and civilization hitherto unknown in Africa. We could not acquit Bowditch of great exaggeration, had not later travellers as well as contemporary explorers confirmed his statements. We can therefore only express our astonishment that such a government, founded on terror alone, could have endured so long.

It is a pleasure to us Frenchmen when we can quote the name of a fellow-countryman amongst the many travellers who have risked their lives in the cause of geographical science. Without abating our critical acumen, we feel our pulse quicken when we read of the dangers and struggles of such travellers as Mollien, Caillié, De Cailliaud, and Letorzec.

Gaspar Mollien was nephew to Napoleon's Minister of the Treasury. He was on board the *Medusa*, but was fortunate enough to escape when that vessel was shipwrecked, and to reach the coast of the Sahara in a boat, whence he made his way to Senegal.

The dangers from which Mollien had just escaped would have destroyed the love of adventure and exploration in a less ardent spirit. They had no such effect upon him. He left St. Louis as soon as ever he obtained the assent of the Governor, Fleuriau, to his proposal to explore the sources of the great rivers of Senegambia, and especially those of the Djoliba.

Mollien started from Djeddeh on the 29th January, 1818, and taking an easterly course between the 15th and 16th parallels of north latitude, crossed the kingdom of Domel, and entered the districts peopled by the Yaloofs. Unable to go by way of Woolli, he decided in favour of the Fouta Toro route, and in spite of the jealousy of the natives and their love of pillage, he reached Bondou without accident. It took him three days to traverse the desert between Bondou and the districts beyond the Gambia, after which he penetrated into Niokolo, a mountainous country, inhabited by the all but wild Peuls and Djallons.

Leaving Bandeia, Mollien entered Fouta Djallon, and reached the sources of the Gambia and the Rio Grande, which are in close proximity. A few days later he came to those of the Falemé; and, in spite of the repugnance and fear of his guide, he made his way into Timbo, the capital of Fouta. The absence of the king and most of the inhabitants probably spared him from a long captivity abbreviated only by torture. Fouta is a fortified town, the king owns houses, with mud walls between three and four feet thick and fifteen high.

At a short distance from Timbo, Mollien discovered the sources of the Senegal—at least what were pointed out to him as such by the blacks; but it was impossible for him to take astronomical observations.

The explorer did not, however, look upon his work as done. He had ever before him the still more important discovery of the sources of the Niger; but the feeble state of his health, the setting in of the rainy season, the swelling of the rivers, the fears of his guides, who refused to accompany him into Kooranko and Soolimano, though he offered them guns, amber beads, and even his horse, compelled him to give up the idea of crossing the Kong mountains, and to return to St. Louis. Mollien had, however, opened several new lines in a part of Senegambia not before visited by any European.

"It is to be regretted," says M. de la Renaudière, "that worn out with fatigue, scarcely able to drag himself along, in a state of positive destitution, Mollien was unable to cross the lofty mountains separating the basin of the Senegal from that of the Djoliba, and that he was compelled to rely upon native information respecting the most important objects of his expedition. It is on the faith of the assertions of the natives that he claims to have visited the sources of the Rio Grande, Falemé, Gambia, and Senegal. If he had been able to follow the course of those rivers to their fountainhead his discoveries would have acquired certainty, which is, unfortunately, now wanting to them. However, when we compare the accounts of other travellers with what he says of the position of the source of the Ba-Fing, or Senegal, which cannot be that of any other great stream, we are convinced of the reality of this discovery at least. It also seems certain that the two last springs are higher up than was supposed, and that the Djoliba rises in a yet loftier locality. The country rises gradually to the south and south-east in parallel terraces. These mountain chains increase in height towards the east, attaining their greatest elevation between lat. 8° and 10° N."

Such were the results of Mollien's interesting journey in the French colony of Senegal. The same country was the starting-point of another explorer, Réné Caillié.

Caillié, who was born in 1800, in the department of the Seine et Oise, had only an elementary education; but reading Robinson Crusoe had fired his youthful imagination with a zeal for adventure, and he never rested until, in spite of his scanty resources, he had obtained maps and books of travel. In 1816, when only sixteen years old, he embarked for Senegal, in the transport- ship *La Loire*.

At this time the English Government was organizing an inland exploring expedition, under the command of Major Gray. To avoid the terrible almamy of Timbo, who had been so fatal to Peddie, the English made for the mouth of the Gambia by sea. Woolli and the Gaboon were crossed, and the explorers penetrated into Bondou, which Mollien was to visit a few years later, a district inhabited by a people as fanatic and fierce as those of Fouta Djallon. The extortions of the almamy were such that under pretext of there being an old debt left unpaid by the English Government, Major Gray was mulcted of nearly all his baggage, and had to send an officer to the Senegal for a fresh supply.

Caillié knowing nothing of this disastrous beginning, and aware that Gray was glad to receive new recruits, left St. Louis with two negroes, and reached Goree. But there some people, who took an interest in him, persuaded him not to take service with Gray, and got him an appointment at Guadaloupe. He remained, however, but six months in that island, and then returned to Bordeaux, whence he started for the Senegal once more.

Partarieu, one of Gray's officers, was just going back to his chief with the merchandise he had procured, and Caillié asked and obtained leave to accompany him, without either pay or a fixed engagement.

Réné Caillié.
(Fac-simile of early engraving.)

The caravan consisted of seventy persons, black and white, and thirty-two richly-laden camels. It left Gandiolle, in Cayor, on the 5th February, 1819, and before entering Jaloof a desert was crossed, where great suffering was endured from thirst. The leader, in order to carry more merchandise, had neglected to take a sufficient supply of water.

At Boolibaba, a village inhabited by Foulah shepherds, the travellers were enabled to recruit, and to fill their leathern bottles for a journey across a second desert.

Avoiding Fouta Toro, whose inhabitants are fanatics and thieves, Partarieu entered Bondou. He would gladly have evaded visiting Boulibané, the capital and residence of the almamy, but was compelled to do so, owing to the refusal of the people to supply grain or water to the caravan, and also in obedience to the strict orders of Major Gray, who thought the almamy would let the travellers pass after paying tribute.

The terrible almamy began by extorting a great number of presents, and then refused to allow the English to visit Bakel on the Senegal. They might, he said, go through his states, those of Kaarta, to Clego, or they might take the Fouta Toro route. Both these alternatives were equally impossible, as in either case the caravan would have to travel among fanatic tribes. The explorers believed the almamy's object was to have them robbed and murdered, without incurring the personal responsibility.

They resolved to force their way. Preparations were scarcely begun for a start, when the caravan was surrounded by a multitude of soldiers, who, taking possession of the wells, rendered it impossible for the travellers to carry out their intentions. At the same time the war-drum was beaten on every side. To fight was impossible; a palaver had to be held. In a word, the English had to own their powerlessness. The almamy dictated the conditions of peace, mulcted the whites of a few more presents, and ordered them to withdraw by way of Fouta Toro.

Yet more—and this was a flagrant insult to British pride—the English found themselves escorted by a guard, which prevented their taking any other route. When night fell they revenged themselves by setting fire to all their merchandise in the very sight of the Foulahs, who had intended to get possession of them. The crossing of Fouta Toro among hostile natives was terribly arduous. The slightest pretext was seized for a dispute, and again and again violence seemed inevitable. Food and water were only to be obtained at exorbitant prices.

At last, one night, Partarieu, to disarm the suspicion of the natives, gave out that he could not carry all his baggage at once, and having first filled his coffers and bags with stones, he decamped with all his followers for the Senegal, leaving his tents pitched and his fires alight. His path was strewn with bales, arms, and animals. Thanks to this subterfuge, and the rapidity of their march, the English reached Bakel in safety, where the French welcomed the remnant of the expedition with enthusiasm.

"He decamped with all his followers."

Caillié, attacked by a fever which nearly proved fatal, returned to St. Louis;

but not recovering his health there, he was obliged to go back to France. Not until 1824 was he able to return to Senegal, which was then governed by Baron Roger, a friend to progress, who was anxious *pari passu*, to extend our geographical knowledge with our commercial relations. Roger supplied Caillié with means to go and live amongst the Bracknas, there to study Arabic and the Mussulman religion.

Life amongst the suspicious and fanatic Moorish shepherds was by no means easy. The traveller, who had great difficulty in keeping his daily journal, was obliged to resort to all manner of subterfuges to obtain permission to explore the neighbourhood of his house. He gives us some curious details of the life of the Bracknas—of their diet, which consists almost entirely of milk; of their habitations, which are nothing more than tents unfitted for the vicissitudes of the climate; of their "*guéhués*" or itinerant minstrels; their mode of producing the excessive *embonpoint* which they consider the height of female beauty; the aspect of the country; the fertility and productions of the soil, &c.

The most remarkable of all the facts collected by Caillié are those relating to the five distinct classes into which the Moorish Bracknas are divided. These are the *Hassanes*, or warriors, whose idleness, slovenliness, and pride exceed belief; the *Marabouts*, or priests; the *Zénagues*, tributary to the Hassanes; the *Laratines*; and the slaves.

The *Zénagues* are a miserable class, despised by all the others, but especially by the *Hassanes*, to whom they pay a tribute, which is of variable amount, and is never considered enough. They do all the work, both industrial and agricultural, and rear all the cattle.

"In spite of my efforts," says Caillié, "I could find out nothing about the origin of this people, or ascertain how they came to be reduced to pay tribute to other Moors. When I asked them any questions about this, they said it was God's will. Can they be a remnant of a conquered tribe? and if so, how is it that no tradition on the subject is retained amongst them. I do not think they can be, for the Moors, proud as they are of their origin, never forget the names of those who have brought credit to their families; and were such the case, the Zénagues, who form the majority of the population, and are skilful warriors, would rise under the leadership of one of their chiefs, and fling off the yoke of servitude."

Laratine is the name given to the offspring of a Moor and a negro slave. Although they are slaves, the Laratines are never sold, but while living in separate camps, are treated very much like the Zénagues. Those who are the sons of Hassanes are warriors, whilst the children of Marabouts are brought up to the profession of their father.

The actual slaves are all negroes. Ill-treated, badly fed, and flogged on the slightest pretext, there is no suffering which they are not called upon to endure.

In May, 1825, Caillié returned to St. Louis. Baron Roger was absent, and his representative was by no means friendly. The explorer had to content himself with the pay of a common soldier until the return of his protector, to whom he sent the notes he had made when amongst the Bracknas, but all his offers of service were rejected. He was promised a certain sum on his return from Timbuctoo; but how was he even to start without private resources?

The intrepid Caillié was not, however, to be discouraged. As he obtained neither encouragement nor help from the colonial government, he went to Sierra Leone, where the governor, who did not wish to deprive Major Laing of the credit of being the first to arrive at Timbuctoo, rejected his proposals.

In the management of an indigo factory, Caillié soon saved money to the extent of two thousand francs, a sum which appeared to him sufficient to carry him to the end of the world. He lost no time in purchasing the necessary merchandise, and joined some Mandingoes and "seracolets," or wandering African merchants. He told them, under the seal of secrecy, that he had been born in Egypt of Arab parents, taken to France at an early age, and sent to Senegal to look after the business of his master, who, satisfied with his services, had given him his freedom. He added, that his chief desire was to get back to Egypt, and resume the Mohammedan religion.

On the 22nd March, 1827, Caillié left Freetown for Kakondy, a village on the Rio Nuñez, where he employed his leisure in collecting information respecting the Landamas and the Nalous, both subject to the Foulahs of Fouta Djallon, but not Mohammedans, and, as a necessary result, both much given to spirituous liquors. They dwell in the districts watered by the Rio Nuñez, side by side with the Bagos, an idolatrous race who dwell at its mouth. The Bagos are light-hearted, industrious, and skilful tillers of the soil; they make large profits out of the sale of their rice and salt. They have no king, no religion but a barbarous idolatry, and are governed by the oldest man in their village, an arrangement which answers very well.

On the 19th April, 1827, Caillié with but one bearer and a guide, at last started for Timbuctoo. He speaks favourably of the Foulahs and the people of Fouta Djallon, whose rich and fertile country he crossed. The Ba-Fing, the chief affluent of the Senegal, was not more than a hundred paces across, and a foot and a half deep where he passed it; but the force of the current, and the huge granite rocks encumbering its bed, render it very difficult and dangerous to cross the river. After a halt of nineteen days in the village of Cambaya, the home of the guide who had accompanied him thus far, Caillié entered Kankan, crossing a district intersected by rivers and large streams, which were then beginning to inundate the whole land.

On the 30th May the explorer crossed the Tankisso, a large river with a rocky bed belonging to the system of the Niger, and reached the latter on the 11th June, at Couronassa.

Caillié crossing the Tankisso.

"Even here," says Caillié, "so near to its source, the Niger is 900 feet wide, with a current of two miles and a half."

Before we enter Kankan with the French explorer, it will be well to sum up what he says of the Foulahs of Fouta. They are mostly tall, well-made men, with chestnut-brown complexions, curly hair, lofty foreheads, aquiline noses, features in fact very like those of Europeans. They are bigoted Mohammedans, and hate Christians. Unlike the Mandingoes, they do not travel, but love their home; they are good agriculturists and clever traders, warlike and patriotic, and they leave none but their old men and women in their villages when they go to war.

The town of Kankan stands in a plain surrounded by lofty mountains. The bombax, baobab, and butter-tree, also called "cé" the "shea" of Mungo Park, are plentiful. Caillié was delayed in Kankan for twenty-eight days before he could get on to Sambatikala; and during that time he was shamefully robbed by his host, and could not obtain from the chief of the village restitution of the goods which had been stolen.

"Kankan," says the traveller, "is a small town near the left bank of the Milo, a pretty river, which comes from the south, and waters the Kissi district, where it takes its rise, flowing thence in a north-westerly direction to empty itself into the Niger, two or three days' journey from Kankan. Surrounded by a thick quick-set hedge, this town, which does not contain more than 6000 inhabitants, is situated in an extensive and very fertile plain of grey sand. On every side are pretty little villages, called *Worondes*, where the slaves live. These habitations give interest to the scene, and are surrounded by very fine plantations; yams, rice, onions, pistachio nuts, &c., are exported in large quantities."

Between Kankan and Wassolo the road led through well cultivated, and, at this time of year, nearly submerged districts. The inhabitants struck Caillié as being of a mild, cheerful, and inquiring disposition. They gave him a cordial welcome.

Several tributaries of the Niger, including the Sarano, were passed before a halt was made at Sigala, the residence of Baranusa, the chief of Wassolo. He was of slovenly habits, like his subjects, and used tobacco both as snuff and for smoking. He was said to be very rich in gold and slaves. His subjects paid him a tribute in cattle; he had a great many wives, each of whom owned a hut of her own, their houses forming a little village, with well cultivated environs. Here Caillié for the first time saw the Rhamnus Lotus mentioned by Park.

On leaving Wossolo, Caillié entered Foulou, whose inhabitants, like those of the former district, are idolaters, of slovenly habits. They speak the Mandingo tongue. At Sambatikala the traveller paid a visit to the almamy.

"We entered," he says, "a place which served him as a bedroom for himself and a stable for his horse. The prince's bed was at the further end. It consisted of a little platform raised six inches from the ground, on which was stretched an ox hide, with a dirty mosquito curtain, to keep off the insects. There was no other furniture in this royal abode. Two saddles hung from stakes driven into the wall; a large straw hat, a drum only used in war-time, a few lances, a bow, a quiver, and some arrows, were the only ornaments. A lamp made of a piece of flat iron set on a stand of the same metal, stood on the ground. This lamp was fed by a kind of vegetable matter, not thick enough to be made into candles."

The almamy soon informed Caillié of an opportunity for him to go to Timeh, whence a caravan was about to start for Jenneh. The traveller then entered the province of Bambarra, and quickly arrived at the pretty little village of Timeh, inhabited by Mohammedan Mandingoes, and bounded on the east by a chain of mountains about 350 fathoms high.

When he entered this village, at the end of July, Caillié little dreamt of the long stay he would be compelled to make in it. He had hurt his foot, and the wound became very much inflamed by walking in wet grass. He therefore decided to let the caravan for Jenneh go on without him, and remain at Timeh until his foot should be completely healed. It would have been too great a risk for him in his state to travel through Bambarra, where the idolatrous inhabitants of the country would be pretty sure to rob him.

"The Bambarras," he says, "have few slaves, go almost naked, and are always armed with bows and arrows. They are governed by a number of petty independent chiefs, who are often at war with one another. They are in fact rude and wild creatures as compared with the tribes who have embraced Mohammedanism."

Caillié was detained at Timeh by the still unhealed wound in his foot, until the 10th November. At that date he proposed starting for Jenneh, but, to quote his own words, "I was now seized with violent pains in the jaws, warning me that I was attacked with scurvy, a terrible malady, all the horrors of which I was to realize. My palate was completely skinned, part of the bone came away, my teeth seemed ready to fall out of the gums, my sufferings were terrible. I feared that my brain might be affected by the agony of pain in my head. I was more than a fortnight without an instant's sleep."

To make matters worse, the wound broke out afresh; and he would have been cured neither of it nor of the scurvy had it not been for the energetic treatment of an old negress, who was accustomed to doctor the scorbutic affections, so common in that country.

On the 9th January, 1828, Caillié left Timeh, and reached Kimba, a little village where the caravan for Jenneh was assembled. Near to this village rises the chain erroneously called Kong, which is the general name for mountain amongst the Mandingoes.

The names of the villages entered by the travellers, and the incidents of the journey through Bambarra, are of no special interest. The inhabitants are accounted great thieves by the Mandingoes, but are probably not more dishonest than their critics.

The Bambarra women all wear a thin slip of wood imbedded in the lower lip, a strange fashion exactly similar to that noticed by Cook amongst the natives of the north-western coast of America. The Bambarras speak Mandingo, though they have a dialect of their own called *Kissour*, about which the traveller could obtain no trustworthy written information.

Jenneh was formerly called "the golden land." The precious metal is not, however, found there, but a good deal is imported by the Boureh merchants and the Mandingoes of Kong.

Jenneh, two miles and a half in circumference, is surrounded by a mud wall ten feet high. The houses, built of bricks baked in the sun, are as large as those of European peasants. They have all terraces, but no outer windows. Numbers of foreigners frequent Jenneh. The inhabitants, as many as eight or ten thousand, are very industrious and intelligent. They hire out their slaves, and also employ them in various handicrafts.

The Moors, however, monopolize the more important commerce. Not a day passes that they do not despatch huge boats laden with rice, millet, cotton, honey, vegetable butter, and other native products.

In spite of this great commercial movement, the prosperity of Jenneh was threatened. Sego Ahmadou, chief of the country, impelled by bigoted zeal, made fierce war upon the Bambarras of Sego, whom he wished to rally round the standard of the Prophet. This struggle did a great deal of harm to the trade of Jenneh, for it interrupted intercourse with Yamina, Sansanding, Bamakou, and Boureh, which were the chief marts for its produce.

The women of Jenneh would not be true to their sex if they did not show some marks of coquetry. Those who aim at fashion pass a ring or a glass ornament through the nostrils, whilst their poorer sisters content themselves with a bit of pink silk.

During Caillié's long stay at Jenneh, he was loaded with kindness and attentions by the Moors, to whom he had told the fabulous tale about his birth in Egypt, and abduction by the army of occupation.

On the 23rd March, the traveller embarked on the Niger for Timbuctoo, on which the sheriff, won over by the gift of an umbrella, had obtained a passage for him. He carried with him letters of introduction to the chief persons in Timbuctoo.

Caillié now passed in succession the pretty villages of Kera, Taguetia, Sankha-Guibila, Diebeh, and Isaca, near to which the river is joined by an important branch, which makes a great bend beyond Sego, catching sight also of Wandacora, Wanga, Corocoïla, and Cona, finally reaching, on the 2nd of April, the mouth of the important Lake Debo.

"Land," says Caillié, "is visible on every side of this lake except on the west, where it widens out like a vast inland sea. Following its northern coast in a west-north-west direction for a distance of fifteen miles, you leave on the left a tongue of level ground, which runs several miles to the south, seeming to bar the passage of the lake, and form a kind of strait. Beyond this barrier the lake stretches away out of sight in the west. The barrier I have just described cuts Lake Debo into two parts, the upper and lower. That navigable to boats contains three islands, and is very wide; it stretches away a short distance on the east, and is supplemented by an immense number of huge marshes."

One after the other, Caillié now passed the fishing village of Gabibi; Tongoon in the Diriman country, a district stretching far away on the east; Codosa, an important commercial town; Barconga, Leleb, Garfolo, Baracondieh, Tircy, Talbocoïla, Salacoïla, Cora, Coratou, where the Tuaricks exact a toll from passing boats, and finally reached Cabra, built on a height out of reach of the overflowing of the Niger, and serving as the port of Timbuctoo.

On the 20th, Caillié disembarked, and started for that city, which he entered at sundown.

"I, at last," cries our hero, "saw the capital of the Soudan, which had so long been the goal of my desires. As I entered that mysterious town, an object of curiosity to the civilized nations of Europe, I was filled with indescribable exultation. I never experienced anything like it, and my delight knew no bounds. But I had to moderate my transports, and it was to God alone I confided them. With what earnestness I thanked Him for the success which had crowned my enterprise and the signal protection He had accorded me in so many apparently insurmountable difficulties and perils. My first emotions having subsided, I found that the scene before me by no means came up to my expectations. I had conceived a very different idea of the grandeur and wealth of this town. At first sight it appeared nothing more than a mass of badly-built houses, whilst on every side stretched vast plains of arid, yellowish, shifting sands. The sky was of a dull red colour on the horizon; all nature seemed melancholy; profound silence prevailed, not so much as the song of a bird was heard. And yet there was something indescribably imposing in the sight of a large town rising up in the midst of the sandy desert, and the beholder cannot but admire the indomitable energy of its founders. I fancy the river formerly passed nearer the town of Timbuctoo; it is now eight miles north of it and five of Cabra."

Timbuctoo, which is neither so large nor so well populated as Caillié expected, is altogether wanting in animation. There are no large caravans constantly arriving in it, as at Jenneh; nor are there so many strangers there as in the latter town; whilst the market, held at three o'clock in the morning on account of the heat, appears deserted.

Timbuctoo is inhabited by Kissour negroes, who seem of mild dispositions, and are employed in trade. There is no government, and strictly speaking no central authority; each town and village has its own chief. The mode of life is patriarchal. A great many Moorish merchants are settled in the town, and rapidly make fortunes there. They receive consignments of merchandise from Adrar, Tafilet, Ghât, Ghâdames, Algiers, Tunis, and Tripoli.

To Timbuctoo is brought all the salt of the mines of Toudeyni, packed on camels. It is imported in slabs, bound together by ropes, made from grass in the neighbourhood of Tandayeh.

Timbuctoo is built in the form of a triangle, and measures about three miles in circumference. The houses are large but not lofty, and are built of round bricks. The streets are wide and clean. There are seven mosques, each surmounted by a square tower, from which the muezzin calls the faithful to prayer. Counting the floating population, the capital of the Soudan does not contain more than from ten to twelve thousand inhabitants.

Timbuctoo, situated in the midst of a vast plain of shifting white sand, trades in salt only, the soil being quite unsuitable to any sort of cultivation. The town is always full of people, who come to exact what they call presents, but what might with more justice be styled forced contributions. It is a public calamity when a Tuarick chief arrives. He remains in the town a couple of months, living with his numerous followers at the expense of the inhabitants, until he has wrung costly presents from them. Terror has extended the domination of these wandering tribes over all the neighbouring peoples, whom they rob and pillage without mercy.

The Tuarick costume is the same as that of the Arabs, with the exception of the head-dress. Day and night they wear a cotton band which covers the eyes and comes down over the nose, so that they are obliged to raise the head in order to see. The same band goes once or twice round the head and hides the mouth, coming down below the chin, so that the tip of the nose is all that is visible.

The Tuaricks are perfect riders, and mounted on first-rate horses or on fleet camels; each man is armed with a spear, a shield, and a dagger. They are the pirates of the desert, and innumerable are the caravans they have robbed, or blackmailed.

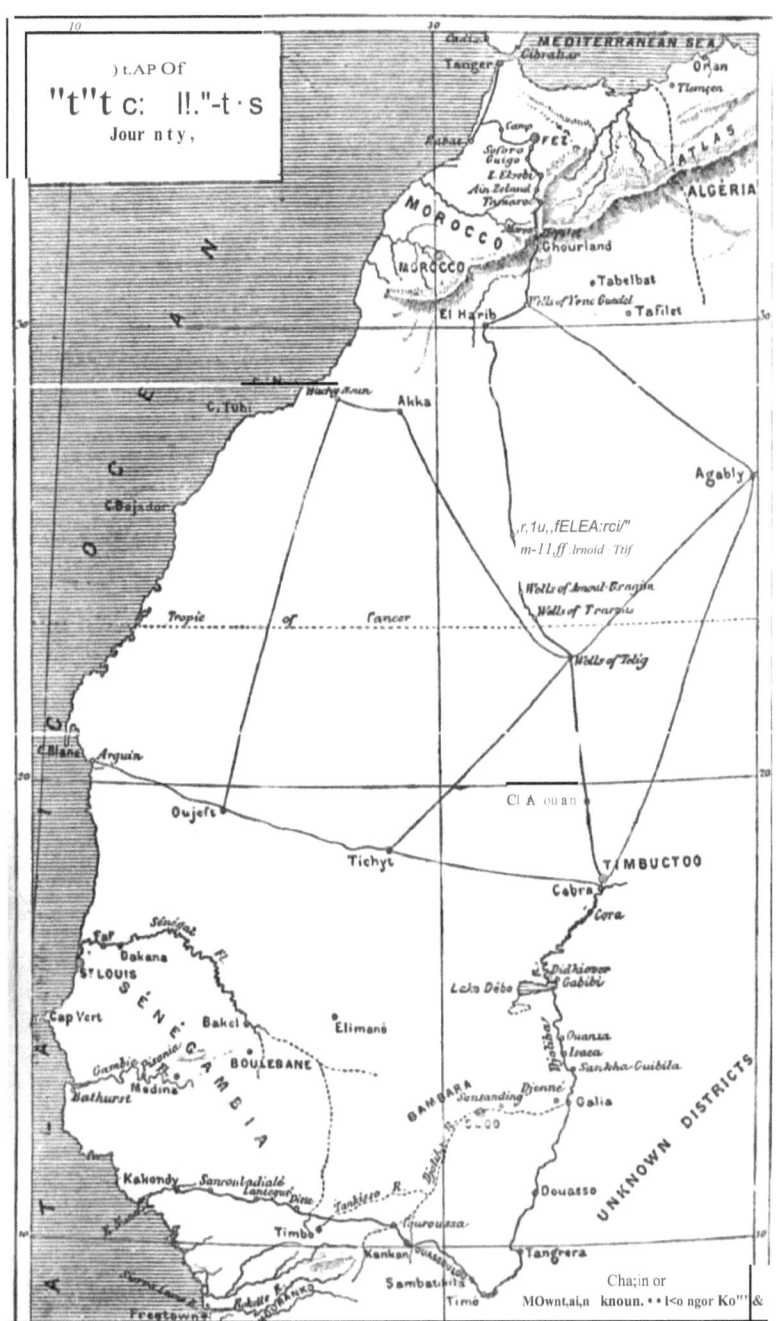

Four days after Caillié's arrival at Timbuctoo, he heard that a caravan was about to start for Talifet; and as he knew that another would not go for three months, fearing detection, he resolved to join this one. It consisted of a large number of merchants, and 600 camels. Starting on the 4th of May, 1828, he arrived, after terrible sufferings from the heat, and a sand-storm in which he was caught, at El Arawan, a town of no private resources, but important as the emporium for the Toudeyni salt, exported at Sansanding, on the banks of the Niger, and also as the halting-place of caravans from Tafilet, Mogadore, Ghât, Drat, and Tripoli, the merchants here exchanging European wares for ivory, gold, slaves, wax, honey, and Soudan stuffs. On the 19th May, the caravan left El Arawan for Morocco, by way of the Sahara. To the traveller's usual sufferings from heat, thirst, and privations of all kinds, was now added the pain of a wound incurred in a fall from his camel. He was also taunted by the Moors, and even by their slaves, who ridiculed his habits and his awkwardness, and even sometimes threw stones at him when his back was turned towards them.

"Often," says Caillié, "one of the Moors would say to me in a contemptuous tone: 'You see that slave? Well I prefer him to you, so you may guess in what esteem I hold you.' This insult would be accompanied with roars of laughter."

Under these miserable circumstances Caillié passed the wells of Trarzas, in whose vicinity salt is found, also those of Amul Gamil, Amul Taf, El Ekreif, surrounded by date-trees, wood, willows, and rushes, and reached Marabouty and El Harib, districts whose inhabitants are disgustingly dirty in their habits.

El Harib lies between two chains of low hills, dividing it from Morocco, to which it is tributary. Its inhabitants, divided into several nomad tribes, employ themselves chiefly in the breeding of camels. They would be rich and contented, but for the ceaseless exactions of the Berber Arabs.

On the 12th July the caravan left El Harib, and eleven days later entered the province of Talifet, famous for its majestic date-trees. At Ghourland, Caillié was welcomed with some kindness by the Moors, though he was not admitted to their houses, lest the women, who are visible only to the men of their own families, should be seen by the irreverent eyes of a stranger.

Caillié visited the market, which is held three times a week near a little village called Boheim, three miles from Ghourland, and was surprised at the variety of articles exposed for sale in it: vegetables, native fruits, fodder for cattle, poultry, sheep, &c. &c., all in large quantities. Water in leather bottles was carried about for sale to all who cared to drink in the exhausting heat, by men who announced their approach by ringing a small hand-bell. Moorish and Spanish coins alone passed current. The province of Tafilet contains several large villages and small towns. Ghourland, El Ekseba, Sosso, Boheim, and Ressant, which our traveller visited, contained some twelve hundred inhabitants each, all merchants and owners of property.

The soil is very productive: corn, vegetables, dates, European fruits, and tobacco, are cultivated in large quantities. Among the sources of wealth in Tafilet we may name very fine sheep, whose beautifully white wool makes very pretty coverlets, oxen, first-rate horses, donkeys, and mules.

As at El-Drah, a good many Jews live in the villages together with Mohammedans. They lead a miserable life, go about half naked, and are constantly struck and insulted. Whether brokers, shoemakers, blacksmiths, porters, or whatever their ostensible occupation, they all lend money to the Moors.

On the 2nd August the caravan resumed its march, and after passing A-Fileh, Tanneyara, Marca, Dayara, Rahaba, El Eyarac, Tamaroc, Ain-Zeland, El Guim, Guigo, and Soporo, Caillié arrived at Fez, where he made a short stay, and then pressed on to Rabat, the ancient Saléh. Exhausted by his long march, with nothing to eat but a few dates, obliged to depend on the charity of the Mussulmans, who as often as not declined to give him anything, and finding at Fez no representative of France but an old Jew named Ismail, who acted as Consular Agent, and who, being afraid of compromising himself, would not let Caillié embark on a Portuguese brig bound for Gibraltar,—the traveller eagerly availed himself of a fortunate chance for going to Tangiers. There he was kindly received by the Vice-Consul, M. Delaporte, who wrote at once to the commandant of the French station at Cadiz, and sent him off bound for that port, disguised as a sailor, in a corvette.

The landing at Toulon of the young Frenchman fresh from Timbuctoo, was a very unexpected event in the scientific world. With nothing to aid him but his own invincible courage and patience, he had brought to a satisfactory conclusion an exploit for which the French and English Geographical Societies had offered large rewards. Alone, without any resources to speak of, without the aid of government or of any scientific society, by sheer force of will, he had succeeded in throwing a flood of new light on an immense tract of Africa.

Caillié was not indeed the first European who had visited Timbuctoo. In the preceding year, Major Laing had penetrated into that mysterious city, but he had paid for his expedition with his life, and we shall presently relate the touching details of his fatal trip.

Caillié had returned to Europe, and brought back with him the curious journal from which our narrative is taken. It is true his profession of the

Mohammedan faith had prevented him from taking astronomical observations, and from making sketches and notes freely, but only at the price of his seeming apostasy could he have passed through the region where the very name of a Christian is held in abhorrence.

How many strange observations, how many fresh and exact details, did Caillié add to our knowledge of North-West Africa! It had cost Clapperton two journeys to traverse Africa from Tripoli to Benin; Caillié had crossed from Senegal to Morocco in one—but at what a price! How much fatigue, how much suffering, how many privations, had the Frenchman endured! Timbuctoo was known at last, as well as the new caravan route across the Sahara by way of the oases of Tafilet and El Harib.

Was Caillié compensated for his physical and mental sufferings by the aid which the Geographical Society sent to him at once, by the prize of 10,000 francs adjudged to him, by the Cross of the Legion of Honour and the fame and glory attached to his name? We suppose he was. He says more than once in his narrative that nothing but his wish to add by his discoveries to the glory of France, his native country, could have sustained him under the trying circumstances and insults to which he was constantly subjected. All honour then to the patient traveller, the sincere patriot, the great discoverer.

We have still to speak of the expedition which cost Alexander Gordon Laing his life; but before giving our necessarily brief account, for his journals were all lost, we must say a few words about his early life and an interesting excursion made by him to Timmannee, Kouran and Soolimana, when he discovered the sources of the Niger.

Laing was born in Edinburgh in 1794, entered the English army at the age of sixteen, and soon distinguished himself. In 1820 he had gained the rank of Lieutenant, and was serving as aide-de-camp to Sir Charles Maccarthy, then Governor General of Western Africa. At this time war was raging between Amara, the Mandingo almamy, and Sannassi, one of his principal chiefs. Trade had never been very flourishing in Sierra Leone, and this state of things dealt it its death-blow. Maccarthy, anxious to put matters on a better footing, determined to interfere and bring about a reconciliation between the rival chiefs. He decided on sending an embassy to Kambia, on the borders of the Scarcies, and from thence to Malacoury and the Mandingo camp. The enterprising character, intelligence, and courage of Laing led to his being chosen by the governor as his envoy, and on the 7th January, 1822, he received instructions to report on the manufactures and topography of the provinces mentioned, and to ascertain the feeling of the inhabitants on the abolition of slavery.

A first interview with Yareddi, leader of the Soolimana troops accompanying the almamy, proved that the negroes of the districts under notice had only the vaguest ideas on European civilization, and that they had had but little intercourse with the whites.

"Every article of our dress," says Laing, "was a subject of admiration; observing me pull off my gloves, Yareddi stared, covered his widely-opened mouth with his hands, and at length exclaimed, 'Alla Akbar!' 'he has pulled the skin off his hands!' By degrees, and as he became more familiar, he alternately rubbed down Dr. Mackie's hair and mine, then indulging himself in a loud laugh, he would exclaim, 'They are not men, they are not men!' He repeatedly asked my interpreter if we had bones?"

These preliminary excursions, during which Laing ascertained that many Soolimanas owned a good deal of gold and ivory, led to his asking the governor's sanction to explore the districts to the east of the colony, with a view to increasing the trade of Sierra Leone by admitting their productions.

Maccarthy liked Laing's proposal and submitted it to the council. It was decided that Laing should be authorized to penetrate into Soolimana by the most convenient route for future communications.

Laing left Sierra Leone on the 16th April, 1824, and rowed up the Rokelle river to Rokon, the chief town of Timmannee. His interview with the King of Rokon was extremely amusing. To do him honour Laing had a salvo of ten charges fired as he came into the court in which the reception was to be held. At the noise the king stopped, drew back, darted a furious look at his visitor, and ran away. It was with great difficulty that the cowardly monarch was induced to return. At last he came back, and seating himself with great dignity in his chair of state he questioned the major:

"He wished to know," says Laing, "why he had been fired at, and was, with some difficulty, persuaded that it had been done out of honour to him. 'Why did you point your guns to the ground?' 'That you might see our intention was to show you respect.' 'But the pebbles flew in my face; why did you not point in the air?' 'Because we feared to burn the thatch on your houses.' 'Well, then, give me some rum.'"

Needless to add that the interview became more cordial after the major had complied with this request!

The portrait of the Timmannee monarch deserves a place in our volume for more than one reason. It is a case of *ab uno disce omnes*."

"Ba-Simera," to quote Laing again, "the principal chief or king of this part of the Timmannee country, is about ninety years of age, with a mottled, shrivelled-up skin, resembling in colour that of an alligator more than that of a human being, with dim, greenish eyes, far sunk in his head, and a bleached, twisted beard, hanging down about two feet from his chin; like the king of the opposite district he wore a necklace of coral and leopard's teeth, but his mantle was brown and dirty as his skin. His swollen legs, like those of an elephant, were to be observed from under his trousers of baft, which might have been originally white, but, from the wear of several years, had assumed a greenish appearance."

Like his predecessors in Africa, Laing had to go through many discussions about the right of passage through the country and bearers' wages, but thanks to his firmness he managed to escape the extortions of the negro kings. The chief halting-places on the route taken by the major were: Toma, where a white man had never before been seen; Balandeko, Roketchnick, which he ascertained to be situated in N. lat. 8° 30', and W. long. 12° 11'; Mabimg, beyond a very broad stream flowing north of the Rokelle; and Ma-Yosso, the chief frontier town of Timmannee. In Timmannee Laing made acquaintance with a singular institution, a kind of free-masonry, known as "Purrah," the existence of which on the borders of the Rio Nuñez had been already ascertained by Caillié.

"Their power" [that of the "Purrah"], says Laing, "supersedes even that of the headmen of the districts, and their deeds of secrecy and darkness are as little called in question, or inquired into, as those of the Inquisition were in Europe, in former years. I have endeavoured in vain to trace the origin, or cause of formation of this extraordinary association, and have reason to suppose, that it is now unknown to the generality of the Timmannees, and may possibly be even so to the Purrah themselves, in a country where no traditionary records are extant, either in writing or in song."

So far as Laing could ascertain Timmannee is divided into three districts. The chief of each arrogates to himself the title of king. The soil is fairly productive, and rice, yams, guavas, earth-nuts, and bananas might be grown in plenty, but for the lazy, vicious, and avaricious character of the inhabitants who vie with each other in roguery.

"I think," says Laing, "that a few hoes, flails, rakes, shovels, &c., would be very acceptable to them, when their respective uses were practically explained; and that they would prove more beneficial both to their interest and ours, than the guns, cocked hats, and mountebank coats, with which they are at present supplied." In spite of our traveller's philanthropic wish, things have not changed since his time. The negroes are just as fond of intoxicating drinks, and their petty kings still go about wearing on grand occasions hats the shape of an accordion, and blue coats with copper buttons, with no shirts underneath. The maternal sentiment did not seem to Laing to be very fully developed amongst the people of Timmannee, for he was twice roundly abused by women for refusing to buy their children of them. A few days later there was a great tumult raised against Laing, the white man who had inflicted a fatal blow on the prosperity of the country by checking its trade. The first town entered in Kouranko was Maboum, and it is interesting to note *en passant* what Laing says of the activity of the inhabitants.

"I entered the town about sunset, and received a first impression highly favourable to its inhabitants, who were returning from their respective labours of the day, every individual bearing about him proofs of his industrious occupation. Some had been engaged in preparing the fields for the crops, which the approaching rains were to mature; others were penning up cattle, whose sleek sides and good condition denoted the richness of their pasturages; the last clink of the blacksmith's hammer was sounding, the weaver was measuring the quantity of cloth he had woven during the day, and the gaurange, or worker in leather, was tying up his neatly-stained pouches, shoes, knife-scabbards, &c. (the work of his handicraft) in a large kotakoo or bag; while the crier at the mosque, with the melancholy call of 'Alla Akbar,' uttered at measured intervals, summoned the dévôts Moslems to their evening devotions."

Had a Marilhat or a Henri Regnault transferred to canvas a scene like this, when the dazzling light of the sun is beginning to die away in green and rose tints, might he not aptly name his painting the *Retour des Champs*, a title so often given to landscapes in our misty climate.

"This scene," adds Laing, "both by its nature and the sentiment which it inspired, formed an agreeable contrast with the noise, confusion, and the dissipation which pervaded a Timmannee town at the same hour; but one must not trust too much to appearances, and I regret to add, that the subsequent conduct of the Kouranko natives did not confirm the good opinion which I had formed of them."

The traveller now passed through Koufoula, where he was very kindly received, crossed a pleasant undulating district shut in by the Kouranko hills and halted at Simera, where the chief ordered his "guiriot" to celebrate in song the arrival of his guest, a welcome neutralized by the fact that the house assigned to Laing let in the rain through its leaky roof and would not let out the smoke, so that, to use his own words, he was more "like a chimney-sweeper" than the white guest of the King of Simera.

Laing afterwards visited the source of the Tongolelle, a tributary of the Rokelle, and then left Kooranko to enter Soolimana. Kooranko, into which our traveller did not penetrate beyond the frontier, is of vast extent and divided into a great number of small states. The inhabitants resemble the

Mandingoes in language and costume, but they are neither so well looking nor so intelligent. They do not profess Mohammedanism and have implicit confidence in their "grigris." They are fairly industrious, they know how to sew and weave. Their chief object of commerce is rosewood or "cam," which they send to the coast. The products of the country are much the same as those of Timmannee.

Komia, N. lat. 9° 22', is the first town in Soolimana. Laing then visited Semba, a wealthy and populous city, where he was received by a band of musicians, who welcomed him with a deafening if not harmonious flourish of trumpets, and he finally reached Falaba, the capital of the country.

The king received Laing with special marks of esteem. He had assembled a large body of troops whom he passed in review, making them execute various manoeuvres accompanied by the blowing of trumpets, beating of tambourines, and the playing of violins and other native instruments. This "fantasia" almost deafened the visitor. Then came a number of *guiriots*, who sang of the greatness of the king, the happy arrival of the major, with the fortunate results which were to ensue from his visit for the prosperity of the country and the development of commerce.

Laing profited by the king's friendliness to ask his permission to visit the sources of the Niger, but was answered by all manner of objections on the score of the danger of the expedition. At last, however, his majesty yielded to the persuasions of his visitor, telling him that "as his heart panted after the water, he might go to it."

The major had not, however, left Falaba two hours before the permission was rescinded, and he had to give up an enterprise which had justly appeared to him of great importance.

A few days later he obtained leave to visit the source of the Rokelle or Sale Kongo, a river of which nothing was known before his time beyond Rokon. From the summit of a lofty rock, Laing saw Mount Loma, the highest of the chain of which it forms part. "The point," says the traveller, "from which the Niger issues, was now shown to me, and appeared to be at the same level on which I stood, viz., 1600 feet above the level of the Atlantic; the source of the Rokelle, which I had already measured, being 1470 feet. The view from this hill amply compensated for my lacerated feet.... Having ascertained correctly the situation of Konkodoogore, and that of the hill upon which I was at this time, the first by observation, and the second by account, and having taken the bearings of Loma from both, I cannot err much in laying down its position in 9° 25' N. and 9° 45' W."

"Laing saw Mount Loma."

Laing had now spent three months in Soolimana, and had made many excursions. It is a very picturesque country, in which alternate hills, valleys, and fertile plains, bordered by woods and adorned with thickets of luxuriant trees.

The soil is fertile and requires very little cultivation; the harvests are abundant and rice grows well. Oxen, sheep, goats, and a small species of poultry, with a few horses, are the chief domestic animals of the people of Soolimana. The wild beasts, of which there are a good many, are elephants, buffaloes, a kind of antelope, monkeys, and leopards.

Falaba, which takes its name from the Fala-ba river, on which it is situated, is about a mile and a half long by one broad. The houses are closer together than in most African towns, and it contains some six thousand inhabitants. Its position as a fortified town is well-chosen. Built on an eminence in the centre of a plain which is under water in the rainy season, it is surrounded by a very strong wooden palisade, proof against every engine of war except artillery.

Strange to say in Soolimana the occupations of men and women seem to be reversed; the latter work in the fields except at seed time and harvest, build the houses, act as masons, barbers, and surgeons, whilst the men attend to the dairy, milk the cows, sew, and wash the linen.

On the 17th September, Laing started on his return journey to Sierra Leone bearing presents from the king, and escorted for several miles by a vast crowd. He finally reached the English colony in safety.

Laing's trip through Timmannee, Kooranko, and Soolimana was not without importance. It opened up districts hitherto unknown to Europeans, and introduced us to the manners, occupations, and trade of the people, as well as to the products of the country. At the same time the course was traced and the source discovered of the Rokelle, whilst for the first time definite information was obtained as to the sources of the Niger, for although our traveller had not actually visited them, he had gone near enough to determine their position approximately.

The results obtained by Laing on this journey, only fired his ambition for further discoveries. He, therefore, determined to make his way to Timbuctoo.

On the 17th June, 1825, he embarked at Malta for Tripoli, where he joined a caravan with which Hateeta, the Tuarick chief, who had made such friends with Lyon, was also travelling as far as Ghât. After two months' halt at Ghadames, Laing again started in October and reached Insalah, which he places a good deal further west than his predecessors had done. Here he remained from November, 1825, to January 1826, and then made his way to the Wâdy Ghât, intending to go from thence at once to Timbuctoo, making a tour of Lake Jenneh or Debbie, visiting the Melli country, and tracing the Niger to its mouth. He would then have retraced his steps as far as Sackatoo, visited Lake Tchad and attempted to reach the hill.

Outside Ghât the caravan with which Laing was travelling was attacked, some say by Tuaricks, others by Berber Arabs, a tribe living near the Niger.

"Laing," says Caillié, who got his information at Timbuctoo, "was recognized as a Christian and horribly ill-treated. He was beaten with a stick until he was left for dead. I suppose that the other Christian whom they told me was beaten to death, was one of the major's servants. The Moors of Laing's caravan picked him up, and succeeded by dint of great care in recalling him to life. So soon as he regained consciousness he was placed on his camel, to which he had to be tied, he was too weak to be able to sit up. The robbers had left him nothing, the greater part of his baggage had been rifled."

Laing arrived at Timbuctoo on the 18th August, 1826, and recovered from his wounds. His convalescence was slow, but he was fortunately spared the extortions of the natives, owing to the letters of introduction he had brought with him from Tripoli and to the sedulous care of his host, a native of that city.

According to Caillié, who quotes this remarkable fact from an old native, Laing retained his European costume, and gave out that he had been sent by his master, the king of England, to visit Timbuctoo and describe the wonders it contained.

"It appears," adds the French traveller, "that Laing drew the plan of the city in public, for the same Moor told me in his naive and expressive language, that he had 'written the town and everything in it.'"

After a careful examination of Timbuctoo, Laing, who had good reason to fear the Tuaricks, paid a visit by night to Cabra, and looked down on the waters of the Niger. Instead of returning to Europe by way of the Great Desert, he was very anxious to go past Jenneh and Sego to the French settlements in Senegal, but at the first hint of his purpose to the Foulahs who crowded to stare at him, he was told that a Nazarene could not possibly be allowed to set foot in their country, and that if he dared attempt it they would make him repent it.

Laing was, therefore, driven to go by way of El Arawan, where he hoped to join a caravan of Moorish merchants taking salt to Sansanding. But five days after he left Timbuctoo, his caravan was joined by a fanatic sheikh, named Hamed-ould-Habib, chief of the Zawat tribe, and Laing was at once arrested under pretence of his having entered their country without authorization. The major being urged to profess Mohammedanism refused, preferring death to apostasy. A discussion then took place between the sheikh and his hired assassins as to how the victim should be put to death, and finally Laing was strangled by two slaves. His body was left unburied in the desert.

This was all Caillié was able to find out when he visited Timbuctoo but one year after Major Laing's death. We have supplemented his accounts by a few details gathered from the reports of the Royal Geographical Society, for the traveller's journal and the notes he took are alike lost to us.

We have already told how Laing managed to fix pretty accurately the position of the sources of the Niger. We have also described the efforts made by Mungo Park and Clapperton to trace the middle portion of the course of that river. We have now to narrate the journeys made in order to examine its mouth and the lower part of its course. The earliest and most successful was that of Richard Lander, formerly Clapperton's servant.

Richard Lander and his brother John proposed to the English Government, that they should be sent to explore the Niger to its mouth. Their offer was accepted, and they embarked on a government vessel for Badagry, where they arrived on the 19th March, 1830.

The king of the country, Adooley, of whom Richard Lander retained a friendly remembrance, was in low spirits. His town had just been burnt, his generals and his best soldiers had perished in a battle with the people of Lagos, and he himself had had a narrow escape when his house and all his treasures were destroyed by fire.

He determined to retrieve his losses, and to do so at the expense of the travellers, who could not get permission to penetrate into the interior of the country until they had been robbed of their most valuable merchandise, and compelled to sign drafts in payment for a gun-boat with a hundred men, for two puncheons of rum, twenty barrels of powder, and a large quantity of merchandise, which they knew perfectly well would never be delivered by this monarch, who was as greedy of gain as he was drunken. As a matter of course the natives followed the example of their chief, vied with him in selfishness, greed, and meanness, regarded the English as fair spoil, and fleeced them on every opportunity.

At last, on the 31st March, Richard and John Lander succeeded in getting away from Badagry; and preceded by an escort sent in advance by the king, arrived at Katunga on the 13th May, having halted by the way at Wow-wow, a good-sized town, Bidjie, where Pearce and Morrison had been taken ill, Jenneh, Chow, Egga, all towns visited by Clapperton, Engua, where Pearce died, Asinara, the first walled city they saw, Bohou, formerly capital of Yariba, Jaguta, Leoguadda, and Itcho, where there is a famous market.

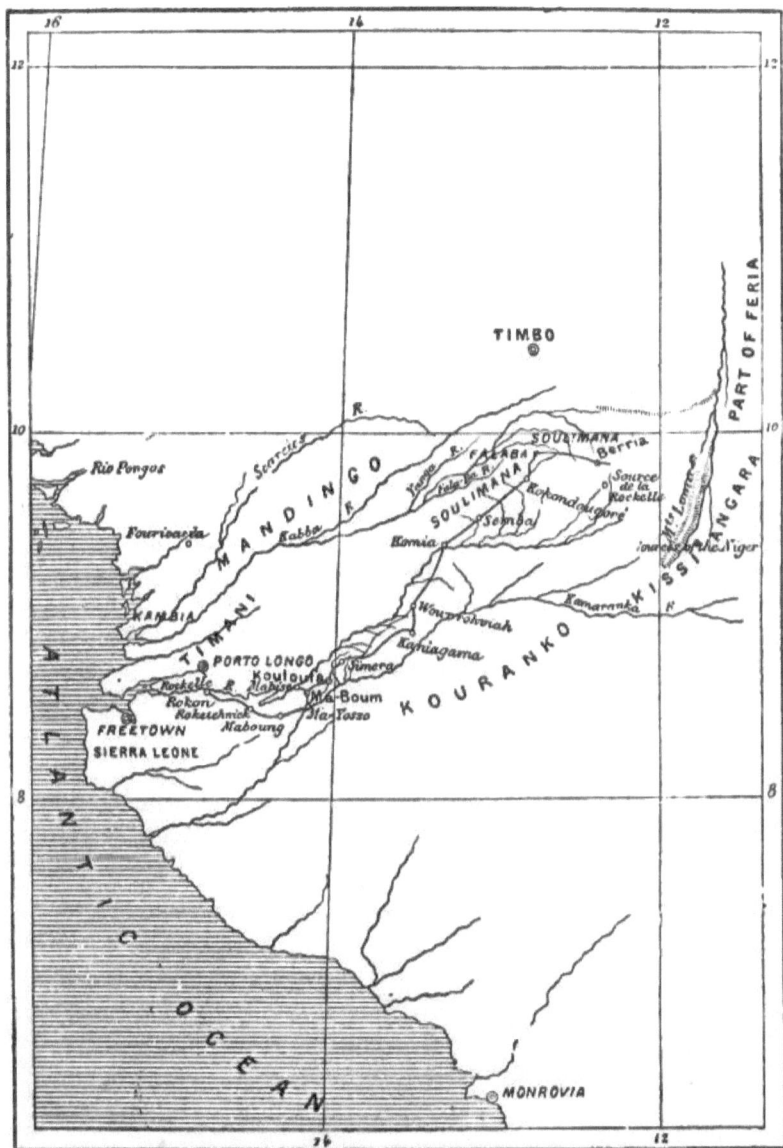

Lower Course of the Niger (after Lander).

At Katunga, according to custom, the travellers halted under a tree before they were received by the king. But being tired of waiting, they presently went to the residence of Ebo, the chief eunuch, and the most influential man about the person of the sovereign. A diabolical noise of cymbals, trumpets, and drums, all played together, announced the approach of the white men, and Mansolah, the king, gave them a most hearty welcome, ordering Ebo to behead every one who should molest them.

The Landers, fearful of being detained by Mansolah until the rainy season, acted on Ebo's advice, and said nothing about the Niger, but merely spoke of the death of their fellow-countryman at Boussa twenty years before, adding that the King of England had sent them to the sultan of Yaourie to recover his papers.

Although Mansolah did not treat the brothers Lander quite as graciously as he had treated Clapperton, he allowed them to go eight days after their arrival.

Of the many details given in the original account of the Landers' journey, of Katunga and the province of Yariba, we will only quote the following:—

"Katunga has by no means answered the expectations we had been led to form of it, either as regards its prosperity, or the number of its inhabitants. The vast plain on which it stands, although exceedingly fine, yields in verdure and fertility, and simple beauty of appearance, to the delightful country surrounding the less celebrated city of Bohoo. Its market is tolerably well supplied with provisions, which are, however, exceedingly dear; insomuch that, with the exception of disgusting insects, reptiles, and vermin, the lower classes of the people are almost unacquainted with the taste of animal food."

Mansolah's carelessness and the imbecile cowardice of his subjects had enabled the Fellatahs to establish themselves in Yarriba, to entrench themselves in its fortified towns, and to obtain the recognition of their independence, until they became sufficiently strong to assume an absolute sovereignty over the whole country.

From Katunga the Landers travelled to Borghoo, by way of Atoupa, Bumbum —a town much frequented by the merchants of Houssa, Borghoo, and other provinces trading with Gonja—Kishi, on the frontiers of Yarriba, and Moussa, on the river of the same name, beyond which they were met by an escort sent to join them by the Sultan of Borghoo. Sultan Yarro received them with many expressions of pleasure and kindness, showing special delight at seeing Richard Lander again. Although he was a convert to Mohammedanism, Yarro evidently put more faith in the superstitions of his forefathers than in his new creed. Fetiches and gri-gris were hung over his door, and in one of his huts there was a square stool, supported on two sides by four little wooden effigies of men. The character, manners, and costumes of the people of Borghoo differ essentially from those of the natives of Yarriba.

"Perhaps no two people in the universe residing so near each other," says the narrative, "differ more widely … than the natives of Yarriba and Borghoo. The former are perpetually engaged in trading with each other from town to town, the latter never quit their towns except in case of war, or when engaged in predatory excursions; the former are pusillanimous and cowardly, the latter are bold and courageous, full of spirit and energy, and never seem happier than when engaged in martial exercises; the former are generally mild, unassuming, humble and honest, but cold and passionless. The latter are proud and haughty, too vain to be civil, and too shrewd to be honest; yet they appear to understand somewhat of the nature of love and the social affections, are warm in their attachments, and keen in their resentments."

On the 17th June our travellers at last came in sight of the city of Boussa. Great was their surprise at finding that town on the mainland, and not, as Clapperton had said, on an island in the Niger. They entered Boussa by the western gate, and were almost immediately introduced to the presence of the king and of the midiki or queen, who told them that they had both that very morning shed tears over the fate of Clapperton.

The Niger or Quorra, which flows below the city, was the first object of interest visited by the brothers.

"This morning," writes the traveller, "we visited the far-famed *Niger* or *Quorra*, which flows by the city about a mile from our residence, and were greatly disappointed at the appearance of this celebrated river. Bleak, rugged rocks rose abruptly from the centre of the stream, causing strong ripples and eddies on its surface. It is said that, a few miles above Boussa, the river is divided into three branches by two small, fertile islands, and that it flows from hence in one continued stream to Funda. The Niger here, in its widest part, is not more than a stone's-throw across at present. The rock on which we sat overlooks the spot where Mr. Park and his associates met their unhappy fate."

Richard Lander made his preliminary inquiries respecting the books and papers belonging to Mungo Park's expedition with great caution. But presently, reassured by the sultan's kindness, he determined to question him as to the fate of the explorer. Yarro was, however, too young at the time of the catastrophe to be able to remember what had occurred. It had taken place two reigns back; but he promised to have a search instituted for relics of the illustrious traveller.

"In the afternoon," says Richard Lander, "the king came to see us, followed by a man with a book under his arm, which was said to have been picked up in the Niger after the loss of our countryman. It was enveloped in a large cotton cloth, and our hearts beat high with expectation as the man was slowly unfolding it, for, by its size, we guessed it to be Mr. Park's Journal; but our disappointment and chagrin were great when, on opening the book, we discovered it to be an old nautical publication of the last century."

There was then no further hope of recovering Park's journal.

On the 23rd June the Landers left Boussa, filled with gratitude to the king, who had given them valuable presents, and warned them to accept no food, lest it should be poisoned, from any but the governors of the places they should pass through. They travelled alongside of the Niger as far as Kagogie, where they embarked in a wretched native canoe, whilst their horses were sent on by land to Yaoorie.

"We had proceeded only a few hundred yards," says Richard Lander, "when the river gradually widened to two miles, and continued as far as the eye could reach. It looked very much like an artificial canal, the steep banks confining the water like low walls, with vegetation beyond. In most places the water was extremely shallow, but in others it was deep enough to float a frigate. During the first two hours of the day the scenery was as interesting and picturesque as can be imagined. The banks were literally covered with hamlets and villages; fine trees, bending under the weight of their dark and impenetrable foliage, everywhere relieved the eye from the glare of the sun's rays, and, contrasted with the lively verdure of the little hills and plains, produced the most pleasing effect. All of a sudden came a total change of scene. To the banks of dark earth, clay, or sand, succeeded black, rugged rocks; and that wide mirror which reflected the skies, was divided into a thousand little channels by great sand-banks."

A little further on the stream was barred by a wall of black rocks, with a single narrow opening, through which its waters rushed furiously down. At this place there is a portage, above which the Niger flows on, restored to its former breadth, repose, and grandeur.

After three days' navigation, the Landers reached a village, where they found horses and men waiting for them, and whence they quickly made their way, through a continuously hilly country, to the town of Yaoorie, where they were welcomed by the sultan, a stout, dirty, slovenly man, who received them in a kind of farm-yard cleanly kept. The sultan, who was disappointed that Clapperton had not visited him, and that Richard Lander had omitted to pay his respects on his return journey, was very exacting to his present guests. He would give them none of the provisions they wanted, and did all he could to detain them as long as possible.

We may add that food was very dear at Yaoorie, and that Richard Lander had no merchandise for barter except a quantity of "Whitechapel sharps, warranted not to cut in the eye," for the very good reason, he tells us, that most of them had no eyes at all, so that they were all but worthless.

They were able, however, to turn to account some empty tins which had contained soups; the labels, although dirty and tarnished, were much admired by the natives, one of whom strutted proudly about for some days wearing an empty tin on his head, bearing four labels of "concentrated essence of meat."

The Sultan would not permit the Englishmen to enter Nyffé or Bornou, and told them there was nothing for them but to go back to Boussa. Richard Lander at once wrote to the king of that town, asking permission to buy a canoe in which to go to Funda, as the road by land was infested by plundering Fellatahs.

At last, on the 26th July, a messenger arrived from the King of Boussa to inquire into the strange conduct of the Sultan of Yaoorie, and the cause of his detention of the white men. After an imprisonment of five weeks the Landers were at last allowed to leave Yaoorie, which was now almost entirely inundated.

The explorers now ascended the Niger to the confluence of the Cubbie, and then went down it again to Boussa, where the king, who was glad to see them again, received them with the utmost cordiality. They were, however, detained longer than they liked by the necessity of paying a visit to the King of Wow-wow, as well as by the difficulty of getting a boat. Moreover, there was some delay in the return of the messengers who had been sent by the King of Boussa to the different chiefs on the banks of the river, and lastly, Beken Rouah (the Dark Water) had to be consulted in order to ensure the safety of the travellers in their journey to the sea.

On taking leave of the king, the brothers were at a loss to express their gratitude for his kindness and hospitality, his zeal in their cause, and the protection he was ever ready to extend during their stay of nearly two months in his capital. The natives showed great regret at losing their visitors, and knelt in the path of the brothers, praying with uplifted hands to their gods on their behalf.

Now began the descent of the Niger. A halt had to be made at the island of Melalie, whose chief begged the white men to accept a very fine kid. We may be sure they were too polite to refuse it. The Landers next passed the large town of Congi, the Songa of Clapperton, and then Inguazilligie, the rendezvous of merchants travelling between Nouffe and the districts north- east of Borghoo. Below Inguazilligie they halted at Patashie, a large fertile island of great beauty, planted with palm groves and magnificent trees.

As this place was not far from Wow-wow, Richard Lander sent a message to the king of that town, who, however, declined to deliver the canoe which had been purchased of him. The messenger failing in his purpose, the brothers were compelled themselves to visit the king, but as they expected, they got only evasive answers. They had now no choice, if they wished to continue their journey, but to make off with the canoes which had been lent them at Patashie. On the 4th October, after further delays, they resumed their course, and being carried down by the current, were soon out of sight of Lever, or Layaba, and its wretched inhabitants.

The first town the brothers came to was Bajiebo, a large and spacious city, which for dirt, noise, and confusion, could not be surpassed. Next came Leechee, inhabited by Nouffe people, and the island of Madje, where the Niger divides into three parts. Just beyond, the travellers suddenly found themselves opposite a remarkable rock, two hundred and eighty feet high, called Mount Kesa, which rises perpendicularly from the centre of the stream. This rock is greatly venerated by the natives, who believe it to be the favourite home of a beneficent genius.

Mount Kesa.
(Fac-simile of early engraving.)

At Belee, a little above Rabba, the brothers received a visit from the "King of the Dark Waters," chief of the island of Zagoshi, who appeared in a canoe of great length and unusual cleanliness, decked with scarlet cloth and gold lace. On the same day they reached the town of Zagoshi, opposite Rabba, and the second Fellatah town beyond Sackatoo.

Mallam Dendo, chief of Zagoshi, was a cousin of Bello. He was a blind and very feeble old man in very bad health, who knew he had but a few years longer to reign, and his one thought was how best to secure the throne to his son.

Although he had received very costly presents, Mallam Dendo was anything but satisfied, and declared that if the travellers did not make him other and more valuable gifts, he would require their guns, pistols, and powder, before he allowed them to leave Zagoshi.

Richard Lander did not know what to do, when the gift of the tobé (or robe) of Mungo Park, which had been restored by the King of Boussa, threw Mallam Dendo into such ecstasies of joy that he declared himself the protector of the Europeans, promised to do all he could to help them to reach the sea, made them a present of several richly-coloured plaited mats, two bags of rice, and a bunch of bananas. These stores came just in time, for the whole stock of cloth, looking-glasses, razors, and pipes was exhausted, and the English had nothing left but a few needles and some silver bracelets as presents for the chiefs on the banks of the Niger.

"Rabba," says Lander, "... seen from Zagoshi, appears to be a large, compact, clean, and well-built town, though it is unwalled, and is not otherwise fenced. It is irregularly built on the slope of a gently-rising hill, at the foot of which runs the Niger; and in point of rank, population, and wealth, it is the second city in the Fellatah dominions, Sackatoo alone being considered as its superior. It is inhabited by a mixed population of Fellatahs, Nyffeans, and emigrants and slaves from various countries, and is governed by a ruler who exercises sovereign authority over Rabba and its dependencies, and is styled sultan or king.... Rabba is famous for milk, oil, and honey. The market, when our messengers were there, appeared to be well supplied with bullocks, horses, mules, asses, sheep, goats, and abundance of poultry. Rice, and various sorts of corn, cotton cloth, indigo, saddles and bridles made of red and yellow leather, besides shoes, boots, and sandals, were offered for sale in great plenty. Although we observed about two hundred slaves for sale, none had been disposed of when we left the market in the evening.... Rabba is not very famous for the number or variety of its artificers, and yet in the manufacture of mats and sandals it is unrivalled. However, in all other handicrafts, Rabba yields to Zagoshi."

The industry and love of labour displayed by the people of the latter town were an agreeable surprise in this lazy country. Its inhabitants, who are hospitable and obliging, are protected by the situation of their island against the Fellatahs. They are independent too, and recognize no authority but that of the "King of the Dark Waters," whom they obey because it is to their interest to do so.

On the 16th October, the Landers at last started in a wretched canoe, for which the king had made them pay a high price, with paddles they had stolen, because no one would sell them any. This was the first time they had been able to embark on the Niger without help from the natives. They went down the river, whose width varies greatly, avoiding large towns as much as possible, for they had no means of satisfying the extortions of the chiefs. No incident of note occurred before Egga was reached, if we except a terrible storm which overtook the travellers when, unable to land in the marshes bordering the river, they had allowed their boat to drift with the current, and during which they were all but upset by the hippopotami playing about on the surface of the water. All this time the Niger flowed in an E.S.E. direction, now eight, now only two miles in width. The current was so rapid that the boat went at the rate of four or five miles an hour.

"They were all but upset."

On the 19th October the Landers passed the mouth of the Coudonia, which Richard had crossed near Cuttup on his first expedition, and a little later they came in sight of Egga. The landing-place was soon reached by way of a bay encumbered with an immense number of large and heavy canoes full of merchandise, with the prows daubed with blood, and covered with feathers, as charms against thieves.

The chief, to whom the travellers were at once conducted, was an old man with a long white beard, whose appearance would have been venerable and patriarchal had he not laughed and played in quite a childish manner. The natives assembled in hundreds to see the strange-looking visitors, and the latter had to place three men as sentinels outside their door to keep the curious at a distance.

Square stool belonging to the King of Bornou.
(Fac-simile of early engraving.)

Lander says that Benin and Portuguese cloths are sold at Egga by many of its
inhabitants, so that it would appear that some kind of communication is kept

up between the sea-coast and this place. The people are very speculative and enterprising, and numbers of them employ all their time solely in trading up and down the Niger. They live entirely in their canoes, over which they have a shed, that answers completely every purpose for which it is intended, so that, in their constant peregrinations, they have no need of any other dwelling or shelter than that which their canoes afford them....

"Their belief," says Lander, "that we possessed the power of doing anything we wished, was at first amusing enough, but their importunities went so far that they became annoying. They applied to us for charms to avert wars and other national calamities, to make them rich, to prevent the crocodiles from carrying off the people, and for the chief of the fishermen to catch a canoe-load of fish every day, each request being accompanied with some sort of present, such as country beer, goora-nuts, cocoa-nuts, lemons, yams, rice, &c., in quantity proportionate to the value of their request.

"The curiosity of the people to see us is so intense, that we dare not stir out of doors, and therefore we are compelled to keep our door open all day long for the benefit of the air, and the only exercise which we can take is by walking round and round our hut like wild beasts in a cage. The people stand gazing at us with visible emotions of amazement and terror; we are regarded, in fact, in just the same light as the fiercest tigers in Europe. If we venture to approach too near the doorway, they rush backwards in a state of the greatest alarm and trepidation; but when we are at the opposite side of the hut they draw as near as their fears will permit them, in silence and caution.

"Egga is a town of vast extent, and its population must be immense. Like all the towns on the banks of the Niger, it is inundated every year. We can but conclude that the natives have their own reasons for building their houses in situations which, in our eyes, are alike so inconvenient and unhealthy. Perhaps it may be because the soil of the surrounding districts consists of a black greasy mould of extraordinary fertility, supplying all the necessaries of life at the cost of very little trouble. Although the King of Egga looked more than a hundred years old, he was very gay and light-hearted. The chief people of the town met in his hut, and spent whole days in conversation. This company of greybeards, for they are all old, laugh so heartily at the sprightliness of their own wit, that it is an invariable practice, when any one passes by, to stop and listen outside, and they add to their noisy merriment so much good-will, that we hear nothing from the hut in which the aged group are revelling during the day but loud peals of laughter and shouts of applause."

One day the old chief wished to show off his accomplishments of singing and dancing, expecting to astonish his visitors.

"He frisked," says Lander, "beneath the burden of five-score, and shaking his hoary locks, capered over the ground to the manifest delight of the bystanders, whose plaudits, though confined, as they always are, to laughter, yet tickled the old man's fancy to that degree, that he was unable to keep up his dance any longer without the aid of a crutch. With its assistance he hobbled on a little while, but his strength failed him; he was constrained for the time to give over, and he set himself down at our side on the threshold of the hut. He would not acknowledge his weakness to us for the world, but endeavoured to pant silently, and suppress loud breathings, that we might not hear him. How ridiculous, yet how natural, is this vanity! He made other unavailing attempts to dance, and also made an attempt to sing, but nature would not second his efforts, and his weak piping voice was scarcely audible. The singers, dancers, and musicians, continued their noisy mirth, till we were weary of looking at and listening to them, and as bedtime was drawing near, we desired them to depart, to the infinite regret of the frivolous but merry old chief."

Mallam-Dendo, however, tried to dissuade the English from continuing the descent of the river. Egga, he said, was the last Nouffe town, the power of the Fellatahs extended no further, and between it and the sea dwelt none but savage and barbarous races, always at war with each other. These rumours and the stories told by the natives to the Landers' people of the danger they would run of being murdered or sold as slaves so terrified the latter, that they refused to embark, declaring their intention of going back to Cape Coast Castle by the way that they came. Thanks to the firmness of the brothers this mutiny was quelled, and on the 22nd October the explorers left Egga, firing a parting salute of three musket-shots. A few miles further down, a sea-gull flew over their heads, a sure sign that they were approaching the sea, and with it, it appeared all but certain, the end of their wearisome journey.

Several small and wretched villages, half under water, and a large town at the foot of a mountain, which looked ready to overwhelm it, the name of which the travellers could not learn, were passed in succession. They met a great number of canoes built like those on the Bonny and Calabar Rivers. The crews stared in astonishment at the white men whom they dared not address. The low marshy banks of the Niger were now gradually exchanged for loftier, richer, and more fertile districts.

Kacunda, where the people of Egga had recommended Lander to halt, is on the western bank of the river. From a distance its appearance is singularly picturesque. The natives were at first alarmed at the appearance of the travellers. An old Mallam acting as Mohammedan priest and schoolmaster took them under his protection, and, thanks to him, the brothers received a warm welcome in the capital of the independent kingdom of Nouffé. The information collected in this town, or rather in this group of four villages, coincided with that obtained at Egga. Richard Lander therefore resolved to make the rest of the voyage by night and to load his four remaining guns and two pistols with balls and shot. To the great astonishment of the natives, who could not understand such contempt of danger, the explorers left Kacunda with three loud cheers, committing their cause to the hands of God. They passed several important towns, which they avoided. The river now wound a great deal, flowing from the south to south-east, and then to the south-west between lofty hills.

On the 25th October, the English found themselves opposite the mouth of a large river. It was the Tchadda or Benuwe. At its junction with the Niger is an important town called Cutum Curaffi. After a narrow escape from being swallowed up in a whirlpool and crushed against the rocks, Lander having found a suitable spot showing signs of habitation, determined to land. That this place had been visited a little time previously, was proved by two burnt out fires with some broken calabashes, fragments of earthenware vessels, cocoa-nut shells, staves of powder-barrels, &c., which the travellers picked up with some emotion, for they proved that the natives had had dealings with Europeans. Some women ran away out of a village which three of Lander's men entered with a view to get the materials for a fire. The exhausted explorers were resting on mats when they were suddenly surrounded by a crowd of half-naked men armed with guns, bows and arrows, cutlasses, iron barbs, and spears. The coolness and presence of mind of the brothers alone averted a struggle, the issue of which could not be dubious. "As we approached," says Lander, "we made all the signs and motions we could with our arms, to deter the chief and his people from firing on us. His quiver was dangling at his side, his bow was bent, and an arrow which was pointed at our breasts already trembled on the string, when we were within a few yards of his person. This was a highly critical moment, the next might be our last. But the hand of Providence averted the blow; for just as the chief was about to pull the fatal cord, a man that was nearest him rushed forward, and stayed his arm. At that instant we stood before him, and immediately held forth our hands; all of them trembled like aspen leaves; the chief looked up full in our faces, kneeling on the ground; light seemed to flash from his dark, rolling eyes, his body was convulsed all over, as though he were enduring the utmost torture, and with a timorous yet undefinable expression of countenance, in which all the passions of our nature were strangely blended, he drooped his head, eagerly grasped our proffered hands, and burst into tears. This was a sign of friendship; harmony followed, and war and bloodshed were thought of no more. It was happy for us that our white faces and calm behaviour produced the effect it did on these people; in another minute our bodies would have been as full of arrows as a porcupine's is full of quills. 'I thought you were children of heaven fallen from the skies,' said the chief, in explanation of this sudden change."

This scene took place in the famous market-town of Bocqua, of which the travellers had so often heard, whither the people come up from the coast to exchange the merchandise of the whites for slaves brought in large numbers from Funda, on the opposite bank.

The information obtained at Bocqua was most satisfactory; the sea was only ten days' journey off. There was no danger in going down the river, the chief said, though the people on the banks were a bad lot.

Following the advice of this chief, the travellers passed the fine town of Atta without stopping, and halted at Abbagaca, where the river divides into several branches, and whose chief showed insatiable greed. Refusing to halt at several villages, whose inhabitants begged for a sight of the white strangers, they were finally obliged to land at the village of Damuggo, where a little man wearing a waistcoat which had once formed part of a uniform, hailed them in English, crying out: "Halloa, ho! you English, come here!" He was an emissary from the King of Bonny come to buy slaves for the master.

The chief of Damuggo, who had never before seen white men, received the explorers very kindly, held public rejoicings in their honour and detained them with constant fêtes until the 4th November. Although the fetich consulted by him presaged that they would meet with a thousand dangers before reaching the sea, this monarch supplied them with an extra canoe, some rowers, and a guide.

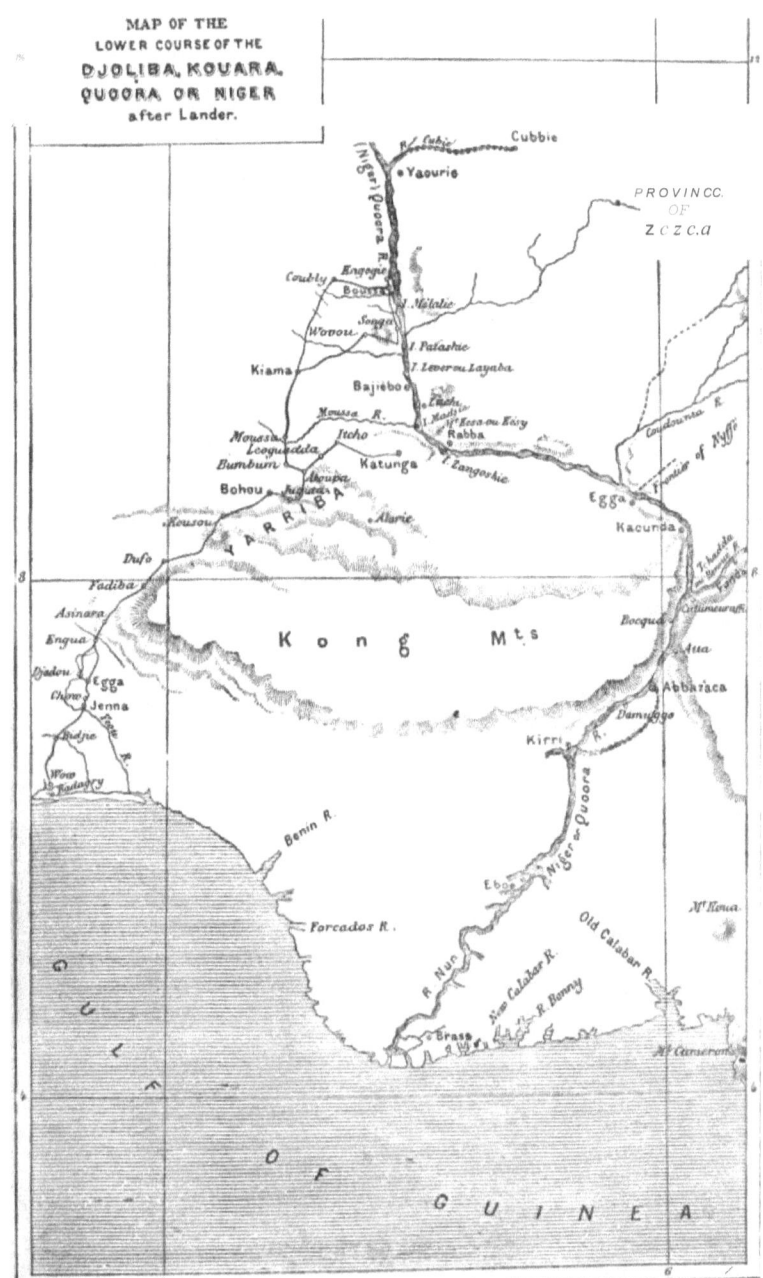

MAP OF THE
LOWER COURSE OF THE
DJOLIBA, KOUARA,
QUOORA, OR NIGER
after Lander.

Gravé par E. Morieu.

The sinister predictions of the fetich were soon fulfilled. John and Richard Lander were embarked in different boats. As they passed a large town called Kirree they were stopped by war-canoes, each containing forty men wearing European clothes, minus the trousers.

Each canoe carried what at first sight appeared to be the Union Jack flying from a long bamboo cane fixed in the stern, a four or six pounder was lashed to each prow, and every black sailor was provided with a musket.

The two brothers were taken to Kirree, where a palaver was held upon their fate. Fortunately the Mallams or Mohammedan priests interfered in their favour, and some of their property was restored to them, but the best part had gone to the bottom of the river with John Lander's canoe.

"To my great satisfaction," says Lander, "I immediately recognized the box containing our books, and one of my brother's journals; the medicine-chest was by its side, but both were filled with water. A large carpet bag, containing all our wearing apparel, was lying cut open, and deprived of its contents, with the exception of a shirt, a pair of trousers, and a waistcoat. Many valuable articles which it had contained were gone. The whole of my journal, with the exception of a note-book with remarks from Rabba to this place, was lost. Four guns, one of which had been the property of the late Mr. Park, four cutlasses, and two pistols, were gone. Nine elephants' tusks, the finest I had seen in the country, which had been given us by the kings of Wow-wow and Boussa; a quantity of ostrich feathers, some handsome leopard skins, a great variety of seeds, all our buttons, cowries, and needles, which were necessary for us to purchase provisions with, all were missing, and said to have been sunk in the river."

This was like going down in port. After crossing Africa from Badagry to Boussa, escaping all the dangers of navigating the Niger, getting free from the hands of so many rapacious chiefs, to be shipwrecked six day's journey from the sea, to be made slaves of or condemned to death just on the eve of making known to Europe the results of so many sufferings endured, so many dangers escaped, so many obstacles happily surmounted! To have traced the course of the Niger from Boussa, to be on the point of determining the exact position of its mouth and then to find themselves stopped by wretched pirates was really too much, and bitter indeed were the reflections of the brothers during the interminable palaver upon their fate.

Although their stolen property was partially restored to them, and the negro who had begun the attack upon them was condemned to be beheaded, the brothers were none the less regarded as prisoners, and they were marched off to Obie, king of the country, who would decide what was to be done with them. It was evident that the robbers were not natives of the country, but had only entered it with a view to pillage. They probably counted on trading in two or three such market-towns as Kirree if they did not meet with any boats but such as were too strong to be plundered. For the rest, all the tribes of this part of the Niger seemed to be at daggers drawn with each other, and the trade in provisions was carried on under arms. After two days' row the canoes came in sight of Eboe, at a spot where the stream divides into three "rivers" of great width, with marshy level banks covered with palm-trees. An hour later one of the boatmen, a native of Eboe, cried, "There is my country." Here fresh difficulties awaited the travellers. Obie, king of Eboe, a young man with a refined and intelligent countenance, received the white men with cordiality. His dress, which reminded his visitors of that of the King of Yarriba, was adorned with such a quantity of coral that he might have been called the coral king.

Obie seemed to be affected by the account the English gave of the struggle in which they had lost all their merchandise, but the aid he gave them was by no means proportioned to the warmth of the sentiments which he expressed, indeed he let them all but die of hunger.

"The Eboe people," says the narrative, "like most Africans, are extremely indolent, and cultivate yams, Indian corn, and plantains only. They have abundance of goats and fowls, but few sheep are to be seen, and no bullocks. The city, which has no other name than the Eboe country, is situated on an open plain; it is immensely large, contains a vast population, and is the capital of a kingdom of the same name. It has, for a series of years, been the principal slave-mart for native traders from the coast, between the Bonny and Old Calabar rivers; and for the production of its palm-oil it has obtained equal celebrity. Hundreds of men from the rivers mentioned above come up for the purpose of trade, and numbers of them are at present residing in canoes in front of the town. Most of the oil purchased by Englishmen at the Bonny and adjacent rivers is brought from thence, as are nearly all the slaves which are annually exported from those places by the French, Spaniards, and Portuguese. It has been told us by many that the Eboe people are confirmed anthropophagi; and this opinion is more prevalent among the tribes bordering on that kingdom, than with the natives of more remote districts."

From what the travellers could learn, it was pretty certain that Obie would not let them go without exacting a considerable ransom. He may doubtless have been driven to this by the importunity of his favourites, but it was more likely the result of the greed of the people of Bonny and Brass, who quarrelled as to which tribe should carry off the English to their country.

A son of the Chief of Bonny, King Pepper, a native named Gun, brother of King Boy, and their father King Forday, who with King Jacket govern the whole of the Brass country, were the most eager in their demands, and produced as proofs of their honourable intentions the testimonials given to them by the European captains with whom they had business relations.

One of these documents, signed James Dow, captain of the brig "Susan" of Liverpool, and dated from the most important river of the Brass Country, September, 1830, ran thus:—

"Captain Dow states that he never met with a set of greater scoundrels than the natives generally, and the pilots in particular."

It goes on in a similar strain heaping curses upon the natives, and charging them with having endeavoured to wreck Dow's vessel at the mouth of the river with a view to dividing his property amongst them. King Jacket was designated as an arrant rogue and a desperate thief. Boy was the only one of common honesty or trustworthiness.

After an endless palaver, Obie declared that according to the laws and customs of the country he had a right to look upon the Landers and their people as his property, but that, not wishing to abuse his privileges, he would set them free in exchange for the value of twenty slaves in English merchandise. This decision, which Richard Lander tried in vain to shake, plunged the brothers into the depths of despair, a state of mind soon succeeded by an apathy and indifference so complete that they could not have made the faintest effort to recover their liberty. Add to these mental sufferings the physical weakness to which they were reduced by want of food, and we shall have some idea of their state of prostration. Without resources of any kind, robbed of their needles, cowries, and merchandise, they were reduced to the sad necessity of begging their bread. "But we might as well have addressed our petitions to the stones or trees," says Lander; "we might have spared ourselves the mortification of a refusal. We never experienced a more stinging sense of our own humbleness and imbecility than on such occasions, and never had we greater need of patience and lowliness of spirit. In most African towns and villages we have been regarded as demigods, and treated in consequence with universal kindness, civility, and veneration; but here, alas, what a contrast! we are classed with the most degraded and despicable of mankind, and are become slaves in a land of ignorance and barbarism, whose savage natives have treated us with brutality and contempt."

It was Boy who finally achieved the rescue of the Landers, for he consented to pay to Obie the ransom he demanded for them and their people. Boy himself was very moderate, asking for nothing in return for his trouble and the risk he ran in taking the white men to Brass, but fifteen bars or fifteen slaves, and a barrel of rum. Although this demand was exorbitant, Lander did not hesitate to write an order on Richard Lake, captain of an English vessel at anchor in Brass river, for thirty-six bars.

The king's canoe, on which the brothers embarked on the 12th November, carried sixty persons, forty of whom were rowers. It was hollowed out of a single tree-trunk, measured more than fifty feet long, carried a four-pounder in the prow, an arsenal of cutlasses and grape-shot, and was laden with merchandise of every kind. The vast tracts of cultivated land on either side of the river showed that the population was far more numerous than would have been supposed. The scenery was flat, open, and varied; and the soil, a rich black mould, produced luxuriant trees, and green shrubs of every shade. At seven p.m. on the 11th November the canoe left the chief branch of the Niger and entered the Brass river. An hour later, Richard Lander recognized with inexpressible delight tidal waves.

A little farther on Boy's canoe came up with those of Gun and Forday. The latter was a venerable-looking old man, in spite of his wretched semi-European semi-native clothing and a very strong predilection for rum, of which he consumed a great quantity, although his manners and conversation betrayed no signs of excessive drinking.

That was a strange escort which accompanied the two Englishmen as far as the town of Brass.

"The canoes," says Lander, "were following each other up the river in tolerable order, each of them displaying three flags. In the first was King Boy, standing erect and conspicuous, his headdress of feathers waving with the movements of his body, which had been chalked in various fantastic figures, rendered more distinct by its natural colour; his hands were resting on the barbs of two immense spears, which at intervals he darted violently into the bottom of the canoe, as if he were in the act of killing some formidable wild animal under his feet. In the bows of all the other canoes fetish priests were dancing, and performing various extraordinary antics, their persons, as well as those of the people with them, being chalked over in the same manner as that of King Boy; and, to crown the whole, Mr. Gun, the little military gentleman, was most actively employed, his canoe now darting before and now dropping behind the rest, adding not a little to the imposing effect of the whole scene by the repeated discharges of his cannon."

Brass consists of two towns, one belonging to Forday, the other to King Jacket. The priests performed some curious ceremonies before disembarking, evidently having reference to the whites. Was the result of the consultation of the fetish of the town favourable or not to the visitors? The way the natives treated them would answer that question. Before he set foot on land Richard Lander, to his great delight, recognized a white man on the banks. He was the captain of a Spanish schooner at anchor in the river. The narrative goes on to say:—

"Of all the wretched, filthy, and contemptible places in this world of ours none can present to the eye of a stranger so miserable an appearance, or can offer such disgusting and loathsome sights, as this abominable Brass Town. Dogs, goats, and other animals run about the dirty streets half-starved, whose hungry looks can only be exceeded by the famishing appearance of the men, women, and children, which bespeaks the penury and wretchedness to which they are reduced; whilst the persons of many of them are covered with odious boils, and their huts are falling to the ground from neglect and decay."

Another place, called Pilot Town by the Europeans, on account of the number of pilots living in it, is situated at the mouth of the river Nun, seventy miles from Brass. King Forday demanded four bars before the Landers left the town, saying it was customary for every white man who came to Brass by the river to make that payment. It was impossible to evade compliance, and Lander drew another bill on Captain Lake. At this price Richard Lander obtained permission to go down in Boy's royal canoe to the English brig stationed at the mouth of the river. His brother and his servants were not to be set free until the return of the king. On his arrival on the brig, Lander's astonishment and shame was extreme when he found that Lake refused to give him any help whatever. The instructions given to the brothers from the ministry were read, to prove that he was not an impostor; but the captain answered,—

"If you think that you have a —— fool to deal with, you are mistaken; I'll not give a —— flint for your bill. I would not give a —— for it."

Overwhelmed with grief at such unexpected behaviour from a fellow-countryman, Richard Lander returned to Boy's canoe, not knowing to whom to apply, and asked his escort to take him to Bonny, where there were a number of English vessels. The king refused to do this, and the explorer was obliged to try once more to move the captain, begging him to give him at least ten muskets, which might possibly satisfy Forday.

"I have told you already," answered Lake, "that I will not let you have even a flint, so bother me no more."

"But I have a brother and eight people at Brass Town," rejoined Lander, "and if you do not intend to pay King Boy, at least persuade him to bring them here, or else he will poison or starve my brother before I can get any assistance from a man-of-war, and sell all my people."

"If you can get them on board," replied the captain, "I will take them away; but as I have told you before, you do not get a flint from me."

At last Lander persuaded Boy to go back and fetch his brother and his people. The king at first declined to do so without receiving some payment on account, and it was only with difficulty that he was induced to forego this demand. When Lake found out that Lander's servants were able-bodied men, who could replace the sailors he had lost by death or who were down with fever, he relented a little. This yielding mood did not, however, last long, for he declared that if John and his people did not come in three days he would start without them. In vain did Richard prove to him beyond a doubt that if he did so the white men would be sold as slaves. The captain would not listen to him, only answering, "I can't help it; I shall wait no longer." Such inhumanity as this is fortunately very rare; and a wretch who could thus insult those not merely his equals, but so much his superiors, ought to be pilloried. At last, on the 24th November, after weathering a strong breeze which made the passage of the bar very rough and all but impossible, John Lander arrived on board. He had had to bear a good many reproaches from Boy, for whom, it must be confessed, there was some excuse; for had he not at his own cost rescued the brothers and their people from slavery, brought them down in his own canoe, and fed them, although very badly, all on the strength of their promise to pay him with as much beef and rum as he could consume? whereas he was, after all, roughly received by Lake, told that his advances would never be refunded, and treated as a thief. Certainly he had cause to complain and any one else would have made his prisoners pay dearly for the disappointment of so many hopes, and the loss of so much money.

For all this, however, Boy brought John Lander safely to the brig. Captain Lake received the traveller pretty cordially, but declared his intention of making the king go back without so much as an obolus. Poor Boy was full of the most gloomy forebodings. His haughty manner was exchanged for an air of deprecating humility. An abundant meal was placed before him, but he scarcely touched it. Richard Lander, disgusted with the stinginess and bad faith of Lake, and unable to keep his promises, ransacked all his possessions; and finding, at last, five silver bracelets and a sabre of native manufacture, which he had brought from Yarriba, he offered these to Boy, who accepted them. Finally, the king screwed up courage enough to make his demand to the captain, who, in a voice of thunder which it was difficult to believe could have come from such a feeble body, declined to accede to it, enforcing his refusal with a shower of oaths and threats, such as made Boy, who saw, moreover, that the vessel was ready to sail, beat a hasty retreat, and hurry off to his canoe.

Thus ended the vicissitudes of the Brothers Lander's journey. They were in some danger in crossing the bar, but that was their last. They reached Fernando Po, and then the Calabar River where they embarked on the *Carnarvon* for Rio Janeiro, at which port Admiral Baker, then commanding the station, got them a passage on board a transport-ship.

On the 9th June they disembarked at Portsmouth. Their first care, after sending an account of their journey to Lord Goderich, then Colonial Secretary, was to inform that official of the conduct of Captain Lake, conduct which was of a nature to compromise the credit of the English Government. Orders were at once given by the minister for the payment of the sums agreed upon, which were perfectly just and reasonable.

Thus was completely and finally solved the geographical problem which had for so many centuries occupied the attention of the civilized world, and been the subject of so many different conjectures. The Niger, or as the natives call it, the Joliba, or Quorra, is not connected with the Nile, and does not lose itself in the desert sands or in the waters of Lake Tchad; it flows in a number of different branches into the ocean on the coast of the Gulf of Guinea, at the point known as Cape Formosa. The entire glory of this discovery, foreseen though it was by scientific men, belongs to the Brothers Lander. The vast extent of country traversed by the Niger between Yaoorie and the sea was completely unknown before their journey.

So soon as the discoveries made by Lander became known in England, several merchants formed themselves into a company for developing the resources of the new districts. In July, 1832, they equipped two steamers, the *Quorra* and *Alburka*, which, under the command of Messrs. Laird, Oldfield, and Richard Lander, appended the Niger as far as Bocqua. The results of this commercial expedition were deplorable. Not only was there absolutely no trade to be carried on with the natives, but the crews of the vessels were decimated by fever. Finally, Richard Lander, who had so often gone up and down the river, was mortally wounded by the natives, on the 27th January, 1834, and died on the morning of 5th February, at Fernando Po.

To complete our account of the exploration of Africa during the period under review, we have still to speak of the various surveys of the valley of the Nile, the most important of which were those by Cailliaud, Russegger, and Rüppell.

Frederic Cailliaud was born at Nantes in 1787, and arrived in Egypt in 1815, having previously visited Holland, Italy, Sicily, part of Greece, and European or Asiatic Turkey, where he traded in precious stones. His knowledge of geology and mineralogy won for him a cordial reception from Mehemet Ali, who immediately on his arrival commissioned him to explore the course of the Nile and the desert.

This first trip resulted in the discovery of emerald mines at Labarah, mentioned by Arab authors, which had been abandoned for centuries. In the excavations in the mountain Cailliaud found the lamps, crowbars, ropes, and tools used in working these mines by men in the employ of Ptolemy. Near the quarries the traveller discovered the ruins of a little town, which was probably inhabited by the ancient miners. To prove the reality of his valuable discovery he took back ten pounds' weight of emeralds to Mehemet Ali.

Another result of this journey was the discovery by the French explorer of the old road from Coptos to Berenice for the trade of India.

From September, 1819, to the end of 1832, Cailliaud, accompanied by a former midshipman named Letorzec, was occupied in exploring all the known oases east of Egypt, and in tracing the Nile to 10° N. lat. On his first journey he reached Wady Halfa, and for his second trip he made that place his starting-point. A fortunate accident did much to aid his researches. This was the appointment of Ismail Pacha, son of Mehemet Ali, to the command of an expedition to Nubia. To this expedition Cailliaud attached himself.

Leaving Daraou in November, 1820, Cailliaud arrived, on the 5th January in the ensuing year, at Dongola, and reached Mount Barka in the Chaguy country, where are a vast number of ruins of temples, pyramids, and other monuments. The fact of this district bearing the name of Merawe had given rise to an opinion that in it was situated the ancient capital of Ethiopia. Cailliaud was enabled to show this to be erroneous.

View of a Merawe temple.
(Fac-simile of early engraving.)

The French explorer, accompanying Ismail Pacha in the character of a mineralogist beyond Berber, on a quest for gold-mines, arrived at Shendy. He then went with Letorzec to determine the position of the junction of the Atbara with the Nile; and at Assour, not far from 17° N. lat., he discovered the ruins of an extensive ancient town. It was Meroë. Pressing on in a southerly direction between the 15th and 16th degrees of N. lat., Cailliaud next identified the mouth of the Bahr-el-Abiad, or White Nile, visited the ruins of Saba, the mouth of the Rahad, the ancient Astosaba, Sennaar, the river Gologo, the Fazoele country, and the Toumat, a tributary of the Nile, finally reaching the Singue country between the two branches of the river. Cailliaud was the first explorer to penetrate from the north so near to the equator; Browne had turned back at 16° 10', Bruce at 11°. To Cailliaud and Letorzec we owe many observations on latitude and longitude, some valuable remarks on the variation of the magnetic needle, and details of the climate, temperature, and nature of the soil, together with a most interesting collection of animals and botanical specimens. Lastly, the travellers made plans of all the monuments beyond the second cataract.

The two Frenchmen had preluded their discoveries by an excursion to the oasis of Siwâh. At the end of 1819 they left Fayum with a few companions, and entered the Libyan desert. In fifteen days, and after a brush with the Arabs, they reached Siwâh, having on their way taken measurements of every part of the temple of Jupiter Ammon, and determined, as Browne had done, its exact geographical position. A little later a military expedition was sent to this same oasis, in which Drovetti collected new and very valuable documents supplementing those obtained by Cailliaud and Letorzec. They afterwards visited successively the oasis of Falafre, never before explored by a European, that of Dakel, and Khargh, the chief place of the Theban oasis. The documents collected on this journey were sent to France, to the care of M. Jomard, who founded on them his work called "Voyage à l'Oasis de Siouah."

A few years later Edward Rüppell devoted seven or eight years to the exploration of Nubia, Sennaar, Kordofan, and Abyssinia in 1824, He ascended the White Nile for more than sixty leagues above its mouth.

Lastly, in 1836 to 1838, Joseph Russegger, superintendent of the Austrian mines, visited the lower portion of the course of the Bahr-el-Abiad. This official journey was followed by the important and successful surveys afterwards made by order of Mehemet Ali in the same regions.

CHAPTER III.

THE ORIENTAL SCIENTIFIC MOVEMENT AND AMERICAN DISCOVERIES.

The decipherment of cuneiform inscriptions, and the study of Assyrian remains up to 1840—Ancient Iran and the Avesta—The survey of India and the study of Hindustani—The exploration and measurement of the Himalaya mountains—The Arabian Peninsula—Syria and Palestine— Central Asia and Alexander von Humboldt—Pike at the sources of the Mississippi, Arkansas, and Red River—Major Long's two expeditions— General Cass—Schoolcraft at the sources of the Mississippi—The exploration of New Mexico—Archæological expeditions in Central America—Scientific expeditions in Brazil—Spix and Martin—Prince Maximilian of Wied-Neuwied—D'Orbigny and American man.

Although the discoveries which we are now to relate are not strictly speaking geographical, they nevertheless throw such a new light on several early civilizations, and have done so much to extend the domain of history and ideas, that we are compelled to dedicate a few words to them.

The reading of cuneiform inscriptions, and the decipherment of hieroglyphics are events so important in their results, they reveal to us so vast a number of facts hitherto unknown, or distorted in the more or less marvellous narratives of the ancient historians Diodorus, Ctesias, and Herodotus, that it is impossible to pass over scientific discoveries of such value in silence.

Thanks to them, we form an intimate acquaintance with a whole world, with an extremely advanced civilization, with manners, habits, and customs differing essentially from our own. How strange it seems to hold in our hands the accounts of the steward of some great lord or governor of a province, or to read such romances as those of *Setna* and the *Two Brothers*, or stories such as that of the *Predestined Prince*.

Those buildings of vast proportions, those superb temples, magnificent hypogæa, and sculptured obelisks, were once nothing more to us than sumptuous monuments, but now that the inscriptions upon them have been read, they relate to us the life of the kings who built them, and the circumstances of their erection.

How many names of races not mentioned by Greek historians, how many towns now lost, how many of the smallest details of the religion, art, and daily life, as well as of the political and military events of the past, are revealed to us by the hieroglyphic and cuneiform inscriptions.

Not only do we now see into the daily life of these ancient peoples, of whom we had formerly but a very superficial knowledge, but we get an idea even of their literature. The day is perhaps not far distant when we shall know as much of the life of the Egyptians in the eighteenth century before Christ as that of our forefathers in the seventeenth and eighteenth centuries of our own era.

Carsten Niebuhr was the first to make and bring to Europe an exact and complete copy of inscriptions at Persepolis in an unknown character. Many attempts had been made to explain them, but all had been vain, until in 1802 Grotefend, the learned Hanoverian philologist, succeeded, by an inspiration of genius, in solving the mystery in which they were enveloped.

Truly these cuneiform characters were strange and difficult to decipher! Imagine a collection of nails variously arranged, and forming groups horizontally placed. What did these groups signify? Did they represent sounds and articulations, or, like the letters of our alphabet, complete words? Had they the ideographic value of Chinese written characters? What was the language hidden in them? These were the problems to be solved! It appeared probable that the inscriptions brought from Persepolis were written in the language of the ancient Persians, but Rask, Bopp, and Lassen had not yet studied the Iranian idioms and proved their affinity with Sanskrit.

It would be beyond our province to give an account of the ingenious deductions, the skilful guesses, and the patient groping through which Grotefend finally achieved the recognition of an alphabetic system of writing, and succeeded in separating from certain groups of words what he believed to be the names of Darius and Xerxes, thus attaining a knowledge of several letters, by means of which he made out other words. It is enough for us to say that the key was found by him, and to others was left the task of completing and perfecting his work.

More than thirty years passed by, however, before any notable progress was made in these studies. It was our learned fellow-countryman Eugène Burnouf who gave them a decided impulse. Turning to account his knowledge of Sanskrit and Zend, he found that the language of the inscriptions of Persepolis was but a Zend dialect used in Bactriana, which was still spoken in the sixth century B.C., and in which the books of Zoroaster were written. Burnouf's pamphlet bears date 1836. At the same period Lassen, a German scholar of Bonn, came to the same conclusion on the same grounds.

The inscriptions already discovered were soon all deciphered; and with the exception of a few signs, on the meaning of which scholars were not quite agreed, the entire alphabet became known. But the foundations alone were laid; the building was still far from finished. The Persepolitan inscriptions appeared to be repeated in three parallel columns. Might not this be a triple version of the same inscription in the three chief languages of the Achæmenian Empire, namely, the Persian, Median, and Assyrian or Babylonian. This guess proved correct; and owing to the decipherment of one of the inscriptions, a test was obtained, and the same plan was followed as that of Champollion with regard to the Rosetta stone, on which was the tri- lingual inscription in Greek, Demotic or Enchorial, and hieroglyphic characters.

In the second and third inscriptions were recognized Syro-Chaldee, which, like Hebrew, Himyaric, and Arabic, belong to the Semitic group, and a third idiom, to which the name of Medic was given, resembling the dialects of the Turks and Tartars. But it would be presumptuous of us to enlarge upon these researches. That was to be the task of the Danish scholar Westergaard, of the Frenchmen De Saulcy and Oppert, and of the Englishmen Morris and Rawlinson, not to mention others less celebrated. We shall have to return to this subject later.

The knowledge of Sanskrit, and the investigation of Brahmanic literature, had inaugurated a scientific movement which has gone on ever since with increasing energy.

Long before Nineveh and Babylon were known as nations, a vast country, called Iran by orientalists, which included Persia, Afghanistan, and Beloochistan, was the scene of an advanced civilization, with which is connected the name of Zoroaster, who was at once a conqueror, a law-giver, and the founder of a religion. The disciples of Zoroaster, persecuted at the time of the Mohammedan conquest, and driven from their ancient home, where their mode of worship was still preserved, took refuge, under the name of Parsees, in the north-west of India.

At the end of the last century, the Frenchman Aquetil Duperron brought to Europe an exact copy of the religious books of the Parsees, written in the language of Zoroaster. He translated them, and for sixty years all the *savants* had found in them the source of all their religious and philological notions of Iran. These books are known under the name of the Zend-Avesta, a word which comprises the name of the language, *Zend*, and the title of the book, *Avesta*.

As the knowledge of Sanskrit increased, however, that branch of science required to be studied afresh by the light of the new method. In 1826 the Danish philologist Rask, and later Eugène Burnouf, with his profound knowledge of Sanskrit, and by the help of a translation in that language recently discovered in India, turned once more to the study of the Zend. In 1834 Burnouf published a masterly treatise on the Yacna, which marked an epoch. From the resemblance between the archaic Sanskrit and the Zend came the recognition of the common origin of the two languages, and the relationship, or rather, the identity, of the races who speak them. Originally the names of the deities, the traditions, the generic appellation, that of Aryan, of the two peoples, are the same, to say nothing of the similarity of their customs. But it is needless to dwell on the importance of this discovery, which has thrown an entirely new light on the infancy of the human race, of which for so many centuries nothing was known.

From the close of the eighteenth century, that is to say from the time when the English first obtained a secure footing in India, the physical study of the country was vigorously carried on, outstripping of course for a time that of the ethnology and kindred subjects, which require for their prosecution a more settled country and less exciting times. It must be owned, however, that knowledge of the races of the country to be controlled is as essential to the government as it is to commercial enterprise; and in 1801 Lord Wellesley, as Governor for the Company, recognizing the importance of securing a good map of the English territories, commissioned Brigadier William Lambton, to connect, by means of a trigonometrical survey, the eastern and western banks of the Indus with the observatory of Madras. Lambton was not content with the mere accomplishment of this task. He laid down with precision one arc of the meridian from Cape Comorin to the village of Takoor-Kera, fifteen miles south-east of Ellichpoor. The amplitude of this arc exceeded twelve degrees. With the aid of competent officers, amongst whom we must mention Colonel Everest, the Government of India would have hailed the completion of the task of its engineers long before 1840, if the successive annexation of new territories had not constantly added to the extent of ground to be covered.

At about the same time with this progress in our knowledge of the geography of India an impulse was given to the study of the literature of India.

In 1776 an extract from the most important native codes, then for the first time translated under the title of the Code of the Gentoos[1] was published in London. Nine years later the Asiatic Society was founded in Calcutta by Sir William Jones, the first who thoroughly mastered the Sanskrit language. In "Asiatic Researches," published by this society, were collected the results of all scientific investigations relating to India. In 1789, Jones published his translation of the drama of S'akuntala, that charming specimen of Hindu literature, so full of feeling and refinement. Sanskrit grammars and dictionaries were now multiplied, and a regular rivalry was set on foot in British India, which would undoubtedly soon have spread to Europe, had not the continental blockade prevented the introduction of works published abroad. At this time an Englishman named Hamilton, a prisoner of war in Paris, studied the Oriental MSS. in the library of the French capital, and taught Frederick Schlegel the rudiments of Sanskrit, which it was no longer necessary to go to India to learn.

[1] Gentoo was the name given by old English writers to the natives of Hindustan, and is now obsolete, having been superseded by that of Hindoo.—*Trans.*

Lassen was Schlegel's pupil, and together they studied the literature and antiquities of India, examining, translating, and publishing the original texts; whilst at the same time Franz Bopp devoted himself to the study of the language, making his grammars accessible to all, and coming to the conclusion which was then startling, although it is now generally accepted, of the common origin of the Indo-European languages.

It was proved that the Vedas, that collection of sacred writings held in too universal veneration to be tampered with, were written in a very ancient and very pure idiom which had not been revived, and whose close resemblance with the Zend, put back the date of the composition of the books beyond the time of the separation of the Aryan family into two branches. The Mahabharata and the Ramayana, dating from the Brahminical or the period succeeding that of the Vedas, were next studied, together with the Puranas. Owing to a profounder knowledge of the language and a more intimate acquaintance with the mythology of the Hindus, scholars were able to fix approximately the date of the composition of these poems, to ascertain the numberless interpolations, and to extract everything of actual historical or geographical value from those marvellous allegories.

The result of these patient and minute investigations was a conviction that the Celtic, Greek, Latin, Germanic, Slave, and Persian languages had one common parent, and that parent none other than Sanskrit. If, then, their language was the same, it followed as a matter of course that the people had been also identical. The differences now existing between these various idioms are accounted for by the successive breakings up of the primitive people, approximate dates enable us to realize the greater or less affinity of those languages with the Sanskrit, and the nature of the words which they have borrowed from it, words corresponding by their nature to the different degrees of advance in civilization.

Moreover a very clear and definite notion was obtained of the kind of life led by the founders of the Indo-European race, and the changes brought about in it by the progress of civilization. The Vedas give us a picture of the Aryan race before it migrated to India, and occupied the Punjab and Cabulistan. By the aid of these poems we can look on at struggles against the primitive races of Hindustan; whose resistance was all the more desperate in that the conqueror, of their caste divisions, left them only the lowest and most degraded. Thanks to the Vedas we can realize every detail of the pastoral and patriarchal life of the Aryans, a life so domestic and unruffled, that we mentally ask ourselves whether the eager strife of the modern peoples is not a poor exchange for the peaceful existence which their few wants secured to their forefathers.

We cannot dwell longer on this subject, but the little that we have said will be enough to show the reader the importance to history, ethnography, and philology, of the study of Sanskrit. For further details we refer him to the special works of Orientalists and to the excellent historical manuals of Robiou, Lenormant, and Maspero. All the scientific results of whatever kind obtained up to 1820 are also skilfully and impartially summed up in Walter Hamilton's large work, "A Geographical, Statistical, and Historical Description of Hindustan, and the neighbouring Countries." This is a book which, by recording the various stages of scientific progress, marks with accuracy the point reached at any given epoch.

After this brief review of the labours of scholars in reference to the intellectual and social life of the Hindus, we must turn to those studies whose aim was a knowledge of the physical character of the country.

One of the most surprising results obtained by the travels of Webb and Moorcroft was the extraordinary height attributed by them to the Himalaya mountains. According to them their elevation exceeded that of the loftiest summits of the Andes. Colonel Colebrook had estimated the average height of the chain at 22,000 feet, and even this would appear to be less than the reality.

Webb measured Yamunavatri, one of the most remarkable peaks of the chain, and estimated its height above the level of the plateau from which it rises as 20,000 feet, whilst the plateau in its turn is 5000 feet above the plain. Not satisfied, however, with what he looked upon as too perfunctory an estimate, he measured, with all possible mathematical accuracy, the Dewalagiri or White Mountain, and ascertained its height to be no less than 27,500 feet.

The most remarkable feature of the Himalaya chain is the succession of these mountains, the ranges of heights rising one above the other. This gives a far more vivid impression of their loftiness than would one isolated peak rising from a plain and with its head lost among the clouds.

The calculations of Webb and Colebrook, were soon verified by the mathematical observations of Colonel Crawford, who measured eight of the highest peaks of the Himalayas. According to him the loftiest of all was Chumulari, situated near the frontiers of Bhoutan and Thibet, which attains to a height of 30,000 feet above the sea-level.

Results such as these, confirmed by the agreement of so many observers, who could not surely all be wrong, took the scientific world by surprise. The chief objection urged was the fact that the snow-line must in these districts be something like 30,000 feet above the sea-level. It appeared, therefore, impossible to believe the assertion of all the explorers, that the Himalayas were covered with forests of gigantic pines. Finally, however, actual personal observation upset theory. In a second journey, Webb climbed the Niti-Ghaut, the loftiest peak in the world, the height of which he fixed at 16,814 feet, and not only did he find no snow, but even the rocks rising 300 feet above it were quite free from snow in summer. Moreover, the steep sides, where breathing was difficult, were clothed with magnificent forests of tapering pines, and firs, and wide-spreading cypress and cedar-trees.

"The high limits of perpetual snow on the Himalaya mountains," says Desborough Cooley, "are justly ascribed by Mr. Webb to the great elevation of the table-land or terrace from which these mountain peaks spring. As the heat of our atmosphere is derived chiefly from the radiation of the earth's surface, it follows that the temperature of any elevated point must be modified in a very important degree by the proximity and extent of the surrounding plains. These observations seem satisfactorily to refute the objections made by certain savants respecting the great height of the Himalaya mountains, which may be, therefore, safely pronounced to be the loftiest mountain chain on the surface of the globe."

We must now refer briefly to an expedition in the latitudes already visited by Webb and Moorcroft. The traveller Fraser, with neither the necessary instruments nor knowledge for measuring the lofty peaks he ascended, was endowed with a great power of observation, and his account of his journey is full of interest, and here and there very amusing. He visited the source of the Jumna, and, at a height of more than 25,000 feet, he found numerous villages picturesquely perched on slopes carpetted with snow. He then made his way to Gangoutri, in spite of the opposition of his guides, who represented the road thither as extremely dangerous, declaring that it was swept by a pestilential wind which would deprive any traveller, who ventured to expose himself to it, of his senses. The explorer, however, was more than rewarded for all his dangers and fatigues by the enjoyment he derived from the grandeur and magnificence of the views he obtained.

"Villages picturesquely perched."

"There is that," says Desborough Cooley in reference to Fraser's journey, "in the appearance of the Himalaya range, which every person who has seen them will allow to be peculiarly their own. No other mountains that I have ever seen bear any resemblance to their character; their summits shoot in the most fantastic and spiring peaks to a height that astonishes, and, when viewed from an elevated situation, almost induce the belief of an ocular deception."

We must now leave the peninsula of the Ganges for that of Arabia, where we have to record the result of several interesting journeys. That of Captain Sadler of the Indian army, claims the first rank. Sent by the Governor of Bombay in 1819, on an embassy to Ibrahim Pacha, who was then at war with the Wahabees, that officer crossed the entire peninsula from Port El Katif on the Persian Gulf to Yambo on the Red Sea.

Unfortunately the interesting account of this crossing of Arabia, never before accomplished by a European, has not been separately published, but is buried in a book which it is almost impossible to obtain, "The Transactions of the Literary Society of Bombay."

At about the same time, 1821-1826, the English Government commissioned Captains Moresby and Haines, of the naval service, to make hydrographical surveys with a view to obtaining a complete chart of the coasts of Arabia. These surveys were to be the foundation of the first trustworthy map of the Arabian peninsula.

We have now only to mention the two expeditions of the French naturalists, Aucher Eloy in the country of Oman, and Emile Botta in Yemen, and to refer to the labours in reference to the idioms and antiquities of Arabia of the French consul at Djedda, Fulgence Fresnel. He was the first, in his letters on the history of the Arabs before Islamism, published in 1836, to explain the Himyarite or Homeric language and to recognize that it resembles rather the early Hebrew and Syriac dialects, than the Arabic of the present day.

At the beginning of this volume we spoke of the explorations and archæological and historical researches of Seetzen and Burckhardt in Syria and Palestine. We have still to say a few words on an expedition the results of which were entirely geographical. We refer to the journey of the Bavarian naturalist Heinrich Schubert.

Schubert was a devout Catholic and an enthusiastic student, and the melancholy scenery of the Holy Land with its wonderful legends, and the lovely banks of the mysterious Nile with its historic memories, had for him an extraordinary fascination. In his account of his journey we find the deep impressions of the believer combined with the scientific observations of the naturalist.

In 1837, Schubert, having crossed Lower Egypt and the peninsula of Sinai, entered the Holy Land. The learned Bavarian pilgrim was accompanied by two friends, Dr. Erdl and Martin Bernatz, a painter.

The travellers landed at El Akabah on the Red Sea, and went with a small Arab caravan to El Khalil, the ancient Hebron. The route they followed had never before been trodden by a European. It led through a wide, flat valley terminating at the Dead Sea; a valley through which the waters of the Dead Sea were supposed at one time to have flowed towards the Red Sea. This hypothesis was shared by Burckhardt and many others who had only seen the district from a distance, and who attributed the cessation of the drainage to an upheaval of the soil. The heights, as taken by the travellers, showed this hypothesis to be altogether erroneous.

In fact from the lower end of the Persian Gulf the country presents a continuous ascent for two or three days' march to the point called by the Arabs the Saddle, from thence it begins to sink and slopes down towards the Dead Sea. The Saddle is about 2100 feet above the sea-level, at least that was the estimate given a year later by Count Bertou, a Frenchman, who visited those localities at that time.

On their way down to the Bituminous Lake, Schubert and his companions took some other barometrical observations, and were very much surprised to find their instrument marking ninety-one feet *below* the Red Sea, the levels gradually decreasing in height as they advanced. At first they thought there must be some mistake, but finally, the evidence was too strong for them, and it became proved beyond a doubt that the Dead Sea could never have emptied its waters into the Red Sea for the very excellent reason that the level of the former is very much lower than that of the latter.

The depression of the Dead Sea is very much more noticeable when Jericho is approached from Jerusalem. In that case the way lies through a long valley with a very rapid slope, all the more remarkable as the hilly plains of Judea, Peræ, and El Harran are very lofty, the latter rising to a height of nearly 3000 feet above the sea-level.

The appearance of the country and the testimony of the instruments were in such contradiction to the prevalent belief, that Messrs. Erdl and Schubert were very unwilling to accept the results obtained, which they attributed to their barometer being out of order and to a sudden disturbance of the atmosphere. But on their way back to Jerusalem the barometer returned to the mean height it had registered before they started for Jericho. There was nothing for it then but to admit, whether they liked it or not, that the Dead Sea was at least 600 feet below the level of the Mediterranean, an estimate, as later researches showed, which fell one-half short of the truth.

This, it will be admitted, was a fortunate rectification, which would have considerable influence, by calling the attention of *savants* to a phenomenon which was soon to be verified by other explorers.

At the same time, the survey of the basin of the Dead Sea was completed and rectified. In 1838, two American Missionaries, Edward Robinson and Eli Smith, gave quite a new impulse to Biblical geography. They were the forerunners of that phalanx of naturalists, historians, archæologists, and engineers, who, under the patronage or in conjunction with the English Exploration Society, were soon to explore the land of the patriarchs from end to end, making maps of it, and achieving discoveries which threw a new light on the history of the ancient peoples who, by turns, were possessors of this corner of the Mediterranean basin.

But it was not only the Holy Land, so interesting on account of the many associations it has for every Christian, which was the scene of the researches of scholars and explorers; Asia Minor was also soon to yield up her treasures to the curiosity of the learned world. That country was visited by travellers in every direction. Parrot visited Armenia; Dubois de Monpereux traversed the Caucasus in 1839. In 1825 and 1826, Eichwald explored the shores of the Caspian Sea; and lastly, Alexander von Humboldt at the expense of the generous Nicholas, Emperor of Russia, supplemented his intrepid work as a discoverer in the New World by an exploration of Western Asia and the Ural Mountains. Accompanied by the mineralogist Gustave Rose, the naturalist Ehrenberg, well known for his travels in Upper Egypt and Nubia, and Baron von Helmersen, an officer of engineers, Humboldt travelled through Siberia, visited the gold and platinum mines of the Ural Mountains, and explored the Caspian steppes and the Altai chain to the frontiers of China. These learned men divided the work, Humboldt taking astronomical, magnetic, and physical observations, and examining the flora and fauna of the country, while Rose kept the journal of the expedition, which he published in German between 1837 and 1842.

Although the explorers travelled very rapidly, at the rate of no less than 11,500 miles in nine months, the scientific results of their journey were considerable. In a first publication which appeared in Paris in 1838, Humboldt treated only the climatology and geology of Asia, but this fragmentary account was succeeded in 1843 by his great work called "Central Asia." "In this," says La Roquette, "he has laid down and systematized the principal scientific results of his expedition in Asia, and has recorded some ingenious speculation as to the shape of the continents and the configuration of the mountains of Tartary, giving special attention to the vast depression which stretches from the north of Europe to the centre of Asia beyond the Caspian Sea and the Ural River."

We must now leave Asia and pass in review the various expeditions in the New World, which have been sent out in succession since the beginning of the present century. In 1807, when Lewis and Clarke were crossing North America from the United States to the Pacific Ocean, the Government commissioned a young officer, Lieutenant Zabulon Montgomery Pike, to examine the sources of the Mississippi. He was at the same time to endeavour to open friendly relations with any Indians he might meet.

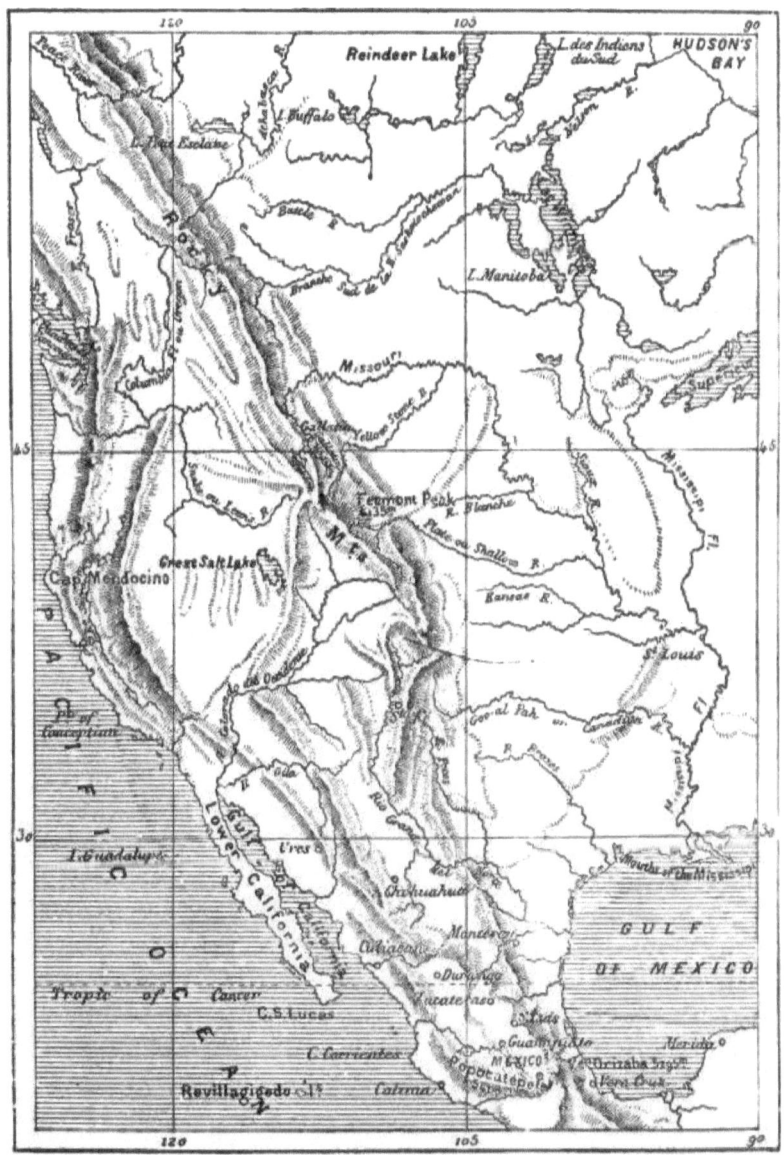

Map of the Missouri.

Pike was well received by the Chief of the powerful Sioux nation and presented with the pipe of peace, a talisman which secured to him the protection of the allied tribes; he ascended the Mississippi, passing the mouths of the Chippeway and St. Peter, important tributaries of that great river. But beyond the confluence of the St. Peter with the Mississippi as far as the Falls of St. Anthony, the course of the main river is impeded by an uninterrupted series of falls and rapids. A little below the 45th parallel of North latitude, Pike and his companions had to leave their canoes and continue their journey in sledges. To the severity of a bitter winter were soon added the tortures of hunger. Nothing, however, checked the intrepid explorers, who continued to follow the Mississippi, now dwindled down to a stream only 300 roods wide, and arrived in February at Leech Lake, where they were received with enthusiasm at the camp of some trappers and fur hunters from Montreal.

Circassians.
(Fac-simile of early engraving.)

After visiting Red Cedar Lake, Pike returned to St. Louis. His arduous and perilous journey had extended over no less than nine months; and although he had not attained its main object, it was not without scientific results. The skill, presence of mind, and courage of Pike were recognized, and the government soon afterwards conferred on him the rank of major, and appointed him to the command of a fresh expedition. This time he was to explore the vast tract of country between the Mississippi and the Rocky Mountains, and to discover the sources of the Arkansas and Red River. With twenty-three companions Pike ascended the Arkansas, a fine river navigable to the mountains in which it rises, that is to say for a distance of 2000 miles, except in the summer, when its bed is encumbered with sand-banks. On this long voyage, winter, from which Pike had suffered so much on his previous trip, set in with redoubled vigour. Game was so scarce that for four days the explorers were without food. The feet of several men were frostbitten, and this misfortune added to the fatigue of the others. The major, after reaching the source of the Arkansas, pursued a southerly direction and soon came to a fine stream which he took for the Red River.

This was the Rio del Norte, which rises in Colorado, then a Spanish province, and flows into the Gulf of Mexico.

From what has been already said of the difficulties which Humboldt encountered before he obtained permission to enter the Spanish possessions in America, we may judge with what jealous suspicion the arrival of strangers in Colorado was regarded. Pike was surrounded by a detachment of Spanish soldiers, made prisoner with all his men, and taken to Santa Fé. Their ragged garments, emaciated forms, and generally miserable appearance did not speak much in their favour, and the Spaniards at first took the Americans for savages. However, when the mistake was recognized, they were escorted across the inland provinces to Louisiana, arriving at Natchitoches on the 1st July, 1807.

The unfortunate end of this expedition cooled the zeal of the government, but not that of private persons, merchants, and hunters, whose numbers were continually on the increase. Many even completely crossed the American continent from Canada to the Pacific. Amongst these travellers we must mention Daniel William Harmon, a member of the North-West Company, who visited Lakes Huron and Superior, Rainy Lake, the Lake of the Woods, Manitoba, Winnipeg, Athabasca, and the Great Bear Lake, all between N. lat. 47° and 58°, and reached the shores of the Pacific. The fur company established at Astoria at the mouth of the Columbia also did much towards the exploration of the Rocky Mountains.

Four associates of that company, leaving Astoria in June, 1812, ascended the Columbia, crossed the Rocky Mountains, and following an east-south-east direction, reached one of the sources of the Platte, descended it to its junction with the Missouri, crossed a district never before explored, and arrived at St.

Louis on the 30th May, 1813.

In 1811, another expedition composed of sixty men, started from St. Louis and ascended the Missouri as far as the settlements of the Ricara Indians, whence they made their way to Astoria, arriving there at the beginning of 1812, after the loss of several men and great suffering from fatigue and want of food.

These journeys resulted not only in the increase of our knowledge of the topography of the districts traversed, but they also brought about quite unexpected discoveries. In the Ohio valley between Illinois and Mexico for instance, were found ruins, fortifications, and entrenchments, with ditches and a kind of bastion, many of them covering five or six acres of ground. What people can have constructed works such as these, which denote a civilization greatly in advance of that of the Indians, is a difficult problem of which no solution has yet been found.

Philologists and historians were already regretting the dying out of the Indian tribes, who, until then, had been only superficially observed, and lamenting their extinction before their languages had been studied. A knowledge of these languages and their comparison with those of the old world, might have thrown some unexpected light upon the origin of the wandering tribes.[2]

[2] The author has evidently not seen Bancroft's "Native Races of the Pacific," an exhaustive work in five volumes, published at New York and San Francisco a few years ago, and which embodies the researches of a number of gentlemen, who collected their information on the spot, and whose contributions to our knowledge of the past and present life of the Indians should certainly not be ignored.—*Trans.*

Simultaneously with the discovery of the ruins the flora and geology of the country began to be studied, and in the latter science great surprises were in store for future explorers. It was so important for the American government to proceed rapidly to reconnoitre the vast territories between the United States and the Pacific, that another expedition was speedily sent out.

In 1819, the military authorities commissioned Major Long to explore the districts between the Mississippi and the Rocky Mountains, to trace the course of the Missouri and of its principal tributaries, to fix the latitude and longitude of the chief places, to study the ways of the Indian tribes, in fact to describe everything interesting either in the aspect of the country or in its animal, vegetable, and mineral productions.

Leaving Pittsburgh on the 5th March, 1819, on board the steamship *Western Engineer*, the expedition arrived in May of the following year at the junction of the Ohio with the Mississippi, and ascended the latter river as far as St. Louis. On the 29th June, the mouth of the Missouri was reached. During the month of July, Mr. Say, who was charged with the zoological observations, made his way by land to Fort Osage, where he was joined by the steamer. Major Long turned his stay at Fort Osage to account by sending a party to examine the districts between the Kansas and the Platte, but this party was attacked, robbed, and compelled to turn back after losing all their horses. After obtaining at Cow Island a reinforcement of fifteen soldiers, the expedition reached Fort Lisa, near Council Bluff, on the 19th September. There it was decided to winter. The Americans suffered greatly from scurvy, and having no medicines to check the terrible disorder, they lost 100 men, nearly a third of the whole party. Major Long, who had meanwhile reached Washington in a canoe, brought back orders for the discontinuation of the voyage up the Missouri, and for a journey overland to the sources of the Platte, whence the Mississippi was to be reached by way of the Arkansas and Red River. On the 6th June, the explorers left Engineer's Fort, as they called their winter quarters, and ascended the Platte Valley for more than a hundred miles, its grassy plains, frequented by vast herds of bisons and deer, supplying them with plenty of provisions.

Those boundless prairies, whose monotony is unbroken by a single hillock, were succeeded by a sandy desert gradually sloping up, for a distance of nearly four hundred miles, to the Rocky Mountains. This desert, broken by precipitous ravines, *cañons*, and gorges, at the bottom of which gurgles some insignificant stream, its banks clothed with stunted and meagre vegetation, produces nothing but cacti with sharp and formidable prickles.

On the 6th July, the expedition reached the foot of the Rocky Mountains. Dr. James scaled one of the peaks, to which he gave his own name, and which rises to a height of 11,500 feet above the sea level.

"From the summit of the peak," says the botanist, "the view towards the north, west, and south-west, is diversified with innumerable mountains all white with snow, and on some of the more distant it appears to extend down to their bases. Immediately under our feet on the west, lay the narrow valley of the Arkansas; which we could trace running towards the north-west, probably more than sixty miles. On the north side of the peak was an immense mass of snow and ice…. To the east lay the great plain, rising as it receded, until, in the distant horizon, it appeared to mingle with the sky."

Here the expedition was divided into two parties, one, under the command of Major Long, to make its way to the sources of the Red River, the other, under Captain Bell, to go down the Arkansas as far as Port Smith. The two detachments separated on the 24th July. The former, misled by the statements of the Kaskaia Indians and the inaccuracy of the maps, took the Canadian for the Red River, and did not discover their mistake until they reached its junction with the Arkansas. The Kaskaias were the most miserable of savages, but intrepid horsemen, excelling in lassoing the wild mustangs which are descendants of the horses imported into Mexico by the Spanish conquerors. The second detachment was deserted by four soldiers, who carried off the journals of Say and Lieutenant Swift with a number of other valuable effects. Both parties also suffered from want of provisions in the sandy deserts, whose streams yield nothing but brackish and muddy water. The expedition brought to Washington sixty skins of wild animals, several thousands of insects, including five hundred new species, four or five hundred specimens of hitherto unknown plants, numerous views of the scenery, and the materials for a map of the districts traversed.

"Excelling in lassoing the wild mustangs."

The command of another expedition was given in 1828 to Major Long, whose services were thoroughly appreciated. Leaving Philadelphia in April, he embarked on the Ohio, and crossed the state of the same name, and those of Indiana and Illinois. Having reached the Mississippi, he ascended that river to the mouth of the St. Peter, formerly visited by Carver, and later by Baron La Hontan. Long followed the St. Peter to its source, passing Crooked Lake and reaching Lake Winnipeg, whence he explored the river of the same name, obtained a sight of the Lake of the Woods and Rainy Lake, and arrived at the plateau which separates the Hudson's Bay valley from that of the St. Lawrence. Lastly, he went to Lake Superior by way of Cold Water Lake and Dog River.

Although all these districts had been constantly traversed by Canadian pathfinders, trappers, and hunters for many years previously, it was the first time an official expedition had visited them with a view to the laying down of a map. The explorers were struck with the beauty of the neighbourhood watered by the Winnipeg. That river, whose course is frequently broken by picturesque rapids and waterfalls, flows between two perpendicular granite walls crowned with verdure. The beauty of the scenery, succeeding as it did to the monotony of the plains and savannahs they had previously traversed, filled the explorers with admiration.

The exploration of the Mississippi, which had been neglected since Pike's expedition, was resumed in 1820 by General Cass, Governor of Michigan. Leaving Detroit at the end of May with twenty men trained to the work of pathfinders, he reached the Upper Mississippi, after visiting Lakes Huron, Superior, and Sandy. His exhausted escort halted to rest whilst he continued the examination of the river in a canoe. For 150 miles the course of the Mississippi is rapid and uninterrupted, but beyond that distance begins a series of rapids extending over twelve miles to the Peckgama Falls.

Above this cataract the stream, now far less rapid, winds through vast savannahs to Leech Lake. Having reached Lake Winnipeg, Cass arrived on the 21st July at a new lake, to which he gave his own name, but he did not care to push on further with his small party of men and inadequate supply of provisions and ammunition.

The source of the Mississippi had been approached, but not reached. The general opinion was that the river took its rise in a small sheet of water known as Deer Lake, sixty miles from Cass Lake. Not until 1832, however, when General Cass was Secretary of State for war, was this important problem solved.

The command of an expedition was then given to a traveller named Schoolcraft, who had in the previous year explored the Chippeway country, north-west of Lake Superior. His party consisted of six soldiers, an officer qualified to conduct hydrographic surveys, a surgeon, a geologist, an interpreter, and a missionary.

Schoolcraft left St. Marie on the 7th June, 1832, visited the tribes living about Lake Superior, and was soon on the St. Louis river. He was then 150 miles from the Mississippi, and was told that it would take him no less than ten days to reach the great river, on account of the rapids and shallows. On the 3rd July, the expedition reached the factory of a trader named Aitkin, on the banks of the river, and there celebrated on the following day the anniversary of the independence of the United States.

Two days later Schoolcraft found himself opposite the Peckgama Falls, and encamped at Oak Point. Here the river winds a great deal amongst savannahs, but guides led the party by paths which greatly shortened the distance. Lake Winnipeg was then crossed, and on the 10th July, Schoolcraft arrived at Lake Cass, the furthest point reached by his predecessors.

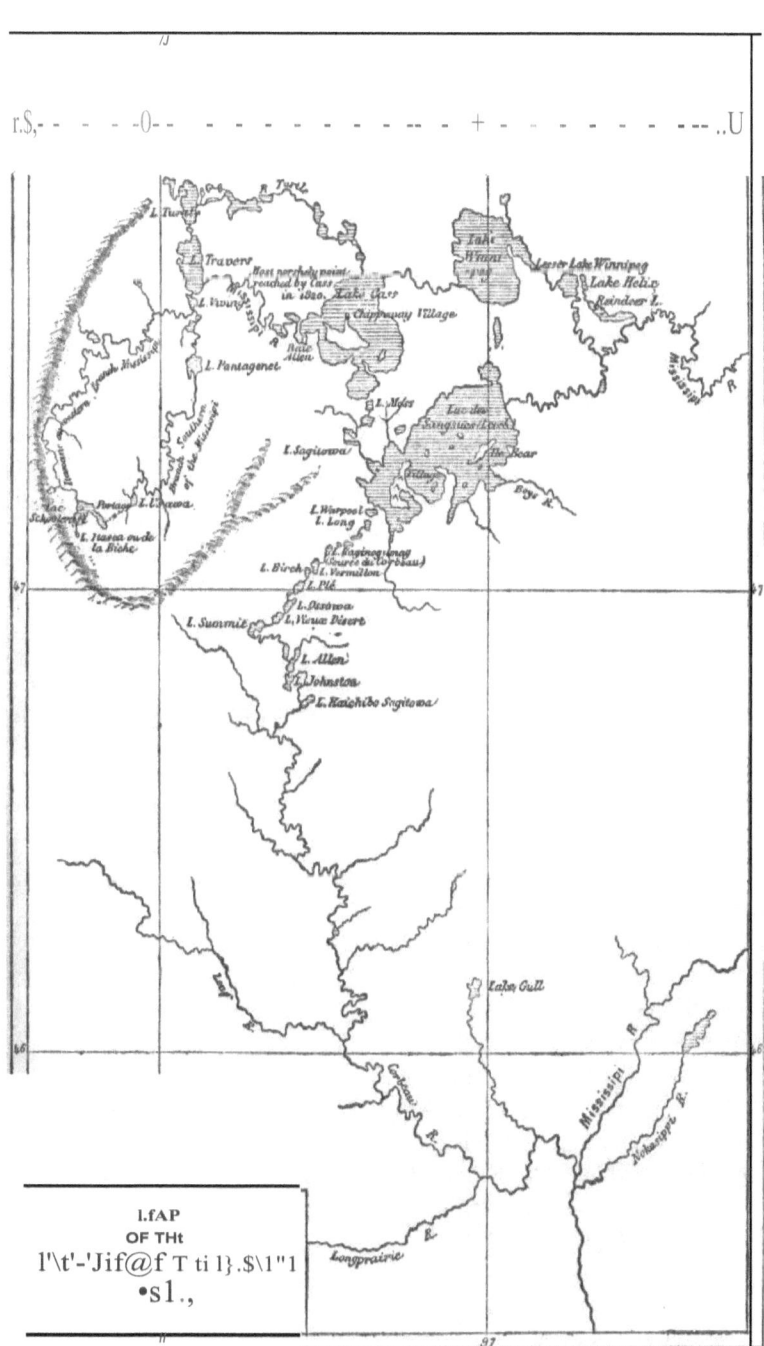

A party of Chippeway Indians led the explorers to their settlement on an island in the river. The friendliness of the natives led Cass to leave part of his escort with them, and, accompanied by Lieutenant Allen, the surgeon Houghton, a missionary, and several Indians, he started in a canoe.

Lakes Tasodiac and Crooked were visited in turn. A little beyond the latter, the Mississippi divides into two branches or forks. The guide took Schoolcraft up the eastern, and after crossing Lakes Marquette, La Salle, and Kubbakanna, he came to the mouth of the Naiwa, the chief tributary of this branch of the Mississippi. Finally, after passing the little lake called Usawa, the expedition reached Lake Itasca, whence issues the Itascan, or western branch of the Mississippi.

Lake Itasca, or Deer Lake, as the French call it, is only seven or eight miles in extent, and is surrounded by hills clothed with dark pine woods. According to Schoolcraft it is some 1500 feet above the sea level; but we must not attach too much importance to this estimate, as the leader of the expedition had no instruments.

On their way back to Lake Cass, the party followed the western branch, identifying its chief tributaries. Schoolcraft then studied the ways of the Indians frequenting these districts, and made treaties with them.

To sum up, the aim of the government was achieved, and the Mississippi had been explored from its mouth to its source. The expedition had collected a vast number of interesting details on the manners, customs, history, and language of the people, as well as numerous new or little known species of flora and fauna.

The people of the United States were not content with these official expeditions, and numbers of trappers threw themselves into the new districts. Most of them being however absolutely illiterate, they could not turn their discoveries to scientific account. But this was not the case with James Pattie, who has published an account of his romantic adventures and perilous trips in the district between New Mexico and New California.

On his way down the River Gila to its mouth, Pattie visited races then all but unknown, including the Yotans, Eiotaws, Papawans, Mokees, Umeas, Mohawas, and Nabahoes, with whom but very little intercourse had yet been held. On the banks of the Rio Eiotario he discovered ruins of ancient monuments, stone walls, moats, and potteries, and in the neighbouring mountains he found copper, lead, and silver mines.

We owe a curious travelling journal also to Doctor Willard, who, during a stay of three years in Mexico, explored the Rio del Norte from its source to its mouth.

Lastly, in 1831 Captain Wyeth and his brother explored Oregon, and the neighbouring districts of the Rocky Mountains.

After Humboldt's journey in Mexico, one explorer succeeded another in Central America. In 1787, Bernasconi discovered the now famous ruins of Palenque. In 1822, Antonio del Rio gave a detailed description of them, illustrated with drawings by Frederick Waldeck, the future explorer of Palenque, that city of the dead.

Between 1805 and 1807, three journeys were successively taken in the province of Chiapa and to Palenque by Captain William Dupaix and the draughtsman Castañeda, and the result of their researches appeared in 1830 in the form of a magnificent work, with illustrations by Augustine Aglio, executed at the expense of Lord Kingsborough.

Lastly, Waldeck spent the years 1832 and 1833 at Palenque, searching the ruins, making plans, sections, and elevations of the monuments, trying to decipher the hitherto unexplained hieroglyphics with which they are covered, and collecting a vast amount of quite new information alike on the natural history of the country and the manners and customs of the inhabitants.

We must also name Don Juan Galindo, a Spanish colonel, who explored Palenque, Utatlan, Copan, and other cities buried in the heart of tropical forests.

View of the Pyramid of Xochicalco.
(Fac-simile of early engraving.)

After the long stay made by Humboldt in equinoctial America, the impulse his explorations would doubtless otherwise have given to geographical science was strangely checked by the struggle of the Spanish colonies with

222

the mother country. As soon, however, as the native governments attained to at least a semblance of stability, intrepid explorers rushed to examine this world, so new in the truest sense, for the jealousy of the Spanish had hitherto kept it closed to the investigations of scientific men.

Many naturalists and engineers now travelled or settled in South America. Soon indeed, that is in 1817-1820, the Austrian and Bavarian Governments sent out a scientific expedition, to the command of which they appointed Doctors Spix and Martins, who collected a great deal of information on the botany, ethnography, and geography of these hitherto little known districts— Martins publishing, at the expense of the Austrian and Bavarian governments, a most important work on the flora of the country, which may be looked upon as a model of its kind.

At the same time the editors of special publications, such as Malte Brun's *Annales des Voyages* and the *Bulletin de la Société de Géographie*, cordially accepted and published all the communications addressed to them, including many on Brazil and the province of Minas Geraës.

About this period too a Prussian Major-General, the Prince of Wied-Neuwied, who had been at leisure since the peace of 1815, devoted himself to the study of natural science, geography, and history, undertaking moreover, in company with the naturalists Freirciss and Sellow, an exploring expedition in the interior of Brazil, having special reference to its flora and fauna.

A few years later, i.e. in 1836, the French naturalist Alcide d'Orbigny, who had won celebrity at a very early age, was appointed by the governing body of the Museum to the command of an expedition to South America, the special object of which was the study of the natural history of the country. For eight consecutive years D'Orbigny wandered about Brazil, Uruguay, the Argentine Republic, Patagonia, Chili, Bolivia, and Peru.

"Such a journey," says Dumour in his funeral oration on D'Orbigny, "in countries so different in their productions, climate, the character of their soil, and the manners and customs of their inhabitants, was necessarily full of ever fresh perils. D'Orbigny, endowed with a strong constitution and untiring energy, overcame obstacles which would have daunted most travellers. On his arrival in the cold regions of Patagonia, amongst savage races constantly at war with each other, he found himself compelled to take part, and to fight in the ranks of a tribe which had received him hospitably. Fortunately for the intrepid student his side was victorious, and he was left free to proceed on his journey."

It took thirteen years of the hardest work to put together the results of D'Orbigny's extensive researches. His book, which embraces nearly every branch of science, leaves far behind it all that had ever before been published on South America. History, archæology, zoology, and botany all hold honoured positions in it; but the most important part of this encyclopædic work is that relating to American man. In it the author embodies all the documents he himself collected, and analyzes and criticizes those which came to him at second hand, on physiological types, and on the manners, languages, and religions of South America. A work of such value ought to immortalize the name of the French scholar, and reflect the greatest honour on the nation which gave him birth.

END OF THE FIRST PART.

PART II.

CHAPTER I.

VOYAGES ROUND THE WORLD, AND POLAR EXPEDITIONS.

The Russian fur trade—Kruzenstern appointed to the command of an expedition—Noukha-Hiva—Nangasaki—Reconnaisance of the coast of Japan—Yezo—The Ainos—Saghalien—Return to Europe—Otto von Kotzebue—Stay at Easter Island—Penrhyn—The Radak Archipelago— Return to Russia—Changes at Otaheite and the Sandwich Islands— Beechey's Voyage—Easter Island—Pitcairn and the mutineers of the *Bounty*—The Paumoto Islands—Otaheite and the Sandwich Islands— The Bonin Islands—Lütke—The Quebradas of Valparaiso—Holy week in Chili—New Archangel—The Kaloches—Ounalashka—The Caroline Archipelago—The canoes of the Caroline Islanders—Guam, a desert island—Beauty and happy situation of the Bonin Islands—The Tchouktchees: their manners and their conjurors—Return to Russia.

At the beginning of the nineteenth century, the Russians for the first time took part in voyages round the world, Until that time their explorations had been almost entirely confined to Asia, and their only mariners of note were Behring, Tchirikoff, Spangberg, Laxman, Krenitzin, and Saryscheff. The last- named took an important part in the voyage of the Englishman Billings, a voyage by the way which was far from achieving all that might have been fairly expected from the ten years it occupied and the vast sums it cost.

Adam John von Kruzenstern was the first Russian to whom is due the honour of having made a voyage round the world under government auspices and with a scientific purpose.

Born in 1770, Kruzenstern entered the English navy in 1793. After six years' training in the stern school which then numbered amongst its leaders the most skilful sailors of the world, he returned to his native land with a profound knowledge of his profession, and with his ideas of the part Russia might play in Eastern Asia very considerably widened.

During a stay of two years at Canton, in 1798 and 1799, Kruzenstern had been witness of the extraordinary results achieved by some English fur traders, who brought their merchandise from the northwest coasts of Russian America. This trade had not come into existence until after Cook's third voyage, and the English had already realized immense sums, at the cost of the Russians, who had hitherto sent their furs to the Chinese markets overland.

In 1785, however, a Russian named Chelikoff founded a fur-trading colony on Kodiak Island, at about an equal distance from Kamtchatka and the Aleutian Islands, which rapidly became a flourishing community. The Russian government now recognized the resources of districts it had hitherto considered barren, and reinforcements, provisions, and stores were sent to Kamtchatka via Siberia.

Kruzenstern quickly realized how inadequate to the new state of things was help such as this, the ignorance of the pilots and the errors in the maps leading to the loss of several vessels every year, not to speak of the injury to trade involved in a two years' voyage for the transport of furs, first to Okhotsk, and thence to Kiakhta.

As the best plans are always the simplest they are sure to be the last to be thought of, and Kruzenstern was the first to point out the imperative necessity of going direct by sea from the Aleutian Islands to Canton, the most frequented market.

On his return to Russia, Kruzenstern tried to win over to his views Count Kuscheleff, the Minister of Marine, but the answer he received destroyed all hope. Not until the accession of Alexander I., when Admiral Mordinoff became head of the naval department, did he receive any encouragement.

Acting on Count Romanoff's advice, the Russian Emperor soon commissioned Kruzenstern to carry out the plan he had himself proposed; and on the 7th August, 1802, he was appointed to the command of two vessels for the exploration of the north-west coast of America.

Although the leader of the expedition was named, the officers and seamen were still to be selected, and the vessels to be manned were not to be had in either the Russian empire or at Hamburg. In London alone were Lisianskoï, afterwards second in command to Kruzenstern, and the builder Kasoumoff, able to obtain two vessels at all suitable to the service in which they were to be employed. These two vessels received the names of the *Nadiejeda* and the *Neva*.

In the meantime, the Russian government decided to avail itself of this opportunity to send M. de Besanoff to Japan as ambassador, with a numerous suite, and magnificent presents for the sovereign of the country.

On the 4th August, 1803, the two vessels, completely equipped, and carrying 134 persons, left the roadstead of Cronstadt. Flying visits were paid to Copenhagen and Falmouth, with a view to replacing some of the salt provisions bought at Hamburg, and to caulk the *Nadiejeda*, the seams of which had started in a violent storm encountered in the North Sea.

After a short stay at the Canary Islands, Kruzenstern hunted in vain, as La Pérouse had done before him, for the Island of Ascension, as to the existence of which opinion had been divided for some three hundred years. He then rounded Cape Frio, the position of which he was unable exactly to determine although he was most anxious to do so, the accounts of earlier travellers and the maps hitherto laid down varying from 23° 6' to 22° 34'. A reconnaissance of the coast of Brazil was succeeded by a sail through the passage between the islands of Gal and Alvaredo, unjustly characterized as dangerous by La Pérouse, and on the 21st December, 1803, St. Catherine was reached.

The necessity for replacing the main and mizzen masts of the *Neva* detained Kruzenstern for five weeks on this island, where he was most cordially received by the Portuguese authorities.

On the 4th February, the two vessels were able to resume their voyage, prepared to face all the dangers of the South Sea, and to double Cape Horn, that bugbear of all navigators. As far as Staten Island the weather was uniformly fine, but beyond it the explorers had to contend with extremely violent gales, storms of hail and snow, dense fogs, huge waves, and a swell in which the vessels laboured heavily. On the 24th March, the ships lost sight of each other in a dense fog a little above the western entrance to the Straits of Magellan. They did not meet again until both reached Noukha-Hiva.

Kruzenstern having given up all idea of touching at Easter Island, now made for the Marquesas, or Mendoza Archipelago, and determined the position of Fatongou and Udhugu Islands, called Washington by the American Captain Ingraham, who discovered them in 1791, a few weeks before Captain Marchand, who named them Revolution Islands. Kruzenstern also saw Hiva-Hoa, the Dominica of Mendaña, and at Noukha-Hiva met an Englishman named Roberts, and a Frenchman named Cabritt, whose knowledge of the language was of great service to him.

The incidents of the stay in the Marquesas Archipelago are of little interest, they were much the same as those related in Cook's Voyages. The total, but at the same time utterly unconscious immodesty of the women, the extensive agricultural knowledge of the natives, and their greed of iron instruments, are commented upon in both narratives.

Nothing is noticed in the later which is not to be found in the earlier narrative, if we except some remarks on the existence of numerous societies of which the king or his relations, priests, or celebrated warriors, are the chiefs, and the aim of which is the providing of the people with food in times of scarcity. In our opinion these societies resemble the clans of Scotland or the Indian tribes of America. Kruzenstern, however, does not agree with us, as the following quotation will show.

"The members of these clubs are distinguished by different tattooed marks upon their bodies; those of the king's club, consisting of twenty-six members, have a square one on their breasts about six inches long and four wide, and to this company Roberts belonged. The companions of the Frenchman, Joseph Cabritt, were marked with a tattooed eye, &c. Roberts assured me that he never would have entered this association, had he not been driven to it by extreme hunger. There was an apparent want of consistency in this dislike, as the members of these companies are not only relieved from all care as to their subsistence, but, even by his own account, the admittance into them is a distinction that many seek to obtain. I am therefore inclined to believe that it must be attended with the loss of some part of liberty."

A reconnaissance of the neighbourhood of Anna Maria led to the discovery of Port Tchitchagoff, which, though the entrance is difficult, is so shut in by land that its waters are unruffled by the most violent storm.

At the time of Kruzenstern's visit to Noukha-Hiva, cannibalism was still largely practised, but the traveller had no tangible proof of the prevalence of the custom. In fact Kruzenstern was very affably received by the king of the cannibals, who appeared to exercise but little authority over his people, a race addicted to the most revolting vices, and our hero owns that but for the intelligent and disinterested testimony of the two Europeans mentioned above he should have carried away a very favourable opinion of the natives.

"In their intercourse with us," he says, "they always showed the best possible disposition, and in bartering an extraordinary degree of honesty, always delivering their cocoa-nuts before they received the piece of iron that was to be paid for them. At all times they appeared ready to assist in cutting wood and filling water; and the help they afforded us in the performance of these laborious tasks was by no means trifling. Theft, the crime so common to all the islanders of this ocean, we very seldom met with among them; they always appeared cheerful and happy, and the greatest good humour was depicted in their countenances…. The two Europeans whom we found here, and who had both resided with them several years, agreed in their assertions that the natives of Nukahiva were a cruel, intractable people, and, without even the exceptions of the female sex, very much addicted to cannibalism; that the appearance of content and good-humour, with which they had so much deceived us, was not their true character; and that nothing but the fear of punishment and the hopes of reward, deterred them from giving a loose to their savage passions. These Europeans described, as eye-witnesses, the barbarous scenes that are acted, particularly in times of war—the desperate rage with which they fall upon their victims, immediately tear off their head, and sip their blood out of the skull,[1] with the most disgusting readiness, completing in this manner their horrible repast. For a long time I would not give credit to these accounts, considering them as exaggerated; but they rest upon the authority of two different persons, who had not only been witnesses for several years to these atrocities, but had also borne a share in them: of two persons who lived in a state of mortal enmity, and took particular pains by their mutual recriminations to obtain with us credit for themselves, but yet on this point never contradicted each other. The very fact of Roberts doing his enemy the justice to allow, that he never devoured his prey, but always exchanged it for hogs, gives the circumstance a great degree of probability, and these reports concur with several appearances we remarked during our stay here, skulls being brought to us every day for sale. Their weapons are invariably adorned with human hair, and human bones are used as ornaments in almost all their household furniture; they also often gave us to understand by pantomimic gestures that human flesh was regarded by them as a delicacy."

[1] "All the skulls which we purchased of them," says Kruzenstern, "had a hole perforated through one end of them for this purpose."

There are grounds for looking upon this account as exaggerated. The truth, probably, lies between the dogmatic assertions of Cook and Forster and those of the two Europeans of Kruzenstern's time, one of whom at least was not much to be relied upon, as he was a deserter.

And we must remember that we ourselves did not attain to the high state of civilization we now enjoy without climbing up from the bottom of the ladder. In the stone age our manners were probably not superior to those of the natives of Oceania.

We must not, therefore, blame these representatives of humanity for not having risen higher. They have never been a nation. Scattered as their homes are on the wide ocean, and divided as they are into small tribes, without agricultural or mineral resources, without connexions, and with a climate which makes them strangers to want, they could but remain stationary or cultivate none but the most rudimentary arts and industries. Yet in spite of all this, how often have their instruments, their canoes and their nets, excited the

230

admiration of travellers.

On the 18th May, 1804, the *Nadiejeda* and the *Neva* left Noukha-Hiva for the Sandwich Islands, where Kruzenstern had decided to stop and lay in a store of fresh provisions, which he had been unable to do at his last anchorage, where seven pigs were all he could get.

This plan fell through, however. The natives of Owhyhee, or Hawaii, brought but a very few provisions to the vessels lying off their south-west coast, and even these they would only exchange for cloth, which Kruzenstern could not give them. He therefore set sail for Kamtchatka and Japan, leaving the *Neva* off the island of Karakakoua, where Captain Lisianskoï relied upon being able to revictual.

New Zealanders.
(Fac-simile of early engraving.)

On the 11th July, the *Nadiejeda* arrived off Petropaulovski, the capital of
Kamtchatka, where the crew obtained the rest and fresh provisions they had

so well earned. On the 30th August, the Russians put to sea again.

Overtaken by thick fogs and violent storms, Kruzenstern now hunted in vain for some islands marked on a map found on a Spanish gallion captured by Anson, and the existence of which had been alternately accepted and rejected by different cartographers, though they appear in La Billardière's map of his voyage.

The navigator now passed between the large island of Kiushiu and Tanega-Sima, by way of Van Diemen Strait, till then very inaccurately defined, rectified the position of the Liu-Kiu archipelago, which the English had placed north of the strait, and the French too far south, and sailed down, surveyed and named the coast of the province of Satsuma.

"This part of Satsuma," says Kruzenstern, "is particularly beautiful: and as we sailed along at a very trifling distance from the land, we had a distinct and perfect view of the various picturesque situations that rapidly succeed each other. The whole country consists of high pointed hills, at one time appearing in the form of pyramids, at others of a globular or conical form, and seeming as it were under the protection of some neighbouring mountain, such as Peak Homer, or another lying north-by-west of it, and even a third farther inland. Liberal as nature has been in the adornment of these parts, the industry of the Japanese seems not a little to have contributed to their beauty; for nothing indeed can equal the extraordinary degree of cultivation everywhere apparent. That all the valleys upon this coast should be most carefully cultivated would not so much have surprised us, as in the countries of Europe, where agriculture is not despised, it is seldom that any piece of land is left neglected; but we here saw not only the mountains even to their summits, but the very tops of the rocks which skirted the edge of the coast, adorned with the most beautiful fields and plantations, forming a striking as well as singular contrast, by the opposition of their dark grey and blue colour to that of the most lively verdure. Another object that excited our astonishment was an alley of high trees, stretching over hill and dale along the coast, as far as the eye could reach, with arbours at certain distances, probably for the weary traveller—for whom these alleys must have been constructed,—to rest himself in, an attention which cannot well be exceeded. These alleys are not uncommon in Japan, for we saw a similar one in the vicinity of Nangasaky, and another in the island of Meac-Sima."

Coast of Japan.

The *Nadiejeda* had hardly anchored at the entrance to Nagasaki harbour before Kruzenstern saw several *daïmios* climb on board, who had come to forbid him to advance further.

Now, although the Russians were aware of the policy of isolation practised by the Japanese government, they had hoped that their reception would have been less forbidding, as they had on board an ambassador from the powerful neighbouring state of Russia. They had relied on enjoying comparative liberty, of which they would have availed themselves to collect information on a country hitherto so little known and about which the only people admitted to it had taken a vow of silence.

They were, however, disappointed in their expectations. Instead of enjoying the same latitude as the Dutch, they were throughout their stay harassed by a perpetual surveillance, as unceasing as it was annoying. In a word, they were little better than prisoners.

Although the ambassador did obtain permission to land with his escort "under arms," a favour never before accorded to any one, the sailors were not allowed to get out of their boat, or when they did land the restricted place where they were permitted to walk was surrounded by a lofty palisading, and guarded by two companies of soldiers.

It was forbidden to write to Europe by way of Batavia, it was forbidden to talk to the Dutch captains, the ambassador was forbidden to leave his house— the word forbidden may be said to sum up the anything but cordial reception given to their visitors by the Japanese.

Kruzenstern turned his long stay here to account by completely overhauling and repairing his vessel. He had nearly finished this operation when the approach was announced of an envoy from the Emperor, of dignity so exalted that, in the words of the interpreter, "he dared to look at the feet of his Imperial Majesty."

This personage began by refusing the Czar's presents, under pretence that if they were accepted the Emperor would have to send back others with an embassy, which would be contrary to the customs of the country; and he then went on to speak of the law against the entry of any vessels into the ports of Japan, and absolutely forbade the Russians to buy anything, adding, however, at the same time, that the materials already supplied for the refitting and revictualling the vessel would be paid for out of the treasury of the Emperor of Japan. He further inquired whether the repairs of the *Nadiejeda* would soon be finished. Kruzenstern understood what was meant as soon as his visitor began to speak, and hurried on the preparations for his own departure.

Truly he had not much reason to congratulate himself on having waited from October to April for such an answer as this. So little were the chief results hoped for by his government achieved, that no Russian vessel could ever again enter a Japanese port. A short-sighted, jealous policy, resulting in the putting back for half a century the progress of Japan.

On the 17th April the *Nadiejeda* weighed anchor, and began a hydrographic survey, which had the best results. La Pérouse had been the only navigator to traverse before Kruzenstern the seas between Japan and the continent. The Russian explorer was therefore anxious to connect his work with that of his predecessor, and to fill up the gaps the latter had been compelled for want of time to leave in his charts of these parts.

"To explore the north-west and south-west coasts of Japan," says Kruzenstern, "to ascertain the situation of the Straits of Sangar, the width of which in the best charts—Arrowsmith's 'South Sea Pilot' for instance, and the atlas subjoined to La Pérouse's Voyage—is laid down as more than a hundred miles, while the Japanese merely estimated it to be a Dutch mile; to examine the west coast of Yezo; to find out the island of Karafuto, which in some new charts, compiled after a Japanese one, is placed between Yezo and Sachalin, and the existence of which appeared to me very probable; to explore this new strait and take an accurate plan of the island of Sachalin, from Cape Crillon to the north-west coast, from whence, if a good harbour were to be found there, I could send out my long boat to examine the supposed passage which divides Tartary from Sachalin; and, finally, to attempt a return through a new passage between the Kuriles, north of the Canal de la Boussole; all this came into my plan, and I have had the good fortune to execute part of it."

Kruzenstern was destined almost entirely to carry out this detailed plan, only the survey of the western coast of Japan and of the Strait of Sangar, with that of the channel closing the Farakaï Strait, could not be accomplished by the Russian navigator, who had, sorely against his will, to leave the completion of this important task to his successors.

Kruzenstern now entered the Corea Channel, and determined the longitude of Tsusima, obtaining a difference of thirty-six minutes from the position assigned to that island by La Pérouse. This difference was subsequently confirmed by Dagelet, who can be fully relied upon.

The Russian explorer noticed, as La Pérouse had done before him, that the deviation of the magnetic needle is but little noticeable in these latitudes.

The position of Sangar Strait, between Yezo and Niphon, being very uncertain, Kruzenstern resolved to determine it. The mouth, situated between Cape Sangar (N. lat. 41° 16′ 30″ and W. long. 219° 46′) and Cape Nadiejeda (N. lat. 41° 25′ 10″, W. long. 219° 50′ 30″), is only nine miles wide; whereas La Pérouse, who had relied, not upon personal observation but upon the map of the Dutchman Vries, speaks of it as ten miles across. Kruzenstern's was therefore an important rectification.

Kruzenstern did not actually enter this strait. He was anxious to verify the existence of a certain island, Karafonto, Tchoka, or Chicha by name, set down as between Yezo and Saghalien in a map which appeared at St. Petersburg in 1802, and was based on one brought to Russia by the Japanese Koday. He then surveyed a small portion of the coast of Yezo, naming the chief irregularities, and cast anchor near the southernmost promontory of the island, at the entrance to the Straits of La Pérouse.

Here he learnt from the Japanese that Saghalien and Karafonto were one and the same island.

On the 10th May, 1805, Kruzenstern landed at Yezo, and was surprised to find the season but little advanced. The trees were not yet in leaf, the snow still lay thick here and there, and the explorer had supposed that it was only at Archangel that the temperature would be so severe at this time of year. This phenomenon was to be explained later, when more was known as to the direction taken by the polar current, which, issuing from Behring Strait, washes the shores of Kamtchatka, the Kurile Islands, and Yezo.

During his short stay here and at Saghalien, Kruzenstern was able to make some observations on the Ainos, a race which probably occupied the whole of Yezo before the advent of the Japanese, from whom—at least from those who have been influenced by intercourse with China—they differ entirely.

Typical Ainos.
(Fac-simile of early engraving.)

"Their figure," says Kruzenstern, "dress, appearance, and their language,
prove that they are the same people, as those of Saghalien, and the captain of

the *Castricum*, when he missed the Straits of La Pérouse, might imagine, as well in Aniwa as in Alkys, that he was but in one island.... The Ainos are rather below the middle stature, being at the most five feet two or four inches high, of a dark, nearly black complexion, with a thick bushy beard, black rough hair, hanging straight down; and excepting in the beard they have the appearance of the Kamtschadales, only that their countenance is much more regular. The women are sufficiently ugly; their colour, which is equally dark, their coal black hair combed over their faces, blue painted lips, and tattooed hands, added to no remarkable cleanliness in their clothing, do not give them any great pretensions to loveliness.... However, I must do them the justice to say, that they are modest in the highest degree, and in this point form the completest contrast with the women of Nukahiva and of Otaheite.... The characteristic quality of an Aino is goodness of heart, which is expressed in the strongest manner in his countenance; and so far as we were enabled to observe their actions, they fully answered this expression.... The dress of the Ainos consists chiefly of the skins of tame dogs and seals; but I have seen some in a very different attire, which resembled the *Parkis* of the Kamtschadales, and is, properly speaking a white shirt worn over their other clothes. In Aniwa Bay they were all clad in furs; their boots were made of seal-skins, and in these likewise the women were invariably clothed."

After passing through the Straits of La Pérouse, Kruzenstern cast anchor in Aniwa Bay, off the island of Saghalien. Here fish was then so plentiful, that two Japanese firms alone employed 400 Ainos to catch and dry it. It is never taken in nets, but buckets are used at ebb-tide.

After having surveyed Patience Gulf, which had only been partially examined by the Dutchman Vries, and at the bottom of which flows a stream now named the Neva, Kruzenstern broke off his examination of Saghalien to determine the position of the Kurile Islands, never yet accurately laid down; and on the 5th June, 1805 he returned to Petropaulovski, where he put on shore the ambassador and his suite.

In July, after crossing Nadiejeda Strait, between Matona and Rachona, two of the Kurile Islands, Kruzenstern surveyed the eastern coast of Saghalien, in the neighbourhood of Cape Patience, which presented a very picturesque appearance, with the hills clothed with grass and stunted trees and the shores with bushes. The scenery of the interior, however, was somewhat monotonous, with its unbroken line of lofty mountains.

The navigator skirted along the whole of this deserted and harbourless coast to Capes Maria and Elizabeth, between which is a deep bay, with a little village of thirty-seven houses nestling at the end, the only one the Russians had seen since they left Providence Bay. It was not inhabited by Ainos, but by

Tartars, of which very decided proof was obtained a few days later.

Kruzenstern next entered the channel separating Saghalien from Tartary, but he was hardly six miles from the middle of the passage when his soundings gave six fathoms only. It was useless to hope to penetrate further. Orders were given to "'bout ship," whilst a boat was sent to trace the coast-line on either side, and to explore the middle of the strait until the soundings should give three fathoms only. A very strong current had to be contended with, rendering this row very difficult, and this current was rightly supposed to be due to the River Amoor, the mouth of which was not far distant.

The advice given to Kruzenstern by the Governor of Kamtchatka, not to approach the coast of Chinese Tartary, lest the jealous suspicions of the Celestial Government should be aroused, prevented the explorer from further prosecuting the work of surveying; and once more passing the Kurile group, the *Nadiejeda* returned to Petropaulovsky.

The Commander availed himself of his stay in this port to make some necessary repairs in his vessel, and to confirm the statements of Captain Clerke, who had succeeded Cook in the command of his last expedition, and those of Delisle de la Croyère, the French astronomer, who had been Behring's companion in 1741.

During this last sojourn at Petropaulovsky, Kruzenstern received an autograph letter from the Emperor of Russia, enclosing the order of St. Anne as a proof of his Majesty's satisfaction with the work done.

On the 4th October, 1805, the *Nadiejeda* set sail for Europe; exploring *en route* the latitudes in which, according to the maps of the day, were situated the islands of Rica-de-Plata, Guadalupas, Malabrigos, St. Sebastian de Lobos, and San Juan.

Kruzenstern next identified the Farellon Islands of Anson's map, now known as St. Alexander, St. Augustine, and Volcanos, and situated south of the Bonin-Sima group. Then crossing the Formosa Channel, he arrived at Macao on the 21st November.

He was a good deal surprised not to find the *Neva* there, as he had given instructions for it to bring a cargo of furs, the price of which he proposed expending on Chinese merchandise. He decided to wait for the arrival of the *Neva*.

Macao seemed to him to be falling rapidly into decay.

"Many fine buildings," he says, "are ranged in large squares, surrounded by courtyards and gardens; but most of them uninhabited, the number of Portuguese residents there having greatly decreased. The chief private houses belong to the members of the Dutch and English factories.... Twelve or fifteen thousand is said to be the number of the inhabitants of Macao, most of whom, however, are Chinese, who have so completely taken possession of the town, that it is rare to meet any European in the streets, with the exception of priests and nuns. One of the inhabitants said to me, 'We have more priests here than soldiers;' a piece of raillery that was literally true, the number of soldiers amounting only to 150, not one of whom is a European, the whole being mulattos of Macao and Goa. Even the officers are not all Europeans. With so small a garrison it is difficult to defend four large fortresses; and the natural insolence of the Chinese finds a sufficient motive in the weakness of the military, to heap insult upon insult."

Just as the *Nadiejeda* was about to weigh anchor, the *Neva* at last appeared. It was now the 3rd November, and Kruzenstern went up the coast in the newly arrived vessel as far as Whampoa, where he sold to advantage his cargo of furs, after many prolonged discussions which his firm but conciliating attitude, together with the intervention of English merchants, brought to a successful issue.

On the 9th February, the two vessels once more together weighed anchor, and resumed their voyage by way of the Sunda Isles. Beyond Christmas Island they were again separated in cloudy weather, and did not meet until the end of the trip. On the 4th May, the *Nadiejeda* cast anchor in St. Helena Bay, sixty days' voyage from the Sunda Isles and seventy-nine from Macao.

"I know of no better place," says Kruzenstern, "to get supplies after a long voyage than St. Helena. The road is perfectly safe, and at all times more convenient than Table Bay or Simon's Bay, at the Cape. The entrance, with the precaution of first getting near the land, is perfectly easy; and on quitting the island nothing more is necessary than to weigh anchor and stand out to sea. Every kind of provision may be obtained here, particularly the best kinds of garden stuffs, and in two or three days a ship may be provided with everything."

On the 21st April, Kruzenstern passed between the Shetland and Orkney Islands, in order to avoid the English Channel, where he might have met some French pirates, and after a good voyage he arrived at Cronstadt on the 7th August, 1806.

Without taking first rank, like the expedition of Cook or that of La Pérouse, Kruzenstern's trip was not without interest. We owe no great discovery to the Russian explorer, but he verified and rectified the work of his predecessors. This was in fact what most of the navigators of the nineteenth century had to do, the progress of science enabling them to complete what had been begun by others.

Kruzenstern had taken with him in his voyage round the world the son of the well-known dramatic author Kotzebue. The young Otto Kotzebue, who was then a cadet, soon gained his promotion, and he was a naval lieutenant when, in 1815 the command was given to him of the *Rurik*, a new brig, with two guns, and a crew of no more than twenty-seven men, equipped at the expense of Count Romantzoff. His task was to explore the less-known parts of Oceania, and to cut a passage for his vessel across the Frozen Ocean. Kotzebue left the port of Cronstadt on the 15th July, 1815, put in first at Copenhagen and Plymouth, and after a very trying trip doubled Cape Horn, and entered the Pacific Ocean on the 22nd January, 1816. After a halt at Talcahuano, on the coast of Chili, he resumed his voyage; sighted the desert island of Salas of Gomez, on the 26th March, and steered towards Easter Island, where he hoped to meet with the same friendly reception as Cook and Pérouse had done before him.

The Russians had, however, hardly disembarked before they were surrounded by a crowd eager to offer them fruit and roots, by whom they were so shamelessly robbed that they were compelled to use their arms in self- defence, and to re-embark as quickly as possible to avoid the shower of stones flung at them by the natives.

The only observation they had time to make during this short visit, was the overthrow of the numerous huge stone statues described, measured, and drawn, by Cook and La Pérouse.

On the 16th April, the Russian captain arrived at the Dog Island of Schouten, which he called Doubtful Island, to mark the difference in his estimate of its position and that attributed to it by earlier navigators. Kotzebue gives it S. lat. 44° 50' and W. long. 138° 47'.

During the ensuing days were discovered the desert island of Romantzoff, so named in honour of the promoter of the expedition; Spiridoff Island, with a lagoon in the centre; the Island Oura of the Pomautou group, the Vliegen chain of islets, and the no less extended group of the Kruzenstern Islands.

On the 28th April, the *Rurik* was near the supposed site of Bauman's Islands, but not a sign of them could be seen, and it appeared probable that the group had in fact been one of those already visited.

As soon as he was safely out of the dangerous Pomautou archipelago Kotzebue steered towards the group of islands sighted in 1788 by Sever, who, without touching at them, gave them the name of Penrhyn. The Russian explorer determined the position of the central group of islets as S. lat. 9° 1' 35" and W. long. 157° 44' 32", characterizing them as very low, like those of the Pomautou group, but inhabited for all that.

At the sight of the vessel a considerable fleet of canoes put off from the shore, and the natives, palm branches in their hands, advanced with the rhythmic sound of the paddles serving as a kind of solemn and melancholy accompaniment to numerous singers. To guard against surprise, Kotzebue made all the canoes draw up on one side of the vessel, and bartering was done with a rope as the means of communication. The natives had nothing to trade with but bits of iron and fish-hooks made of mother-of-pearl. They were well made and martial-looking, but wore no clothes beyond a kind of apron.

At first only noisy and very lively, the natives soon became threatening. They thieved openly, and answered remonstrances with undisguised taunts. Brandishing their spears above their heads, they seemed to be urging each other on to an attack.

When Kotzebue felt that the moment had come to put an end to these hostile demonstrations, he had one gun fired. In the twinkling of an eye the canoes were empty, their terrified crews unpremeditatingly flinging themselves into the water with one accord. Presently the heads of the divers reappeared, and, a little calmed down by the warning received, the natives returned to their canoes and their bartering. Nails and pieces of iron were much sought after by these people, whom Kotzebue likens to the natives of Noukha-Hiva. They do not exactly tatoo themselves, but cover their bodies with large scars.

"In the twinkling of an eye the canoes were empty."

A curious fashion not before noticed amongst the islanders of Oceania prevails amongst them. Most of them wear the nails very long, and those of the chief men in the canoes extended three inches beyond the end of the finger.

Thirty-six boats, manned by 360 men, now surrounded the vessel, and Kotzebue, judging that with his feeble resources and the small crew of the *Rurik* any attempt to land would be imprudent, set sail again without being able to collect any more information on these wild and warlike islanders.

Continuing his voyage towards Kamtchatka, the navigator sighted on the 21st May two groups of islands connected by a chain of coral reefs. He named them Kutusoff and Suwaroff, determined their position, and made up his mind to come back and examine them again. The natives in fleet canoes approached the *Rurik*, but, in spite of the pressing invitation of the Russians, would not trust themselves on board. They gazed at the vessel in astonishment, talked to each other with a vivacity which showed their intelligence, and flung on deck the fruit of the pandanus-tree and cocoa-nuts.

Their lank black hair, with flowers fastened in it here and there, the ornaments hung round their necks, their clothing of "two curiously-woven coloured mats tied to the waist" and reaching below the knee, but above all their frank and friendly countenances, distinguished the natives of the Marshall archipelago from those of Penrhyn.

On the 19th June the *Rurik* put in at New Archangel, and for twenty-eight days her crew were occupied in repairing her.

On the 15th July Kotzebue set sail again, and five days later disembarked on Behring Island, the southern promontory of which he laid down in N. lat. 55° 17' 18" and W. long. 194° 6' 37".

The natives Kotzebue met with on this island, like those of the North American coast, wore clothes made of seal-skin and the intestines of the walrus. The lances used by them were pointed with the teeth of these amphibious animals. Their food consisted of the flesh of whales and seals, which they store in deep cellars dug in the earth. Their boats were made of leather, and they had sledges drawn by dogs.

Their mode of salutation is strange enough, they first rub each other's noses and then pass their hands over their own stomachs as if rejoicing over the swallowing of some tid-bit. Lastly, when they want to be very friendly indeed, they spit in their own palms and rub their friends' faces with the spittle.

The captain, still keeping his northerly course along the American coast, discovered Schichmareff Bay, Saritschiff Island, and lastly, an extensive gulf, the existence of which was not previously known. At the end of this gulf Kotzebue hoped to find a channel through which he could reach the Arctic Ocean, but he was disappointed. He gave his own name to the gulf, and that of Kruzenstern to the cape at the entrance.

Driven back by bad weather, the *Rurik* reached Ounalashka on the 6th September, halted for a few days at San Francisco, and reached the Sandwich Islands, where some important surveys were made and some very curious information collected.

On leaving the Sandwich Islands, Kotzebue steered for Suwaroff and Kutusoff Islands, which he had discovered a few months before. On the 1st January, 1817, he sighted Miadi Island, to which he gave the name of New Year's Island. Four days later he discovered a chain of little low wooded islands set in a framework of reefs, through which the vessel could scarcely make its way.

Just at first the natives ran away at the sight of Lieutenant Schischmaroff, but they soon came back with branches in their hands, shouting out the word *aidara* (friend). The officer repeated this word and gave them a few nails in return, for which the Russians received the collars and flowers worn as neck-ornaments by the natives.

This exchange of courtesies emboldened the rest of the islanders to appear, and throughout the stay of the Russians in this archipelago these friendly demonstrations and enthusiastic but guarded greetings were continued. One native, Rarik by name, was particularly cordial to the Russians, whom he informed that the name of his island and of the chain of islets and *attolls*[2] connected with it was Otdia. In acknowledgment of the cordial reception of the natives, Kotzebue left with them a cock and hen, and planted in a garden laid out under his orders a quantity of seeds, in the hope that they would thrive; but in this he did not make allowance for the number of rats which swarmed upon these islands and wrought havoc in his plantations.

[2] Attolls are coral islands like circular belts surrounding a smooth lagoon.—*Trans.*

On the 6th February, after ascertaining from what he was told by a chief named Languediak, that these sparsely populated islands were of recent formation, Kotzebue put to sea again, having first christened the archipelago Romantzoff.

The next day a group of islets, on which only three inhabitants were found, had its name of Eregup changed to that of Tchitschakoff, and then an enthusiastic reception was given to Kotzebue on the Kawen Islands by the tamon or chief. Every native here fêted the new-comers, some by their silence —like the queen forbidden by etiquette to answer the speeches made to her— some by their dances, cries, and songs, in which the name of Totabou (Kotzebue) was constantly repeated. The chief himself came to fetch Kotzebue in a canoe, and carried him on his shoulders through the breakers to the beach.

In the Aur group the navigator noticed amongst a crowd of natives who climbed on to the vessel, two natives whose faces and tattooing seemed to mark them as of alien race. One of them, Kadu by name, especially pleased the commander, who gave him some bits of iron, and Kotzebue was surprised that he did not receive them with the same pleasure as his companions. This was explained the same evening. When all the natives were leaving the vessel, Kadu earnestly begged to be allowed to remain on the *Rurik*, and never again to leave it. The commander only yielded to his wishes after a great deal of persuasion.

"Kadu," says Kotzebue, "had scarcely obtained permission, when he turned quickly to his comrades, who were waiting for him, declared to them his intention of remaining on board the ship, and distributed his iron among the chiefs. The astonishment in the boats was beyond description: they tried in vain to shake his resolution; he was immovable. At last his friend Edock came back, spoke long and seriously to him, and when he found that his persuasion was of no avail, he attempted to drag him by force; but Kadu now used the right of the strongest, he pushed his friend from him, and the boats sailed off. His resolution being inexplicable to me, I conceived a notion that he perhaps intended to steal during the night, and privately to leave the ship, and therefore had the night-watch doubled, and his bed made up close to mine on the deck, where I slept, on account of the heat. Kadu felt greatly honoured to sleep close to the tamon of the ship."

Born at Ulle, one of the Caroline Islands, more than 300 miles from the group where he was now living, Kadu, with Edok and two other fellow-countrymen, had been overtaken, when fishing, by a violent storm. For eight months the poor fellows were at the mercy of the winds and currents on a sea now smooth, now rough. They had never throughout this time been without fish, but they had suffered the cruelest tortures from thirst. When their stock of rain-water, which they had used very sparingly, was exhausted, there was nothing left to them to do but to fling themselves into the sea and try to obtain at the bottom of the ocean some water less impregnated with salt, which they brought to the surface in cocoa-nut shells pierced with a small opening. When they reached the Aur Islands, even the sight of land and the immediate prospect of safety did not rouse them from the state of prostration into which they had sunk.

The sight of the iron instruments in the canoe of the strangers led the people of Aur to decide on their massacre for the sake of their treasures; but the tamon, Tigedien by name, took them under his protection.

Three years had passed since this event, and the men from the Caroline Islands, thanks to their more extended knowledge, soon acquired a certain ascendancy over their hosts.

When the *Rurik* appeared, Kadu was in the woods a long way from the coast. He was sent for at once, as he was looked upon as a great traveller, and he might perhaps be able to say what the great monster approaching the island was. Now Kadu had more than once seen European vessels, and he persuaded his friends to go and meet the strangers, and to receive them kindly.

Such had been Kadu's adventures. He now remained on the *Rurik*, identified the other islands of the Archipelago, and lost no time in facilitating intercourse between the Russians and the natives. Dressed in a yellow mantle, and wearing a red cap like a convict, Kadu looked down upon his old friends, and seemed not to recognize them. When a fine old man with a flowing beard, named Tigedien, came on board, Kadu undertook to explain to him and his companions the working of the vessel and the use of everything about the ship. Like many Europeans, he made up for his ignorance by imperturbable assurance, and had an answer ready for every question.

Interrogated on the subject of a little box from which a sailor took a black powder and applied it to his nostrils, Kadu glibly told some most extraordinary stories, and wound up with a practical illustration by putting the box against his own nose. He then flung it from him, sneezing violently and screaming so loud that his terrified friends fled away on every side; but when the crisis was over he managed to turn the incident to his own advantage.

Kadu gave Kotzebue some general information about the group of islands then under examination, and the Russians spent a month in taking surveys, &c. All these islands, which the natives call Radack, were under the control of one tamon, a man named Lamary. A few years later Dumont d'Urville gave the name of Marshall to the group. According to Kadu, another chain of islets, attolls, and reefs was situated some little distance off on the west.

Kotzebue had not time to identify them, and steering in a northerly direction he reached Ounalashka on the 24th April, where he had to repair the serious damage sustained by the *Rurik* in two violent storms. This done, he took on board some baidares (boats cased in skins to make them water-tight), with fifteen natives of the Aleutian Islands, who were used to the navigation of the Polar seas, and resumed his exploration of Behring Strait.

Kotzebue had suffered very much from pain in his chest ever since when, doubling Cape Horn, he had been knocked down by a huge wave and flung overboard, an accident which would have cost him his life had he not clung to some rope. The consequences were so serious to his health that when, on the 10th July, he landed on the island of St. Lawrence, he was obliged to give up the further prosecution of his researches.

On the 1st October the *Rurik* made a second short halt at the Sandwich Islands where seeds and animals were landed, and at the end of the month the explorers landed at Otdia in the midst of the enthusiastic acclamations of the natives. The cats brought by the visitors were welcomed with special enthusiasm, for the island was infested with immense numbers of rats, who worked havoc on the plantations. Great also was the rejoicing over the return of Kadu, with whom the Russians left an assortment of tools and weapons, which made their owner the wealthiest inhabitant of the archipelago.

Interior of a house at Radak.
(Fac-simile of early engraving.)

On the 4th November the *Rurik* left the Radak Islands, after identifying the Legiep group, and cast anchor off Guam, one of the Marianne islands, where she remained until the end of the month. A halt of some weeks at Manilla enabled the commander to collect some curious information about the Philippine Islands, to which he would have to return later.

After escaping from the violent storms encountered in doubling the Cape of Good Hope, the *Rurik* cast anchor on the 3rd August, 1818, in the Neva, opposite Count Romantzoff's palace.

These three years of absence had been turned to good account by the hardy navigators. In spite of the smallness of their number and the poverty of their equipments, they had not been afraid to face the terrors of the deep, to venture amongst all but unknown archipelagoes, or to brave the rigours of the Arctic and Torrid zones. Important as were their actual discoveries, their rectification of the errors of their predecessors were of yet greater value. Two thousand five hundred species of plants, one third of which were quite new, with numerous details respecting the language, ethnography, religion, and customs of the tribes visited, formed a rich harvest attesting the zeal, skill, and knowledge of the captain as well as the intrepidity and endurance of his crew.

When, therefore, the Russian government decided, in 1823, to send reinforcements to Kamtchatka to put an end to the contraband trade carried on in Russian America, the command of the expedition was given to Kotzebue. A frigate called the *Predpriatie* was placed at his disposal, and he was left free to choose his own route both going and returning.

Kotzebue had gone round the world as a midshipman with Kruzenstern, and that explorer now entrusted to him his eldest son, as did also Möller, the Minister of Marine, a proof of the great confidence both fathers placed in him.

The expedition left Cronstadt on the 15th August, 1823, reached Rio Janeiro in safety, doubled Cape Horn on the 15th January, 1824, and steered for the Pomautou Archipelago, where Predpriatie Island was discovered and the islands of Araktschejews, Romantzoff, Carlshoff, and Palliser were identified. On the 14th March anchor was cast in the harbour of Matavar, Otaheite.

View of Otaheite.

Since Cook's stay in this archipelago a complete transformation had taken place in the manners and customs of the inhabitants.

In 1799 some missionaries settled in Otaheite, where they remained for ten years, unfortunately without making a single conversion, and we add with regret without even winning the esteem or respect of the natives. Compelled at the end of these ten years, in consequence of the revolutions which convulsed Otaheite, to take refuge at Eimeo and other islands of the same group, their efforts were there crowned with more success. In 1817, Pomaré, king of Otaheite, recalled the missionaries, made them a grant of land, and declared himself a convert to Christianity. His example was soon followed by a considerable number of natives.

Kotzebue had heard of this change, but he was not prepared to find European customs generally adopted.

At the sound of the discharge announcing the arrival of the Russians, a boat, bearing the Otaheitian flag, put off from shore, bringing a pilot to guide the *Predpriatie* to its anchorage.

The next day, which happened to be Sunday, the Russians were surprised at the religious silence which prevailed throughout the island when they landed. This silence was only broken by the sound of canticles and psalms sung by the natives in their huts.

The church, a plain, clean building of rectangular form, roofed with reeds and approached by a long avenue of palms, was well filled with an attentive, orderly congregation, the men sitting on one side, the women on the other, all with prayer-books in their hands. The voices of the neophytes often joined in the chant of the missionaries, unfortunately with better will than correctness or appropriateness.

If the piety of the islanders was edifying, the costumes worn by these strange converts were such as somewhat to distract the attention of the visitors. A black coat or the waistcoat of an English uniform was the only garment worn by some, whilst others contented themselves with a jacket, a shirt, or a pair of trousers. The most fortunate were wrapped in cloth mantles, and rich and poor alike dispensed with shoes and stockings.

The women were no less grotesquely clad. Some wore men's shirts, white or striped as the case might be, others a mere piece of cloth; but all had European hats. The wives of the Areois[3] wore coloured robes, a piece of great extravagance, but with them the dress formed the whole costume.

[3] The Areois are a curious vagrant set of people, who have been found in these regions, who practise the singular and fatal custom of killing their children at birth, because of a traditional law binding them to do so.—*Trans.*

On the Monday a most imposing ceremony took place. This was the visit to Kotzebue of the queen-mother and the royal family. These great people were preceded by a master of ceremonies, who was a sort of court fool wearing nothing but a red waistcoat, and with his legs tattooed to represent striped trousers, whilst on the lower portion of his back was described a quadrant divided into minute sections. He performed his absurd capers, contortions, and grimaces with a gravity infinitely amusing.

The queen regent carried the little king Pomaré III. in her arms, and beside her walked his sister, a pretty child of ten years old. The royal infant was dressed in European style, like his subjects, and like them, he wore nothing on his feet. At the request of the ministers and great people of Otaheite, Kotzebue had a pair of boots made for him, which he was to wear on the day of his coronation.

Great were the shouts of joy, the gestures of delight, and the envious exclamations over the trifles distributed amongst the ladies of the court, and fierce were the struggles for the smallest shreds of the imitation gold lace given away.

What important matter could have brought so many men on to the deck of the frigate, bearing with them quantities of fruits and figs? These eager messengers were the husbands of the disappointed ladies of Otaheite who had not been present at the division of the gold lace more valuable in their eyes than rivers of diamonds in those of Europeans.

At the end of ten days, Kotzebue decided to leave this strange country, where civilization and barbarism flourished side by side in a manner so fraternal, and steered for the Samoa Archipelago, notorious for the massacre of the companions of La Pérouse.

How great was the difference between the Samoans and the Otaheitians! Wild and fierce, suspicious and threatening, the natives of Rose Island could scarcely be kept off the deck of the *Predpriatie*, and one of them at the sight of the bare arm of a sailor made a savage and eloquent gesture showing with what pleasure he could devour the firm and doubtless savoury flesh displayed to view.

The insolence of the natives increased with the arrival of more canoes from the shore, and they had to be beaten back with boathooks before the *Predpriatie* could get away from amongst the frail boats of the ferocious islanders.

Upolu or Oyalava, Platte and Pola or Savai Islands, which with Rose Island form part of the Navigator or Samoan group, were passed almost as soon as they were sighted; and Kotzebue steered for the Radak Islands, where he had been so kindly received on his first voyage. This time, however, the natives were terrified at sight of the huge vessel, and piled up their canoes or fled into the interior, whilst on the beach a procession was formed, a number of islanders with palm branches in their hands advancing to meet the intruders and beg for peace.

At this sight, Kotzebue flung himself into a boat with the surgeon Eschscholtz, and rowing rapidly towards the shore, shouted: "Totabou aïdara" (Kotzebue, friend). An immediate change was the result; the petitions the natives were going to address to the Russians were converted into shouts and enthusiastic demonstrations of delight, some rushing forwards to welcome their friend, others running over to announce his arrival to their fellow- countrymen.

The commander was very pleased to find that Kadu was still living at Aur, under the protection of Lamary, whose countenance he had secured at the price of half his wealth.

Of all the animals left here by Kotzebue, the cats, now become wild alone, had survived, and thus far they had not destroyed the legions of rats with which the island was overrun.

The explorer remained several days with his friends, whom he entertained with dramatic representations; and on the 6th May he made for the Legiep group, the examination of which he had left uncompleted on his last voyage. After surveying it, he intended to resume his exploration of the Radak Islands, but bad weather prevented this, and he had to set sail for Kamtchatka.

The crew here enjoyed the rest so fully earned, from the 7th June to the 20th July, when Kotzebue set sail for New Archangel on the American coast, where he cast anchor on the 7th August.

The frigate, which was here to take the place of the *Predpriatie*, was not however ready for sea until the 1st March of the following year, and Kotzebue turned the delay to account by visiting the Sandwich Islands, where he cast anchor off Waihou in December, 1824.

The harbour of Hono-kourou or Honolulu is the safest of the archipelago; a good many vessels therefore put in there even at this early date, and the island of Waihou bid fair to become the most important of the group, supplanting Hawaii or Owhyee. The appearance of the town was already semi-European, stone houses replaced the primitive native huts, regular streets with shops, café, public-houses, much patronized by the sailors of whalers and fur-traders, together with a fortress provided with cannon, were the most noteworthy signs of the rapid transformation of the manners and customs of the natives.

Fifty years had now elapsed since the discovery of most of the islands of Oceania, and everywhere changes had taken place as sudden as those in the

Sandwich Islands.

"The fur trade," says Desborough Cooley, carried on with the north-west coast of America, "has effected a wonderful revolution in the Sandwich Islands, which from their situation offered an advantageous shelter for ships engaged in it. Among these islands the fur-traders wintered, refitted their vessels, and replenished their stock of fresh provisions; and, as summer approached, returned to complete their cargo on the coast of America. Iron tools and, above all, guns were eagerly sought for by the islanders in exchange for their provisions; and the mercenery traders, regardless of consequences, readily gratified their desires. Fire-arms and ammunition being the most profitable stock to traffic with were supplied them in abundance. Hence the Sandwich islanders soon became formidable to their visitors; they seized on several small vessels, and displayed an energy tinctured at first with barbarity, but indicating great capabilities of social improvement. At this period, one of those extraordinary characters which seldom fail to come forth when fate is charged with great events, completed the revolution, which had its origin in the impulse of Europeans. Tame-tame-hah, a chief, who had made himself conspicuous during the last and unfortunate visit of Cook to those islands, usurped the authority of king, subdued the neighbouring islands with an army of 16,000 men, and made his conquests subservient to his grand schemes of improvement. He knew the superiority of Europeans, and was proud to imitate them. Already, in 1796, when Captain Broughton visited those islands, the usurper sent to ask him whether he should salute him with great guns. He always kept Englishmen about him as ministers and advisers. In 1817, he is said to have had an army of 7000 men, armed with muskets, among whom were at least fifty Europeans. Tame-tame-hah, who began his career in blood and usurpation, lived to gain the sincere love and admiration of his subjects, who regarded him as more than human, and mourned his death with tears of warmer affection than often bedew the ashes of royalty."

One of the guard of the King of the Sandwich Islands.
(Fac-simile of early engraving.)

Such was the state of things when the Russian expedition put in at Waihou. The young king Rio-Rio was in England with his wife, and the government of the archipelago was in the hands of the queen-mother, KaahouManou.

Kotzebue took advantage of the latter and of the first minister both being absent on a neighbouring island, to pay a visit to another wife of Kamea-Mea.

"The apartment," says the traveller, "was furnished in the European fashion, with chairs, tables, and looking-glasses. In one corner stood an immensely large bed with silk curtains; the floor was covered with fine mats, and on these, in the middle of the room, lay Nomahanna, extended on her stomach, her head turned towards the door, and her arms supported on a silk pillow.... Nomahanna, who appeared at the utmost not more than forty years old, was exactly six feet two inches high, and rather more than two ells in circumference.... Her coal-black hair was neatly plaited, at the top of a head as round as a ball; her flat nose and thick projecting lips were certainly not very handsome, yet was her countenance on the whole prepossessing and agreeable."

The "good lady" remembered having seen Kotzebue ten years before. She, therefore, received him graciously, but she could not speak of her husband without tears in her eyes, and her grief did not appear to be assumed. In order that the date of his death should be ever-present to her mind she had had the inscription 6th May, 1819, branded on her arm.

A zealous Christian, like most of the population, the queen took Kotzebue to the church, a vast but simple building, not nearly so crowded as that at Otaheite. Nomahanna seemed to be very intelligent, she knew how to read and was specially enthusiastic about writing, that art which connects us with the absent. Being anxious to give the commander a proof alike of her affection and of her acquirements she sent him a letter by hand which it had taken her several weeks to concoct.

The other ladies did not like to be outdone, and Kotzebue found himself overwhelmed with documents. The only means to check this epistolary inundation was to weigh anchor, which the captain did without loss of time.

Before his departure he received queen Nomahanna on board. Her Majesty appeared in her robes of ceremony, consisting of a magnificent peach- coloured silk dress embroidered with black, evidently originally made for a European, and consequently too tight and too short for its wearer. People could, therefore, see not only the feet, beside which those of Charlemagne would have looked like a Chinaman's, and which were cased in huge men's boots, but also a pair of fat, brown, naked legs resembling the balustrades of a terrace. A collar of red and yellow feathers, a garland of natural flowers, serving as a gorget, and a hat of Leghorn straw, trimmed with artificial flowers, completed this fine but absurd costume.

Nomahanna went over the ship, asking questions about everything, and at last, worn out with seeing so many wonders, betook herself to the captain's cabin, where a good collation was spread for her. The queen flung herself upon a couch, but the fragile article of furniture was unable to sustain so much majesty, and gave way beneath the weight of a princess, whose *embonpoint* had doubtless had a good deal to do with her elevation to such high rank.

After this halt Kotzebue returned to New Archangel, where he remained until the 30th July, 1825. He then paid another visit to the Sandwich Islands a short time after Admiral Byron had brought back the remains of the king and queen. The archipelago was then at peace, its prosperity was continually on the increase, the influence of the missionaries was confirmed, and the education of the young monarch was in the hands of Missionary Bingham. The inhabitants were deeply touched by the honours accorded by the English to the remains of their sovereigns, and the day seemed to be not far distant when European customs would completely supersede those of the natives.

Some provisions having been embarked at Waihou, the explorer made for Radak Islands, identified the Pescadores, forming the southern extremity of that chain, discovered the Eschscholtz group, a short distance off, and touched at Guam on the 15th October. On the 23rd January, 1826, he left Manilla after a stay of some months, during which constant intercourse with the natives had enabled him to add greatly to our knowledge of the geography and natural history of the Philippine islands. A new Spanish governor had arrived with a large reinforcement of troops, and had so completely crushed all agitation that the colonists had quite given up their scheme of separating themselves from Spain.

On the 10th July, 1826, the *Predpriatie* returned to Cronstadt, after a voyage extending over three years, during which she had visited the north-west coast of America, the Aleutian Islands, Kamtchatka, and the Sea of Oktoksh; surveyed minutely a great part of the Radak Islands, and obtained fresh information on the changes through which the people of Oceania were passing. Thanks to the ardour of Chamisso and Professor Eschscholtz, many specimens of natural history had been collected, and the latter published a description of more than 2000 animals, as well as some curious details on the mode of formation of the Coral islands in the South Seas.

The English government had now resumed with eagerness the study of the tantalizing problem, the solution of which had been sought so long in vain. We allude to the finding of the north-west passage. When Parry by sea and Franklin by land were trying to reach Behring Strait, Captain Frederick William Beechey received instructions to penetrate as far north as possible by way of the same strait so as to meet the other explorers, who would doubtless arrive in a state of exhaustion from fatigue and privation.

The *Blossom*, Captain Beechey commander, set sail from Spithead on the 19th May, 1825, and after doubling Cape Horn on the 26th December, entered the Pacific Ocean. After a short stay off the coast of Chili, Beechey visited Easter Island, where the same incidents which had marked Kotzebue's visit were repeated. The same eager reception on the part of the natives, who swam to the *Blossom* or brought their paltry merchandise to it in canoes, and the same shower of stones and blows from clubs when the English landed, repulsed, as in the Russian explorer's time, with a rapid discharge of shot.

On the 4th December, Captain Beechey sighted an island completely overgrown with vegetation. This was the spot famous for the discovery on it of the descendants of the mutineers of the *Bounty*, who landed on it after the enactment of a tragedy, which at the end of last century had excited intense public interest in England.

In 1781 Lieutenant Bligh, one of the officers who had distinguished himself under Cook, was appointed to the command of the *Bounty*, and received orders to go to Otaheite, there to obtain specimens of the breadfruit-tree and other of its vegetable productions for transportation to the Antilles, then generally known amongst the English as the Western Indies. After doubling Cape Horn, Bligh cast anchor in the Bay of Matavai, where he shipped a cargo of breadfruit-trees, proceeding thence to Ramouka, one of the Tonga Isles, for more of the same valuable growth. Thus far no special incident marked the course of the voyage, which seemed likely to end happily. But the haughty character and stern, despotic manners of the commander had alienated from him the affections of nearly the whole of his crew. A plot was formed against him which was carried out before sunrise on the 28th April, off Tofona.

Surprised by the mutineers whilst still in bed, Bligh was bound and gagged before he could defend himself, and dragged on deck in his night-shirt, and after a mock trial, presided over by Lieutenant Christian Fletcher, he, with eighteen men who remained faithful to him, was lowered into a boat containing a few provisions, and abandoned in the open sea.

After enduring agonies of hunger and thirst, and escaping from terrible storms and from the teeth of the savage natives of Tofona, Bligh succeeded in reaching Timor Island, where he received an enthusiastic welcome.

"I now desired my people to come on shore," says Bligh, "which was as much as some of them could do, being scarce able to walk; they, however, were helped to the house, and found tea with bread and butter provided for their breakfast.... Our bodies were nothing but skin and bones, our limbs were full of sores, and we were clothed in rags; in this condition, with the tears of joy and gratitude flowing down our cheeks, the people of Timor beheld us with a mixture of horror, surprise, and pity.... Thus, through the assistance of Divine Providence, we surmounted the difficulties and distresses of a most perilous voyage."

Perilous, indeed, for it had lasted no less than forty-one days in latitudes but little known, in an open boat, with insufficient food, want and exposure causing infinite suffering. Yet in this voyage of more than 1500 leagues but one man was lost, a sailor who fell a victim at the beginning of the journey to the natives of Tofona.

The fate of the mutineers was strange, and more than one lesson may be learnt from it.

They made for Otaheite, where provisions were obtained, and those who had been least active in the mutiny were abandoned, and thence Christian set sail with eight sailors, who elected to remain with him, and some twenty-two natives, men and women from Otaheite and Toubonai. Nothing more was heard of them!

As for those who remained at Otaheite, they were taken prisoners in 1791 by Captain Edwards of the *Pandora*, sent out by the English Government in search of them and the other mutineers, with orders to bring them to England. Of the ten who were brought home by the *Pandora*, only three were condemned to death.

Twenty years passed by before the slightest light was thrown on the fate of Christian and those he took with him.

In 1808 an American trading-vessel touched at Pitcairn, there to complete her cargo of seal-skins. The captain imagined the island to be uninhabited, but to his very great surprise a canoe presently approached his ship manned by three young men of colour, who spoke English very well. Greatly astonished, the commander questioned them, and learnt that their father had served under Bligh.

The fate of the latter was now known to the whole world, and its discussion had lightened the tedious hours in the forecastles of vessels of every nationality, and the American captain, reminded by the singular incident related above of the disappearance of so many of the mutineers of the *Bounty*, landed on the island, where he met an Englishman named Smith, who had belonged to the crew of that vessel, and who made the following confession.

When he left Otaheite, Christian made direct for Pitcairn, attracted to it by its lonely situation, south of the Pomautou Islands, and out of the general track of vessels. After landing the provisions of the *Bounty* and taking away all the fittings which could be of any use, the mutineers burnt the vessel not only with a view to removing all trace of their whereabouts, but also to prevent the escape of any of their number.

From the first the sight of the extensive marshes led them to believe the island to be uninhabited, and they were soon convinced of the justice of this opinion. Huts were built and land was cleared; but the English charitably assigned to the natives, whom they had carried off or who had elected to join them, the position of slaves. Two years passed by without any serious dissensions arising, but at the end of that time the natives laid a plot against the whites, of which, however, the latter were informed by an Otaheitan woman, and the two leaders paid for their abortive attempt with their lives.

Two more years of peace and tranquillity ensued, and then another plot was laid, this time resulting in the massacre of Christian and five of his comrades. The murder, however, was avenged by the native women, who mourned for their English lovers and killed the surviving men of Otaheite.

A little later the discovery of a plant, from which a kind of brandy could be made, caused the death of one of the four Englishmen still remaining, another was murdered by his companions, a third died a natural death, and the last one, Smith, took the name of Adams and lived on at the head of a community, consisting of ten women and nineteen children, the eldest of whom were but seven or eight years old.

This man, who had reflected on his errors and repented of them, now led a new life, fulfilling the duties of father, priest, and sovereign, his combined firmness and justice acquiring for him an all-powerful influence over his motley subjects.

This strange teacher of morality, who in his youth had set all laws at defiance, and to whom no obligation was sacred, now preached pity, love, and sympathy, arranged regular marriages between the children of different parents, his little community thriving lustily under the mild yet firm control of one who had but lately turned from his own evil ways.

Such at the time of Beechey's arrival was the state of the colony at Pitcairn. The navigator, well received by the inhabitants, whose virtuous conduct recalled the golden age, remained amongst them eighteen days. The village consisted of clean, well-built huts, surrounded by pandanus and cocoa-palms; the fields were well cultivated, and under Adams' tuition the young people had made implements of agriculture of really extraordinary excellence. The faces of these half breeds were good-looking and pleasant in expression, and their figures were well-proportioned, showing unusual muscular development.

"The village consisted of clean, well-built huts."

After leaving Pitcairn, Beechey visited Crescent, Gambier, Hood, Clermont, Tonnerre, Serles, Whitsunday, Queen-Charlotte, Tehaï, and the Lancer Islands, all in the Pomautou group, and an islet to which he gave the name of

Byam-Martin.

Here the explorer met a native named Ton-Wari, who had been shipwrecked in a storm. Having left Anaa with 500 fellow-countrymen in three canoes to render homage to Pomaré III., who had just ascended the throne, Ton-Wari had been driven out of his course by westerly winds. These were succeeded by variable breezes, and provisions were soon so completely exhausted that the survivors had to feed on the bodies of those who were the first to succumb. Finally Ton-Wari arrived at Barrow Island in the centre of the Dangerous Archipelago, where he obtained a small stock of provisions, and after a long delay, his canoe having been stove in off Byam-Martin, once more put to sea.

Beechey yielded under considerable persuasion to Ton-Wari's entreaty to be received on board with his wife and children and taken to Otaheite. The next day, by one of those strange chances seldom occurring except in fiction, Beechey stopped at Heïon, where Ton-Wari met his brother, who had supposed him to be long since dead. After the first transports of delight and surprise the two natives sat down side by side, and holding each others hands related their several adventures.

Beechey left Heïon on the 10th February, sighted Melville and Croker Islands, and cast anchor on the 18th off Otaheite, where he had some difficulty in obtaining provisions. The natives now demanded good Chilian dollars and European clothing, both of which were altogether wanting on the *Blossom*.

After receiving a visit from the queen-mother, Beechey was invited to a *soirée* given in his honour in the palace at Papeïti. When the English arrived, however, they found everybody sound asleep, the hostess having forgotten all about her invitation, and gone to bed earlier than usual. She received her guests none the less cordially however, and organized a little dance in spite of the remonstrances of the missionaries; only the *fête* had to be conducted so to speak in silence, that the noise might not reach the ears of the police on duty on the beach. From this incident we can guess the amount of liberty the missionary Pritchard allowed to the most exalted personages of Otaheite. What must the discipline then have been for the common herd of the natives!

On the 3rd April the young king paid a visit to Beechey, who gave him, on behalf of the Admiralty, a fine fowling-piece. Very friendly was the intercourse which ensued, and the good influence the English missionaries had obtained was strengthened by the cordiality and tact of the ship's officers.

Leaving Otaheite on the 26th April, Beechey reached the Sandwich Islands, where he remained some ten days, and then set sail for Behring Strait and the Arctic Ocean. His instructions were to skirt along the North American coast as far as the state of the ice would permit. The *Blossom* made a halt in Kotzebue Bay, a desolate, forbidding, and inhospitable spot, where the English had several interviews with the natives without obtaining any information about Franklin and his people. At last Beechey sent forward one of the ship's boats, under command of Lieutenant Elson, to seek the intrepid explorer. Elson was, however, unable to pass Point Barrow (N. lat. 71° 23') and was compelled to return to the *Blossom*, which in her turn was driven back to the entrance of the strait by the ice on the 13th October, the weather being clear and the frost of extreme severity.

In order to turn to account the winter season, Beechey visited San Francisco and cast anchor yet again off Honolulu in the Sandwich Islands. Thanks to the liberal and enlightened policy of the government, this archipelago was now rapidly growing in prosperity. The number of houses had increased, the town was gradually acquiring a European appearance, the harbour was frequented by numerous English and American vessels, and a national navy numbering five brigs and eight schooners had sprung into being. Agriculture was in a flourishing condition; coffee, tea, spices, were cultivated in extensive plantations, and efforts were being made to utilize the luxuriant sugar-cane forests native to the archipelago.

After a stay in April at the mouth of the Canton River, the explorers surveyed the Liu-Kiu archipelago, a chain of islands connecting Japan with Formosa, and the Bonin-Sima group, districts in which no animals were seen but big green turtles.

This exploration over, the *Blossom* resumed her northerly course, but the atmospheric conditions were less favourable than before, and it was impossible this time to penetrate further than N. lat. 70° 40'. Beechey left provisions, clothes, and instructions on the coast in this neighbourhood in case Parry or Franklin should get as far. The explorer then cruised about until the 6th October, when he decided with the greatest regret to return to England. He touched at Monterey, San Francisco, San-Blas, and Valparaiso, doubled Cape Horn, cast anchor at Rio de Janeiro, and finally arrived off Spithead on the 21st October.

A Morai at Kayakakoua.
(Fac-simile of early engraving.)

We must now give an account of the expedition of the Russian Captain Lütke,
which was fruitful of most important results. The explorer's own relation of
his adventures is written in a most amusing and spirited style, and from it we

shall therefore quote largely.

The *Seniavine* and the *Möller* were two transport ships built in Russia, both of which were good sea-going boats. The latter, however, was a very slow sailer, which unfortunately kept the two vessels apart for the greater part of the voyage. Lütke commanded the *Seniavine*, and Stanioukowitch the *Möller*.

The two vessels set sail from Cronstadt on the 1st September, 1828, and touched at Copenhagen and Plymouth, where scientific instruments were purchased. Hardly had they left the Channel before they were separated. The *Seniavine*, whose movements we shall most particularly follow, touched at Teneriffe, where Lütke hoped to meet his consort.

From the 4th to the 8th November, Teneriffe had been devastated by a terrific storm such as had not been seen since the Conquest. Three vessels had perished in the very roadstead of Santa Cruz, and two others thrown upon the coast had gone to pieces. Torrents swollen by a tremendous downpour had destroyed gardens, walls, and buildings, laid waste plantations, all but demolished one fort, swept down a number of houses in the town, and rendered several streets impassable. Three or four hundred persons had met their deaths in this convulsion of nature, and the damage done was estimated at several millions of piastres.

In January the two vessels met again at Rio de Janeiro, and kept together as far as Cape Horn, where they encountered the usual storms and fogs, and were again separated. The *Seniavine* then made for Conception.

"On the 15th May," says Lütke, "we were not more than eight miles from the nearest coast, but a dense fog hid it from us. In the night this fog lifted, and at daybreak a scene of indescribable grandeur and magnificence met our eyes. The serrated chain of the Andes, with its pointed peaks, stood out against an azure blue sky lit up by the first rays of the morning sun. I will not add to the number of those who have exhausted themselves in vain efforts to transmit to others their own sensations at the first sight of such scenes. They are as indescribable as the majesty of the scene itself. The variety of the colours, the light, which as the sun rose gradually spread over the sky, and the clouds were alike of inimitable beauty. To our great regret this spectacle, like everything most sublime in nature, did not last long. As the atmosphere became flooded with light the huge masses of clouds seemed with one accord to plunge into the deep, and the sun, appearing above the horizon, removed every trace of them."

Lütke's opinion of Conception does not agree with that of some of his predecessors. He had not yet forgotten the exuberant richness of the vegetation of the Bay of Rio de Janeiro, so that he found this new coast poor.

As far as he could judge, during a very short stay, the inhabitants were more affable and civilized than the people of the same class in many other countries.

When he reached Valparaiso, Lütke met the *Möller* setting sail for Kamtchatka. The crews bid each other good-bye, and thenceforth the two vessels took different directions.

The first excursion of the officers and naturalists of Lütke's party was to the celebrated "quebradas."

"These," says the explorer, "are ravines in the mountains, crowded so to speak with the little huts containing the greater part of the people of Valparaiso. The most densely populated of these 'quebradas' is that rising at the south-west corner of the town. The granite, which is there laid bare, serves as a strong foundation for the buildings, and protects them from the destructive effects of earthquakes. Communication between the town and the different houses is carried on by means of narrow paths without supports or steps, which are carried along the slopes of the rocks, and on which the children play and run about like chamois. The few houses here belong to foreigners. Little paths lead up to them, and some have steps, which the Chilians look upon as a superfluous and altogether useless luxury. A staircase of tiled or palm-branch roofs below and above an amphitheatre of gates and gardens present a curious spectacle. At first I kept up with the naturalists, but they presently brought me to a place where I could not advance or retire a step, which decided me to return with one of my officers, and to leave them there with a hearty wish that they might bring their heads back safely to our lodgings. As for myself I expected to lose mine a thousand times before I got down again."

On their return from an arduous excursion, a few leagues from Valparaiso, the marines were astonished at being arrested as they rode into the town, by a patrol, who in spite of their remonstrances compelled them to dismount.

"It was Holy Thursday," says Lütke, "and from that day to Holy Saturday no one is here permitted under pain of a severe penalty either to ride, sing, dance, play on any instrument, or wear a hat. All business, work, and amusement are strictly forbidden during that time. The hill in the centre of the town with the theatre upon it is converted for the time being into a Golgotha. In the centre of a railed-in space rises a crucifix with numerous tapers and flowers about it and female figures kneeling on either side representing the witnesses of the Passion of our Lord. Pious souls come here to obtain absolution from their sins by loud prayers. I saw none but female penitents, not a single man was there amongst them. Most of them were doubtless very certain of obtaining the divine favour, for they came up playing and laughing, only assuming a contrite air when close to the object of their devotion, before which they knelt for a few minutes, resuming their pranks and laughter again directly they turned away."

The intolerance and superstition met with by the visitors at every turn made the explorer reflect deeply. He regretted seeing so much force and so many resources which might have promoted the intellectual progress and material prosperity of the country wasted on perpetual revolutions.

To Lütke nothing less resembled a valley of Paradise than Valparaiso and its environs: rugged mountains, broken by deep *quebradas*, a sandy plain, in the centre of which rises the town, with the lofty heights of the Andes in the background, do not, strictly speaking, form an Eden.

The traces of the terrible earthquake of 1823 were not yet entirely effaced, and here and there large spaces covered with ruins were still to be seen.

On the 15th April, the *Seniavine* set sail for New Archangel, where she arrived on the 24th June, after a voyage unmarked by any special incident. The necessity for repairing the effects of the wear and tear of a voyage of ten months, and of disembarking the provisions for the company of which the *Seniavine* was the bearer, detained Captain Lütke in the Bay of Sitka for five weeks.

This part of the coast of North America presents a wild but picturesque appearance. Lofty mountains clothed to their very peaks with dense and gloomy forests form the background of the picture. At the entrance of the bay rises Mount Edgecumbe, an extinct volcano 2800 feet above the sea-level. On entering the bay the visitor finds himself in a labyrinth of islands, behind which rise the fortress, towers, and church of New Archangel, which consists of but one row of houses with gardens, a hospital, a timber-yard, and outside the palisades a large village of Kaloche Indians. At this time the population consisted of a mixture of Russians, Creoles, and Aleutians, numbering some 800 altogether, of whom three-eighths were in the service of the company. This population, however, fluctuates very much according to the season. In the summer almost every one is away at the chase, and no sooner does autumn bring the people before they are all off again fishing.

New Archangel does not offer too many attractions in the way of amusements. Truth to tell, it is one of the dullest places imaginable, inexpressibly gloomy, where autumn seems to reign all through the year except for three months, when snow falls continuously. All this, however, does not of course affect the passing visitor, and for the resident there is nothing to keep up his spirits but a good stock of philosophy or a stern determination not to die of hunger. There is a good deal of remunerative trade with California, the natives, and foreign vessels.

The chief furs obtained by Aleutians who hunt for the Company are those of the otter, the beaver, the fox, and the *souslic*. The natives also hunt the walrus, seal, and whale, not to speak of the herring, the cod, salmon, turbot, lote, perch, and tsouklis, a shell fish found in Queen Charlotte's Islands, used by the Company as a medium of exchange with the Americans.

As for these Americans they seem to be all of one race between the 46th and 60th degrees of N. lat., such at least is the conclusion to which we are led by the study of their manners, customs, and languages.

The Kaloches of Sitka claim a man of the name of Elkh as the founder of their race, favoured by the protection of the raven, first cause of all things.[4] Strange to say, this bird also plays an important part amongst the Kadiaks, who are Esquimaux. According to Lütke, the Kaloches have a tradition of a deluge and some fables which recall those of the Greek mythology.

[4] The raven was regarded by these races with superstitious dread, as having the power of healing diseases, &c.—*Trans.*

Their religion is nothing more than a kind of Chamanism or belief in the power of the Chamans or magicians to ward off diseases, &c. They do not recognize a supreme God, but they believe in evil spirits, and in sorcerers who foretell the future, heal the sick, and transmit their office from father to son.

They believe the soul to be immortal, and that the spirits of their chieftains do not mix with those of the common people. Slaves are slaves still after death; the far from consolatory nature of this creed is obvious. The government is patriarchal; the natives are divided into tribes, the members of which have the figures of animals as signs, after which they are also sometimes named. We meet for instance with the wolf, the raven, the bear, the eagle, &c.

The slaves of the Kaloches are prisoners taken in war, and very miserable is their lot. Their masters hold the power of life and death over them. In some ceremonies, that on the death of a chief, for instance, the slaves who are no longer of use are sacrificed, or else their liberty is given to them.[5]

[5] The aim being to give up the slaves as property, it was a matter of indifference whether they were killed or set at liberty.—*Trans.*

Suspicious and crafty, cruel and vindictive, the Kaloches are neither better nor worse than the neighbouring tribes. Hardened to fatigue, brave but idle, they leave all the housework to their wives, of whom they have many, polygamy being an institution amongst them.

On leaving Sitka, Lütke made for Ounalashka. Ilioluk is the chief trading establishment on that island, but it only contains some twelve Russians and ten Aleutians of both sexes.

This island has a good many productions which tend to make life pass pleasantly. It is rich in good pastures, and cattle-breeding is largely carried on, but it is almost entirely wanting in timber, the inhabitants being obliged to pick up the *débris* flung up by the sea, which sometimes includes whole trunks of cypress, camphor-trees, and a kind of wood which smells like roses.

At the time of Lütke's visit the people of the Fox Islands had adopted to a great extent Russian manners and costumes. They were all Christians. The Aleutians are a hardy, kind-hearted, agile race, almost living on the sea.

Since 1826 several eruptions of lava have caused terrible devastation in these islands. In May, 1827, the Shishaldin volcano opened a new crater, and vomited forth flames.

Lütke's instructions obliged him to explore St. Matthew's Island, which Cook had called Gore Island. The hydrographical survey was successful beyond the highest expectations, but the Russians could do nothing towards learning anything of the natural history of the island, for they were not allowed to land at all.

In the meantime the winter with its usual storms and fogs was rapidly drawing on. It was of no use hoping to get to Behring Strait, and Lütke therefore made for Kamtchatka after touching at Behring Island. He remained three weeks at Petropaulovsky, which he employed in landing his cargo and preparing for his winter campaign.

Lütke's instructions were now to spend the winter in the exploration of the Caroline Islands. He decided to go first to Ualan Island, which had been discovered by the French navigator Duperrey. Here a safe harbour enabled him to make some experiments with the pendulum.

On his way Lütke sought in vain for Colonnas Island in N. lat. 26° 9', W. long. 128°. He was equally unsuccessful in his search for Dexter and St. Bartholomew Islands, though he identified the Brown coral group discovered by Butler in 1794 and arrived safely off Ualan on the 4th December.

From the first the relations between the natives of this island and the Russians were extremely satisfactory. Many of the former came on board, and showed so much confidence in their visitors as to remain all night, though the vessel was still in motion.

It was only with great difficulty that the *Seniavine* entered Coquille harbour. Following the example of Duperrey, who had set up his observatory on the islet of Matanial, Lütke landed there and took his observations, whilst his people traded with the natives, who were, throughout his stay, peaceful, friendly, and civil. To check their thieving propensities, however, a chief was kept as a hostage for a couple of days, and one canoe was burnt, these new measures being completely successful.

"We are glad to be able to declare in the face of the world," says Lütke, "that our stay of three weeks at Ualan cost not a drop of human blood, but that we were able to leave these friendly islanders without enlightening them further on the use of our fire-arms, which they looked upon as suitable only for the killing of birds. I don't think there is another instance of the kind in the records of any previous voyages in the South Seas."

Native of Ualan.
(Fac-simile of early engraving.)

After leaving Ualan, Lütke had a vain search for the Musgrave Islands, marked on Kruzenstern's map, and soon discovered a large island, surrounded by a coral reef, which had escaped the notice of Duperrey, and is known as Puinipet, or Pornabi. Some very large and fine canoes, each manned by fourteen men, and some smaller ones, worked by two natives only, soon surrounded the vessel. Their inmates, with fierce faces and blood-shot eyes, were noisy and blustering, and did a good deal of shouting, gesticulating, and dancing before they could make up their minds to trust themselves on board the *Seniavine*.

It would have been impossible to land, except by force, as the native canoes completely surrounded the vessel, and when an attempt at disembarkation was made, the savages surrounded the ship's boat, only retiring before the warlike attitude of the sailors and a volley from the guns of the *Seniavine*.

Lütke had not time to examine thoroughly his discovery, to which he gave the name of the Seniavine Archipelago. The information he collected on the people of the Puinipet Islands is, therefore, not very trustworthy. According to him they do not belong to the same race as those of Ualan, but resemble rather the Papuans, the nearest of whom are those of New Ireland, seven hundred miles away.

After another vain search, this time for Saint Augustine's Island, he sighted the Cora of Los Vaherites, also called Seven, or Raven Island, discovered in 1773 by the Spaniard Felipe Tompson.

The navigator next saw the Mortlock Archipelago, the old Lugunor group, known to Torrés as the Lugullos, the people of which resemble those of Ualan. He landed on the principal of these islands, which he found to be one huge garden of cocoa palms and breadfruit-trees.

The natives enjoy a centre degree of civilization. They weave and dye the fibres of the banana and cocoa-nut palms, as do those of Ualan and Puinipet. Their fishing-tackle does credit to their inventive faculties, especially a sort of case constructed of small sticks and split bamboo-canes, which the fish cannot get out of when once in. They also use nets of the shape of large wallets, lines, and harpoons.

Their canoes, in which they spend more than half their lives, are wonderfully adapted to their requirements. The large ones, which are a very great trouble to build, and which are kept in sheds constructed specially for them, are twenty-six feet long, two and a half wide, and four deep. They are furnished with gimbals, the cross-pieces being connected by a rafter. On the other side there is a small platform, four feet square, and furnished with a roof, under which they are accustomed to keep their provisions. These pirogues have a triangular sail, which is made of matting woven from bandanus leaves, and is attached to two yards. In tacking about they drop the sail, and turn the mast towards the other end of the canoe, to which, at the same time, they have passed the fastening of the sail, so that the pirogue moves forward by its other extremity.

Lütke next sighted the Namuluk group, the inhabitants of which do not differ at all from the people of Lugunor, and he proved the identity of Hogolu Island —already described by Duperrey—with Quirosa. He then visited the Namnuïto group, the first stratum of a number of islands, or of one large island which will some day exist in this part of the world.

Lütke, who was in want of biscuits and other articles, which he hoped to obtain at Guam, or from vessels at anchor in that port, now set sail for the Marianne Islands, where he counted upon being able to repeat some new experiments with the pendulum, in which Freycinet had found an important anomaly of gravitation.[6]

[6] "From numerous experiments," says Freycinet, "with the pendulum, collected at our observatory at Agagna, in lat. 13° 27′ 511″ 5 N. ... at the level of the sea, and with the thermometer at +20° centig., we were shown that the pendulum which, in the same circumstances, would make at Paris 86,400 oscillations in 24 mean solar hours would here make 86,295 [osc].013 in the same time."—*Trans.*

Great, however, was his surprise when he arrived to find not a sign of life at Guam. No flags waved above the two ports, the silence of death reigned everywhere, and but for the presence of a schooner at anchor in the inner harbour, it might have been a desert island. There was hardly anybody about on shore, and the few people there were were half savage, from whom it was all but impossible to obtain the slightest information. Fortunately, an English deserter came and offered his services to Lütke, who sent him to the governor with a letter, which elicited a satisfactory reply.

The governor was the same Medinella whose hospitality had been lauded by Kotzebue and Freycinet. There was, therefore, no difficulty in obtaining permission to set up an observatory, and to take to it the necessary provisions. The stay at Guam was, however, saddened by an accident to Lütke, who wounded himself severely in the thumb with his own gun when hunting.

The repairing and refitting of the *Seniavine*, with the taking in of wood and water, delayed the explorer at Guam until the 19th March. During this time Lütke was able to verify the information collected ten years ago by Freycinet in his stay of two months in the Governor's own house. Things had not changed at all since the French traveller's visit.

As it was not yet time to go north, Lütke made for the Caroline Islands, *viâ* the Swedes Islands. The inhabitants seemed to him to be better made than their neighbours on the west, from whom, however, they differ in no other particulars. The Faraulep, Ulie, Ifuluk, and Euripeg Islands were successively examined, and on the 27th April the explorer started for the Bonin Islands, where he learnt that his exploration of that group had been anticipated by Beechey. He, therefore, took no hydrographical surveys. Two of the crew of a whaling-vessel, which had been shipwrecked on the coast, were still living at Bonin Sima.

Since the rise of the great fisheries, this Archipelago has been frequented by numerous whalemen, who here find a safe port at all seasons, plenty of wood and water, turtles for six months of the year, fish, and immense quantities of anti-scorbutic plants, including the delicious savoy cabbage.

"The majestic height and the vigour of the trees," says Lütke, "the productions of the tropical and temperate zones, alternating with each other, bear witness at once to the fertility of the soil and the salubrity of the climate. Most of our vegetables and pot-herbs, perhaps, indeed, all of them would certainly flourish well, as would also wheat, rice, and maize, nor could a better climate be desired for the cultivation of the vine. Domestic animals of every kind and bees would multiply rapidly. In a word, a small and industrious colony would shortly convert this little group into a fertile and flourishing settlement."

On the 9th June, after a week's delay for want of wind, the *Seniavine* entered Petropaulovsky, where it was retained taking in provisions until the 26th. A whole series of surveys were taken during this interval, of the coasts of Kamtchatka, and of the Kodiak and Tchouktchi districts, interrupted, however, by visits to Karaghinsk Island, the bay of St. Lawrence, and the gulf of Santa Cruz.

During one of these visits, the captain met with a strange adventure. He had been for several days on a friendly footing with the Tchouktchis, whose knowledge of the people and customs of Russia he endeavoured to increase.

"These natives," he says, "were friendly and polite, and endeavoured to pay back our jokes and tricks in our own coin. I softly patted the cheek of a sturdy Tchouktchi as a sign of kindly feeling, and suddenly received in return a box on the ear which knocked me down. Recovered from my astonishment, there I saw my Tchouktchi with a laughing face, looking like a man who has just given proof of his politeness and tact. He too had meant to give me merely a gentle tap, but it was with a hand only accustomed to deal with reindeer."

The travellers were also witnesses of some proofs of the skill of a Tchouktchi conjurer, or chaman, who went behind a curtain, from which his audience soon heard a voice like the howl of a wild beast, accompanied by blows on a tambourine with a whale-bone. The curtain then rose, revealing the sorcerer balancing himself, and accompanying his own voice with blows on his drum, which he held close to his ear. Presently he flung off his jacket, leaving himself naked to the waist, took a polished stone, which he gave to Lütke to hold, took it away again, and as he passed one hand over the other the stone disappeared. Then showing a tumour on his shoulder, he pretended that the stone was in it; turned over the tumour, extracted the stone from it, and prophesied a favourable issue of the journey of the Russians.

The conjuror was congratulated on his skill, and a knife was given to him as a token of gratitude. Taking this knife in his hand, he put out his tongue, and began to cut it. His mouth became full of blood, and he finally cut a piece of his tongue off, and held the piece out in his hand. Here the curtain fell, probably because the skill of the professor of legerdemain could go no further.

The people inhabiting the north-east corner of Asia are known under the general name of Tchouktchis. This includes two races, one nomad, like the Samoyedes, called the Reindeer Tchouktchis; the other, living in fixed habitations, called the sedentary Tchouktchis. The mode of life, the physiognomy, and the very language of these two races differ. The idiom spoken by the sedentary Tchouktchis has great affinity with that of the Esquimaux, whom they also resemble in their mode of building their huts and leather boats, and in the instruments they use.

Sedentary Tchouktchis.

Lütke did not see many Reindeer Tchouktchis, so that he could add nothing to the information obtained by his predecessors. He was of opinion, however, that they had been painted in unfairly gloomy colours, and that their turbulence and wildness had been grossly exaggerated.

The sedentary Tchouktchis, generally called Namollos, spend the winter in sheds, and the summer in huts covered with skins. The latter usually each serve for several families.

"The sons and their wives, the daughters and their husbands," says the narrative, "live together with their parents, and *vice versâ*. Each family occupies one division of the back part of the hut, curtained off from the others. The curtains are made of reindeer-skins, sewn into the shape of a bell. They are fastened to the beams of the ceiling, and reach to the ground. With the aid of the grease they burn in cold weather, two, three, and sometimes more persons so warm the air with their breath in these hermetically sealed positions that all clothing is superfluous, even with the severest frost, but only Tchouktchi lungs are fitted to respire in such an atmosphere. In the outer part of the hut cooking-utensils, pottery, baskets, seal-skin trunks, &c., are kept. Here too is the hearth, if we can so call the spot where burn a few sticks of brushwood, painfully collected in the marsh, or when they are not to be obtained, whale-bones floating in grease. Round about the hut on wooden dryers, black and disgusting looking pieces of seal's flesh are exposed to view." These people lead a miserable life. They feed upon the half-raw flesh of seals and walruses hunted by themselves, or on that of whales flung up by the waves on the beach. The dog is the only domestic animal they possess, and they treat it badly enough, although the poor creatures are very affectionate and render them great services, now towing along their canoes, now dragging their sledges over the snow.

After a second stay of five weeks at Petropaulovski, the *Seniavine* left Kamtchatka, on the 10th of November, on its way back to Europe. Before reaching Manilla, Lütke made a cruise in the northern part of the Caroline Archipelago, which he had not had time to visit during the preceding winter. He saw in succession the islands of Marileu, Falulu, Faïu, Namuniuto, Magur, Faraulep, Eap, Mogmog, and found at Manilla the sloop, the *Möller* which was waiting his arrival.

The Caroline Archipelago embraces an immense space, and the Marianne Islands, as well as the Radak group, might fitly be included in it, as containing a population perfectly identical in race. For a long time the old geographers had had for their guidance only the charts of missionaries who, lacking alike the education and the appliances necessary to estimate accurately the size, position, and relative distance of all these archipelagoes, had attached notable importance to them, and often fixed at a considerable number of degrees the extent of a group which covered only a few miles.

Thus navigators accepted their guidance with wise caution. Freycinet was the first to infuse a little order into this chaos, and, thanks to his meeting with Kadu and Don Louis Torrès, he was able to identify later with earlier discoveries. Lütke did his part—and that not a small part—in the settling of an accurate and scientific chart of an archipelago which had long been the terror of navigators.

The learned Russian explorer is not of the same opinion as Lesson, one of his predecessors, who connected all the inhabitants of the Caroline group with the Mongolian race, under the name of the "Mongolo-Pelagian" branch. He rather sees in them, as did Chamisso and Balbi, a branch of the Malay family, which has peopled Eastern Polynesia. Whilst Lesson compares the people of the Carolines with the Chinese and Japanese, Lütke, on the other hand, finds in their great, projecting eyes, thick lips, and *retroussé* nose, a family likeness to the people of the Sandwich and Tonga Islands. The language does not suggest the slightest comparison with Japanese, whilst it shows a great resemblance to that of the Tonga Islands.

Lütke spent the time of his sojourn at Manilla in laying in stores, and repairing the sloop, and, on the 30th of January, he left that Spanish possession for Russia, which he reached on the 6th of September, 1829, casting anchor in the roads of Cronstadt.

It remains now to tell how it had fared with the sloop, the *Möller*, after the separation at Valparaiso. Arriving at Kamtchatka from Otaheite, she had left part of her cargo at Petropaulovski, and thereafter—in August, 1827—had set sail for Ounalashka, where she had remained for a month. After an examination of the west coast of America, which was cut short by unfavourable weather, and a stay at Honolulu, which extended to February, 1828, she had discovered the island Möller, noted the Necker, Gardner, and Lisiansky Islands, and marked, at a distance of six miles southwards, a very dangerous reef.

The sloop had then coasted the island of Curè, the French Frigate Shoal the reef Maro, Pearl Island, and the Isle of Hermes; and, after having made search for several islands marked upon Arrowsmith's charts, had at length reached Kamtchatka. At the end of April, she had set sail for Ounalashka and taken observations of the north coast of the Alaska peninsula. In September the *Möller* rejoined the *Seniavine*, and, from that period until their return to Russia, they were no more separated, save for brief intervals.

As one may judge from the sufficiently detailed account which has just been given, this expedition did not fail to bring about results of importance to geographical science. We must add that the different branches of natural history, physics, and astronomy, owe to it equally numerous and important additions.

CHAPTER II.

FRENCH CIRCUMNAVIGATORS.

The journey of Freycinet—Rio de Janeiro and its gipsy inhabitants—The Cape and its wines—The Bay of Sharks—Stay at Timor—Ombay Island and its cannibal inhabitants—The Papuan Islands—The pile dwellings of the Alfoers—A dinner with the Governor of Guam—Description of the Marianne Islands and their inhabitants—Particulars concerning the Sandwich Islands—Port Jackson and New South Wales—Shipwreck in Berkeley Sound—The Falkland Islands—Return to France—The voyage of the *Coquille* under the command of Duperrey—Martin-Vaz and Trinidad—The Island of St. Catharine—The independence of Brazil—Berkeley Sound and the remains of the *Uranie*—Stay at Conception—The civil war in Chili—The Araucanians—Discoveries in the Dangerous Archipelago—Stay at Otaheite and New Ireland—The Papuans—Stay at Ualan—The Caroline Islands and their inhabitants—Scientific results of the expeditions.

The expedition under the command of Louis Claude de Saulces de Freycinet was the result of the leisure which the Peace of 1815 brought to the French navy. The idea was started by one of its most adventurous officers, the same who had accompanied Baudin in his survey of the Australian coasts, and to him was entrusted the task of carrying it out. It was the first voyage which had not hydrography alone for its object. Its chief aim was to survey the shape of the land in the southern hemisphere, and to make observations in terrestrial magnetism, without, at the same time, omitting to give attention to all natural phenomena, and to the manners, customs, and languages of indigenous races. Purely geographical inquiries, though not altogether omitted from the programme, had the least prominent place in it.

Among the medical officers of the navy, Freycinet found MM. Quoy, Gaimard, and Gaudichaud, whose attainments in natural history qualified them for being valuable coadjutors; and he also chose to accompany him several distinguished officers who had risen to high rank in the navy, the best known being Duperrey, Lamarche, Berard, and Odet-Pellion, who subsequently became, one a member of the Institute, the others superior officers or admirals.

No less care was exercised by Freycinet in composing his crew chiefly of sailors who were also skilled in some trade; so that out of the 120 men who manned the corvette *Uranie*, no less than fifty could serve on occasion as carpenters, ropemakers, sailmakers, blacksmiths, or other mechanics.

The *Uranie*, amply supplied with stores for two years, and provided with all sorts of apparatus of proved utility, iron cisterns for fresh water, machines for distilling salt water, preserved provisions, remedies for scurvy, &c. At last, on the 17th of September, 1817, she set sail from Toulon. On board, disguised as a sailor, was the commander's wife, who was not to be deterred from joining her husband by the dangers and hardships of so protracted a voyage.

Together with all these provisions for bodily comfort, Freycinet took with him a stock of the best scientific instruments, together with minute instructions from the Institute intended to direct his researches, and to suggest the experiments best adapted to promote the progress of science.

The *Uranie* reached Rio de Janeiro on the 6th of December, having put in at Gibraltar, and made a short stay at Teneriffe, one of the Canaries, which, as Freycinet wittily observes, were not Fortunate Islands for his crew, all communication with the land being forbidden by the governors.

During their stay at Rio de Janeiro the officers took a great many magnetical observations and made experiments with the pendulum, whilst the naturalists scoured the country for new specimens and curiosities, making large and important collections.

The original records of the voyage contain a long narrative of the discovery and colonization of Brazil, and detailed information on the customs and manners of the people, on the temperature and the climate, as well as a minute description of the principal buildings and the suburbs of Rio de Janeiro itself. The most curious part of this account is that which touches upon the gipsies, who, at that time, were to be met with at Rio de Janeiro.

"Worthy descendants of the Pariahs of India, whence these gipsies without doubt originally came," says Freycinet, "they are noted like their ancestors for every vicious practice and criminal propensity. Most of them, possessing immense wealth, make a great display in dress and in horses, especially at their weddings, which are celebrated with much expense; and they find their chief pleasure either in riotous debauchery or in sheer idleness. Knaves and liars, they cheat as much as they can in trade, and are also clever smugglers. Here, as elsewhere, these detestable people intermarry only among their own race. They speak a jargon of their own with a peculiar accent. The government most unaccountably tolerates the nuisance of their presence, and goes so far as to appropriate to their exclusive use two streets in the neighbourhood of the Campo de Santa Anna."

A little further on the traveller remarks,—

Any one who saw Rio de Janeiro only by day would come to the conclusion that the population consisted entirely of negroes. The respectable classes never go out except in the evening, unless compelled by some pressing circumstance or for the performance of religious duties; and it is in the evening that the ladies especially show themselves. During the day all remain indoors, and pass the time between their couches and their looking-glasses. The only places where a man can enjoy the society of the ladies are the theatres and the churches."

During the sail from Brazil to the Cape of Good Hope nothing occurred deserving special mention. On the 7th March the *Uranie* anchored in Table Bay. After a quarantine of three days, the travellers obtained permission to land, and were received with a hearty welcome by Governor Somerset. As soon as a place suitable for their reception had been found, the scientific instruments were brought on shore, and the usual experiments were made with the pendulum, and the variations of the magnetic needle observed.

MM. Quoy and Gaimard, the naturalists, in company with several officers of the staff, made scientific excursions to Table Mountain and to the famous vineyards of Constantia. M. Gaimard observes, "The vines that we rode amongst are in the midst of alleys of oak and of pine; and the vine-stems, planted at the distance of four feet from one another, are not supported by props. Every year the vines are pruned, and the earth about them, which is of a sandy nature, is turned up. We noticed here and there plenty of peaches, apricots, apples, pears, citrons, as well as small plots cultivated as kitchen-gardens. On our return, M. Colyn insisted on our tasting the several sorts of wine which he produces,—Constantia properly so-called, both red and white, Pontac, Pierre, and Frontignac. The wine produced in other localities, which is called *Cape wine par excellence*, is manufactured from a muscatel grape of a dark straw colour, which seemed to me in flavour preferable to the grape of Provence. We have just said that there are two sorts of Constantia, the red and the white; they are both produced from muscatel grapes of different colours. People at the Cape generally prefer Frontignac to all the other wines produced from the vintages of Constantia."

Exactly a month after quitting the southern extremity of Africa, the *Uranie* cast anchor off Port Louis in the Isle of France, which, since the Treaties of 1815, has been in the hands of the English. The necessity for careening the ship, that it might be thoroughly examined, and the copper sheathing repaired, led to a much longer stay in this port than Freycinet had calculated upon; but our travellers found no cause to regret the delay, for the society of Port Louis fully sustained its old reputation for generous hospitality. The time passed quickly in excursions, receptions, dinners, balls, horse-races, and all sorts of festivities. It was, therefore, not without some regret that the French guests bade adieu to a place where they had been received with so much kindness both by their old compatriots and by those who had so lately been their bitter enemies.

The stay of the *Uranie* at the Isle of France had not, however, been sufficiently long to allow Freycinet to investigate many subjects of much interest, but this omission was remedied by the polite readiness shown by some of the leading residents in supplying him with valuable papers on the agriculture of the island, its commerce, its financial position, the industrial pursuits, and the social condition of the people, the correct appreciation of which demanded a more careful and minute examination than a mere passing traveller could possibly give to them. Since the island had come under English administration, it appeared that a number of new roads had been planned out, and a policy of reform had supplanted a benumbing system of routine fatal to all activity and progress.

Bourbon was the next place touched at by the *Uranie*, where the supplies of which the travellers stood in need were to be procured from the government stores. She cast anchor off St. Denis on the 19th July, 1818, remaining in the roadstead of St. Paul until the 2nd August, when she set sail for the Bay of Sharks, on the western shores of Australia. There is little of interest to be noted in connexion with the stay at Bourbon beyond the steady increase of the population and of trade which had taken place during the century preceding the arrival of the French expedition in 1717. According to Gentil de Barbinais, there were living in the island only 900 free people, amongst whom were no more than six white families, and 1100 slaves. At the last census taken in 1817, these numbers had risen to 14,790 whites, 4342 free blacks, 49,759 slaves, making a total of 68,898 inhabitants. This large and rapid increase must be attributed partly to the salubrity of the climate, but chiefly to the freedom of trade, of which the island had for some time enjoyed the advantage.

After a fortunate voyage of forty days, the *Uranie* cast anchor at the entrance of the Bay of Sharks on the 12th September. A party was at once despatched to Dirk Hartog, in order to determine the latitude and longitude of Cape Levaillant, and to bring on board the corvette a certain metal plate which had been left there by the Dutch at a remote period, and had been seen by Freycinet in 1801. Whilst this party were away, the two alembics were set to work to distil sea-water, which was effected so successfully that as long as the vessel stayed there, no other water was drunk but that obtained by this process, and all on board were satisfied with it.

On landing, the party sent to Dirk Hartog, got a view of the natives, who were armed with javelins and clubs, but had not a vestige of clothing. They, however, refused to have any close communications with the white strangers, keeping themselves at a respectful distance, and not handling any of the presents offered them without a previous careful inspection.

Although the Bay of Sharks had been minutely explored at the time of the expedition under Baudin, there still remained a hydrographical gap to be filled up on the eastern side of Hamelin Bay. Accordingly Duperrey proceeded there to complete the survey of that part of the coast. At the same time Gaimard, the naturalist, not disposed to rest satisfied with the interviews which as yet he had been able to obtain with the natives of the country, whom the sound of the fire-arms had summarily dispersed, decided upon penetrating into the interior, to gain some information respecting their mode of life. His companion and himself lost their way, as also did Riche in 1792 upon Nuyt's Land, where for three days they underwent severe sufferings from thirst, not being able to find a single rivulet or spring in the country.

The Expedition were well pleased when the inhospitable shores of Endracht disappeared from view. They had a pleasant passage in lovely weather, and over an unruffled sea, to the island of Timor, where on the 9th October the *Uranie* cast anchor in the roadstead of Coupang, and the travellers met with a cordial reception from the Portuguese authorities. But they found that the prosperity which had made the colony an object of wonder and admiration to the French travellers who had visited it with Baudin, had passed away. The Rajah of Amanoubang, the district where the sandal-tree grows in such abundance, who was formerly a tributary prince, was carrying on war to gain independence. The hostilities which were proceeding were not only detrimental to the interests of the colony, but also made it very difficult for Freycinet to purchase the commodities of which he stood in need. Some of the staff set off to pay a visit to the Rajah Peters de Banacassi, whose residence was not more than three-quarters of a league from Coupang. Peters, then eighty years of age, must have been a remarkably fine man. He gave them an audience surrounded by his attendants, who treated him with profound respect, and among whom were conspicuous several warriors of gigantic stature. The dwelling that served for the royal palace was rudely constructed, yet the French travellers saw with lively surprise that articles of luxury were plentiful, and they observed also some muskets of good manufacture and great value.

Notwithstanding the excessive heat of the climate, the thermometer rising in the open air to 45°, and in the shade to 33°, and even to 35°, the commander and his officers carried on with unremitting zeal the observations and surveys which it was the object of the Expedition to make. A few fell victims to their own imprudence, for in defiance of the earnest warnings of Freycinet, some of the young officers and the seamen chose to sally forth in the middle of the day, and with the view of fortifying themselves against the injurious effects of their dangerous freak, drank and ate plentifully of cold water and sour fruits. The result was that in a short time five of the most imprudent were confined to their hammocks with dysentery. This necessitated a departure from Timor; so the *Uranie* weighed anchor and set sail on the 23rd October.

At first the corvette sailed rapidly along the north coast of Timor, for the purpose of making a survey, but when she had reached the narrowest part of the Channel of Ombay, she encountered such violent currents that—the winds being slight and contrary—it was only with great difficulty she was able to regain the course which she had lost during the calm. No less than nineteen days were wasted in this trying situation; though certain of the officers took advantage of the delay to land on the nearest point of the island of Ombay, where the coast had a very inviting appearance. They went on shore near a village called Bitouka, and advanced to meet a body of the natives, armed with shields and cuirasses made of buffalo-skin, and carrying bows, arrows, and daggers. Savages though they were, they had quite the air of warriors, and were not at all afraid of fire-arms; on the contrary, they argued that the loading of the gun caused loss of time, for while that operation was going on, they could fire off a great number of arrows.

Gaimard writes, "The points of the arrows were of hard wood, or of bone, and some of iron. The arrows themselves, displayed fan-wise, were fastened on the left side of the warrior to the belt of his sword or dagger. Most of these people wore bundles of palm-leaves, slit so as to allow red or black coloured strips of the same to be passed through to hold them together, which were attached to the belt or the right thigh. The rustling sound produced with every movement of the wearers of this singular ornament, increased by knocking against the cuirass or the buckler, with the addition of the tinkling of little bells, which also formed part of the warrior's equipment, altogether made such a jumble of discordant sounds that we could not refrain from laughing. Far from taking offence, our Ombayan friends joined heartily in our merriment. M. Arago[1] greatly excited their astonishment by performing some sleight-of-hand tricks. We then took our way straight to the village of Bitouka, which was situated on a rising ground. In passing one of their cottages we happened to see about a score of human jawbones suspended from the roof, and anxious to get possession of one or two, I offered the most valuable articles I had about me in exchange. The answer was, 'palami,' they are sacred. We ascertained afterwards that these were the jawbones of their enemies, preserved as trophies of victory."

[1] Jacques Arago, brother of the illustrious astronomer.

Warriors of Ombay and Guebeh.
(Fac-simile of early engraving.)

This excursion derived greater interest from the circumstance of the island of Ombay having been up to that time rarely visited by Europeans; and the few vessels that had effected any landing brought mournful accounts of the warlike and ferocious temper of the natives, and even in some instances of their cannibal propensities. Thus in 1802 the merchant-ship *Rose* had her small boat carried off, and the crew were detained as prisoners by the savages. Ten years later, the captain of the ship *Inacho*, who landed by himself, received several arrow wounds. Again, in 1817, an English frigate sent the cutter ashore for the purpose of getting wood, when a scrimmage took place between the crew and the natives, which ended in the former being killed and eaten. The day after, an armed sloop was despatched in quest of the missing crew; but nothing was found save some fragments of the cutter and the bloody remains of the unfortunate men.

In view of these facts the French travellers must be congratulated on having escaped being entrapped by the savage cannibals, which would undoubtedly have been attempted had the *Uranie* stayed long enough at Ombay.

On the 17th of November the anchor was let go at Dili.

After the customary interchange of compliments with the Portuguese governor, Freycinet made known the requirements of the expedition, and received a friendly assurance that the necessary provisions should be instantly forthcoming. The reception given to all the members of the expedition was both hearty and liberal, and when Freycinet took his leave, the governor, wishing that he should carry away some souvenir of his visit, presented him with two boys and two girls, of the ages of six and seven, natives of Failacor, a kingdom in the interior of Timor. To insure the acceptance of this present, the governor, D. José Pinto Alcofarado d'Azevado e Souza, stated that the race to which the children belonged was quite unknown in Europe. In spite of all the strong and conclusive reasons that Freycinet gave to explain why he felt compelled to decline the present, he was obliged to take charge of one of the little boys, who subsequently received the name of Joseph Antonio in baptism, but when sixteen years old died of some scrofulous disease at Paris.

On a first examination it would appear that the population of Timor belonged altogether to the Asiatic race; but so far as any reliance can be placed upon somewhat extended researches, there is reason to think that in the unfrequented mountains in the centre of the island there exists a race of negroes with woolly hair, and savage manners, of the type of the indigenous races of New Guinea and New Ireland, whom one is led to consider the primitive population. This line of research, commenced at the close of the eighteenth century by an Englishman of the name of Crawford, has been in our time carried forward with striking results by the labours of the learned Doctors Broca and E. Hamy, to the latter of whom the reading public are indebted for the pleasing and instructive papers on primitive populations which have appeared in *Nature* and in the journals of the Royal Geographical Society.

After leaving Timor the *Uranie* proceeded towards the Strait of Bourou, and in passing between the islands of Wetter and Roma got sight of the picturesque island of Gasses, clothed in the brightest and thickest verdure imaginable. The corvette was then drifted by currents almost as far as the island of Pisang, near which she fell in with three dhows, manned by natives of the island of Gueby. These people have an olive complexion, broad flat noses, and thick lips; some are strong, looking robust and athletic, others are slender and weakly in appearance; and others, again, thickset and repulsive- looking. The only clothing worn by the majority at this time was a pair of drawers fastened with a handkerchief round the waist.

A landing was effected on the little island of Pisang. It was found to be of volcanic origin, and the soil, formed from the decomposition of trachytic lava, was evidently very fertile. From Pisang the corvette made her way among islands, till then scarcely known, to Rawak, where she cast anchor at noon on the 16th of December. This island, though small, is inhabited; but though our navigators were often visited by the natives of Waigiou, opportunities for studying this species of the human family have been rare. Moreover, it ought to be mentioned that through ignorance of the language of the indigenous tribes, and the difficulty of making them understand through the medium of Malayan, of which they know only a few words, even those few opportunities have not been turned to much account. As soon as a suitable position was found, the instruments were set up, and the usual physical and astronomical observations were made in conjunction with geographical researches.

Rawak hut on piles.
(Fac-simile of early engraving.)

The islands which Freycinet calls the islands of the Papuans are Rawak, Boni,
Waigiou, and Manouran, which are situated almost immediately below the

equator. The largest of these, Waigiou, is not less than seventy-two miles from one side to the other; the low shorage consists mainly of swamp and morass, while the banks, which run up steeply, are surrounded by coral reefs, and are full of small caves hollowed out by the waves. All the islets are clothed with vegetation of surprising beauty. They abound with magnificent trees, amongst which the "Barringtonia" may be recognized, with its voluminous trunk always leaning towards the sea, allowing the tips of the branches to touch the water; the "scoevola lobelia," fig-trees, mangroves, the casuarinæ, with their straight and slender stems shooting up to the height of forty feet, the rima, the takanahaka, with its trunk more than twenty feet in circumference; the cynometer, belonging to the family of leguminous plants, bright from its topmost to its lowest branches with pale red flowers and golden fruits; and besides these rarer trees, palms, nutmeg-trees, roseapple-trees, banana-trees, flourish in the low and moist ground.

The luxuriant vegetation of the Papuan Islands.

The fauna, however, has not attained to the same exceptionally fine development as the flora. At Rawak the phalanger and the sheepdog in a wild state were the only quadrupeds met with. In Waigiou, the boar called barberossa, and a diminutive of the same race were found. But as to the feathered tribe, they were not so numerous as one might have supposed; the plants yielding grain necessary for the sustenance of birds not being able to thrive in the dense shade of the forests. Hornbills are here met with, whose wings, furnished with long feathers separated at the tips, make a very loud noise when they fly; great quantities of parrots, kingfishers, turtle-doves, piping-crows, brown hawks, crested pigeons, and possibly also birds of paradise, though the travellers did not see any specimens.

The Papuans themselves are positively repulsively ugly. To quote the words of Odet-Pellion, "a flat skull, a facial angle of 75°, a large mouth, eyes small and sunken, a thick nose, flat at the end and pressed down on the upper lip, a scanty beard, a peculiarity of the people of those regions already noticed, shoulders of a moderate size, a prominent belly, and slight lower limbs; these are the chief characteristics of the Papuans. Their hair both in its nature and mode of arrangement varies a good deal. Most commonly it is dressed with great pains into a matted structure not less than eight inches in height; composed of a mass of soft downy hair curling naturally; or it is frizzed up, till it positively bristles, and with the assistance of a coating of grease, is plastered round the skull in the shape of a globe. A long wooden comb of six or seven teeth is also often stuck in, not so much to aid in keeping the mass together as to give a finishing touch of ornament."

These unfortunate people are afflicted with the terrible scourge of leprosy, which is so prevalent that at least a tenth part of the population are infested with the disease. The cause of this dreadful malady must be sought in the insalubrity of the climate, the miasma from the marshes, which are overflowed with sea-water every flood tide, the neighbourhood of the burial- places, which are badly kept, and perhaps also to the consumption of shell- fish which these natives devour greedily.

All the houses, whether inland or on the coast, are built on piles. Many of these dwellings are erected in places extremely difficult of access. They are made by thrusting stakes into the earth, to which transverse beams are fastened with ropes made of fibre, and on these a flooring is laid of palm- leaves, trimmed and strongly intertwined one with another. These leaves, made to lap over in an artistic fashion, are also used for the roof of the house, which has only one door. Should the dwellings be built over the water, communication is carried on between them and the shore by means of a kind of bridge resting upon trestles, the movable flooring of which can be quickly taken up. Every house is also surrounded by a kind of balcony furnished with a balustrade.

The travellers could not obtain any information as to the friendly disposition of these natives. Whether the whole tribe consists of large communities united under one chief or several, whether each community obeys only its own proper head, whether the population is numerous or not, are all points which could not be ascertained. The name by which they call themselves is Alfourous. They appeared to talk in several distinct dialects, which differ remarkably from Papuan or Malay.

The inhabitants of this group seem to be a very industrious race. They manufacture all sorts of fishing apparatus very cleverly; they are expert in finding their way through the forests; they know how to prepare the pith of the sago-plant, and to make ovens for the cooking of the sago; they can turn pottery ware, weave mats, carpets, baskets, and can also carve idols and figures. In the harbour of Boni on the coast of Waigiou, MM. Quoy and Gaimard noticed a statue moulded in white clay, under a sort of canopy close to a tomb. It represented a man standing upright, of the natural height, with his hands raised towards heaven. The head was of wood, with the cheeks and eyes inlaid with small pieces of white shell.

On the 6th of January, 1819, having taken in supplies at Rawak, the *Uranie* proceeded on her voyage, and soon came in sight of the Ayou islands, mere sand-banks surrounded by breakers, of which few geographical details had been known up to that time. There was much to be done in the way of accurate survey, but unfortunately the hydrographers were sorely hindered in their work by the fever which they and some forty of the crew had contracted at Rawak. Sailing on, the Anchoret Islands came in sight on the 12th of February, and on the day following the Amirantes, but the *Uranie* did not attempt to make for the land. Shortly after passing the Amirantes, the corvette sighted St. Bartholomew, which the inhabitants call Poulousouk. It belongs to the Caroline archipelago. A busy trade, always attended with much uproar, was soon set on foot with the indigenous people, who resisted all persuasion to come on board, conducting all their transactions, nevertheless, with admirable good faith, in no instance showing any dishonest tendencies. One after another Poulouhat, Alet, Tamatam, Allap, Tanadik, all islands belonging to this archipelago, passed before the admiring gaze of the French navigators. At length, on the 17th of March, 1819, just eighteen months from the time of quitting France, Freycinet got sight of the Marianne Islands, and cast anchor in the roads of Umata on the coast of Guam. Just as the officers of the expedition were ready to go on shore, the governor of the island, D. Medinilla y Pineda, accompanied by his lieutenant, Major D. Luis de Torrès, came on board to bid them welcome. These gentlemen showed a polite anxiety to learn what the explorers stood in need of, and engaged that all their wants should be supplied with the least possible delay.

No time was lost in looking for a place suited for conversion into a temporary hospital, and one being found, the sick on board, to the number of twenty, were removed to it for treatment the very next day.

A dinner to the staff of the expedition was given by the governor, and all the officers assembled in his house at the appointed hour. They found a table covered with light cakes and fruits, in the midst of which were two bowls of hot punch. Some surprise escaped the guests, in private remarks to one another, at this singular kind of banquet. Could it be a fast-day? Why did no one sit down? But as there was no interpreter to clear up these points, and as it would have been unbecoming to ask for an explanation, they kept their difficulties for solution among themselves, and paid attention to the good things before them. Soon a fresh surprise came; the table was cleared and covered with various sorts of prepared dishes—in short, a substantial and sumptuous dinner was served. The collation which had been taken at the commencement, called in the language of the country "Refresco," had been intended only to whet the appetites of the guests for what was to follow.

After this, luxurious dinners became quite the rage at Guam. Two days subsequent to the governor's banquet, the officers found themselves at a dinner-party of fifty guests, where no less than forty-four separate dishes were served at each of the three courses of which the dinner consisted. Freycinet, from information he had received, relates that "this dinner cost the lives of two oxen and three fat pigs, to say nothing of poultry, game, and fish. Such a slaughter, I should think, has not been known since the marriage-feast of Gamache. No doubt our host considered that persons who had undergone so many privations during a protracted voyage ought to be compensated with an unusually profuse entertainment. The dessert showed no falling off either in abundance or in variety; it was succeeded by tea, coffee, creams, liqueurs of every description; and as the 'Refresco' had been served as usual an hour previous to dinner, it will be admitted without question that at Guam the most intrepid gourmand could find no other cause for disappointment but the limited capacity of the human stomach."

However, the objects of the mission were not interfered with by all this dining and festivity. Natural history excursions, magnetical observations, the geographical survey of the island of Guam, entrusted to Duperrey, were all being pushed forward simultaneously. But in the meantime the corvette had got to moorings in the deep water off the port of St. Louis, while the chief of the Staff, as well as the sick, were housed at Agagna, the capital of the island and the seat of government. At that place, in honour of the French visitors, cock-fights took place, a kind of sport very popular in all the Spanish possessions in Oceania; dances also were given, the figures in which, it was said, contained allusions to events in the history of Mexico. The dancers, students of the Agagna college, were dressed in rich silks, imported a long time previously by the Jesuits from New Spain. Then came combats with sticks in which the Carolins took part; which again were succeeded, almost uninterruptedly by other amusements. But what Freycinet considered of most value was the mass of information concerning the customs and manners of the former inhabitants of the islands, which he obtained through Major D. Luis Torrès; who, himself born in the country, had made a constant study of this subject. Of this interesting information use will be made when the subject is presently resumed, but first some notice must be taken of an excursion to the islands Rota and Tinian, the latter of which had already become known to us through the narratives of former travellers.

A performer of the dances of Montezuma.
(Fac-simile of early engraving.)

On the 22nd April a small fleet of eight proas conveyed MM. Berard, Gaudichaud, and Jacques Arago to Rota, where their arrival occasioned great surprise and alarm, explained by the fact that a report had gained currency in the island that the corvette was manned with rebels from America.

Beyond Rota the proas reached Tinian, where the arid plains recalled to the travellers the desolate coasts of the land of Endracht, testifying to the considerable changes that must have taken place there since the time when Lord Anson described the place as a terrestrial Paradise.

The Marianne archipelago was discovered by Magellan on the 6th March, 1521, and at first received the name of *Islas de las velas latinas*, the Isles of the lateen sails, but subsequently that of the *Ladrones*, or the Robbers. If one may trust Pigafetta, the illustrious admiral saw no islands but Tinian, Saypan, and Agoignan. Five years later they were visited by the Spaniard Loyasa, whose cordial reception was quite a contrast to that of Magellan; and in 1565 the islands were declared to be Spanish territory by Miguel Lopez de Legaspi. It was not, however, until 1669 that they were colonized and evangelized by Father Sanvitores. It will be understood that we should not follow Freycinet's narrative of past events in the history of this archipelago, were it not that the manuscripts and works of every kind which he was permitted to consult enabled him to treat the subject *de novo*, and throw upon it the light of real knowledge.

The admiration, still lingering in the minds of the travellers, which had been aroused by the incredible fertility of the Papuan Islands and the Moluccas was no doubt calculated to weaken the impression produced by any of the Marianne Islands. The forests of Guam, though well stocked, did not present the gigantic appearance common to forest scenery in the tropics. They extended over a large part of the island, yet there were also immense spaces devoted to pasturage, where not a breadfruit-tree nor a cocoa-nut palm was to be seen. In the depths of the forests, moreover, the conquerors of the islands had created artificial glades, in order that the herds of horned cattle which they had introduced might find food and also enjoy shelter from the sun.

Agoignan, an island with a very rocky coast, presented from a distance an arid and barren appearance, but is in reality thickly clothed with trees even to the summit of its highest mountains.

Rota is a regular jungle, an almost impenetrable mass of brushwood, above which rise thickets of rimas, tamarind, fig, and palm trees. Tinian, too, presents anything but an agreeable appearance. The French explorers altogether missed the charming scenes described in such glowing colours by their predecessors, but the appearance of the soil, and the immense number of dead trees, led them to the conclusion that old accounts were not altogether exaggerated, especially as the southern portion of the island is now rendered quite inaccessible by its dense forests.

At the time of Freycinet's visit the population of these islands was of a very mixed character, the aborigines being quite in the minority. The more highly born of the natives were formerly bigger, stronger, and better made than Europeans, but the race is degenerating, and the primitive type in its purity is now only to be met with in Rota.

Capital swimmers and divers, able to walk immense distances without fatigue, every man of them had to prove his proficiency in these exercises on his marriage; but although this proficiency has been in some measure kept up, the leading characteristic of the people of the Marianne group is idleness, or perhaps to be more strictly accurate, indifference.

Marriages are contracted at a very early age, the bridegroom being generally between fifteen and eighteen, the bride between twelve and fifteen. A numerous progeny is the result of these unions; instances being on record of twenty-two children born of one mother.

Not only do the people of Guam suffer from many diseases, such as lung complaints, smallpox, &c., introduced by Europeans; but also from some which seem to be endemic, or in any case to have assumed a type peculiar to the place and altogether abnormal. Such are elephantiasis and leprosy, three varieties of which are met with at Guam, differing from each other alike in their symptoms and their effects.

Before the conquest, the people of the Mariannes lived on the fruit of the rima or bread-tree, rice, sago, and other farinaceous plants. Their mode of cooking these articles was extremely simple, though not so much so as their style of dress, for they went about in a state of nature, unrelieved even by the traditional fig-leaf.

At the present time children still wear no clothing till they are about ten years old. Alluding to this peculiar custom, Captain Pages, writing at the close of last century, says, "I found myself near a house, in front of which an Indian girl, about eleven years old, was squatted on her heels in the full blaze of the sun, without a vestige of clothing on. Her chemise lay folded on the ground in front of her. When she saw me approaching, she got up quickly and put it on again. Although still far from decently clothed, for only her shoulders were covered by it, she now considered herself properly dressed, and stood before me quite unembarrassed."

Judging from the remains nearly everywhere to be met with, such as the ruins of dwellings originally supported by masonry pillars, it is plain that the population was formerly considerable. The earliest traveller who has made any reference to this subject is Lord Anson. He has given a somewhat fanciful description, which, however, the explorers in the *Uranie* were able to corroborate, as will be seen from the following extract.

"The description found in the narrative of Lord Anson's voyage is correct; but the ruins and the branches of the trees that have in some way twined themselves about the masonry pillars, wear now a very different aspect from what they did in his time. The sharp edges of the pillars have got rubbed away, and the half-globes that surmounted them have no longer their former roundness."

Ruins of ancient pillars at Tinian.
(Fac-simile of early engraving.)

Of the structures of more recent date only a sixth part are of stone. At Agagna may be counted several buildings possessing some interest on account of their size, if not on that of their elegance, grandeur, or the fineness of their proportions. These are the College of St. John Lateran, the church, the clergy-house, the governor's palace, and the taverns.

Before the Spaniards established their sway in these islands, the natives were divided into three classes, the nobility, the inferior nobility, and the commonalty. These last, the Pariahs of the country, Freycinet remarks, though without citing his authority, were of a more diminutive stature than the other inhabitants. This difference of height is, however, scarcely a sufficient reason for pronouncing them to be of a different race from the other two classes; is it not more reasonable to conclude it to be the result of the degrading servitude to which they have been subjected? These plebeians could under no circumstances raise themselves to a higher class; and a seafaring life was forbidden to them. Each of the three castes had its own sorceresses and priestesses, or medicine-women, who each devoted her attention to the treatment of some one disorder; only no reason, however, for crediting them with any special skill in its cure.

The business of canoe-building was monopolized by the nobles; who, however, allowed the inferior nobles to assist in their construction. The making of canoes was to them a work of the utmost importance, and the nobles maintained it as one of their most valuable privileges. The language spoken in the Philippine group, though it has some affinity with the Malay and Tagala dialects, has all the same a distinctive character of its own. Freycinet's narrative also contains much information on the extremely singular customs of the former population of the Mariannes, which are beyond our province, though well worthy of the attention of the philosopher and historian.

The *Uranie* had been now more than two months at anchor. It was full time to resume the work of exploration. Freycinet and his staff, therefore, devoted the few remaining days of their stay to the task of paying farewell visits and expressing their gratitude for the hearty kindness which had been so profusely shown to them. The governor, however, not only declined to admit his claim to thanks from the French travellers for the hospitable attentions heaped upon them for upwards of two months; but also refused to accept any payment for the supplies which had been furnished for the refitting of the corvette. He even went so far as to write a letter of apology for the scantiness of the provisions, the result of the drought which had desolated Guam for the previous six months, and which had prevented him from doing things as he could have wished. The final farewell took place off Agagna. "It was impossible," says Freycinet, "to take leave of the amiable man, who had loaded us with so many proofs of his friendly disposition, without being deeply affected. I was too much moved to be able to find expression for the feelings with which my heart was filled; but the tears which filled my eyes must have been to him a surer evidence than any words could have been of my gratitude and my regret."

From the 5th to the 16th June the *Uranie* occupied in an exploring cruise round the north of the Marianne Islands, in the course of which were made the observations of which the substance has been given above. The commander, wishing to make a quick passage to the Sandwich Islands, then took advantage of a breeze to gain a higher latitude, where he hoped to meet with favourable winds. But as the explorers penetrated further and further into this part of the Pacific Ocean, cold and dense fogs wrapped them round, permeating the whole vessel with damp, equally unpleasant and injurious to health. However, the crew suffered no worse inconvenience than slight colds; in fact, the change had rather a bracing effect than otherwise on men now for some time accustomed to the enervating heat of the tropics.

On the 6th August the south point of Hawaï was doubled, and Freycinet made for the western side of the island, where he hoped to find a safe and convenient anchorage. A dead calm prevailing, the first and second days were spent in opening relations with the natives. The women came off in crowds immediately on the arrival of the ship, with the view of carrying on their usual trade, but the commander laid an interdict on their coming on board.

The first piece of news given to the captain by one of the Areois[2] was that King Kamahamaha was dead, and that his young son Rio Rio had succeeded him. Taking advantage of a change of wind the *Uranie* sailed on to the Bay of Karakakoa, and Freycinet was about to send an officer in advance to take soundings, when a canoe put off from the shore, having on board the governor of the island, Prince Kouakini, otherwise John Adams,[3] who promised the captain that he would find boats suitable for the taking of the necessary supplies to the corvette. This young man, about nine and twenty years of age, almost a giant in stature, but well proportioned, surprised Freycinet by the extent of his information. On being informed that the corvette was on a voyage of discovery, he inquired, "Have you doubled Cape Horn or did you come round the Cape of Good Hope?" He then asked for the latest information about Napoleon, and wished to know whether it was true that the island of St. Helena had been swallowed up with all its inhabitants! A story he had evidently heard from some facetious whalemen, but had not entirely believed.

[2] See previous footnote.

[3] It was the custom for the chiefs in these parts to assume new names, often for the most trifling reasons.—*Trans.*

Kouakini next apprised Freycinet that though actual disturbances had not broken out on the death of Kamahamaha, yet that some of the chiefs having asserted claims to independence, the stability of the monarchy was in some danger. As a result the political situation was strained and the government was in some perplexity, a state of things which probably would soon terminate, especially if the commandant would consent to make some declaration in favour of the youthful sovereign. Freycinet landed with the prince, to pay him a return visit; and, on entering his house, was introduced to his wife, a very corpulent woman, who was lying on a European bedstead covered with matting. After this visit, the captain and his host went to visit the widows of Kamahamaha, the prince's sisters, but not being able to see them, they proceeded to the yards and workshops of the deceased king. Here were four sheds sacred to the building of large war-canoes, and others containing European boats. Farther on were seen wood for building purposes, bars of copper, quantities of fishing-nets, a forge, a cooper's workshop, and lastly, some cases belonging to the prime minister, Kraimokou, filled with all necessary appliances for navigation, such as compasses, sextants, thermometers, watches, and even a chronometer. Strangers were not allowed to inspect two other magazines in which were stored powder and other war-materials, strong liquors, iron, &c. All these places were for the present abandoned by the new sovereign, who held his court at Koaihai Bay.

Freycinet, on receiving an invitation from the king, made ready to visit him there, under the guidance of a native pilot who showed himself most attentive, and was very skilful in forecasting the weather. "The monarch," writes Freycinet, "was waiting for me on the beach, dressed in the full uniform of an English captain, and surrounded by the whole of his suite. In spite of the terrible barrenness of this side of the island, the spectacle of the grotesque assemblage of men and women was not without grandeur and beauty. The king himself stood in front with his principal officers a little distance behind him; some wearing splendid mantles made of red or yellow feathers, or of scarlet cloth; others in short tippets of the same kind, but in which the two glaring colours were relieved with black; a few had helmets on their heads. This striking picture was further diversified by a number of soldiers grouped here and there, and clad in various and strange costumes."

The sovereign now under notice was the same, who, with his young and charming wife, undertook at a later period a voyage to England, where they both died. Their remains were brought back to Hawaï by Captain Byron in the frigate *La Blonde*.

Freycinet seized this opportunity to repeat his request for supplies of fresh provisions, and the king promised that two days should not pass before his wishes should be fully complied with. However, although the good faith of the young monarch was above suspicion, the commander soon discovered that most of the chiefs had no intention of obeying their sovereign's orders.

Some little time after this, the principal officers of the staff went to pay a visit to the widows of Kamahamaha. The following amusing description of their lively reception is given by M. Quoy:—"A strange spectacle," he says, "met our view on our entrance into an apartment of narrow dimensions, where eight lumps of half naked humanity lay on the ground with their faces downwards. It was not an easy task to find space to lay ourselves down according to custom in the same manner. The attendants were constantly on the move, some carrying fans made of feathers to whisk away the flies; another a lighted pipe, which was passed from one prostrate figure to another, each taking a whiff or two, while the rest were engaged in shampooing the royal personages.... Conversation, it may readily be imagined, was not well maintained under these trying circumstances, and had it not been for some excellent watermelons which were handed to us, the tedium of the interview would have been insupportable."

Freycinet next went to pay a visit to the famous John Young, who had been for so long a time the faithful friend and sagacious adviser of King Kamahamaha. Although he was then old and in bad health, he was not the less able to supply Freycinet with some valuable information about the Sandwich Islands, where he had lived for thirty years, and in the history of which he had played a prominent part.

Kraimokou, the minister, during a visit which he was paying on board the *Uranie*, had caught sight of the Abbé de Quelen, the chaplain, whose costume puzzled him a good deal. As soon as he had learned that the strangely dressed person was a priest, he expressed to the commandant a desire to receive baptism. His mother, he said, had been admitted to that sacrament upon her deathbed, and she had obtained from him a promise to submit himself to the same ceremony as soon as he met with a convenient opportunity. Freycinet gave his consent, and endeavoured to make the proceeding as solemn as possible, all the more because Rio Rio requested permission to be present at it with all his suite. Every one behaved with the utmost decorum and reverence while the ceremony was taking place; but immediately on its close there was a general rush to the collation which the commandant had ordered to be prepared. It was wonderful to see how rapidly the bottles of wine and the flasks of rum and of brandy were emptied, and to witness the speedy disappearance of the viands with which the table had been covered. Fortunately the day was coming to a close, or Rio Rio and the majority of his officers and courtiers would not have been in a condition to reach the shore.

In spite of this, however, it was necessary to comply with his request for two additional bottles of brandy, that he might, as he said, drink the health of the commander and success to his voyage, a request which all his attendants felt bound in politeness to make likewise.

"It is not an over-statement," observes Freycinet, "to say that in the short space of two hours our distinguished guests drank and carried away what would have been sufficient to supply the wants of ten ordinary persons for three months." Several presents had been exchanged between the royal pair and the commander. Among those made by the young queen was a cloak of feathers, a kind of garment which had become exceedingly scarce in the Sandwich Islands.

Freycinet was about to set sail again, when he learnt from an American captain that a merchant-vessel was lying off the island of Miow, having a large quantity of biscuit and rice on board, which there was no doubt might be purchased. This information determined Freycinet to anchor first off Raheina, among other reasons, because it was there that Kraimokou had undertaken to deliver a number of pigs, which were required for the use of the crew. But the minister displayed signal bad faith in the transaction; he tendered miserably poor pigs, and demanded an extravagantly high price; so that it was necessary to have recourse to threats before the business could be satisfactorily arranged. In this matter Kraimokou was under the misguidance of an English runaway convict from Port Jackson, and most probably had the native been left to obey the promptings of his own nature he would have acted on this occasion with the good faith and the sense of honour which were his usual characteristics.

On reaching the island of Waihou, Freycinet dropped anchor off Honolulu. The hearty welcome he received from the European residents made him regret that he had not come here direct to begin with; for he was able without any delay to procure all the supplies which he had found so much difficulty in getting together at the two other islands. Boki, the governor of Waihou, received baptism from the chaplain of the *Uranie*. He was prompted apparently by no other motive than a wish to do as his brother had done, who had previously received this sacrament. He was far from having the air of intelligence common to the other natives of the various islands of the Sandwich group hitherto visited.

Many observations on these natives are made in the narrative of the expedition, which are too interesting to be passed over without a brief summary here. All navigators are agreed in considering that the class of chiefs belong to a race excelling the other inhabitants, both in intelligence and in stature. It is very unusual to find one who is less than six feet in height.

Obesity is very common, but chiefly among the women, who while still quite young often become enormously corpulent. The Sandwich type is strongly marked and distinct. Pretty women are numerous; but the blessing of length of days is seldom enjoyed. An old man of seventy is a rare phenomenon. This early decline and premature death must be ascribed to the persistent dissipation in which the people pass their lives.

On leaving the Sandwich Islands, Freycinet found it necessary to notice carefully the curves of the magnetic equator in low latitudes.[4] Accordingly, he crowded all sail in an easterly direction. On the 7th October the *Uranie* entered the southern hemisphere, and on the 19th of the same month the Dangerous Islands came in sight. To the eastward of the Navigators' archipelago, an island was discovered, not marked on the charts, which was named "Rose," after Madame Freycinet. This was the only actual discovery of the voyage.

[4] This refers to the line made up of the succession of points at which the magnetic needle ceases to indicate.—*Trans.*

The position of the islands of Pylstaart and Howe was next rectified, and on the 13th November the lights of Port Jackson, or Sydney, were at last sighted.

Freycinet had fully expected to find the town enlarged during the sixteen years that had passed since his last visit; but his astonishment was great indeed at the sight of a large and prosperous European city, set down in the midst of scenery which might almost be called wild. But as the travellers made excursions in various directions, fresh signs of the progress which the colony had made were forced on their attention. Fine roads carefully kept, bordered with the eucalyptus, styled by Pérou "the giant of the Australian forests," well constructed bridges, distances marked by milestones, proved the existence of a well organized local administration; whilst the charming cottages, the numerous herds of cattle, and the carefully cultivated fields, bore testimony to the industry and perseverance of the new colonists.

Governor Macquarie, and the principal authorities of the province vied with each other in showing attention to the French travellers, who, however, persisted in declining all but a single invitation, lest the work of the mission should not receive its fair share of attention. The entertainment given by the governor took place at his country house at Paramatta, whither the officers of the expedition proceeded by water, accompanied by a military band. Several of them also visited the little town of Liverpool, built in a pleasant situation on the banks of the river George. Excursions too were made to the little villages of Richmond and Windsor, which were growing up near Hawkesbury river. At the same time a party of the staff joined in a kangaroo hunt, and crossing the Blue Mountains penetrated the Bathurst settlement.

Through the friendly relations which Freycinet had established with the residents during his two visits, he was able to collect numerous interesting details respecting the Australian colony. Therefore the chapter that he devotes to New South Wales, recording the marvellous and rapid advance of this effort at colonization, excited a lively interest in France, where the development and growing prosperity of Australia were very imperfectly known. Freycinet's narrative was there quite a new revelation, well calculated to excite inquiry, and which had, moreover, the advantage of showing the exact condition of the colony so late as the year 1825.

The chain of mountains at some distance from the coast, known by the name of the Australian Alps, separates New South Wales from the interior of the Australian continent. For twenty-five years this chain formed a barrier against all communication with the country beyond; but now, thanks to the energy of Governor Macquarie, the barrier has been removed. A zigzag road has been cut in the rock, thus opening the way to the colonization of wide spreading plains watered by important rivers. The loftiest summits of this chain, nearly 10,000 feet in height, are covered with snow even in the middle of summer. Whilst the elevation of the principal peaks, Mount Exmouth, Mount Cunningham, and others was being taken, it was discovered that so far from Australia possessing only one large watercourse, the Swan River, it had several, the chief being Hawkesbury River, formed by the confluence of the Nepean, the Grose, and the Brisbane; the river Murray not being yet known. At the period under notice a commencement had been made in the working of coal-mines, slate quarries, layers of solid carbonate of iron, sandstone, chalk, porphyry and jasper; but the presence of gold, the metal that was to effect so rapid a development of the young colony, had not as yet been established.

The nature of the soil varies. On the sea-coast it is barren, able only to support the growth of a few stunted trees; but inland the traveller meets with fields clothed with a rich vegetation, vast pasturages in which here and there rise a few tall shrubs, and forests where giant trees entwined with an inextricable growth of underwood, defy all attempts to penetrate to their recesses.

An Australian farm near the Blue Mountains.
(Fac-simile of early engraving.)

One circumstance which much surprised travellers was the apparent homogeneity of race throughout the whole of this immense continent. Take the aborigines at the Bay of Sharks, or in the land of Endracht, or by the Swan

River, or at Port Jackson, and the same complexion, and the same kind of hair, the same features, the same physique, all prove indisputably that they have sprung from one common origin. Those dwelling by the rivers or on the sea coast subsist chiefly on shell or other fish, but those living in the interior trust to hunting for their food, and will eat indiscriminately the flesh of the opossum or the kangaroo, not rejecting even lizards, snakes, worms, or ants, the last named of which they manufacture into a sort of paste with the addition of their eggs and the roots of ferns. All over the continent the practice of the aborigines is to go completely naked; though they have no objection to put on any articles of European clothing that they can get possession of. It is said that in 1820 at Port Jackson there was a laughable caricature of the European style of dress to be seen in the person of an ancient negress who went about clothed in some pieces of an old woollen blanket, wearing on her head a bonnet of green silk. A few of the aborigines, however, make themselves cloaks of opossum or kangaroo skin, stitching the pieces together with the nerve-fibres of the cassowary; but this kind of garment is of rare occurrence.

Though their hair is smooth, they plaster it with grease and arrange it in curls. Then inserting in the middle a tuft of grass, they raise a strange and comical superstructure, surmounted by a few cockatoo feathers; or failing these, they fasten on, with the aid of a resinous gum, a few human teeth, or some bits of bone, a dog's tail, or one or two fish bones. Although the practice of tattooing is not much in favour among the natives of New Holland, some are occasionally to be seen who have succeeded by means of sharp shells in cutting symmetrical figures upon their skins. A more general custom is that of painting on their bodies monstrous designs in red and white colours which, on their dark skins, give them an almost diabolical aspect.

These savages formerly believed that after death they would take the form of children, and be transported to the clouds or to the summits of lofty trees, where, in a sort of aërial paradise, they would be regaled with plentiful repasts. But since the arrival of the Europeans their faith on this point has undergone some change, their present belief being, that metamorphosed into whites they will go to inhabit some far-off land. It is also an article of their creed that the whites themselves are no other than their own ancestors, who, having been killed in battle, have assumed the form of Europeans.

Native Australians.

The census of 1819—one of the strictest hitherto instituted—gives the number of the colonists at 25,425; this return, it must be understood, does not take in the soldiers. The women being very much in the minority, the mother-country had made efforts to remedy the inconvenience resulting from this great disparity of the sexes, by promoting the immigration of young women, who soon married and founded families of a higher tone of morality than that of the convicts.

Freycinet devotes a very long chapter in his narrative to all matters connected with political economy. The various soils and the crops suited to them; industrial pursuits; the breeding of cattle; farming economy; manufactures; foreign trade; means of communication; government;—all these subjects are treated comprehensively on the authority of documents then newly compiled, and with an ability that could scarcely have been expected from a man who had not given special attention to questions of this nature. He has, moreover, added a close inquiry into the regimen which the convicts were subjected to from the time of their arrival in the colony, the punishments they had to undergo, as also the encouragements and rewards which were readily granted to them, when earned by good behaviour. The chapter concludes with reflections full of learning and sound judgment on the probable development and future prosperity of the Australian colony.

After this long and fruitful stay in New Holland, the *Uranie* put to sea on the 25th December, 1819, and steered so as to pass to the south of New Zealand and Campbell Island, with the view of doubling Cape Horn. A few days afterwards ten fugitive convicts were discovered on board; but the corvette had left the shores of Australia too far behind to allow of their restoration. The coast of Tierra del Fuego was reached without anything worthy of special notice having occurred during a very prosperous voyage, with a prevailing west wind. On the 5th February, Cape Desolation was sighted. Having doubled Cape Horn without any difficulty, the *Uranie* let go her anchor in the Bay of Good Success, where the shores, lined with grand forest-trees and echoing to the sound of waterfalls, presented a scene totally different from the sterile desolation generally characterizing this quarter of the globe. No long stay was, however, made there; the corvette resuming her voyage, lost no time in entering the Strait of Le Maire, notwithstanding a dense haze. Here she met with a heavy swell, a strong gale, and a mist so thick that land, sea, and sky were confounded in one general obscurity. The rain and the heavy spray raised by the storm, and the coming on of night, made it necessary to put the *Uranie* under a close-reefed topsail and jib, under which pressure of sail she behaved splendidly. The only available course was to run before the wind, and the travellers had just begun to feel thankful for their good fortune in being driven by the storm far away from the land, when the cry was heard, "Land close ahead!"

All hearts sunk with despair; shipwreck and death seemed inevitable.

Freycinet alone, after a brief instant of hesitation, recovered his self-command. It was impossible that land could be ahead. He, therefore, kept on his northerly course, bearing a little east, and the correctness of his calculations was soon verified. On the next day but one the weather grew calmer; observations were taken, and as they proved the vessel to have run a great distance from the Bay of Good Success, the commander had to choose between a detention off the coast of South America, or off the Falkland Islands. The island of Conti, the Bay of Marville, and Cape Duras, were successively observed through the haze, whilst a favourable breeze speeded the corvette on her course to Berkeley Sound, fixed on as the best place for the next halt.

Mutual congratulations were already being exchanged on the happy termination of the dangerous struggle, and on the fortunate escape from any serious accident during so hazardous a trip. The sailors all rejoiced, to use the words of Byron, that—

But a severe trial was still in store for them!

On entering Berkeley Sound, every man was at his post, ready to let go the anchor. The look-outs were on the watch, men were stationed in the main-shrouds to heave the lead. Then first at twenty, after at eighteen fathoms, the presence of rocks was reported. The ship was now about half a league off shore, and Freycinet thought it prudent to put her off about two points. This precaution proved fatal, for the corvette suddenly struck violently on a hidden rock. As she struck, the soundings gave fifteen fathoms to starboard, and twelve to larboard. The reef against which the corvette had run, was, therefore, not so wide as the vessel itself; in fact, it was but the pointed summit of a rock.

The immediate rising of pieces of wood to the surface of the water at once gave reason for fears that the injury was serious. There was a rush to the pumps. Water was pouring into the hold. Freycinet had sent for a sail, and had it passed under the vessel in such a manner that the pressure of the water forcing it into the leak in a measure stopped it up. But it was of no avail. Although the whole ship's company, officers and sailors alike, worked at the pumps, no more could be done than just keep the water from gaining on the vessel. There was nothing for it but to run her ashore. This decision, painful as it was, had to be carried out, and it was indeed no easy task. On every side the land was girded with rocks, and only at the very bottom of the bay was there a strip of sandy beach favourable for running the ship aground. Meanwhile the wind had become contrary, night was approaching, the vessel was already half full of water. The distress of the commander can be imagined. But there was no alternative, so the vessel was stranded on Penguin Island.

"This effected," to quote Freycinet, "the men were so exhausted that it was necessary to cease further work of every kind, and to allow the crew an interval of rest, all the more indispensable on account of the hardships and dangers which our present disastrous situation must entail upon all. As for myself, repose was out of the question. Tormented by a thousand harassing reflections, I could scarcely credit my own existence. The sudden transition from a position where all things seemed to smile on me, to that in which I found myself at that moment, weighed on my spirits like a horrible nightmare. It was difficult to regain the composure necessary to face fairly the painful trial. All my companions had done their duty in the frightful accident, which had all but lost us our lives, and I am glad to be able to do justice to their admirable conduct.

"As soon as daylight revealed the nature of the country, a mournful gloomy look settled upon every countenance. Not a tree, not so much as a blade of grass was to be seen, not a sound was to be heard, and the silent desolation around reminded us of the Bay of Sharks."

But there was no time to be lost in vain lamentations. Was the sea to be allowed to swallow up the journals and observations, the precious results of so much labour and so many hardships?

All the papers were saved. The same good fortune did not, unfortunately, attend the collections. Several cases of specimens which were at the bottom of the hold were entirely lost; others were damaged by the sea water. The collections that sustained the chief injury were those of natural history, and the herbarium that had been put together with infinite trouble by Gaudichaud. The merino sheep, generously presented to the expedition by Mr. MacArthur, of Sydney, which it was hoped could be acclimatized in France, were brought on shore, as also were all the animals still alive.

A few tents were pitched, first for the sick, happily not very numerous, and then for the officers and the crew. The provisions and ammunition taken out of the ship were carefully deposited in a place where they would be sheltered from the inclemency of the weather. The alcoholic liquors were allowed to remain on board until the time arrived for quitting the scene of the shipwreck, and during the three months of the expedition's stay here, not a single theft of rum or of brandy came to light, although no one had anything to drink but pure water.

The efforts of the whole of the expedition were steadily applied to the task of trying to repair the main injuries sustained by the *Uranie*, with the exception of a few sailors told off to provide, by hunting and fishing, for the subsistence of the community. The lakes were frequented by numbers of sea-lions, geese, ducks, teal, and snipe, but it was no easy matter to procure, at one time, a sufficient quantity of these animals to serve for the food of the entire crew; at the same time, the expenditure of powder was necessarily considerable. As good luck would have it, gulls abounded in sufficient numbers to furnish a hundred and twenty men with food for four or five months, and these creatures were so stupid as to allow themselves to be knocked on the head with a stick. A few horses were also killed which had relapsed into a wild state since the departure of the colony founded by Bougainville.

By the 28th February the painful conclusion was come to, that with the slender resources available, it was impracticable to repair the damage done to the *Uranie*, especially as the original injury had been aggravated by the repeated shocks occasioned by thumping on the beach. "What was to be done?" Should the explorers calmly wait until some vessel chanced to put in at Berkeley Sound? This would be to leave the sailors with nothing to do, and this enforced idleness would open the door to disorder and insubordination. Would it not be better to build a small vessel out of the wreckage of the

Uranie? As it happened, there was a large sloop belonging to the ship; if the sides were raised, and a deck added, it might be possible to reach Monte Video, and there obtain the assistance of a vessel capable of bringing off in safety the members of the expedition and all the cargo worth preserving. This latter plan met with the approval of Freycinet, and a decision once come to, not a moment was wasted.

The sailors, animated with fresh energy, rapidly pushed on the work. Now was proved the sound judgment of the commander when manning the corvette at Toulon, in selecting sailors who were also skilled in some mechanical employment. Blacksmiths, sail-makers, rope-makers, sawyers, all worked with zeal at the different tasks assigned to them.

No doubts were entertained of the success of the voyage before them. Monte Video was separated from the Falkland Islands by but three hundred and fifty nautical miles, and with the winds prevailing in these latitudes at this time of year, this distance could be traversed in a few days by the *Esperance*—for so the transformed sloop was named. To provide, at the same time, against the possible contingency of the frail vessel failing to reach the Rio de la Plata, Freycinet determined to commence the construction of a schooner of a hundred tons, as soon as the sloop had taken her departure. Notwithstanding the incessant demands on the energies of all made by the arduous and varied tasks involved in reconstruction and refitting of the new vessel, the usual astronomical and physical observations, the natural history researches and the hydrographical surveys, were not neglected. No one could have imagined that the stay in Berkeley Sound was anything more than an ordinary halt for exploring purposes.

At last the sloop was finished and safely launched. The instructions for Captain Duperrey, appointed to take command, were all drawn up; the crew was selected; the provisions were on board; in two days the adventurers were to sail, when on the 19th March, 1820, the cry was raised, "A sail! a sail!" A sloop under full sail was seen entering the bay.

A cannon was fired several times to attract attention, and in a short time the master of the new arrival was on shore. In a few words Freycinet explained to him the misadventure which had led to the residence of the explorers upon this desolate coast. The master stated in reply that he was under the orders of the captain of an American ship, the *General Knox*, engaged in the seal- fishery at West Island, to the west of the Falklands. An officer was at once deputed to go and ascertain from the captain what succour he could render to the French travellers. The result of the interview was a demand for 135,750 francs for the conveyance of the shipwrecked strangers to Rio—an unworthy advantage to take of the necessities of the unfortunate. To such a bargain the

French officer was unwilling to agree without the consent of his commander; so he begged the American captain to sail for Berkeley Sound. While these negotiations were going on, however, another ship, the *Mercury*, under command of Captain Galvin, had made its appearance in the bay. The *Mercury* was bound from Buenos Ayres to Valparaiso with cannon, but just before doubling Cape Horn she had sprung a leak, and was compelled to put in at the Falkland Islands to make the necessary repairs. It was a fortunate incident for the Frenchmen, who knew they could turn to account the competition which must result from the arrival of two ships.

The *Mercury* at anchor in Berkeley Sound.

Freycinet at once made an offer to Captain Galvin to repair the damage the *Mercury* had sustained, with the materials and the labour at his command, asking in return for this service a free passage for himself and his companions to Rio de Janeiro.

At the end of fifteen days the repairs of the *Mercury* were completed. While they were going on, the negotiation with the *General Knox* was terminated by a positive refusal on the part of Freycinet to agree to the extravagant terms proposed by the American captain. It took several days to come to a settlement with Captain Galvin, who finally made the following agreement.

1. Captain Galvin engaged to convey to Rio the wrecked persons, their papers, collections, and instruments, as well as all the cargo saved out of the *Uranie* that could be got on board.

2. Freycinet and his people were during the passage to subsist entirely on the provisions set apart for them.

3. That the captain was to receive the sum of 97,740 francs within ten days of their arrival at Rio. By the acceptance of these truly extortionate conditions a bargain, which had cost much dispute, was finally settled.

Before leaving the Falklands, however, the naturalist, Gaudichaud, planted its destitute shores with several sorts of vegetables, which he thought likely to be of service to future voyagers who might be detained there.

A few particulars regarding this archipelago will not be without interest. The group, lying between 50° 57', and 52° 45' S. latitude, and 60° 4', 63° 48' west of the meridian of Paris, consists of several islets and two principal islands, named Conti and Maidenland. Berkeley Sound, situated in the extreme east of the Conti Island, is a wide opening, rather deep than extensive, with a shelving rocky coast. The temperature of the islands is milder than one would expect from the high latitude. Snow does not fall in any great quantity, and does not remain even on the summits of the highest hills longer than for about two months. The streams are never frozen, and the lakes and marshes are never covered with ice hard enough to bear the weight of a man, for more than twenty-four hours consecutively. From the observations of Weddell, who visited these parts between 1822 and 1824, the temperature must have risen considerably during the last forty years in consequence of a change in the direction taken by the icebergs which melt away in the mid-Atlantic. M. Quoy, the naturalist, judging from the shallowness of the sea between the Falkland Islands and South America, as well as the resemblance of their grassy plains to the pampas of Buenos Ayres, is of opinion that they once formed part of the continent. These plains are low, marshy, covered with tall grass and shrubs, and are inundated in the winter. Peat is abundant and makes excellent fuel. The character of the soil has proved an obstacle to the growth of the trees which Bougainville endeavoured to acclimatize, of which scarce a vestige remained at the time of Freycinet's visit. The plant which reaches the greatest height and grows most plentifully is a species of sword-grass, excellent food for cattle, and serving also as a place of shelter to numbers of seals and multitudes of gulls. It is this high grass which sailors have taken from a distance for bushes. The only vegetables growing on these islands of any use to man are celery, scurvy-grass, watercress, dandelion, raspberries, sorrel, and pimpernel.

Both French and Spanish colonists had at different times imported into these islands oxen, horses, and pigs, which had multiplied to a singular extent in the island of Conti; but the persistent hunting of them by the crews of the whaling ships must tend to considerably reduce their numbers. The only quadruped indigenous to the Falkland Islands is the Antarctic dog, the muzzle of which strikingly resembles that of the fox. It has therefore had the name dog-fox, or wolf-fox, given to it by whalers. These animals are so fierce that they rushed into the water to attack Byron's sailors. They, however, find rabbits enough, whose reproductive powers are limitless, to satisfy them; but the seals, which the dogs attack without any fear, manage to escape from them.

The *Mercury* set sail on the 28th of April, 1821, to convey Freycinet and his crew to the port of Rio de Janeiro. But one point Captain Galvin had failed to take into his reckoning,—his ship, equipped under the flag of the Independent State of Buenos Ayres, then at war with the Portuguese, would be seized on entering the harbour of Rio, and he himself with all his crew would be made prisoners. On this he endeavoured to make Freycinet cancel the engagement between them, hoping to prevail on him to land at Monte Video. But as Freycinet would not agree to this proposal on any ground, a new contract had to be substituted for the original one. According to the latter arrangement Freycinet became proprietor of the *Mercury* on behalf of the French navy by payment of the sum stipulated under the first contract. The ship was renamed the *Physicienne*, and reached Monte Video on the 8th of May, where the command was taken over by Freycinet. The stay at Monte Video was made use of for arming the vessel, arranging its trim, repairing the rigging, taking on board the supply of water and provisions requisite for the trip to Rio de Janeiro; before reaching which port, however, several serious defects in the ship had been discovered. The appearance of the *Physicienne* was so distinctly mercantile that on entering the port of Rio, though the flag of a man-of-war was flying at the masthead, the customs officers were deceived and proposed to inspect her as a merchant-vessel. Extensive repairs were absolutely necessary, and the making of them compelled Freycinet to remain at Rio until the 18th of September. He was then able to take his departure direct for France; and on the 13th of November, 1820, he cast anchor in the port of Havre, after an absence of three years and two months, during which time he had sailed over 18,862 nautical miles.

A few days after his return, Freycinet proceeded to Paris, suffering from a severe illness, and forwarded to the secretary of the Academy of Sciences the scientific records of the voyage, which made no less than thirty-one quarto volumes. At the same time, the naturalists attached to the expedition, MM. Quoy, Gaimard, and Gaudichaud, submitted the specimens which they had collected. Among these were four previously unknown species of mammiferous animals, forty-five of fishes, thirty of reptiles, besides rare kinds of molluscs, polypes, annelides, &c., &c.

The rules of the French service required that Freycinet should be summoned before a council of war to answer for the loss of his ship. The trial terminated in a unanimous verdict of acquittal from all blame, the council expressing at the same time their hearty acknowledgment of the energy and ability displayed by the commander, approving, moreover, the skilful and careful measures he had taken to remedy the disastrous results of his shipwreck. A few days after, being received by the king, Louis XVIII., his Majesty, accompanying him to the door, said, "You entered here the captain of a frigate, you depart the captain of a ship of the line. Offer me no thanks; reply in the words used by Jean Bart to Louis XIV., 'Sire, you have done well!'"

From that time Freycinet devoted himself entirely to the task of publishing the notes of his travels. The meagre account which has been given here will serve to show how extensive these notes were. But the extreme conscientiousness of the explorer prevented him from publishing anything which was not complete, and he was bent on placing his work in advance of the recognized boundaries of knowledge at that date. Even the mere classification of the vast quantity of material which he had collected during his voyage demanded a large expenditure of time. Thus it was that when surprised by death on the 18th of August, 1842, he had not put the last finishing touch to one of the most curious and novel divisions of his work, that relating to the languages of Oceania with special reference to that of the Marianne Islands.

At the close of the year 1821 the Marquis de Clermont Tonnerre, then Minister of Marine, received the scheme of a new voyage from two young officers, MM. Duperrey and Dumont d'Urville. The former, second in command to Freycinet on board the *Uranie*, after having rendered valuable assistance to the expedition by his scientific researches and surveys, had within the year returned to France; the other, the colleague of Captain Garnier, had brought himself into notice during the hydrographical cruises in the Mediterranean and Black Seas, which it had fallen to Captain Garnier to complete. He had a fine taste for botany and art, and had been one of the first to draw attention to the artistic value of the Venus of Milos which had just been discovered. These two young *savants* proposed in the plan submitted by them to make special researches into three departments of natural science—magnetism, meteorology, and the configuration of the globe. "In the geographical department," said Duperrey, "we would propose to verify or to rectify, either by direct, or by chronometrical observations, the position of a great number of points in different parts of the globe, especially among the numerous island groups of the Pacific Ocean, notorious for shipwrecks, and so remarkable for the character and the form of the shoals, sandbanks, and reefs, of which they in part consist; also to trace new routes through the Dangerous Archipelago and the Society Islands, side by side with those taken by Quiros, Wallis, Bougainville, and Cook; to carry on hydrographical surveys in continuation of those made in the voyages of D'Entrecasteaux and of Freycinet in Polynesia, New Holland, and the Molucca Islands; and particularly to visit the Caroline Islands, discovered by Magellan, about which, with the exception of the eastern side, examined in our own time by Captain Kotzebue, we have only very vague information, communicated by the missionaries, and by them learnt from stories told by savages who had lost their way and were driven in their canoes upon the Marianne Islands. The languages, character, and customs of these islanders must also receive special and careful attention."

The naval doctors, Garnon and Lesson, were placed in charge of the natural history department, whilst the staff was composed of officers most remarkable for their scientific attainments, among whom may be mentioned MM. Lesage, Jacquinot, Bérard, Lottin, De Blois, and De Blosseville.

The Academy of Sciences took up the plan of research submitted by the originators of this expedition with much enthusiasm, and furnished them with minute instructions, in which were set forth with care the points on which accurate scientific information was especially desirable. At the same time the instruments supplied to the explorers were the most finished and complete of their kind.

The vessel chosen for the expedition was the *Coquille*, a small ship, not drawing more than from twelve to thirteen feet of water, which was lying in ordinary at Toulon. The time spent in refitting, stowing the cargo, arming the ship, prevented the expedition from starting earlier than the 11th of August, 1822. The island of Teneriffe was reached on the 28th of the same month, and there the officers hoped to be able to make a few gleanings after the rich harvest of knowledge which their predecessors had reaped; but the Council of Health in the island, having received information of an outbreak of yellow fever on the shores of the Mediterranean, imposed on the *Coquille* a quarantine of fifteen days. It happened, however, that at that period political opinion was in a state of fervid excitement at Teneriffe, and party spirit ran so high in society that the inhabitants found it hard to come together without also coming to blows. Under these circumstances it is easy to imagine that the French officers did not indulge in violent regrets over the privations which they had to sustain. The eight days during which their stay at Teneriffe lasted were given up exclusively to the revictualling of the ship, and to magnetic and astronomical observations.

Towards the end of September anchor was weighed, and on the 6th of October the work of surveying the islands of Martin-Vaz and of Trinidad was commenced. The former are nothing more than bare rocks rising out of the sea, of a most forbidding aspect. The island of Trinidad is high land, rugged and barren, with a few trees crowning the southern point. This island is none other than the famous Ascençao—now called Ascension—which for three centuries had been the object of exploring research. In 1700 it was taken possession of by the celebrated Halley in the name of the English Government, but it had to be ceded to the Portuguese, who formed a settlement there. La Pérouse found it still in existence at the same place in 1785. The settlement, which turned out expensive and useless, was abandoned a short time after the visit just referred to, and the island was left in the occupation of the dogs, pigs, and goats, whose progenitors had entered the island in company with the early colonists.

When he left the island of Trinidad, Duperrey purposed to steer a direct course for the Falkland Islands; but an accidental damage, in the repair of which no time was to be lost, compelled him to alter his course for the island of St. Catherine, where only he could obtain without any delay the wood required for new yards and masts, as well as provisions, which from their abundance could there be bought very cheap. As he drew near to the island he was delighted with the grand and picturesque scene presented by its dense forests, where laurel-trees, sassafras, cedars, orange-trees, and mangroves intermingled with banana and other palms, with their feathery foliage waving gracefully in the breeze. Just four days before the corvette anchored off St. Catherine, Brazil had cast off the authority of the mother-country, and declared its independence by the proclamation of Prince Don Pedro d'Alcantara as Emperor. This led the commander to despatch a mission consisting of MM. d'Urville, de Blosseville, Gabert, and Garnot to the capital of the island, Nossa-Senhora-del-Desterro, to make inquiries about the political change, and learn how far it might modify the friendly relations of the country with France. It appeared that the administration of the province was in the hands of a Junto, but orders were at once given to allow the French travellers to cut what wood they might stand in need of, and the Governor of the Fort of Santa Cruz was requested to further the scientific inquiries of the Expedition by all the means at his command. As to provisions, however, there was considerable difficulty, for the merchants had transferred their funds to Rio, in apprehension of what the political change might result in. It is probable that this circumstance accounts for the commander of the *Coquille* finding the course of business not run smooth in a port which had received the warm recommendations of Captains Kruzenstern and Kotzebue.

The narrative of the travellers states that "the inhabitants were living in expectation of the island being shortly attacked with the view to recolonization, which they considered would be tantamount to their enslavement. The decree issued on the 1st August, 1822, calling on all Brazilians to arm themselves for the defence of their shores and proclaiming under all circumstances a war of partisans had given rise to these fears. The measures which Prince Don Pedro propounded were equally generous and vigorous, and had created a favourable opinion of his character and of his desire to promote freedom. Full of confidence in his purposes, the strong party in favour of independence were filled with enthusiasm expressing itself all the more boisterously as for so long a time their fervid aspirations had been kept under restraint. They now gave open demonstration of their joy by making the towns of Nossa-Senhora-del-Desterro, Laguna, and San Francisco one blaze of light with their illuminations, and marching through the streets singing verses in honour of Don Pedro."

But the excitement which had been thus strikingly manifested in the towns was not shared by the quiet peace-loving dwellers in the rural districts, to whose breasts political passion was an entire stranger. And there cannot be a doubt that, if Portugal had been in a position to enforce her decrees by the despatch of a fleet, the province would have been easily reconquered.

The *Coquille* set sail again on the 30th October. When to the east of Rio de la Plata she was caught in one of those formidable gales, there called *pampero*, but had the good fortune to weather it without sustaining any damage.

While in this part of the ocean Duperrey made some interesting observations on the current of the Plate River. Freycinet had already established the fact of its flowing at the rate of two miles and a half an hour, at a distance of a hundred leagues to the east of Monte Video. It was reserved to the commander of the *Coquille* to ascertain that the current is sensibly felt at a much greater distance; he proved moreover that the water of the river resisted by that of the ocean is forcibly divided into two branches running in the direction of the two banks of the river at its mouth; and finally he accounts for the comparative shallowness of the sea down to the shores of the Magellan Strait by the immense residuum of earth held in suspension by the waters of the La Plata and deposited daily along the coast of South America.

Before entering Berkeley Sound the *Coquille*, driven by a favourable breeze, passed immense shoals of whales and dolphins, flocks of gulls and numerous flying fish, the ordinary tenants of those tempestuous regions. The Falkland Isles were reached, and Duperrey with a few of his fellow-travellers felt a lively pleasure at revisiting the land which had been to them a place of refuge for three months after their shipwreck in the *Uranie*. They paid a visit to the spot where the camp had been pitched. The remains of the corvette were almost entirely imbedded in sand, and what was visible of it bore marks of the appropriations which had been made by the whalers who had followed them in that place. On all sides were scattered miscellaneous fragments, carronades with the knobs broken off, pieces of the rigging, tattered clothes, shreds of sails, unrecognizable rags, mingled with the bones of the animals which the castaways had killed for food. "This scene of our recent calamity," Duperrey observes, "wore an aspect of desolation which was rendered still gloomier by the barrenness of the land and the dark rainy weather prevailing at the time of our visit. Nevertheless, it had for us an inexplicable sort of attraction and left a melancholy impression on our minds, which was not effaced till long after we had left the Falkland Islands well behind us."

The wreck of the *Uranie*.

The stay of Duperrey at the Falklands was prolonged to the 17th December. He took up his residence in the midst of the ruins of the settlement founded by Bougainville, in order to execute certain repairs which the condition of his vessel required. The crew provided themselves by fishing and hunting with an ample supply of food; everything necessary was found in abundance, except fruit and vegetables; and having laid in abundant stores, all prepared to confront the dangers of the passage round Cape Horn.

At first the *Coquille* had to struggle against strong winds from the south-west and violent currents; these were succeeded by squalls and hazy weather until the island of Mocha was reached on the 19th January, 1823. Of this island a brief mention has already been made. Duperrey places it in 38° 20′ 30″ S. lat., and 76° 21′ 55″ W. long., and reckons it to be about twenty-four miles in circumference. Consisting of a chain of mountains of moderate elevation, sloping down towards the sea, it was the rendezvous of the early explorers of the Pacific. It furnished the ships touching there, now a merchantman, now a pirate, with horses and with wild pigs, the flesh of which had a well-known reputation for delicacy of flavour. Here was also a good supply of pure fresh water, as well as of some European fruits, such as apples, peaches, and cherries, the growth of trees planted here by those who first took possession of the island. In 1823, however, these resources had all but disappeared, through the wasteful practices of improvident whalers. At no great distance might be seen the two round eminences which mark the mouth of the river Bio-Bio, the small island of Quebra-Ollas, and that of Quiriquina, and, these passed, the Bay of Conception opened to view, where was a solitary English whaler about to double the Cape, to which was entrusted the correspondence for home, as well as the notes of the work that had already been accomplished.

On the day after the arrival of the *Coquille*, as soon as the morning sun had lit up the bay, the melancholy and desolate appearance of the place, which had taken every one by surprise on the previous evening, became still more depressing. The name of the town was Talcahuano; and the picture it presented was one of houses in ruins and silent streets. A few wretched canoes, ready to fall to pieces, were on the beach; near them loitered a few poorly clad fishermen; while in front of the tumble-down cottages and roofless huts sat women in rags employed in combing one another's hair. In contrast with this human squalor, the surrounding hills and woods, the gardens and the orchards, were clothed in the most splendid foliage; on every side flowers displayed their gorgeous colours, and fruits proclaimed their ripeness in tints of gold.

Overhead a glowing sun, a sky without a cloud, completed the bitter irony of the spectacle. All this ruin, desolation, and wretchedness were the outward and visible signs of a series of revolutions. At St. Catherine the French travellers had been witnesses of the declaration of Brazilian independence; on the opposite side of the continent they were spectators of the downfall of Director O'Higgins. This official had evaded the summons of the Congress, had sacrificed the interests of the agricultural community to those of the traders and merchants, by the imposition of direct taxes and the lowering of customs duties; was openly accused, as well as his ministers, of peculation; and as the result of all this malversation the greater part of the population had risen in revolt. The movement against O'Higgins was led by a General D. Ramon Freire y Serrano, who gave formal assurances to the explorers that the political disturbance should be no impediment to the revictualling of the *Coquille*.

On the 26th January two corvettes arrived at Conception. They brought a regiment under the command of a French official, Colonel Beauchef, who came to assist General Freire. The regiment, which had been organized by the exertions of Colonel Beauchef, was in point of steadiness, discipline, and knowledge of drill, one of the smartest in the Chilian army.

On the 2nd February the officers of the *Coquille* proceeded to Conception, to pay a visit to General Freire. The nearer they approached the city the more fields were lying waste, the more ruined houses were seen, the fewer people were visible, while their clothing had almost reached the vanishing-point. At the entrance of the town itself stood a mast, with the head of a notorious bandit affixed to the top, one Benavidez, a ferocious savage, more wild beast than man, whose name was long execrated in Chili for the horrible atrocities he had committed.

The interior of the town was found as desolate in appearance as the approach to it. Having been set fire to by each party that had successively been victorious, Conception was nothing more than a heap of ruins, amongst which loitered a little remnant of scantily clothed inhabitants, the wretched residuum of a once flourishing population. Grass was growing in the streets, the bishop's palace and the cathedral were the only buildings still standing, and these, roofless and gutted, would not be able much longer to resist the dilapidating influence of the climate.

General Freire, before placing himself in opposition to O'Higgins, had arranged a peace with the Araucanians, an indigenous tribe distinguished for their bravery, who had not only maintained their own independence but were always ready, when opportunity offered, to encroach on the Spanish territory. Some of these natives were employed as auxiliary troops in the Chilian army. Duperrey saw them, and, having obtained from General Freire and Colonel Beauchef trustworthy information, has given a not very flattering description of them, of which the substance shall be here given.

The Araucanians are of an ordinary stature, in complexion copper-coloured, with small, black, vivacious eyes, a rather flat nose, and thick lips; the result of which is an expression of brutal ferocity. Divided into tribes, each one jealous of another, all animated by an unbridled lust of plunder, and ever on the move, their lives are spent in perpetual warfare. The mounted Araucanian is armed with a long lance, a long cutlass, sabre-shaped, called a "*Machete*,"[5] and the lasso, in the use of which they are extremely expert, while the horse he rides is usually swift.

[5] This is a weapon shorter than a sword and longer than a dagger.—*Trans.*

"Sometimes they are known," says Duperrey, "to receive under their protection vanquished enemies and become their defenders; but the motive prompting them to this seemingly generous conduct is always one of special vindictiveness; the fact being that their real object is the total extermination of some tribe allied with the opposite party. Among themselves hatred is the ruling passion; it is the only enduring bond of fidelity. All display undoubted courage, spirit, recklessness, implacability towards their enemies, whom they massacre with a shocking insensibility. Haughty in manner and revengeful in disposition, they treat all strangers with unqualified suspicion, but they are hospitable and generous to all whom they take as friends. All their passions are easily excited, but they are inordinately sensitive with regard to their liberty and their rights, which they are ever ready to defend sword in hand. Never forgetting an injury, they know not how to forgive; nothing less than the life-blood of their enemies can quench their thirst for vengeance."

Duperrey pledges himself to the truth of the picture which he has here drawn of these savage children of the Andes, who at least deserve the credit of having from the sixteenth century to the present day managed to preserve their independence against the attacks of all invaders.

After the departure of General Freire, and the troops he led away with him, Duperrey took advantage of the opportunity to get his vessel provisioned as quickly as possible. The water and the biscuits were soon on board; but longer time was necessary to procure supplies of coal, which, however, was to be got without any other expense save that of paying the muleteers, who transported it to the beach from a mine scarcely beneath the level of the earth, where it was to be picked up for nothing.

Although the events happening at Conception during the detention there of the *Coquille* were far from being cheerful, the prevailing depression could not hold out against the traditional festivities of the Carnival. Dinners, receptions, and balls recommenced, and the departure of the troops made itself felt only in the paucity of cavaliers. The French officers, in acknowledgment of the hospitable welcome offered to them, gave two balls at Talcahuano, and several families came from Conception for the sole purpose of being present at them.

Unfortunately, Duperrey's narrative breaks off at the date of his quitting Chili, and there is no longer any official record from which to gather the details of a voyage so interesting and successful. Far from being able to trace step by step from original documents the course of the expedition, as has been done in the case of other travellers, we are obliged in our turn to epitomize other epitomes now lying before us. It is an unpleasing task; as little agreeable to the reader as it is difficult for the writer, who, while bound to respect facts, is no longer able to enliven his narrative with personal observations, and the generally lively stories of the travellers themselves. However, some few of the letters of the navigator to the Minister of Marine have been published, from which have been extracted the following details.

On the 15th February, 1823, the *Coquille* set sail from Conception for Payta, the place where, in 1595, Alvarez de Mendana and Fernandez de Quiros took ship on the voyage of discovery that has made their names famous; but after a fortnight's sail the corvette was becalmed in the vicinity of the island of Laurenzo, and Duperrey resolved to put in at Callao to obtain fresh provisions. It need not be said that Callao is the port of Lima; so the officers could not lose the opportunity of paying a visit to the capital of Peru. They were not fortunate in the time of their visit. The ladies were away for sea- bathing at Miraflores, and the men of most distinction in the place had gone with them. The travellers were thus compelled to rest content with an inspection of the chief residences and public buildings of the city, returning to Callao on the 4th March. On the 9th of the same month the *Coquille* anchored at Payta.

The situation of this place between the terrestrial and magnetic equators was most favourable for conducting observations on the variations of the magnetic needle. The naturalists also made excursions to the desert of Pierra, where they collected specimens of petrified shells imbedded in a tertiary stratum precisely similar to that in the suburbs of Paris. As soon as all the sources of scientific interest at Payta had been exhausted the *Coquille* resumed her voyage, setting sail for Otaheite. During the sail thither a circumstance occurred which might have materially delayed the progress of the expedition, if not have led to its total destruction. On the night of the 22nd April, the *Coquille* being in the waters of the Dangerous Archipelago, the officer of the watch all at once heard the sound of breakers dashing over reefs. He immediately made the ship lie to, and at daybreak the peril which had been escaped became manifest. At the distance of barely a mile and a half from the corvette lay a low island, well wooded, and fringed with rocks along its entire extent. A few people lived on it, some of whom approached the vessel in a canoe, but none of them would venture on board. Duperrey had to give up all thoughts of visiting the island, which received the name of Clermont-Tonnerre. On all sides the waves broke violently on the rocks, and he could do no more than coast it from end to end at a little distance.

The next and following days some small islands of no note were discovered, to which were given the names of Augier, Freycinet, and Lostanges.

At length, as the sun rose on the 3rd May, the verdant shores and woody mountains of Otaheite came in sight. Duperrey, like preceding visitors, could not help noticing the thorough change which had been effected in the manners and practices of the natives. Not a canoe came alongside the *Coquille*. It was the hour of Divine worship when the corvette entered the Bay of Matavai, and the missionaries had collected the whole population of the island, to the number of seven thousand, inside the principal church of Papahoa to discuss the articles of a new code of laws. The Otaheitan orators, it seems, would not yield the palm to those of Europe. There were not a few of them gifted with the valuable talent of being able to talk for several hours without saying anything, and to make an end of the most promising undertakings with the flowers of their rhetoric. A description of one of these meetings is given by D'Urville.

"M. Lejeune, the draughtsman of the expedition, went by himself to be present at the meeting held the next day, when certain political questions were submitted to the popular assembly. It lasted for several hours, during which the chiefs took it in turn to speak. The most brilliant speaker of the gathering was a chief called Tati. The chief point of discussion was the imposition of an annual poll-tax at the rate of five measures of oil per man. Then came a question as to the taxes which were to be levied, whether they should be on behalf of the king, or on behalf of the missionaries. After some time, we arrived at the conclusion that the first question had been answered in the affirmative; but that the second, the one relating to the missionaries, had been postponed by themselves from a forecast of its probable failure. About four thousand persons were present at this kind of national congress."

Two months before, Otaheite had renounced the English flag, in order to adopt one of its own, but that pacific revolution in no wise diminished the confidence which the people placed in their missionaries. The latter received the French travellers in a friendly manner, and supplied them at the usual prices with the stores of which they stood in need.

But what seemed especially curious in the reforms effected by the missionaries was the total change in the behaviour of the women. From being, according to the statements of Cook, Bougainville, and contemporary explorers, compliant to an unheard of degree, they had become most modest, reserved, and decently conducted; so that the whole island wore the air of a convent, a revolution as amusing as it was unnatural.

From Otaheite the *Coquille* proceeded to the adjacent island of Borabora, belonging to the same group, where European customs had been adopted to the same extent; and on the 9th June, steering a westerly course, made a survey in turn of the islands Salvage, Coa, Santa Cruz, Bougainville, and Bouka; finally coming to an anchor in the harbour of Praslin, on the coast of New Ireland, famous for its beautiful waterfall. "The friendly relations which were established with the natives there were the means of extending our knowledge of the human race by the observation of some peculiarities which had not fallen under the notice of preceding travellers." The sentence just quoted from an abridged account appearing in the "Annals of Voyages," which merely excites curiosity without satisfying it, causes us here to express our regret that the original narrative of the voyage has not been published in its entirety.

The waterfall of Port Praslin.
(Fac-simile of early engraving.)

The student Porel de Blossville—the same who afterwards lost his life with the *Lilloise* in the Polar regions—undertook a journey to the village of Praslin, in spite of all the means adopted by the savages to deter him. When there he was shown a kind of temple, where several ill-shaped, grotesque idols had been set up on a platform surrounded by walls.

Great pains were taken to prepare a chart of St. George's Channel, after which Duperrey paid a visit to the islands previously surveyed by Schouten to the north-east of New Guinea. Three days—the 26th, 27th, and 28th—were devoted to a survey of them. The explorer, after this, searched ineffectually for the islands Stephen and De Carteret, and after comparing his own route with that taken by D'Entrecasteaux in 1792, he came to the conclusion that this group must be identical with that of Providence, discovered long since by Dampier.

On the 3rd of September the north cape of New Guinea was recognized. Three days later the *Coquille* entered the narrow and rocky harbour of Offak on the north-west coast of Waigiou, one of the Papuan islands. The only navigator who has mentioned this harbour is Forest. Duperrey therefore felt unusual satisfaction at having explored a corner of the earth all but untrodden by the foot of the European. It was also an interesting fact for geographers that the existence of a southern bay, separated from Offak by a very narrow isthmus, was established.

Two officers, MM. d'Urville and de Blossville, were employed in this work, which MM. Berard, Lottin, and de Blois de la Calande connected with that accomplished by Duperrey on the coast during the cruise of the *Uranie*. This land was found to be particularly rich in vegetable products, and D'Urville was able there to form the nucleus of a collection as valuable for the novelty as the beauty of its specimens.

D'Urville and Lesson, full of curiosity to study the inhabitants, who belonged to the Papuan race, started for the shore immediately after the corvette arrived at the island in a boat manned with seven sailors. They had already walked some distance in a deluge of rain, when all at once they found themselves opposite a cottage built upon piles, and covered over with leaves of the plane-tree.

Cowering amongst the bushes, at a little distance, was a young female savage, who seemed to be watching them. A few paces nearer was a heap of about a dozen cocoa-nuts freshly gathered, placed well in sight, apparently intended for the refreshment of the visitors. The Frenchmen came to understand that this was a present offered by the youthful savage of whom they had caught a glimpse, and proceeded to feast on the fruits so opportunely placed at their disposal. The native girl, soon gathering confidence from the quiet behaviour of the strangers, came forward, crying, "*Bongous!*" (good!), making signs to show that the cocoa-nuts had been presented by herself. Her delicate attention was rewarded by the gift of a necklace and earrings.

When D'Urville regained the boat he found a dozen Papuans playing, eating, and seeming on the best possible terms with the boatmen. "In a short time," he says, "they had surrounded me, repeating, '*Captain, bongous*,' and offering various tokens of good will. These people are, in general, of diminutive stature, their constitution is slight and feeble; leprosy is a common disease among them; their voice is soft, their behaviour grave, polite, and even marked with a certain air of melancholy that is habitually characteristic of them."

Natives of New Guinea.
(Fac-simile of early engraving.)

Among the antique statues of which the Louvre is full, there is one of
Polyhymnia, which is celebrated above the rest for an expression of

melancholy pensiveness not usually found among the ancients. It is a singular circumstance that D'Urville should have observed among the Papuans the very expression of countenance distinguishing this antique statue. On board the corvette another company of natives were conducting themselves with a calmness and reserve, offering a marked contrast to the usual manner of the greater part of the inhabitants of the lands of Oceania.

The same impression was made on the French travellers during a visit paid to the rajah of the island, as also during his return visit on board the *Coquille*. In one of the villages on this southern bay was observed a kind of temple, in which were to be seen several rudely carved statues, painted over with various colours, and ornamented with feathers and matting. It was quite impossible to obtain the slightest information on the subject of the worship which the natives paid to these idols.

The *Coquille* set sail again on the 16th September, coasting along the north side of the islands lying between Een and Yang, and after a brief stay at Cayeli reached Amboyna, where the remarkably kind reception given by M. Merkus, the governor of the Molucca Island, afforded the staff an interval of rest from the continual labours of this troublesome voyage. The 27th October saw the corvette again on its course, steering towards Timor and westward of the Turtle and Lucepara Islands. Duperrey next determined the position of the island of Vulcan; sighted the islands of Wetter, Baba, Dog, Cambing, and finally, entering the channel of Ombay, surveyed a large number of points in the chain of islands stretching from Pantee and Ombay in the direction of Java. After having made a chart of Java, and an ineffectual search for the Trial Islands in the place usually assigned to them, Duperrey steered for New Holland, but through contrary winds was not able to sail along the western coast of the island. On the 10th January he at length rounded Van Diemen's Island, and six days after that sighted the lights of Port Jackson, coming to an anchor off Sydney the following day.

The governor, Sir Thomas Brisbane, who had received previous intimation of the arrival of the Expedition, gave the officers a cordial welcome, forwarded with all the means at his command the revictualling of the corvette, and rendered friendly assistance in the repairs which the somewhat shattered condition of the ship rendered necessary. He also provided means to enable MM. d'Urville and Lesson to make an excursion, full of interest, beyond the Blue Mountains into the plain of Bathurst, the resources of which were as yet but imperfectly known to Europeans.

Duperrey did not leave Australia until the 20th of March. On this occasion he directed his course towards New Zealand, which had been rather overlooked in former voyages. The vessel came to an anchor in the Bay of Manawa, forming the southern part of the grand Bay of Islands. Here the officers occupied their leisure in scientific and geographical observations, and in making researches in natural history. At the same time, the frequent intercourse of the explorers with the natives threw quite a new light upon their manners, their religious notions, their language, and on their attitude of hostility up to that time to the teaching of the missionaries. What these savages most appreciated in European civilization was well-finished weapons —of which at that time they possessed a great quantity—for by their help they were the better able to indulge their sanguinary instincts.

The stay of the *Coquille* at New Zealand terminated on the 17th of April, when a *détour* was made northwards as far as Rotuma, discovered, but not visited, by Captain Wilson in 1797. The inhabitants, gentle and hospitable, took great pains to furnish the navigators with the provisions they required. But it was not long before the Frenchmen discovered that these gentle islanders, taking advantage of the confidence which they had known how to create, had carried off a number of articles that it afterwards cost much trouble to make them restore. Stringent orders were given, and all thieves caught in the act were flogged in the presence of their fellow-countrymen, who, however, as well as the culprits themselves, treated the affair only as a joke.

Among these savages four Europeans were observed, who had a long time before deserted from the whale-ship *Rochester*. They were no better clothed than the natives, and were tatooed and smeared with a yellow powder after the native fashion; so that it would have been hard to recognize them but for their white skins and more intelligent looks. They were quite content with their lot, having married wives and reared families at Rotuma, where, escaping the cares, the troubles, and the difficulties of civilized life, they reckoned on ending their days in comfort. One among them asked to be allowed to remain on board the *Coquille*, a favour which Duperrey was ready to grant, but the chief of the island was unwilling, until he learned that two convicts from Port Jackson asked permission to stay on shore.

Although these people, hitherto little known, offered a most interesting subject of study to the naturalists, it was necessary to depart, so the *Coquille* proceeded to survey the Coral Isles and St. Augustin, discovered by Maurelle in 1781. Then came Drummond Island, where the inhabitants, dark complexioned, with slight limbs, and unintelligent faces, offered to exchange some triangular shells, commonly called holy water cups, for knives and fishhooks; next the islands of Sydenham and Henderville, where the inhabitants go entirely naked; after them, Woolde, Hupper, Hall, Knox, Charlotte, Mathews, which form the Gilbert Archipelago; and finally the

Marshall and Mulgrave groups.

On the 3rd of June Duperrey came in sight of the island of Ualan, which had been discovered in 1804 by an American, Captain Croser. As it was not marked upon any chart, the commander decided upon making an exact and particular survey of it. No sooner had the anchor touched the bottom than Duperrey, accompanied by some of his officers, made for the shore. The inhabitants turned out to be a mild and obliging race, who made their visitors presents of cocoa-nuts and the fruit of the bread-tree, conducting them through most picturesque scenery to the dwelling of their principal chief, or "Uross-ton," as he was called. Dumont d'Urville has given the following sketch of the country through which the travellers passed on their way to the residence of the chief.

"We glided calmly across a magnificent basin girdled in by a well-wooded shore, the foliage a bright green. Behind us rose the lofty hill-tops, carpeted with verdure, from which shot up the light and graceful stems of the cocoa palms. Out of the sea to the front rose the little island of Leilei, covered with the pretty cottages of the islanders, and crowned with a verdant mound. If this pleasant prospect be further brightened by a magnificent day, in a delicious climate, some notion may be formed of the sensations we experienced as we proceeded in a sort of triumphal procession, surrounded by a crowd of simple, gentle, kind attendants."

The number of persons accompanying the boats D'Urville estimated at about 800. On arriving before a neat and charming village, with well paved streets, they divided themselves, the men standing on one side, the women on the other, maintaining an impressive silence. Two chiefs advanced, and taking the travellers by the hand, conducted them to the dwelling of the "Uross-ton." The crowd, still silent, remained outside while the Frenchmen entered the chief's house. The "Uross-ton" shortly made his appearance, a pale and shrivelled old man, bowed down under the weight of fourscore years. The Frenchmen politely rose on his entering the room, but they were apprised by a whisper of disapproval from those standing about that this was a violation of the local etiquette. The crowd in front prostrated themselves on the ground. The chiefs themselves could not withhold that mark of respect. The old man, recovering from a momentary surprise at the boldness of the strangers, called upon his subjects to keep silence, then seated himself near the travellers. In return for the trifling presents which were made to him and his wife, he vouchsafed marks of goodwill in the shape of slight pats on the cheek, the shoulder, or the thigh. But the gratitude of these sovereigns was expressed only by the gift of seven so-called "*tots*"—probably pieces of cloth—four of which were of very fine tissue.

Meeting with the Chief of Ualan.

After the audience was over the travellers proceeded to look round the village, where they were astonished to find two immense walls made of coral, some blocks of which were of immense size and weight.

Notwithstanding a few acts of petty theft committed by the chiefs, the ten days during which the expedition remained at the island passed without disturbance; the good understanding on which the intercourse between the Frenchmen and the Ualanese was based never suffered a moment's interruption. Duperrey remarks that "it is easy to predict that this island of Ualan will one day become of considerable importance. It is situated in the midst of the Caroline group, in the course of ships sailing from New Holland to China, and presents good ports for careening vessels, ample supplies of water, and provisions of various kinds. The inhabitants are generous and peaceably disposed, and they will soon be in a position to supply a kind of food most essential to sailors, from the progeny of the sows that we left with them, a gift which excited a very lively gratitude."

Subsequent events, however, have not verified the forecast made by Duperrey. Although a route from Europe to China, by the south of Van Diemen's Island, passes near the coast of Ualan, the island is of little more value now than it was fifty years ago. Steam has completely revolutionized the conditions of navigation. Sailors at the commencement of the century could not possibly foresee the radical changes which the introduction of this agent would produce.

The *Coquille* had not gone more than two days' sail from Ualan, when on the 17th, 18th, and 23rd June were discovered several new islands, which by the native inhabitants were called Pelelap, Takai, Aoura, Ougai, and Mongoul. These are the groups usually called Mac-Askyll and Duperrey, the people resembling those of Ualan, who, as well as those of the Radak Islands, give to their chiefs the title of "Tamon."

On the 24th of the same month the *Coquille* found herself in the middle of the Hogoleu group, which Kotzebue had looked for in too high a latitude, the commander recognizing their bearings by means of certain names given by the natives, which were found entered in the chart of Father Cantova. The hydrographical survey of this group, contained within a circumference of at least thirty leagues, was executed by M. Blois from the 24th to the 27th June. The islands are for the most part high, terminating in volcanic peaks; but some are of opinion, judging from the arrangement of the lagoon, that they are of madreporic formation. They are tenanted by a race of diminutive, badly-shaped people, subject moreover to repulsive complaints. If ever the converse of the phrase *mens sana in corpore sano* can find a just application, it must be here, for these natives are low in the scale of intelligence, and inferior by many degrees to the people of Ualan. Even at that time foreign styles of dress appeared to have found their way into the islands. Some of the people were wearing conical-shaped hats, after the Chinese fashion; others had on garments of plaited straw, with a hole in the middle to allow the head to pass through, reminding one of the "Poncho" of the South American; but they held in contempt such trumpery as looking-glasses, necklaces, or bells, asking rather for axes and steel weapons, evidences of frequent intercourse with Europeans.

The islands of Tamatan, Fanendik, and Ollap, called "The Martyrs" on old maps, were next surveyed; afterwards an ineffectual search was made for the islands of Namoureck and Ifelouk about the position assigned to them by Arrowsmith and Malaspina; and then, by way of continuing the exploration of the north side of New Guinea, the *Coquille* put in at the port of Doreï, on the south-east coast of the island, where a stay was made until the 9th August.

Whether estimated by the addition made to natural history, or to geography, or to astronomy, or to science in general, no more profitable a sojourn could have been made than this. The indigenous inhabitants of New Guinea belong to the purest race of Papuans. Their dwellings are huts built upon piles, the entrance to them being made by means of a piece of wood with notches cut in it to serve for steps; this is drawn up into the interior every night. The natives dwelling on the coast are always at war with those in the interior, the Harfous or Arfakis negroes.

Guided by a young Papuan, D'Urville succeeded in making his way to the place where these last-mentioned dwelt. He found them gentle, hospitable, courteous creatures, not in the least like the portrait drawn of them by their enemies.

After the stay at New Guinea, the *Coquille* again sailed through the Moluccas, put in for a short time at Sourabaya, upon the coast of Java, and on the 30th October reached the islands of Bourbon and Mauritius. At length, having on the way stopped at St. Helena, where the officers paid a visit to the tomb of Napoleon, and at Ascension, where an English colony had been established since 1815, the corvette entered Marseilles on the 24th April, 1825, concluding a voyage that had occupied thirty-one months and three days, over 24,894 nautical miles, without the loss of a single life, or any cases of sickness, and without any damage being sustained by the ship. A success in every way so distinguished covered with glory the young commander of the expedition and all its officers, who had manifested such untiring energy in the prosecution of scientific inquiries, yielding a rich harvest of valuable results.

Fifty-two charts and plans carefully drawn up; collections of natural specimens of all kinds, both numerous and curious; copious vocabularies, by the help of which it may be possible to throw new light on the migrations of the Oceanic peoples; interesting intelligence regarding the productions of the places visited; the condition of commerce and industrial pursuits;

observations relating to the shape of the globe; magnetical, meteorological, and botanical researches; such formed the bulk of the valuable freight of knowledge brought home by the *Coquille*. The scientific world waited eagerly for the time when this store of information should be thrown open to the public.

II.

Expedition of Baron de Bougainville—Stay at Pondicherry—The "White Town" and the "Black Town"—"Right-hand" and "Left-hand"—Malacca—Singapore and its prosperity—Stay at Manilla—Touron Bay—The monkeys and the people—The marble rocks of Faifoh—Cochin-Chinese diplomacy—The Anambas—The Sultan of Madura—The straits of Madura and Allas—Cloates and the Triad Islands—Tasmania—Botany Bay and New South Wales—Santiago and Valparaiso—Return *viâ* Cape Horn—Expedition of Dumont d'Urville in the *Astrolabe*—The Peak of Teneriffe—Australia—Stay at New Zealand—Tonga-Tabu—Skirmishes—New Britain and New Guinea—First news of the fate of La Pérouse—Vanikoro and its inhabitants—Stay at Guam—Amboyna and Menado—Results of the expedition.

The expedition, the command of which was entrusted to Baron de Bougainville, was, strictly speaking, neither a scientific voyage nor a campaign of discovery. Its chief purpose was to unfurl the French flag in the extreme East, and to impress upon the governments of that region the intention of France to protect her nationalities and her interests, everywhere and at all times. The chief instructions given to the commander were that he was to convey to the sovereign of Cochin-China a letter from the king, together with some presents, to be placed on board the frigate *Thetis*.

M. de Bougainville was also, whenever possible, without such delays as would prejudice the main object of the expedition, to take hydrographic surveys, and to collect information upon the commerce, productions, and means of exchange, of the countries visited.

Two vessels were placed under the orders of M. de Bougainville. One, the *Thetis*, was an entirely new frigate, carrying forty-four cannons and three hundred sailors, no French frigate of this strength, except the *Boudeuse*, having ever before accomplished the voyage round the world; the other, the sloop *Espérance*, had twenty carronades upon the deck, and carried a hundred and twenty seamen.

The first of these vessels was under the direct orders of Baron de Bougainville, and his staff consisted of picked officers, amongst whom we may mention Longueville, Lapierre, and Baudin, afterwards captain, vice- admiral, and rear-admiral. The *Espérance* was commanded by Frigate- Captain De Nourquer du Camper, who, as second in command of the frigate *Cleopatra*, had already explored a great part of the course of the new expedition. It numbered among its officers, Turpin, afterwards vice-admiral, deputy, and aide-de-camp of Louis Philippe; Eugène Penaud, afterwards general officer, and Médéric Malavois, the future governor of Senegal.

Not one notable scientific man, such as those who had been billeted in such numbers on the *Naturalist* and other circumnavigating vessels, had embarked upon those of Baron de Bougainville, to whom it was a constant matter of regret, a regret intensified by the fact that the medical officers, with so many under their care, could not be long absent from the vessels when in port. M. de Bougainville's journal of the voyage opens with this judicious remark:—

"It was not many years ago a dangerous enterprise to make a voyage round the world, and scarce half a century has elapsed since the time when an expedition of this kind would have sufficed to reflect glory upon the man who directed it. This was 'the good old time,' the golden age of the circumnavigator, and the dangers and privations against which he had to struggle were repaid a hundredfold, when, rich in valuable discoveries, he hailed on his return the shores of his native land. But this is all over now; the *prestige* has gone, and we make our tour of the globe nowadays as we should then have made that of France."

What would Baron Yves-Hyacinth Potentien de Bougainville, the son of the vice-admiral, senator, and member of the *Institut*, say to-day to our admirable steamships of perfect form, and charts of such minute exactitude that distant voyages appear a mere joke.

On the 2nd March, 1824, the *Thetis* quitted the roads at Brest to take up at Bourbon her companion, the *Espérance*, which, having started some time before, had set sail for Rio de Janeiro. A short stay at Teneriffe, where the *Thetis* was only able to purchase some poor wine and a very small quantity of the provisions needed; a view of the Cape Verd Islands and the Cape of Good Hope in the distance, and a hunt for the fabulous island of Saxemberg, and some rocks no less fictitious, were the only incidents of the voyage to Bourbon, where the *Espérance* had already arrived.

Bourbon was at this time so familiar a point with the navigators that there was little to be said about it, when its two open roads of St. Denis and St. Paul had been mentioned. St. Denis, the capital, situated on the north of Bourbon, and at the extremity of a sloping table-land, was, properly speaking, merely a large town, without enclosure or walls, and each house in it was surrounded by a garden. There were no public buildings or places of interest worth mentioning except the governor's palace, situated in such a position as to command a view of the whole road; the botanic garden and the "Jardin de Naturalisation," which dates from 1817. The former, which is in the centre of the town, contains some beautiful walks, unfortunately but little frequented, and it is admirably kept. The eucalyptus, the giant of the Australian forests, the *Phormium tenax*, the New Zealand hemp-plant, the casuarina (the pine of Madagascar), the baobab, with its trunk of prodigious size, the carambolas, the sapota, the vanilla, combined to beautify this garden, which was refreshed by streams of sparkling water. The second, upon the brow of a hill, formed of terraces rising one above the other, to which several brooklets give life and fertility, was specially devoted to the acclimatisation of European trees and plants. The apple, peach, apricot, cherry, and pear-trees, which have thriven well, have already supplied the colony with valuable shoots. The vine was also grown in this garden, together with the tea-plant, and several rarer species, amongst which Bougainville noted with delight the "Laurea argentea," with its bright leaves.

On the 9th June the two vessels left the roads of St. Denis. After having doubled the shoals of La Fortune and Saya de Malha, and passed off the Seychelles, whilst among the atolls to the south of the Maldive Islands, which are level with the surface of the water and covered with bushy trees ending in a cluster of cocoas, they sighted the island of Ceylon and the Coromandel coast, and cast anchor before Pondicherry.

Natives of Pondicherry.

Ancient idols near Pondicherry.
(Fac-simile of early engraving.)

This part of India is far from answering to the "enchantress" idea which the
dithyrambic descriptions of writers who have celebrated its marvels have led

Europeans to form. The number of public buildings and monuments at Pondicherry will scarcely bear counting, and when one has visited the more curious of the pagodas, and the "boilers," whose only recommendation is their utility, there is nothing very interesting, except the novelty of the scenes met with at every turn. The town is divided into two well-defined quarters. The one called the "white town," dull and deserted in spite of its coquettish- looking buildings, and the far more interesting "black town," with its bazaars, its jugglers, its massive pagodas, and the attractive dances of the bayadères.

"The Indian population upon the coast of Coromandel," says the narrative, "is divided into two classes,—the 'right-hand' and the 'left.' This division originated under the government of a nabob against whom the people revolted; those who remained faithful to the prince being distinguished by the designation of 'right-hand,' and the rest by that of 'left-hand.' These two great tribes, which divide between them almost equally the entire population, are in a chronic state of hostility against the holders of the ranks and prerogatives obtained by the friends of the prince. The latter, however, retain the offices in the gift of the government, whilst the others are engaged in commerce. To maintain peace amongst them it was necessary to allow them to retain their ancient processions and ceremonies.... The 'right-hand' and 'left-hand' are subdivided into eighteen castes or guilds, full of pretensions and prejudices, not diminished even by the constant intercourse with Europeans which has now for centuries been maintained. Hence have arisen feelings of rivalry and contempt, which would be the source of sanguinary wars, were it not that the Hindus have a horror of bloodshed, and that their temperament renders them averse to conflict. These two facts, i.e. the gentleness of the native disposition and the constant presence of an element of discord amongst the various tribes, must ever be borne in mind if we would understand the political phenomenon of more than fifty millions of men submitting to the yoke of some five and twenty or thirty thousand foreigners."

The *Thetis* and the *Espérance* quitted the roadstead of Pondicherry on the 30th July, crossed the Sea of Bengal, sighted the islands of Nicobar and Pulo-Penang, with its free port capable of holding 300 ships at a time. They then entered the Straits of Malacca, and remained in the Dutch port of that name from the 24th to the 26th July, to repair damages sustained by the *Espérance*, so that she might hold out as far as Manilla. The intercourse of the explorers with the Resident and the inhabitants generally were all the more pleasant that it was confirmed by banquets given on land and on board the *Thetis* in honour of the kings of France and the Netherlands. The Dutch were expecting soon to cede this station to the English, and this cession took place shortly afterwards. It must be added, with regard to Malacca, that in point of fertility of soil, pleasantness of situation and facilities for obtaining all really necessary supplies, it was superior to its rivals.

Bougainville set out again on August 26th, and was tossed about by head-winds, and troubled alike by calms and storms during the remainder of his passage through the straits. As these latitudes were more frequented than any others by Malay pirates, the commandant placed sentries on the watch and took all precautions against surprise, although his force was strong enough to be above fearing any enemy. It was no uncommon thing to see fly-boats manned by a hundred seamen, and more than one merchant-ship had recently fallen a prey to these unmolested and incorrigible corsairs. The squadron, however, saw nothing to awake any suspicions, and continued its course to Singapore.

The population of this town is a curious mixture of races, and our travellers met with Europeans engaged in the chief branches of commerce; Armenian and Arabian merchants, and Chinese; some planters, others following the various trades demanded by the requirements of the population. The Malays, who seemed out of place in an advancing civilization, either led a life of servitude, or slept away their time in indolence and misery whilst the Hindus, expelled from their country for crime, practised the indescribable trades which in all great cities alone save the scum from dying of starvation. It was only in 1819 that the English procured from the Malayan sultan of Johore the right to settle in the town of Singapore; and the little village in which they established themselves then numbered but 150 inhabitants, although, thanks to Sir Stamford Raffles, a town soon rose on the site of the unpretending cabins of the natives. By a wise stroke of policy all customs-duties were abolished; and the natural advantages of the new city, with its extensive and secure port, were supplemented and perfected by the hand of man.

The garrison numbered only 300 sepoys and thirty gunners; there were as yet no fortifications, and the artillery equipment consisted merely of one battery of twenty cannons, and as many bronze field-pieces. Indeed, Singapore was simply one large warehouse, to which Madras sent cotton cloth; Calcutta, opium; Sumatra, pepper; Java, arrack and spices; Manilla, sugar and arrack; all forthwith despatched to Europe, China, Siam, &c. Of public buildings there appeared to be none. There were no stores, no careening-wharves, no building-yards, no barracks, and the visitors noticed but one small church for native converts.

The squadron resumed its voyage on the 2nd September, and reached the harbour of Cavité without any mishap. Meanwhile, M. du Camper, commander of the *Espérance* who had, during a residence of some years, become acquainted with the principal inhabitants, was ordered to go to Manilla, that he might inform the Governor-General of the Philippines of the arrival of the frigates, the reasons of their visit, &c., and at the same time gauge his feelings towards them, and form some idea of the reception the French might expect. The recent intervention of France in the affairs of Spain placed them indeed in a very delicate position with the then governor, Don Juan Antonio Martinez, who had been nominated to his post by the very Cortés which had just been overthrown by their government. The fears of the commandant, however, were not confirmed, for he met with the warmest kindness and most cordial co-operation from the Spanish authorities.

Cavité Bay, where the vessels cast anchor, was constantly encumbered with mud, but it was the chief port in the Philippine Islands, and there the Spaniards owned a very well supplied arsenal in which worked Indians from the surrounding districts, who though skilful and intelligent were excessively lazy. Whilst the *Thetis* was being sheathed, and the extensive repairs necessary to the *Espérance* were being carried out, the clerks and officers were at Manilla, seeing about the supply of provisions and cordage. The latter, which was made of "abaca," the fibre of a banana, vulgarly called "Manilla hemp," although recommended on account of its great elasticity, was not of much use on board ship. The delay at Manilla was rendered very disagreeable by earthquakes and typhoons, which are always of constant occurrence there. On October 24th there was an earthquake of such violence that the governor, troops, and a portion of the people were compelled hastily to leave the town, and the loss was estimated at 120,000*l.* Many houses were thrown down, eight people were buried in the ruins, and many others injured. Scarcely had the inhabitants begun to breathe freely again, when a frightful typhoon came to complete the panic. It lasted only part of the night of the 31st October, and the next day, when the sun rose, it might have been looked upon as a mere nightmare had not the melancholy sight of fields laid waste, and of the harbour with six ships lying on their sides, and all the others at anchor, almost entirely disabled, testified to the reality of the disaster. All around the town the country was devastated, the crops were ruined, the trees—even the largest of them—violently shaken, the village destroyed. It was a heart- rending spectacle! The *Espérance* had its main-mast and mizen-mast lifted several feet above deck, and its barricadings were carried off; the *Thetis*, more fortunate than its companion, escaped almost uninjured in the dreadful tempest.

The laziness of the workpeople, and the great number of holidays in which they indulge, early decided Bougainville to part for a time from his convoy, and on December 12th he set sail for Cochin-China. Before following the French to the little-frequented shores of that country, however, we must survey with them Manilla and its environs. The Bay of Manilla is one of the most extensive and beautiful in the world; numerous fleets might find anchorage in it; and its two channels were not yet closed to foreign vessels, and in 1798 two English frigates had been allowed to pass through them and carry off numerous vessels under the very guns of the town. The horizon is shut in by a barrier of mountains, ending on the south of the Taal, a volcano now almost extinct, but the eruptions of which have often caused frightful calamities. In the plains, framed in rice plantations, several hamlets and solitary houses give animation to the scene. Opposite to the mouth of the bay rises the town, containing 60,000 inhabitants, with its lighthouse and far-extending suburbs. It is watered by the Passig, a river issuing from Bay Lake, and its exceptionally good situation secures to it advantages which more than one capital might envy. The garrison, without including the militia, consisted at that time of 2200 soldiers; and, in addition to the military navy, always represented by some vessel at anchor, a marine service had been organized for the exclusive use of the colony, to which the name of "sutil" had been given, either on account of the small size, or the fleetness of the vessels employed. This service, all appointments in which are in the gift of the governor-general, is composed of schooners and gun-sloops, intended to protect the coasts and the trading-vessels against the pirates of Sulu. But it cannot be said that the organization, imposing as it is, has achieved any great results. Of this Bougainville gives the following curious illustration:—In 1828 the Suluans seized 3000 of the inhabitants upon the coast of Luzon, and an expedition sent against them cost 140,000 piastres, and resulted in the killing of six men!

Near the Bay of Manilla.
(Fac-simile of early engraving.)

Great uneasiness prevailed in the Philippines at the time of the visit of the *Thetis* and the *Espérance*, and a political reaction which had steeped the metropolis in blood had thrown a gloom over every one. On December 20th,

1820, a massacre of the whites by the Indians; in 1824, the mutiny of a regiment, and the assassination of an ex-governor, Senor de Folgueras, had been the first horrors which had endangered the supremacy of the Spanish.

The Creoles, who, with the Tagalas, were alike the richest and most industrious classes of the true native population, at this time gave just cause for uneasiness to the government, because they were known to desire the expulsion of all who were not natives of the Philippines; and when it is borne in mind that they commanded the native regiments, and held the greater part of the public offices, it is easy to see how great must have been their influence. Well might people ask whether they were not on the eve of one of those revolutions which lost to Spain her fairest colonies.

Until the *Thetis* reached Macao, she was much harassed by squalls, gales, heavy showers, and an intensity of cold, felt all the more keenly by the navigators after their experience for several months of a temperature of 75¾° Fahrenheit. Scarcely was anchor cast in the Canton river before a great number of native vessels came to examine the frigate, offering for sale vegetables, fish, oranges, and a multitude of trifles, once so rare, now so common, but always costly.

"The town of Macao," says the narrative, "shut in between bare hills, can be seen from afar; the whiteness of its buildings rendering it very conspicuous. It partly faces the coast, and the houses, which are elegantly built, line the beach, following the natural contour of the shore. The parade is also the finest part of the town, and is much frequented by foreigners; behind it, the ground rises abruptly, and the façades of the buildings, such as convents, noticeable for their size and peculiar architecture, rise, so to speak, from the second stage; the whole being crowned by the embattled walls of the forts, over which floated the white flag of Portugal.

"At the northern and southern extremities of the town, facing the sea, are batteries built in three stages; and near the first, but a little further inland, rises a church with a very effective portico and fine external decorations. Numerous *sampangs*, junks, and fishing-boats anchored close in shore, give animation to the scene, the setting of which would be much brightened if the heights overlooking the town were not so totally wanting in verdure."

Situated as it is in the high road, between China and the rest of the world, Macao, once one of the chief relics of Portuguese colonial prosperity, long enjoyed exceptional privileges, all of which were, however, gone by 1825, when its one industry was a contraband trade in opium.

The *Thetis* only touched at Macao to leave some missionaries, and to hoist the French flag, and Bougainville set sail again on January 8th.

Nothing worthy of notice occurred on the voyage from Macao to Touron Bay. Arrived there, Bougainville learned that the French agent, M. Chaigneu, had left Hué for Saigon, with the intention of there chartering a barque for Singapore, and in the absence of the only person who could further his schemes he did not know with whom to open relations. Fearing failure as an inevitable result of this *contretemps* he at once despatched a letter to Hué, explaining the object of his mission, and expressing a wish to go with some of his officers to Saigon. The time which necessarily elapsed before an answer was received was turned to account by the French, who minutely surveyed the bay and its surroundings, together with the famous marble rocks, the objects of the curious interest of all travellers. Touron Bay has been described by various authors, notably by Horsburgh, as one of the most beautiful and vast in the universe; but such is not the opinion of Bougainville, who thinks these statements are to be taken with a great deal of reservation. The village of Touron is situated upon the sea-coast, at the entrance of the channel of Faifoh, from the right bank of which rises a fort with glacis, bastions, and a dry moat, built by French engineers.

The French being looked upon as old allies were always received with kindness and without suspicion. It had not, apparently, been so with the English, who had not been permitted to land, whilst the sailors on board the *Thetis* were at once allowed to fish and hunt, and to go and come as they chose, every facility for obtaining fresh provisions being also accorded to them. Thanks to this latitude, the officers were able to scour the country and make interesting observations. One of them, M. de la Touanne, gives the following description of the natives:—"They are rather under than over middle height, and in this respect they closely resemble the Chinese of Macao. Their skin is of a yellowish-brown, and their heads are flat and round; their faces are without expression, their eyes are as melancholy, but their eyebrows are not so strongly marked as those of the Chinese. They have flat noses and large mouths, and their lips bulge out in a way rendered the more disagreeable as they are always black and dirty from the habit indulged in, by men and women alike, of chewing areca nut mixed with betel and lime. The women, who are almost as tall as the men, have not a more pleasant appearance; and the repulsive filthiness, common to both sexes, is enough without anything else to deprive them of all attractiveness."

Women of Touron Bay.

What strikes one most is the wretchedness of the inhabitants as compared with the fertility of the soil, and this shocking contrast betrays alike the selfishness and carelessness of the government and the insatiable greed of the mandarins. The plains produce maize, yams, manioc, tobacco, and rice, the flourishing appearance of which testifies to the care bestowed upon them; the sea yields large quantities of delicious fish, and the forests give shelter to numerous birds, as well as tigers, rhinoceroses, buffaloes, and elephants, and troops of monkeys are to be met with everywhere, some of them four feet high, with bodies of a pearl-grey colour, black thighs, and red legs. They wear red collars and white girdles, which make them look just as if they were clothed. Their muscular strength is extraordinary, and they clear enormous distances in leaping from branch to branch. Nothing can be odder than to see some dozen of these creatures upon one tree indulging in the most fantastic grimaces and contortions. "One day," says Bougainville, "when I was at the edge of the forest, I wounded a monkey who had ventured forth for a stroll in the sunshine. He hid his face in his hands and sent forth such piteous groans that more than thirty of his tribe were about him in a moment. I lost no time in reloading my gun not knowing what I might have to expect, for some monkeys are not afraid of attacking men; but the troop only took up their wounded comrade, and once more plunged into the wood."

Another excursion was made to the marble rocks of the Faifoh River, where are several curious caves, one containing an enormous pillar suspended from the roof and ending abruptly some distance from the ground; stalactites were seen, but the sound of a water-fall was heard from the further end. The French also visited the ruins of an ancient building near a grotto, containing an idol, and with a passage opening out of one corner. This passage Bougainville followed. It led him into an "immense rotunda lighted from the top, and ending in an arched vault, at least sixty feet high. Imagine the effect of a series of marble pillars of various colours, some from their greenish colour, the result of old age and damp, looking as if cast in bronze, whilst from the roof hung down creepers, now in festoons, now in bunches, looking for all the world like candelabra without the lights. Above our heads were groups of stalactites resembling great organ-pipes, altars, mutilated statues, hideous monsters carved in stone, and even a complete pagoda, which, however, occupied but a very small space in the vast enclosure. Fancy such a scene in an appropriate setting, the whole lit up with a dim and wavering light, and you can perhaps form some idea how it struck me when it first burst upon me."

On the 20th of January, 1825, the *Espérance* at last rejoined the frigate; and, two days later, two envoys arrived from the court at Hué, with orders to ask Bougainville for the letter of which he was the bearer. But, as the latter had received orders to deliver it to the Emperor in person, this request involved a long series of puerile negotiations. The formalities by which the Cochin-Chinese envoys were, so to speak, hemmed in, reminded Bougainville of the anecdote of the envoy and the governor of Java, who, rivalling each other in their gravity and diplomatic prudence, remained together for twenty-four hours without exchanging a word. The commander was not the man to endure such trial of patience as this, but he could not obtain the necessary authorization of his explorations, and the negotiations ended in an exchange of presents, securing nothing in fact but an assurance from the Emperor that he would receive with pleasure a visit of the French vessels to his ports, if their captain and officers would conform to the laws of the Empire. Since 1817 the French had been pretty well the only people who had done any satisfactory business with the people of Cochin-China, a state of things resulting from the presence of French residents at the court of Hué, on whom alone of course depended the maintenance of the exceptionally cordial relations so long established between them and the government to which they were accredited.

The two ships left Touron Bay on the 17th February for the Anambas Archipelago, which had not as yet been explored; and, on the 3rd of March, they came in sight of it, and found it to bear no resemblance whatever to the islands of the same name, marked upon the English map of the China Sea. Bougainville was agreeably surprised to see a large number of islands and islets, the bays, &c., of which were sure to afford excellent anchorage during the monsoons. The explorers penetrated to the very heart of the archipelago, and made a hydrographic survey of it. Whilst the small boats were engaged upon this task, two prettily built canoes approached, from one of which a man of about fifty came on board the *Thetis*, whose breast was seamed with scars, and from whose right-hand two fingers were missing. The sight of the rows of guns and ammunition, however, so terrified him that he beat a hasty retreat to his canoe, though he had already got as far as the orlop-deck. Next day two more canoes approached, manned by fierce-looking Malays, bringing bananas, cocoa-nuts, and pineapples, which they bartered for biscuits, a handkerchief, and two small axes. Several other interviews took place with islanders, armed with the kriss, and short two-edged iron pikes, who were very evidently pirates by profession.

Although the French explored but a part of the Anamba group, the information they collected was extremely interesting on account of its novelty. The first requisite of a large population is plenty of fresh water, and there is apparently very little of it in the Anambas. Moreover, the cultivable soil is not very deep, and the mountains are separated by narrow ravines, not by plains, so that agriculture is all but out of the question. Even the native trees, with the exception of the cocoa-palm, are very stunted. The population was estimated by a native at not more than 2000, but Bougainville thought even that too high a figure. The fortunate position of the Anambas—they are passed by all vessels trading with China, whichever route may be taken—long since brought them to the notice of navigators; and we must attribute to their lack of resources the neglect to which they have been abandoned. The small amount of cordiality and confidence met with by Bougainville from the inhabitants, the high price of provisions, and the destructive nature of the monsoons in the Sunda waters, determined him to cut short his survey and to make with all speed for Java, where his instructions compelled him to touch. The 8th of March was fixed for the departure of the two vessels, which sighted Victory, Barren, Saddle, and Camel Islands, passed through the Gasper Straits—the passage of which did not occupy more than two hours, although it often takes several days with an unfavourable wind—and cast anchor at Surabaya, where the explorers were met with the news of the death of Louis XVIII. and the accession of Charles X. As the cholera, which had claimed 300,000 victims in Java in 1822, was still raging, Bougainville took the precaution of keeping his crew on board under shelter from the sun, and expressly forbade any intercourse with vessels laden with fruit, the use of which is so dangerous to Europeans, especially during the rainy season then setting in. In spite of these wise orders, however, dysentery attacked the crew of the *Thetis*, and too many fell victims to it.

The town of Surabaya is situated one league from the mouth of the river, and it can only be reached by towing up the stream. Its approaches are lively, and everything bears witness to the presence of an active commercial population. An expedition to the island of Celebes having exhausted the resources of the government and the magazines being empty, Bougainville had to deal direct with the Chinese merchants, who are the most bare-faced robbers on the face of the globe, and now resorted to all manner of cunning and knavery to get the better of their visitors. The stay at Surabaya, therefore, left a very disagreeable impression on all. It was quite different, however, with regard to the reception met with from the chief personages of the colony, for there was every reason to be satisfied with the conduct of all connected with the government.

To go to Surabaya without paying a visit to the Sultan of Madura, whose reputation for hospitality had crossed the seas, would have been as impossible as it is to visit Paris without going to see Versailles and Trianon. After a comfortable lunch on shore, therefore, the staff of the two vessels set out in open carriages and four; but the roads were so bad and the horses so worn out that they would many a time have stuck in the mud if men stationed at the dangerous places had not energetically shoved at the wheels. At last they arrived at Bankalan, and the carriages drew up in the third court of the palace at the foot of a staircase, at the top of which the hereditary prince and the prime minister awaited the arrival of the travellers. Prince Adden Engrate belonged to the most illustrious family of the Indian Archipelago. He wore the undress uniform of a Java chief, consisting of a long flowered petticoat of Indian make, scarcely allowing the Chinese slippers to be seen, a white vest with gold buttons, and a small skirted waistcoat of brown cloth, with diamond buttons. A handkerchief was tied about his head, on which he wore a visor-cap, his ease and dignity of bearing alone saving him from looking like the grotesque figure of a carnival amazon. The palace or "kraton" consisted of a series of buildings with galleries, kept delightfully cool by awnings and curtains, whilst lustres, tasty European furniture, pretty hangings, glass and crystal ornaments decorated the vast halls and rooms. A suite of private apartments, with no opening to the court, but with a view of the gardens, is reserved for the "Ratu" (sovereign) and the harem.

The reception was cordial, and the repast, served in European style, was delicious. "The conversation," says Bougainville, "was conducted in English, and many toasts were proposed, the prince drinking our healths in tea poured from a bottle, and to which he helped himself as if it had been Madeira. Being head of the church as well as of the state, he strictly obeys the precepts of the Koran, never drinking wine, and spending a great part of his time at the mosque; but he is not the less sociable, and his talk bears no trace of the austerity to be expected in that of one who leads so regular a life. This life is not, however, all spent in prayer, and the scenes witnessed by us would give a very false impression if we did not know that great latitude is allowed on this point to the followers of the prophet."

In the afternoon the Frenchmen visited several coach-houses, containing very handsome carriages, some of which, built on the island, were so well-made that it was absolutely impossible to distinguish them from those which had been imported. Some archery was then witnessed, and joined in, after which, on the return to the palace, the visitors were welcomed by the sound of melancholy music, speedily interrupted, however, by the barking and fantastical dancing of the prince's fool, who showed wonderful agility and suppleness. To this dance, or rather to these postures of a bayadère, succeeded the excitement of vingt-et-un, followed by well-earned repose. Next day there were new entertainments and new exercises; beginning with wrestling-matches for grown men and for youths, and proceeding with quail-fights, and feats performed by a camel and an elephant. After lunch Bougainville and his party had a drive and some archery, and witnessed sack-races, basket-balancing, &c. In this way, they were told, the sultan passed all his time. Most striking is the respect and submission shown by all to this sovereign. No one ever stands upright before him, but all prostrate themselves before addressing him. All his subjects do but "wait at his feet," and even his own little child of four years clasps his tiny hands when he speaks to his father.

While at Surabaya, Bougainville took the opportunity of visiting the volcano of Brumo, in the Tengger Mountains; and this excursion, in which he explored the island for a hundred miles, from east to west, was one of the most interesting undertaken by him. Surabaya contains some curious buildings and monuments, most of them the work of a former governor, General Daendels; such are the "Builder's Workshop," the "Hôtel de la Monnaie" (the only establishment of the kind in Java), and the hospital, which is built on a well-chosen site, and contains 400 beds. The island of Madura, opposite to Surabaya, is at least 100 miles in length, by fifteen or twenty in breadth, and does not yield produce sufficient to maintain the population, sparse as it is. The sovereignty of this island is divided between the sultans of Bankalan and Sumanap, who furnish annually six hundred recruits to the Dutch, without counting extraordinary levies.

On the 20th April, symptoms of dysentery showed themselves amongst the crews. Two days later therefore the vessel set sail, and it took seven good days to get beyond the straits of Madura. They returned along the north coast of Lombok, and passed through the Allas Straits, between Lombok and Sumbawa. The first of these islands, from the foot of the mountains to the sea, presents the appearance of a green carpet, adorned with groups of trees of elegant appearance, and upon its coast there is no lack of good anchorage, whilst fresh water and wood are plentiful. On the other side, however, there are numerous peaks of barren aspect, rising from a lofty table-land, the approach to which is barred by a series of rugged and inaccessible islands, known as Lombok, the coral-beds and treacherous currents about which must be carefully avoided. Two stoppages at the villages of Baly and Peejow, with a view to taking in fresh provisions, enabled the officers to make a hydrographical chart of this part of the coast of Lombok. Upon leaving the strait, Bougainville made an unsuccessful search for Cloates Island. That he did not find it is not very wonderful, as during the last eight years many ships have passed over the spot assigned to it upon the maps. The "Triads," on the other hand, i.e. the rocks seen in 1777 by the *Freudensberg Castle*, are, in Captain King's opinion, the Montepello Islands, which correspond perfectly with the description of the Danes.

Bougainville had instructions to survey the neighbourhood of the Swan River, where the French Government hoped to find a place suitable for the reception of the wretches then huddled together in their convict-prisons; but the flag of England had just been unfurled on the shores of Nuyts and Leuwin, in King George's Sound, Géographe Bay, the little Leschenault inlet, and on the Swan River, so that there was no longer any reason for a new exploration. Everything in fact had combined to prevent it; the delays to which the expedition had been subjected had indeed been so serious that instead of arriving in these latitudes in April, they did not reach them until the middle of May, there the very heart of winter. Moreover, the coast offers no shelter, for so soon as the wind begins to blow, the waves swell tremendously, and the memory of the trials which the *Géographe* had undergone at the same season of the year was still fresh in the minds of the French. The *Thetis* and the *Espérance* were pursued by the bad weather as far as Hobart Town, the chief English station upon the coast of Tasmania, where the commander was very anxious to put in. He was, however, driven back by storms to Port Jackson, which is marked by a very handsome lighthouse, a granite tower seventy-six feet high, with a lantern lit by gas, visible at a distance of nine leagues.

Entrance to Sydney Bay.

Sir Thomas Brisbane, the governor, gave a cordial reception to the expedition, and at once took the necessary steps to furnish it with provisions. This was done by contract at low prices, and the greatest good faith was shown in carrying out all bargains. The sloop had to be run ashore to have its sheathing repaired, but this, with some work of less importance necessary to the *Thetis*, did not take long. The delay was also turned to account by the whole staff, who were greatly interested in the marvellous progress of this penal colony. While Bougainville was eagerly reading all the works which had as yet appeared upon New South Wales, the officers wandered about the town, and were struck dumb with amazement at the numberless public buildings erected by Governor Macquarie, such as the barracks, hospital, market, orphanages, almshouses for the aged and infirm, the prison, the fort, the churches, government-house, the fountains, the town gates, and last but not least, the government-stables, which are always at first sight taken for the palace itself. There was, however, a dark side to the picture. The main thoroughfares, though well-planned, were neither paved nor lighted, and were so unsafe at night, that several people had been seized and robbed in the very middle of George Street, the best quarter of Sydney. If the streets in the town were unsafe, those in the suburbs were still more so. Vagrant convicts overran the country in the form of bands of "bushrangers," who had become so formidable that the government had recently organized a company of fifty dragoons for the express purpose of hunting them down. All this did not, however, hinder the officers from making many interesting excursions, such as those to Paramatta, on the banks of the Nepean, a river very deeply embanked, where they visited the Regent Ville district; and to the "plains of Emu," a government agricultural-station, and a sort of model farm. They went to the theatre, where a grand performance was given in their honour. The delight sailors take in riding is proverbial, and it was on horseback that the French crossed the Emu plains. The noble animals, imported from England, had not degenerated in New South Wales; they were still full of spirit as one of the young officers found to his cost, when, as he was saying in English to Sir John Cox, acting as cicerone to the party, "I do love this riding exercise," he was suddenly thrown over his horse's head and deposited on the grass before he knew where he was. The laugh against him was all the more hearty as the skilful horseman was not injured.

Beyond Sir John Cox's plantations extends the unbroken "open forest," as the English call it, which can be crossed on horseback, and consists chiefly of the eucalyptus, acacias of various kinds, and the dark-leaved casuarinas. The next day, an excursion was made up the river Nepean, a tributary of the Hawkesbury, on which trip many valuable facts of natural history were obtained, Bougainville enriching his collection with canaries, waterfowl, and a very pretty species of kingfisher and cockatoos. In the neighbouring woods was heard the unpleasant cry of the lyre-pheasant and of two other birds, which feebly imitate the tinkling of a hand-bell and the jarring noise of the saw. These are not, however, the only feathered fowl remarkable for the peculiarity of their notes; we must also mention the "whistling-bird," the "knife-grinder," the "mocking-bird," the "coachman," which mimics the crack of the whip, and the "laughing jackass," with its continual bursts of laughter, which have a strange effect upon the nerves. Sir John Cox presented the commander with two specimens of the water-mole, also called the ornithorhynchus, a curious amphibious creature, the habits of which are still little known to European naturalists, many museums not possessing a single specimen.

Another excursion was made in the Blue Mountains, where the famous "King's Table-land" was visited, from which a magnificent view was obtained. The explorers gained with great difficulty the top of an eminence, and an abyss of 1600 feet at once opened beneath them; a vast green carpet stretching away to a distance of some twenty miles, whilst on the right and left were the distorted sides of the mountain, which had been rudely rent asunder by some earthquake, the irregularities corresponding exactly with each other. Close at hand foams a roaring, rushing torrent, flinging itself in a series of cascades into the valley beneath, the whole passing under the name of "Apsley's Waterfall." This trip was succeeded by a kangaroo hunt in the cow-pastures with Mr. Macarthur, one of the chief promoters of the prosperity of New South Wales. Bougainville also turned his stay at Sydney to account by laying the foundation-stone of a monument to the memory of La Pérouse. This cenotaph was erected in Botany Bay, upon the spot where the navigator had pitched his camp.

"Apsley's Waterfall."

On September 21st the *Thetis* and the *Espérance* at last set sail; passing off Pitcairn Island, Easter Island, and Juan Fernandez, now a convict settlement for criminals from Chili, after having been occupied for a half-century by Spanish vine-growers.

On the 23rd November the *Thetis*, which had been separated from the *Espérance* during a heavy storm, anchored off Valparaiso, where it met Admiral de Rosamel's division. Great excitement prevailed in the roadstead, for an expedition against the island of Chiloë, which still belonged to Spain, was being organized by the chief director, General Ramon Freire y Serrano, of whom we have already spoken.

Bougainville, like the Russian navigator Lütke, is of opinion that the position of Valparaiso does not justify its reputation. The streets are dirty and narrow, and so steep that walking in them is very fatiguing. The only pleasant part is the suburb of Almendral, which, with its gardens and orchards, would be still more agreeable but for the sand-storms prevalent throughout nearly the whole of the year. In 1811, Valparaiso numbered only from four to five thousand inhabitants; but in 1825 the population had already tripled itself, and the increase showed no sign of ceasing. When the *Thetis* touched at Valparaiso, the English frigate, the *Blonde*, commanded by Lord Byron, grandson of the explorer of the same name, whose discoveries are narrated above, was also at anchor there. By a singular coincidence Byron had raised a monument to the memory of Cook in the island of Hawaii, at the very time when Bougainville, the son of the circumnavigator, met by Byron in the Straits of Magellan, was laying the foundation-stone of the monument to the memory of La Pérouse in New South Wales.

Bougainville turned the delay necessary for the revictualling of his division to account by paying a visit to Santiago, the capital of Chili, thirty-three leagues inland. The environs of Chili are terribly bare, without houses or any signs of cultivation. Its steeples alone mark the approach to it, and one may fancy oneself still in the outskirts when the heart of the city is reached. There is, however, no lack of public buildings, such as the Hôtel de la Monnaie, the university, the archbishop's palace, the cathedral, the church of the Jesuits, the palace, and the theatre, the last of which is so badly lighted that it is impossible to distinguish the faces of the audience. The promenade, known as La Cañada, has now supplanted that of L'Alameda on the banks of the river Mapocha, once the evening rendezvous. The objects of interest in the town exhausted, the Frenchmen examined those in the neighbourhood, visiting the Salto de Agua, a waterfall of 1200 feet in height, the ascent to which is rather arduous, and the Cerito de Santa-Lucia, from which rises a fortress, the sole defence of the town.

The season was now advancing, and no time was to be lost if the explorers wished to take advantage of the best season for doubling Cape Horn. On the 8th January, 1826, therefore, the two vessels once more put to sea, and rounded the Cape without any mishap, though landing at the Falklands was rendered impossible by fog and contrary winds. Anchor was cast on the 28th March in the roadstead of Rio Janeiro, and, as it turned out, at a time most favourable for the French to form an accurate opinion alike on the city and the court.

"The emperor," says Bougainville, "was upon a journey at the time of our arrival, and his return was the occasion of fêtes and receptions which roused the population to activity, and broke for a time the monotony of ordinary life in Rio, that dullest and dreariest of towns to the foreigner. Its environs, however, are charming; nature has in them been lavish of her riches; and the vast harbour, the Atlantic, rendezvous of the commercial world, presents a most animated scene. Innumerable ships, either standing in or getting under weigh, small craft cruising about, a ceaseless roar of cannon from the forts and men-of-war, exchanging signals on the occasion of some anniversary or the celebration of some festival of the church, whilst visits were constantly being exchanged between the officers of the various foreign vessels and the diplomatic agents of foreign powers at the court of Rio."

The division set sail again on the 11th April, and arrived at Brest on the 24th June, 1826, without having put into port since it left Rio Janeiro. We must remember that if Bougainville did not make any discoveries on this voyage, he had no formal instructions to do so, his mission being merely to unfurl the flag of France where it had as yet been rarely seen. None the less do we owe to this general officer some very interesting, and in some cases new information on the countries visited by him. Some of the surveys made by his expedition may be of service to navigators, and it must be owned that the hydrographical researches which alone could be undertaken in the absence of scientific men were carefully made, and resulted in the obtaining of numerous and accurate data. We can but sympathize with the commander of the *Thetis*, in his expression of regret, in the preface to his journal, that neither the Government nor the *Académie des Sciences* had seen fit to turn his expedition to account to obtain new results supplementary of the rich harvest gleaned by his predecessors.

The expedition next sent out under the command of Captain Dumont d'Urville was merely intended by the minister to supplement and consolidate the mass of scientific data collected by Captain Duperrey in his voyage from 1822 to 1824. As second in command to Duperrey, and the originator and organizer of the new exploring expedition, D'Urville had the very first claim to be appointed to its command. The portions of Oceania he proposed to visit were New Zealand, the Fiji Islands, the Loyalty Islands, New Britain, and New Guinea, all of which he considered urgently to demand the consideration alike of the geographer and the traveller. What he effected in this direction we shall ascertain by following him step by step. An interest of another character also attaches to this trip, but it will be well to quote on this point the instructions given to the navigator.

"An American captain," writes the Minister of Marine, "said that he saw in the hands of the natives of an isle situated between New Caledonia and the Louisiade Archipelago a cross of St. Louis and some medals, which he imagined to be relics of the wrecked vessel of the celebrated La Pérouse, whose loss is so deeply and justly regretted. This is, of course, but a feeble reason for hoping that some of the victims of the disaster still survive; but you, sir, will give great satisfaction to his Majesty, if you are the means of restoring any one of the poor shipwrecked mariners to their native land after so many years of misery and exile."

The aims of the expedition were therefore manifold, and by the greatest chance it was able to achieve them nearly all. D'Urville received his appointment in December, 1825, and was permitted himself to choose all who were to accompany him. He named as second in command Lieutenant Jacquinot, and as scientific colloborateurs Messrs. Quoy and Gaimard, who had been on board the *Uranie*, and as surgeon Primevère Lesson. The *Coquille*, the excellent qualities of which were well known to D'Urville, was the vessel selected; and the commander having named her the *Astrolabe* in memory of La Pérouse, embarked in her a crew of twenty-four men. Anchor was weighed on the 25th April, and the mountains of Toulon with the coast of France were soon out of sight.

After touching at Gibraltar, the *Astrolabe* stopped at Teneriffe to take in fresh provisions before crossing the Atlantic, and D'Urville took advantage of this delay to ascend the peak, accompanied by Messrs. Quoy, Gaimard, and several officers, a bad road, very arduous for pedestrians, leading the first part of the way over fields of scoria, though as Laguna is approached the scenery improves. This town, of a considerable size, contains but a small, indolent, and miserable population.

Between Matunza and Orotara the vegetation is magnificent, and the luxuriant foliage of the vine enhances the beauty of the view. Orotara is a small seaboard town, with a port affording but little shelter. It is well-built and laid out, and would be comfortable enough if the streets were not so steep as to make traffic all but impossible. After three-quarters of an hour's climb through well-cultivated fields, the Frenchmen reached the chestnut-tree region, beyond which begin the clouds, taking the form of a thick moist fog, very disagreeable to the traveller. Further on comes the furze region, beyond which the atmosphere again becomes clear, vegetation disappears, the ground becomes poorer and more barren. Here are met with decomposed lava, scoria, and pumice-stones in great abundance, whilst below stretches away the boundless sea of clouds.

Thus far hidden by clouds or by the lofty mountains surrounding it, the peak at last stands forth distinctly, the incline becomes less steep, and those vast plains of intensely melancholy appearance, called Cañadas by the Spanish, on account of their bareness, are crossed. A halt is made for lunch at the Pine grotto before climbing the huge blocks of basalt ranged in a circle about the crater, now filled in with ashes from the peak, and forming its enceinte. The peak itself is next attached, the ascent of which is broken one-third of the way up by a sort of esplanade called the Estancia de los Ingleses. Here our travellers passed the night, not perhaps quite so comfortably as they would have done in their berths, but without suffering too much from the feeling of suffocation experienced by other explorers. The fleas, however, were very troublesome, and their unremitting attacks kept the commander awake all night.

At four a.m. the ascent was resumed, and a second esplanade, called the Alta Vista, was soon reached, beyond which all trace of a path disappears, the rest of the ascent being over rough lava as far as the Chahorra Cone, with here and there, in the shade, patches of unmelted snow. The peak itself is very steep, and its ascent is rendered yet more arduous by the pumice-stone which rolls away beneath the feet.

"At thirty-five minutes past six," says M. Dumont d'Urville, "we arrived at the summit of the Chahorra, which is evidently a half-extinct crater. Its sides are thin and sloping, it is from sixty to eighty feet deep, and the whole surface is strewn with fragments of obsidian, pumice-stones, and lava. Sulphureous vapour, forming a kind of crown of smoke, is emitted from it, whilst the atmosphere at the bottom is perfectly cool. At the summit of the peak the thermometer marked 11°, but in my opinion it was affected by the presence of the fumerolles, for when at the bottom of the crater it fell rapidly from 19° in the sun to 9° 5' in the shade."

The descent was accomplished without accident by another route, enabling our travellers to examine the Cueva de la Nieve, and to visit the forest of Aqua Garcia, watered by a limpid stream, and in which D'Urville made a rich collection of botanical specimens.

In Major Megliorini's rooms at Santa Cruz the commander was shown, together with a number of weapons, shells, animals, fish, &c., a complete mummy of a Guanche, said to be that of a woman. The corpse was sewn up in skins, and seemed to be that of a woman five feet four high, with regular features and large hands. The sepulchral caves of the Guanches also contained earthenware, wooden vases, triangular seals of baked clay, and a great number of small discs of the same material, strung together like chaplets, which may have been used by this extinct race for the same purposes as the "quipos" of the Peruvians.

On the 21st June the *Astrolabe* once more set sail and touched at La Praya, and at the Cape Verd Islands, where D'Urville had hoped to meet Captain King, who would have been able to give him some valuable hints on the navigation of the coast of New Guinea. King, however, had left La Praya thirty-six hours previously, and the *Astrolabe* therefore resumed her voyage the next day, i.e. on the 30th June.

On the last day of July the rocks of Martin-Vaz and Trinity Island were sighted, and the latter appearing perfectly barren, a little dried-up grass and a few groups of stunted trees, dotted about amongst the rocks, being the only signs of vegetation.

D'Urville had been very anxious to make some botanical researches on this desert island, but the surf was so rough that he was afraid to risk a boat in it.

On the 4th August the *Astrolabe* sailed over the spot laid down as "Saxembourg" Island, which ought to be finally erased from French as it has been from English charts; and after a succession of squalls, which tried her sorely, she arrived off St. Paul and Amsterdam Islands, finally anchoring on the 7th October in King George's Sound, on the coast of Australia. In spite of the roughness of the sea, and constant bad weather throughout his voyage of 108 days, D'Urville had carried on all his usual observations on the height of the waves, which he estimated at 80 and occasionally as much as 100 feet, off Needle Bank; the temperature of the sea at various depths, &c.

Captain Jacquinot having found a capital supply of fresh water on the right bank of Princess Royal Harbour, and at a little distance a site suitable for the erection of an observatory, the tents were soon pitched by the sailors, and several officers made a complete tour of the bay, whilst others opened relations with the aborigines, one of whom was induced to go on board, though it was only with the greatest difficulty that he was persuaded to throw away his *Banksia*, a cone used to retain heat, and to keep the stomach and the front part of the body warm. He remained quietly enough on board for two days, however, eating and drinking in front of the kitchen fire. In the meantime his fellow-countrymen on land were peaceable and well-disposed, even bringing three of their children into the camp.

During this halt a boat arrived manned by eight Englishmen, who asked to be taken on board as passengers, and told such a very improbable story of having been deserted by their captain, that D'Urville suspected them of being escaped convicts; a suspicion which became a conviction, when he saw the wry faces they made at his proposal to send them back to Port Jackson. The next day, however, one took a berth as sailor, and two were received as passengers; whilst the other five decided to remain on land and drag out a miserable existence amongst the natives.

All this time hydrographical and astronomical observations were being made, and the hunters and naturalists were trying to obtain specimens of new varieties of fauna and flora. The delays extending to October 24th enabled the explorers to regain their strength, after their trying voyage, to make the necessary repairs, take in wood and water, draw up a map of the whole neighbourhood, and to collect numerous botanical and zoological specimens. His observations of various kinds made D'Urville wonder that the English had not yet founded a colony on King George's Sound, admirably situated as it is, not only for vessels coming direct from Europe, but for those trading between the Cape and China, or bound for the Sunda Islands, and delayed by the monsoons. The coast was explored as far as West Port, preferred by D'Urville to Port Dalrymple, the latter being a harbour always difficult and often dangerous either to enter or to leave. West Port moreover, was as yet only known from the reports of Baudin and Flinders, and it was therefore better worth exploring than a more frequented district. The observations made in King George's Sound were therefore repeated at West Port, resulting in the following conclusions:—

"It affords," says D'Urville, "an anchorage alike easy to reach and to leave, the bottom is firm, and wood is abundant and easily procurable. In a word, when a good supply of fresh water is found, and that will probably be soon, West Port will rise to a position of great importance in a channel such as Bass's Straits, when the winds often blow strongly from one quarter for several days together, the currents at the same time rendering navigation difficult."

From November 19th to December 2nd the *Astrolabe* cruised along the coast, touching only at Jervis Bay, remarkable for its magnificent eucalyptus forests.

Eucalyptus forest of Jervis Bay.

The reception given to the French at Port Jackson, by Governor Darling and the colonial authorities, was none the less cordial for the fact that the visits made by D'Urville to various parts of New Holland had greatly amazed the

English Government.

During the last three years Port Jackson had increased greatly in size and improved in appearance; though the population of the whole colony only amounted to 50,000, and that in spite of the constant foundation of new English settlements. The commander took advantage of his stay in Sydney to forward his despatches to France, together with several cases of natural history specimens. This done and a fresh stock of provisions having been laid in, he resumed his voyage.

New Guinea hut on piles.
(Fac-simile of early engraving.)

It would be useless to linger with Dumont d'Urville at New South Wales, to the history of which, and its condition in 1826, he devotes a whole volume of his narrative. We have already given a detailed account of it, and it will be better to leave Sydney with our traveller, on the 19th December, and follow him to Tasman Bay, through calms, head-winds, currents, and tempests, which prevented his reaching New Zealand before the 14th January, 1827. Tasman Bay, first seen by Cook on his second voyage, had never yet been explored by any expedition, and on the arrival of the *Astrolabe* a number of canoes, containing some score of natives, most of them chiefs, approached. These natives were not afraid to climb on board, some remaining several days, whilst later arrivals drew up within reach, and a brisk trade was opened. Meanwhile several officers climbed through the thick furze clothing the hills overlooking the bay, and the following is D'Urville's verdict on the desolate scene which met their view.

"Not a bird, not an insect, not even a reptile to be seen, the solemn, melancholy silence is unbroken by the voice of any living creature." From the summit of these hills the commander saw New Bay, that known as Admiralty, which communicates by a current with that in which the *Astrolabe* was anchored; and he was anxious to explore it, as it seemed safer than that of Tasman, but the currents several times brought his vessel to the very verge of destruction; and had the *Astrolabe* been driven upon the rocky coast, the whole crew would have perished, and not so much as a trace of the wreck would have been left. At last, however, D'Urville succeeded in clearing the passage with no further loss than that of a few bits of the ship's keel.

"To celebrate," says the narrative, "the memory of the passage of the *Astrolabe*, I conferred upon this dangerous strait the name of the 'Passe des Français'" (French Pass), "but, unless in a case of great necessity, I should not advise any one else to attempt it. We could now look calmly at the beautiful basin in which we found ourselves; and which certainly deserves all the praise given to it by Cook. I would specially recommend a fine little harbour, some miles to the south of the place, where the captain cast anchor. Our navigation of the 'Passe des Français' had definitively settled the insular character of the whole of the district terminating in the 'Cape Stephens' of Cook. It is divided from the mainland of Te-Wahi-Punamub[1] by the Current Basin. The comparison of our chart with that of the strait as laid down by Cook will suffice to show how much he left to be done."

[1] Now "South Island."—*Trans.*

The *Astrolabe* soon entered Cook's Strait, and sailing outside Queen Charlotte's Bay, doubled Cape Palliser, a headland formed of some low hills. D'Urville was greatly surprised to find that a good many inaccuracies had crept into the work of the great English navigator, and in that part of the account of his voyage which relates to hydrography, he quotes instances of errors of a fourth, or even third of a degree.

The commander then resolved to make a survey of the eastern side of the northern island Ika-Na-Mawi. On this island pigs were to be found, but no "*pounamon*" the green jade which the New Zealanders use in the manufacture of their most valuable tools; strange to say, however, jade is to be found on the southern island, but there are no pigs.

Two natives of the island, who had expressed a wish to remain on board the corvette, became quite low-spirited as they watched the coast of the district where they lived disappear below the horizon. They then began to repent, but too late, the intrepidity which had prompted them to leave their native shores; for intrepid they justly deserve to be called, seeing that again and again they asked the French sailors if they were not to be eaten, and it took several days of kind treatment to dispel this fear from their minds.

New Zealanders.
(Fac-simile of early engraving.)

D'Urville continued to sail northward up the coast until the capes, named by Cook Turn-again and Kidnappers, had been doubled, and Sterile Island with its "Ipah" came in sight. In the Bay of Tolaga, as Cook called it, the natives brought alongside the corvette pigs and potatoes, which they readily exchanged for articles of little value. On other canoes approaching, the New Zealanders who were on board the vessel urged the commander to fire upon and kill their fellow-countrymen in the boats; but as soon as the latter climbed up to the deck, the first arrivals advanced to greet them with earnest assurances of friendship. Conduct so strangely inconsistent is the outcome of the compound of hatred and jealousy mutually entertained for each other by these tribes. "They all desire to appropriate to themselves exclusively whatever advantage may be obtained from the visits of foreigners, and they are distressed at the prospect of their neighbours getting any share." Proof was soon afforded that this explanation is the right key to their behaviour.

Upon the *Astrolabe* were several New Zealanders, but among them was a certain *"Shaki"* who was recognized as a chief by his tall stature, his elaborate tattooing, and the respectful manner in which he was addressed by his fellow-islanders. Seeing a canoe manned by not more than seven or eight men approaching the corvette, this *"Shaki"* and the rest came to entreat D'Urville most earnestly to kill the new arrivals, going so far as to ask for muskets that they might themselves fire upon them. However, no sooner had the last comers arrived on board than all those who were there already overwhelmed them with courtesies, while the *"Shaki"* himself, although he had been one of the most sanguinary, completely changed his tone and made them a present of some axes he had just obtained. After the chief men of a warlike and fierce appearance, with faces tattooed all over, had been a few minutes on board, D'Urville was preparing to ask them some questions, with the aid of a vocabulary published by the missionaries, when all at once they turned away from him, leaped into their canoes and pushed out into the open sea. This sudden move was brought about by their countrymen, who, for the purpose of getting rid of them, slily hinted that their lives were in danger, as the Frenchmen had formed a plot to kill them.

It was in the Bay of Tolaga, the right name of which is Houa-Houa, that D'Urville found the first opportunity of gaining some information about the "kiwi," by means of a mat decorated with the feathers of that bird, such mats being articles of luxury among these islanders. The "kiwi" is about the size of a small turkey, and, like the ostrich, has not the power of flying. It is hunted at night by the light of torches and with the assistance of dogs. It is this bird which is also known under the name of the "apteryx." What the natives told D'Urville about it was in the main accurate. The apteryx, with the tail of a fowl and a plumage of a reddish-brown, has an affinity to the ostrich; it inhabits damp and gloomy woods, and never comes out even in search of food except in the evening. The incessant hunting of the natives has considerably diminished the numbers of this curious species, and it is now very rare.

D'Urville made no pause in the hydrographical survey of the northern island of New Zealand, keeping up daily communication with the natives, who brought him supplies of pigs and potatoes. According to their own statements, the tribes were perpetually at war with one another, and this was the true cause of the decrease in the population of these islands. Their constant demand was for fire-arms; failing to obtain these, they were satisfied if they could get powder in exchange for their own commodities.

On the 10th February, when not far from Cape Runaway, the corvette was caught in a violent storm, which lasted for thirty-six hours, and she was more than once on the point of foundering. After this, she made her way into the Bay of Plenty, at the bottom of which rises Mount Edgecumbe; then keeping along the coast, the islands of Haute and Major were sighted; but during this exploration of the bay, the weather was so severe that the chart of it then laid down cannot be considered very trustworthy. After leaving this bay, the corvette reached the Bay of Mercury; surveyed Barrier Island, entered Shouraki or Hauraki Bay, identified the Hen and Chickens and the Poor Knights Islands, finally arriving at the Bay of Islands. The native tribes met with by D'Urville in this part of the island were busy with an expedition against those of Shouraki and Waikato Bays. For the purpose of exploring the former bay, which had been imperfectly surveyed by Cook, D'Urville sailed back to it, and discovered that that part of New Zealand is indented with a number of harbours and gulfs of great depth, each one being safer, if possible, than the other. Having been informed that by following the direction of the Wai Magoia, a place would be reached distant only a very short journey from the large port of Manukau, he despatched some of his officers by that route, and they verified the correctness of the information he had received. This discovery, observes Dumont d'Urville, may become of great value to future settlements of Shouraki Bay; and this value will be still farther increased should the new surveys prove that the port of Manukau is accessible to vessels of a certain size, for such a settlement would command two seas, one on the east and the other on the west.

One of the "Rangatiras," as the chiefs of that quarter of the island are called, Rangui by name, had again and again begged the commander to give him some lead to make bullets with; a request which was always refused. Just before setting sail, D'Urville was informed that the deep-sea lead had been carried off; and he at once reproached Rangui in severe terms, telling him that such petty larcenies were unworthy of a man in a respectable position. The chief appeared to be deeply moved by the reproach, and excused himself by saying that he had no knowledge of the theft, which must have been committed by some stranger. "A short time afterwards," the narrative goes on to say, "my attention was drawn to the side of the ship by the sound of blows given with great force, and piteous cries proceeding from the canoe of Rangui. There I saw Rangui and Tawiti striking blow after blow with their paddles upon an object resembling the figure of a man covered with a cloak. It was easy to perceive that the two wily chiefs were simply beating one of the benches of the canoe. After this farce had been played for some little time, Rangui's paddle broke in his hands. The sham man was made to appear to fall down, when Rangui, addressing me, said that he had just killed the thief, and wished to know whether that would satisfy me. I assured him that it would, laughing to myself at the artifice of these savages; an artifice, for that matter, such as is often to be met with among people more advanced in civilization."

D'Urville next surveyed the lovely island of Wai-hiki, and thus terminated the survey of the Astrolabe Channel and Hauraki Bay. He then resumed his voyage in a northerly direction towards the Bay of Islands, sailing as far as Cape Maria Van Diemen, the most northerly point of New Zealand, where, say the Waïdonas, "the souls of the departed gather from all parts of Ika-Na- Mawi, to take their final flight to the realms of light or to those of eternal darkness."

The Bay of Islands, at the time when the *Coquille* put in there, was alive with a pretty considerable population, with whom the visitors soon became on friendly terms. Now, however, the animation of former days had given place to the silence of desolation. The Ipah, or rather the Pah of Kahou Wera, once the abode of an energetic tribe, was deserted, war had done its customary destructive work in the place. The Songhui tribe had stolen the possessions, and dispersed the members of the tribe of Paroa.

The Bay of Islands was the place chosen for their field of effort by the English missionaries, who, notwithstanding their devotion to their work had not made any progress among the natives. The unproductiveness of their labours was only too apparent.

The survey of the eastern side of New Zealand, a hydrographical work of the utmost importance, terminated at this point. Since the days of Cook no exploration of anything like such a vast extent of the coast of this country had been conducted in so careful a manner, in the face of so many perils. The sciences of geography and navigation were both signally benefited by the skilful and detailed work of D'Urville, who had to give proof of exceptional qualities in the midst of sudden and terrible dangers. However, on his return to France, no notice was taken of the hardships he had undergone, or the devotion to duty he had shown; he was left without recognition, and duties were assigned to him, the performance of which could bring no distinction, for they could have been equally well discharged by any ordinary ship's captain.

Leaving New Zealand on the 18th of March, 1827, D'Urville steered for Tonga Tabou, identified to begin with the islands Curtis, Macaulay, and Sunday; endeavoured, but without success, to find the island of Vasquez de Mauzelle, and arrived off Namouka on the 16th of April. Two days later he made out Eoa; but before reaching Tonga Tabou he encountered a terrible storm which all but proved fatal to the *Astrolabe*. At Tonga Tabou he found some Europeans, who had been for many years settled on the island; from them he received much help in getting to understand the character of the natives. The government was in the hands of three chiefs, called *Equis*, who had shared all authority between them since the banishment of the *Tonï Tonga*, or spiritual chief, who had enjoyed immense influence. A Wesleyan mission was in existence at Tonga; but it could be seen at a glance that the Methodist clergy had not succeeded in acquiring any influence over the natives. Such converts as had been made were held in general contempt for their apostasy.

When the *Astrolabe* had reached the anchorage, after her fortunate escape from the perils from contrary winds, currents, and rocks, which had beset her course, she was at once positively overwhelmed with the offer of an incredible quantity of stores, fruits, vegetables, fowls, and pigs, which the natives were ready to dispose of for next to nothing. For equally low prices D'Urville was able to purchase, for the museum, specimens of the arms and native productions of the savages. Amongst them were some clubs, most of them made of casuarina wood, skilfully carved, or embossed in an artistic manner with mother-of-pearl or with whalebone. The custom of amputating a joint or two of the fingers or toes, to propitiate the Deity, was still observed, in the case of a near relative being dangerously ill.

From the 28th of April the natives had manifested none but the most friendly feelings; no single disturbance had occurred; but on the 9th of May, while D'Urville, with almost all his officers, went to pay a visit to one of the leading chiefs, named Palou, the reception accorded to them was marked by a most unusual reserve, altogether inconsistent with the noisy and enthusiastic demonstrations of the preceding days. The distrust evinced by the islanders aroused that of D'Urville, who, remembering how few were the men left on board the *Astrolabe*, felt considerable uneasiness. However, nothing unusual happened during his absence from the ship. But it was only the cowardice of Palou which had caused the failure of a conspiracy, aiming at nothing less than the massacre, at one blow, of the whole of the staff, after which there would have been no difficulty in prevailing over the crew, who were already more than half-disposed to adopt the easy mode of life of the islanders. Such at least was the conclusion the commander came to, and subsequent events showed that he was right.

These apprehensions determined D'Urville to leave Tonga Tabou as quickly as possible, and on the 13th every preparation was made to set sail on the following day. The apprentice Dudemaine was walking about on the large island, whilst the apprentice Faraquet, with nine men, was engaged on the small island, Pangaï Modou, in getting fresh water, or studying the tide, when Tahofa, one of the chiefs, with several other islanders, then on board the *Astrolabe*, gave a signal. The canoes pushed off at once and made for the shore. On trying to discover the cause of this sudden retreat, it was observed that the sailors on the island Pangaï Modou were being forcibly dragged off by the natives. D'Urville was about to fire off a cannon, when he decided that it would be safer to send a boat to shore. This boat took off the two sailors and the apprentice Dudemaine, but was fired upon when despatched shortly afterwards to set fire to the huts, and to try to capture some natives as hostages. One native was killed and several others were wounded, whilst a corporal of the marines received such severe bayonet wounds, that he died two hours later.

Attack from the natives of Tonga Tabou.

D'Urville's anxiety about the fate of his sailors, and of Faraquet, who was in command of them, knew no bounds. Nothing was left for him to do but to make an attack upon the sacred village of Mafanga, containing the tombs of several of the principal families. But on the following day a crowd of natives so skilfully surrounded the place with embankments and palisades, that it was impossible to hope to carry it by an attack. The corvette then drew nearer to the shore, and began to cannonade the village, without, however, doing any other damage than killing one of the natives. At length the difficulty of obtaining provisions, the rain, and the continual alarm in which the firing of the Frenchmen kept them, induced the islanders to offer terms of peace. They gave up the sailors, who had all been very well treated, made a present of pigs and bananas; and on the 24th of May the *Astrolabe* took her final departure from the Friendly Islands.

It was quite time indeed that this was done, for D'Urville's situation was untenable, and in a conversation with his boatswain he ascertained that not more than half a dozen of the sailors could be relied on; all the others were ready to go over to the side of the savages.

Tonga Tabou is of madreporic formation, with a thick covering of vegetable soil, favourable to an abundant growth of shrubs and trees. The cocoa-tree, the stem of which is slenderer than elsewhere, and the banana-tree here shoot up with wonderful rapidity and vigour. The aspect of the land is flat and monotonous, so that a journey of one or two miles will give as fair an impression of the country as a complete tour of the island. The number of the population who have the true Polynesian cast of countenance may be put down at about 7000. D'Urville says "they combine the most opposite qualities. They are generous, courteous, and hospitable, yet avaricious, insolent, and always thoroughly insincere. The most profuse demonstration of kindness and friendship may at any moment be interrupted by an act of outrage or robbery, should their cupidity or their self-respect be ever so slightly roused."

In intelligence the natives of Tonga are clearly far superior to those of Otaheite. The French travellers could not sufficiently admire the astonishing order in which the plantations of yams and bananas were kept, the excessive neatness of their dwellings, and the beauty of the garden-plots. They even knew something of the art of fortification, as D'Urville ascertained by an inspection of the fortified village of Hifo, defended with stout palisades, and surrounded by a trench between fifteen and twenty feet wide, and half filled with water.

On the 25th of May, D'Urville began the exploration of the Viti or Fiji Archipelago. At the outset he was so fortunate as to fall in with a native of Tonga who was living on the Fiji Islands for purposes of trade, and had previously visited Otaheite, New Zealand, and Australia. This man, as well as a Guam islander, proved most useful to the commander in furnishing him with the names of more than 200 islands belonging to this group, and in acquainting him beforehand with their position, and that of the reefs in their neighbourhood. At the same time, Gressier, the hydrographer, collected all the materials requisite for preparing a chart of the Fiji Islands.

At this station a sloop was put under orders to proceed to the island of Laguemba, where was an anchor which D'Urville would have been well pleased to obtain, as he had lost two of his own while at Tonga. On arrival at the island, Lottin, who was in command of the sloop, observed on the shore none but women and children; armed men, however, soon came running up, made the women leave the place, and were preparing to seize the sloop and make the sailors prisoners. Their intentions were too plain to leave room for any doubt on the subject, so Lottin at once gave orders to draw up the grapnel, and got away into the open sea before there was time for an encounter to take place.

During eighteen consecutive days, in the face of bad weather and a rough sea, the *Astrolabe* cruised through the Fiji Archipelago, surveyed the islands of Laguemba, Kandabou, Viti-Levou, Oumbenga Vatou Lele, Ounong Lebou, Malolo, and many others, giving special attention to the southern islands of the group, which up to that period had remained almost entirely unknown.

The population of this group, if we accept D'Urville's account, form a kind of transition between the copper-coloured, or the Polynesian, and the black or Melanesian races. Their strength and vigour are in proportion to their tall figures, and they make no secret of their cannibal propensities.

On the 11th of June the corvette set sail for the harbour of Carteret; surveyed one by one the islands of Erronan and Annatom, the Loyalty Islands, of which group D'Urville discovered the Chabrol and Halgan Islands, the little group of the Beaupie Islands, the Astrolabe reefs, all the more dangerous as they are thirty miles distant from the Beaupie Islands, and sixty from New Caledonia. The island of Huon, and the chain of reefs to the north of New Caledonia, were subsequently surveyed. From this point D'Urville reached the Louisiade Archipelago in six days, but the stormy weather there encountered determined him to abandon the course he had planned out, and not to pass through Torres Straits. He thought that an early examination of the southern coast of New Britain, and of the northern coast of New Guinea, would be the most conducive to the interests of science.

Rossel Island and Cape Deliverance were next sighted; and the vessel was steered for New Ireland, with a view to obtaining fresh supplies of wood and water. Arriving there on the 5th of July in such gloomy, rainy weather, that it was with no small difficulty that the entrance of the harbour of Carteret, where D'Entrecasteaux made a stay of eight days, was made out; whilst there the travellers received several visits from the score of natives, who seem to make up the total population of the place. They were creatures possessed of scarcely any intelligence, and quite destitute of curiosity about objects that they had not seen before. Neither did their appearance lead to the slightest prepossession in their favour. They wore no vestige of clothing; their skin was black and their hair woolly; and the partition of the nostrils had a sharp bone thrust through by way of ornament. The only object that they showed any eagerness to possess was iron, but they could not be made to understand that it was only to be given in exchange for fruits or pigs. Their expression was one of sullen defiance, and they refused to guide any one whatever to their village. During the unprofitable stay of the corvette in this harbour, D'Urville had a serious attack of enteritis, from which he suffered much for several days.

On the 19th July the *Astrolabe* went to sea again and coasted the northern side of New Britain, the object of this cruise was frustrated by rainy and hazy weather. Continual squalls and heavy showers compelled the vessel to put off again as soon as it had succeeded in nearing the land. His experience on this coast D'Urville thus describes:—"One who has not had, as we have, a practical acquaintance with these seas, is unable to form any adequate conception of these incredible rains. Moreover, to obtain a just estimate of the cares and anxieties which a voyage like ours entails, there must be a liability to the call of duties similar to those which we had to discharge. It was very seldom that our horizon lay much beyond the distance of 200 yards, and our observations could not possibly be other than uncertain, when our own true position was doubtful. Altogether, the whole of our work upon New Britain, in spite of the unheard of hardships that fell to our lot and the risks which the *Astrolabe* had to run, cannot be put in comparison for a moment, as respects accuracy, with the other surveys of the expedition."

As it was impracticable to fall back upon the route by the St. George's Channel, D'Urville had to pass through Dampier's Strait, the southern entrance to which is all but entirely closed by a chain of reefs, which were grazed more than once by the *Astrolabe*.

The charming prospect of the western coast of New Britain excited intense admiration both in Dampier and D'Entrecasteaux; an enthusiasm fully shared by D'Urville. A safe roadstead enclosed by land forming a semicircle, forests whose dark foliage contrasted with the golden colour of the ripening fields, the whole surmounted by the lofty peaks of Mount Gloucester, and this variety still further enhanced by the undulating outlines of Rook Island, are the chief features of the picture here presented by the coast of New Britain.

Lofty mountains clothed with dense and gloomy forests.

On issuing from the strait the mountains of New Guinea rose grandly in the distance; and on a nearer approach they were seen to form a sort of half-circle shutting in the arm of the sea known as the Bay of Astrolabe. The Schouten Islands, the Creek of the Attack (the place where D'Urville had to withstand

393

an onset of savages), Humboldt Bay, Geelwinck Bay, the Traitor Islands, Tobie and Mysory, the Arfak Mountains, were one after another recognized and passed, when the *Astrolabe* at length came to an anchor in Port Dorei, in order to connect her operations with those accomplished by the *Coquille*.

Friendly intercourse was at once established with the Papuans of that place, who brought on board a number of birds of paradise, but not much in the shape of provisions. These natives, are of so gentle and timid a disposition, that only with great reluctance will they risk going into the woods through fear of the Arfakis, who dwell on the mountains, and are their sworn enemies.

One of the sailors engaged in getting fresh water was wounded with an arrow shot by one of these savages, whom it was impossible to punish for a dastardly outrage prompted by no motive whatever.

The land here is everywhere so fertile that it requires no more than turning over and weeding, in order to yield the most abundant harvests; yet the Papuans are so lazy and understand so little of the art of agriculture, that the growth of food plants is often allowed to be choked with weeds. The inhabitants belong to several races. D'Urville divides them into three principal varieties: the Papuans, a mixed breed, belonging more or less to the Malay or Polynesian race; and the Harfous or Alfourous, who resemble the common type of Australians; New Caledonians and the ordinary black Oceanic populations. These latter would appear to be the true indigenous people of the country.

On the 6th September the *Astrolabe* again put to sea, and after an uninteresting stay at New Guinea, in the course of which scarcely any specimens of natural history were obtained, except a few mollusca, and still less exact information regarding the customs, religion, or language of its diversified population, steered for Amboyna, which was reached without any accident on the 24th September. The governor, M. Merkus, happened to be on circuit; but his absence was no obstacle to the supply of all the stores needed by the commander. The reception given by the authorities and the society of the place was of a very cordial kind, and everything was done to compensate the French explorers for the hardships undergone in their long and troublesome voyage.

From Amboyna D'Urville proceeded to Hobart Town in Tasmania, a place not visited by any French vessel since the time of Baudin, arriving on the 27th December, 1827. Thirty-five years previously D'Entrecasteaux had met on the shores of this island only a few wretched savages; and ten years later Baudin found it quite deserted. The first piece of news that Dumont d'Urville learnt on entering the river Derwent, before even casting anchor at Hobart Town, was that Captain Dillon, an Englishman, had received certain information, when at Tucopia, of the shipwreck of La Pérouse at Vanikoro; and that he had brought away the hilt of a sword which he believed to have belonged to that navigator. On his arrival at Calcutta Dillon communicated his information to the governor, who without delay despatched him with instructions to rescue such of the shipwrecked crew as might still be alive, and collect whatever relics could be found of the vessels. To D'Urville this intelligence was of the highest interest, seeing that he had been specially instructed to search for whatever might be calculated to throw any light upon the fate of the unfortunate navigator, and he had while at Namouka obtained proof of the residence for a time of La Pérouse at the Friendly Islands.

In the English colony itself there was some difference of opinion as to the credit which Captain Dillon's story was entitled to receive; but the report which that officer had made to the Governor-General of India, quite removed any doubt from the mind of D'Urville. Abandoning, therefore, all further plans with reference to New Zealand, he decided upon proceeding at once in the *Astrolabe*, in the track of Dillon, to Vanikoro, which he then knew only by the name of Mallicolo.

Natives of Vanikoro.
(Fac-simile of early engraving.)

The following is the statement of the circumstances as made by Dillon.
During a stay made by the ship *Hunter* at the Fiji Islands, three persons, a

Prussian named Martin Bushart, his wife, and a Lascar, called Achowlia, were received on board, endeavouring to escape from the horrible fate awaiting them, which had already befallen the other European deserters settled in that archipelago, that of being devoured by the savages; this unhappy trio merely begged to be put on shore at the first inhabited island which the *Hunter* might touch at. Accordingly, they were left on one of the Charlotte Islands, Tucopia, in 12° 15' S. lat, and 169° W. long. In the month of May, 1836, Dillon, who had been one of the crew of the ship *Hunter*, paid a visit to the island of Tucopia, with a view of ascertaining what had become of the people put on shore in 1813. There he found the Lascar and the Prussian; the former of whom sold him a silver sword-hilt. As might have been expected, Dillon was curious to know how the natives of that island had come into possession of such an article. The Prussian then related that on his arrival at Tucopia he had found many articles of iron, such as bolts, axes, knives, spoons, and other things, which he was told had come from Mallicolo, a group of islands situated about two days canoe sail to the east of Tucopia. By further interrogatories, Dillon learnt that two vessels had been thrown upon the coasts many years previously, one of which had perished entirely with all on board, whilst the crew of the second had constructed out of the wreck of their ship a little boat, in which they had put to sea, leaving some of their number at Mallicolo. The Lascar said he had seen two of these men, who had acquired a well-merited influence through services rendered to chiefs.

Dillon tried in vain to persuade his informant to take him to Mallicolo, but was more successful with the Prussian, who took him within sight of the island, called Research by D'Entrecasteaux, on which, however, Dillon was unable to land on account of the dead calm and his want of provisions.

On hearing his account, on his arrival at Pondicherry, the governor entrusted him with the command of a boat specially constructed for exploring purposes. This was in 1827. Dillon now touched at Tucopia, where he obtained interpreters and a pilot, and thence went to Mallicolo, where he learnt from the natives that the strangers had stayed there five months to build their vessel, and that they had been looked upon as supernatural visitors, an idea not a little confirmed by their singular behaviour. They had been seen, for instance, to talk to the moon and stars through a long stick, their noses were immense, and some of them always remained standing, holding bars of iron in their hands. Such was the impression left on the minds of the natives by the astronomical observations, cocked hats, and sentinels of the French.

Dillon obtained from the natives a good many relics of the expedition, and he also saw at the bottom of the sea, on the coral reef on which the vessel had struck, some bronze cannons, a bell, and all kinds of rubbish, which he reverently collected and carried to Paris, arriving there in 1828, and receiving from the king a pension of 4000 francs as a reward for his exertions. All doubt was dispelled when the Comte de Lesseps, who had landed at Kamtchatka from La Pérouse's party, identified the cannons and the carved stern of the *Boussole*, and the armorial bearings of Colignon, the botanist, were made out on a silver candlestick. All these interesting and curious facts, however, D'Urville did not know until later; at present he had only heard Dillon's first report. By chance, or perhaps because he was afraid of being forestalled, the captain had not laid down the position of Vanikoro or the route he followed on the way from Tucopia, which island D'Urville supposed to belong to the Banks or Santa Cruz group, each as little known as the other.

Before following D'Urville, however, we must pause with him for awhile at Hobart Town, which he looked upon even then as a place of remarkable importance. "Its houses," he says, "are very spacious, consisting only of one story and the ground-floor, though their cleanness and regularity give them a very pleasant appearance. Walking in the streets, which are unpaved, though some have curb stones, is very tiring; and the dust always rising in clouds is very trying to the eyes. The Government house is pleasantly situated on the shores of the bay, and will be greatly improved in a few years if the young trees planted about it thrive. Native timber is quite unsuitable for ornamental purposes."

The stay at Hobart Town was turned to account to complete the stock of provisions, anchors, and other very requisite articles, and also to repair the vessel and the rigging, the latter being sorely dilapidated.

On the 5th January the *Astrolabe* once more put to sea, surveyed Norfolk Island on the 20th, Matthew Volcano six days later, Erronan on the 28th, and the little Mitre Island on the 8th February, arriving the next day off Tucopia, a small island three or four miles in circumference with one rather pointed peak covered with vegetation. The eastern side of Tucopia is apparently inaccessible from the violence of the breakers continually dashing on to its beach. The eagerness of all was now great, and was becoming unbounded when three boats, one containing a European, were seen approaching. This European turned out to be the Prussian calling himself Bushart, who had lately gone with Dillon to Mallicolo, where the latter remained a whole month, and where he really obtained the relics of the expedition as D'Urville had heard at Hobart Town. Not a single Frenchman now remained on the island; the last had died the previous year. Bushart at first consented, but declined at the last moment, to go with D'Urville or to remain on the *Astrolabe*.

Vanikoro is surrounded by reefs, through which, not without danger, the

Astrolabe found a passage, casting anchor in the same place as Dillon had done, namely in Ocili Bay. The scene of the shipwreck was on the other side of the bay. It was not easy to get information from the natives, who were avaricious, untrustworthy, insolent, and deceitful. An old man, however, was finally induced to confess that the whites who had landed on the beach at Vanon had been received with a shower of arrows, and that a fight ensued in which a good many natives had fallen; as for the *maras* (sailors) they had all been killed, and their skulls buried at Vanon. The rest of the bones had been used to tip the arrows of the natives.

A canoe was now sent to the village of Nama, and after considerable hesitation the natives were induced by a promise of some red cloth to take the Frenchmen to the scene of the shipwreck about a mile off, near Païon and opposite Ambi, where amongst the breakers at the bottom of a sort of shelving beach anchors, cannons, and cannonballs, and many other things were made out, leaving no doubt as to the facts in the minds of the officers of the *Astrolabe*. It was evident to all that the vessel had endeavoured to get inside the reefs by a kind of pass, and that she had run aground and been unable to get off. The crew may then have saved themselves at Païon, and according to the account of some natives they built a little boat there, whilst the other vessel, which had struck on the reef further out, had been lost with all on board.

Chief Moembe had heard it said that the inhabitants of Vanon had approached the vessel to pillage it, but had been driven back by the whites, losing twenty men and three chiefs. The savages in their turn had massacred all the French who landed, except two, who lived on the island for the space of three months.

Another chief, Valiko by name, said that one of the boats had struck outside the reef opposite Tanema after a very windy night, and that nearly all its crew had perished before they could land. Many of the sailors of the second vessel had got to land, and built at Païon a little boat out of the pieces of the large ship wrecked. During their stay at Païon quarrels arose, and two sailors with five natives of Vanon and one from Tanema were killed. At the end of five months the Frenchmen left the island.

Lastly, a third old man told how some thirty sailors belonging to the first vessel had joined the crew of the second, and that they had all left at the end of six or seven months. All these facts, which had so to speak to be extracted by force, varied in their details; the last, however, seemed most nearly to approach the truth. Amongst the objects picked up by the *Astrolabe* were an anchor weighing about 1800 pounds, a cast-iron cannon, a bronze swivel, a copper blunderbuss, some pig lead, and several other considerably damaged articles of little interest. These relics, with those collected by Dillon, are now in the Naval Museum at the Louvre.

D'Urville did not leave Vanikoro without erecting a monument to the memory of his unfortunate fellow-countrymen. This humble memorial was placed in a mangrove grove off the reef itself. It consists of a quadrangular prism, made of coral slabs six feet high, surmounted by a pyramid of Koudi wood of the same height, bearing on a little plate of lead the following inscription,—

> ## À la Mémoire
> ## DE LA PÉROUSE,
> ### Et de ses Compagnons
> ### L'Astrolabe
> ### 14 *Mars*, 1828.

As soon as this task was accomplished, D'Urville prepared to set sail again, as it was time he did, for the damp resulting from the torrents of rain had engendered serious fevers, prostrating no less than twenty-five of the party. The commander would have to make haste if he wished to keep a crew fit to execute the arduous manoeuvres necessary to the exit of the vessel from a narrow pass strewn with rocks.

The last day passed by the *Astrolabe* at Vanikoro would have shown the truth to D'Urville had he needed any enlightening as to the true disposition of the natives. The following is his account of the last incidents of this dangerous halt.

"At eight o'clock, I was a good deal surprised to see half a dozen canoes approaching from Tevaï, the more so, that two or three natives from Manevaï who were on board showed no uneasiness, although they had told me a few days before that the people of Tevaï were their mortal enemies. I expressed my surprise to the Manevaians, who merely said, with an evident air of equivocation, that they had made their peace with the Tevaians, who were only bringing some cocoa-nuts. I soon saw, however, that the new comers were carrying nothing but bows and arrows in first rate condition. Two or three of them climbed on board, and in a determined manner came up to the main watch to look down into the orlop-deck to find out how many men were disabled, whilst a malignant joy lit up their diabolical features. At this moment some of the crew told me that two or three of the Manevaï men on board had done the same thing during the last three or four days, and M. Gressien, who had been watching their movements since the morning, thought he had seen the warriors of the two tribes meet on the beach and have a long conference together. Such behaviour gave proof of the most treacherous intentions, and I felt the danger to be imminent. I at once ordered the natives to leave the vessel and return to the canoes, but they had the audacity to look at me with a proud and threatening expression, as if to defy me to put my order into execution. I merely had the armoury, generally kept jealously closed, opened, and with a severe look I pointed to it with one hand, whilst with the other I motioned the savages to the canoes. The sudden apparition of twenty shining muskets, the powers of which they understood, made them tremble, and relieved us of their ominous presence."

"I merely had the armoury opened."

Before leaving the scene of this melancholy story, we will glean a few details from D'Urville's account of it. The Vanikoro, Mallicolo, or, as Dillon calls it, the La Pérouse group, consists of two islands, Research and Tevaï. The former is no less than thirty miles in circumference, whilst the latter is only nine miles round. Both are lofty, clothed with impenetrable forests almost to the beach, and surrounded by a barrier of reefs thirty-six miles in circumference, with here and there a narrow strait between them. The inhabitants, who are lazy, slovenly, stupid, fierce, cowardly, and avaricious, do not exceed twelve or fifteen hundred in number. It was unfortunate for La Pérouse to be shipwrecked amongst such people, when he would have received a reception so different on any other island of Polynesia. The women are naturally ugly, and the hard work they have to do, with their general mode of life, render their appearance yet more displeasing. The men are rather less ill-favoured, though they are stunted and lean, and covered with ulcers and leprosy scars. Arrows and bows are their only weapons, and, according to themselves, the former, with their very fine bone tips, soldered on with extremely tenacious gum, inflict mortal wounds. They therefore value them greatly, and the visitors had great trouble to obtain any.

Reefs off Vanikoro.

On the 17th March the *Astrolabe* at length issued from amongst the terrible reefs encircling Vanikoro. D'Urville had intended to survey Tamnako, Kennedy, Nitendi, and the Solomon Islands, where he hoped to meet with traces of the survivors from the shipwreck of the *Boussole* and the *Astrolabe*. But the melancholy condition of the crew, pulled down as they were by fever, and the illness of most of the officers, with the absence of any safe anchorage in this part of Oceania, decided him to make for Guam, where he thought a little rest might possibly be obtained. This was a very grave dereliction from the instructions which ordered him to survey Torres Straits, but the fact of forty sailors being *hors de combat* and on the sick-list, will suffice to prove how foolish it would have been to make so perilous an attempt.

Not until the 26th April was Hogoley Archipelago sighted, where D'Urville bridged over the gaps left by Duperrey in his exploration, and only on the 2nd May did the coasts of Guam come in sight. Anchor was cast at Umata, where a supply of fresh water was easily found, and the climate much milder than at Agagna. On the 29th May, however, when the expedition set sail again, the men were not by any means all restored to health, which D'Urville attributed to the excesses in the way of eating indulged in by the sick, and the impossibility of getting them to keep to a suitable diet.

The good Medinilla, of whom Freycinet had such reason to speak favourably, was still governor of Guam. He did not this time, it is true, show so many kind attentions to the present expedition, but that was because a terrible drought had just devastated the colony, and a rumour had got afloat that the illness the crew of the *Astrolabe* was suffering from was contagious. Umata too was a good distance from Agagna, so that D'Urville could not visit the governor in his own home. Medinilla, however, sent the expedition fresh provisions and fruits in such quantities as to prove he had lost none of his old generosity.

After leaving Guam D'Urville surveyed, under sail, the Elivi, the Uluthii of Lütke, Guapgolo and the Pelew group of the Caroline Archipelago, was driven by contrary winds past Waigiou, Aiou, Asia, and Guebek, and finally entered Bouron Straits and cast anchor off Amboine, where he was cordially received by the Dutch authorities, and obtained news from France to the effect that the Minister of Marine had taken no notice of all the work, fatigue, and perils of the expedition, for not one officer had received advancement.

The receipt of this news caused considerable disappointment and discouragement, which the commander at once tried to remove. From Amboine the *Astrolabe* steered, *viâ* Banka Strait, for Uanado, with its well-armed and equipped fort, forming a pleasant residence. Governor Merkus obtained for D'Urville's natural history collections some fine *barberosas*, a *sapioutang*—the latter a little animal of the size of a calf, with the same kind of muzzle, paws, and turned-back horns—serpents, birds, fishes, and plants.

According to D'Urville the people of the Celebes resemble in externals the

Polynesians rather than the Malays. They reminded him of the natives of Otaheite, Tonga Tabou, and New Zealand, much more than of the Papuans of Darei Harbour, the Harfous of Bouron, or the Malays, with their square bony faces. Near Manado are some mines of auriferous quartz, of which the commander was able to obtain a specimen, and in the interior is the lake of Manado, said to be of immense depth, and which is the source of the torrent of the same name that dashes in the form of a magnificent waterfall over a basalt rock eighty feet high, barring its progress to the sea. D'Urville, accompanied by the governor and the naturalists of the expedition, explored this beautiful lake, shut in by volcanic mountains, with here and there a few fumerolles still issuing from them, and ascertained the depth of the water to be no more than twelve or thirteen fathoms, so that in the event of its ever drying up, its basin would form a perfectly level plain.

On the 4th August anchor was weighed at Manado, where the sufferers from fever and dysentery had not got much better, and on the 29th of the same month the expedition arrived at Batavia where it only remained three days. The rest of the voyage of the *Astrolabe* was in well-known waters. Mauritius was reached in due course, and there D'Urville met Commander Le Goarant, who had made a trip to Vanikoro in the corvette *La Bayonnaise*, and who told D'Urville that he had not attempted to enter the reef, but had only sent in some boats to reconnoitre. The natives had respected the monument to the memory of La Pérouse, and had been reluctant even to allow the sailors of the *Bayonnaise* to nail a copper plate upon it.

On the 18th November the corvette left Mauritius, and after touching at the Cape, St. Helena, and Ascension, arrived on the 25th March, 1829, at Marseilles, exactly thirty-five months after her departure from that port. To hydrographical science, if to nothing else, the results of the expedition were remarkable, and no less than forty-five new charts were produced by the indefatigable Messrs. Gressien and Paris. Nothing will better bring before us the richness of harvest of natural history specimens than the following quotation from Cuvier's report:—

"They (the species brought home by Quoy and Gaimard) amount to thousands in the catalogues, and no better proof can be given of the activity of our naturalists than the fact that the directors of the Jardin du Roi do not know where to store the results of the expedition, especially those now under notice. They have had to be stowed away on the ground-floor, almost in the cellars, and the very warehouses are now so crowded—no other word would do as well—that we have had to divide them by partitions to make more stowage."

The geological collections were no less numerous; one hundred and eighty-seven species or varieties of rock attest the zeal of Messrs. Quoy and

Gaimard, while M. Lesson, junior, collected fifteen or sixteen hundred plants; Captain Jacquinot made a number of astronomical observations; M. Lottin studied magnetism, and the commander, without neglecting his duties as a sailor and leader of the expedition, made experiments on submarine temperature and meteorology, and collected an immense mass of information on philology and ethnography.

We cannot better conclude our account of this expedition than with the following quotation from Dumont d'Urville's memoirs, given in his biography by Didot:—

"This adventurous expedition surpassed all previous ones, alike in the number and gravity of the dangers incurred, and the extent of the results of every kind obtained. An iron will prevented me from ever yielding to any obstacle. My mind once made up to die or to succeed, I was free from any hesitation or uncertainty. Twenty times I saw the *Astrolabe* on the eve of destruction without once losing hope of her salvation. A thousand times did I risk the very lives of my companions in order to achieve the object of my instructions, and I can assert that for two consecutive years we daily incurred more real perils than we should have done in the longest ordinary voyage. My brave and honourable officers were not blind to the dangers to which I daily exposed them, but they kept silence, and nobly fulfilled their duty."

From this admirable harmony of purpose and devotion resulted a mass of discoveries and observations in every branch of human knowledge, of all of which an exact account was given by Rossel, Cuvier, Geoffrey St. Hilaire, Desfontaines, and others, all competent and disinterested judges.

CHAPTER III.

POLAR EXPEDITIONS.

Bellinghausen, yet another Russian explorer—Discovery of the islands of Traversay, Peter I., and Alexander I.—The whaler, Weddell—The Southern Orkneys—New Shetland—The people of Tierra del Fuego—John Biscoe and the districts of Enderby and Graham—Charles Wilkes and the Antarctic Continent—Captain Balleny—Dumont d'Urville's expedition in the *Astrolabe* and the *Zelée*—Coupvent Desbois and the Peak of Teneriffe—The Straits of Magellan—A new post-office shut in by ice—Louis Philippe's Land—Across Oceania—Adélie and Clarie Lands—New Guinea and Torres Strait—Return to France—James Clark Rosset—Victoria.

We have already had occasion to speak of the Antarctic regions, and the explorations made there in the seventeenth, and at the end of the eighteenth century, by various navigators, nearly all Frenchmen, amongst whom we must specially note La Roche, discoverer of New Georgia, in 1675, Bouvet, Kerguelen, Marion, and Crozet. The name of Antarctic is given to all the islands scattered about the ocean which are called after navigators, as well as those of Prince Edward, the Sandwich group, New Georgia, &c.

It was in these latitudes that William Smith, commander of the brig *William*, trading between Monte Video and Valparaiso, discovered, in 1818, the Southern Shetland Islands, arid and barren districts covered with snow, on which, however, collected vast herds of seals, animals of which the skins are used as furs, and which had not before been met with in the Southern Seas. The news of this discovery led to a rush of whaling-vessels to the new hunting-grounds, and between 1821 and 1822 the number of seals captured in this archipelago is estimated at 32,000, whilst the quantity of sea-elephant oil obtained during the same time may be put down at 940 tons. As males and females were indiscriminately slaughtered, however, the new fields were soon exhausted. The survey of the twelve principal islands, and of the innumerable and all but barren rocks, making up this archipelago, occupied but a short time.

Hunting sea-elephants.

Two years later Botwell discovered the Southern Orkneys, and then Palmer and other whalemen sighted, or thought they sighted, districts to which they gave the names of Palmer and Trinity.

More important discoveries were, however, to be made in these hyberborean regions, and the hypothesis of Dalrymple, Buffon, and other scholars of the eighteenth century, as to the existence of a southern continent, forming, so to speak, a counterpoise to the North Pole, was to be unexpectedly confirmed by the work of these intrepid explorers.

The navy of Russia had now for some years been rapidly gaining in importance, and had played no insignificant part in scientific research. We have related the interesting voyages of most Russian circumnavigators; but we have still to speak of Bellinghausen's voyage round the world, which occupies a prominent place in the history of the exploration of the Antarctic seas.

The *Vostok*, Captain Bellinghausen, and the *Mirni*, commanded by Lieutenant Lazarew, left Cronstadt on the 3rd July, 1819, *en route* for the Antarctic Ocean. On the 15th December Southern Georgia was sighted, and seven days later an island was discovered in the south-east, to which the name of Traversay was given, and the position of which was fixed at 52° 15' S. lat., and 27° 21' W. long., reckoning from the Paris meridian.

Continuing their easterly course in S. lat. 60° for 400 miles as far as W. long. 187°, the explorers then bore south to S. lat. 70°, where their further progress was arrested by a barrier of ice.

Bellinghausen, nothing daunted, tried to cut his way eastwards into the heart of the Polar Circle, but at 44° E. long, he was compelled to return northwards. After a voyage of forty miles a large country hove in sight, which a whaler was to discover twelve years later when the ice had broken up.

Back again in S. lat. 62°, Bellinghausen once more steered eastwards without encountering any obstacles, and on the 5th March, 1820, he made for Port Jackson to repair his vessels.

The whole summer was given up by the Russian navigator to a cruise about Oceania, when he discovered no less than seventeen new islands, and on the 31st October he left Port Jackson on a new expedition. The first places sighted on this trip were the Macquarie Islands; then cutting across the 60th parallel, S. lat. in E. long. 160°, the explorers bore east between S. lat. 64° and 68° as far as W. long. 95°. On the 9th January, Bellinghausen reached 70° S. lat., and the next day discovered, in S. lat. 69° 30', W. long. 92° 20', an island, to which he gave the name of Peter I., the most southerly land hitherto visited. Then fifteen degrees further east, and in all but the same latitude, he sighted some more land which he called Alexander I.'s Land. Scarcely 200 miles distant from Graham's Land, it appeared likely to be connected with it, for the sea between the two districts was constantly discoloured, and many other facts pointed to the same conclusion.

From Alexander I.'s Land the two vessels, bearing due north, and passing Graham's Land, made for New Georgia, arriving there in February. Thence they returned to Cronstadt, the port of which they entered in July 1821, exactly two years after they left it, having lost only three men out of a crew of 200.

We would gladly have given further details of this interesting expedition, but we have not been able to obtain a sight of the original account published in Russian at St. Petersburg, and we have had to be content with the *résumé* brought out in one of the journals of the Geographical Society in 1839.

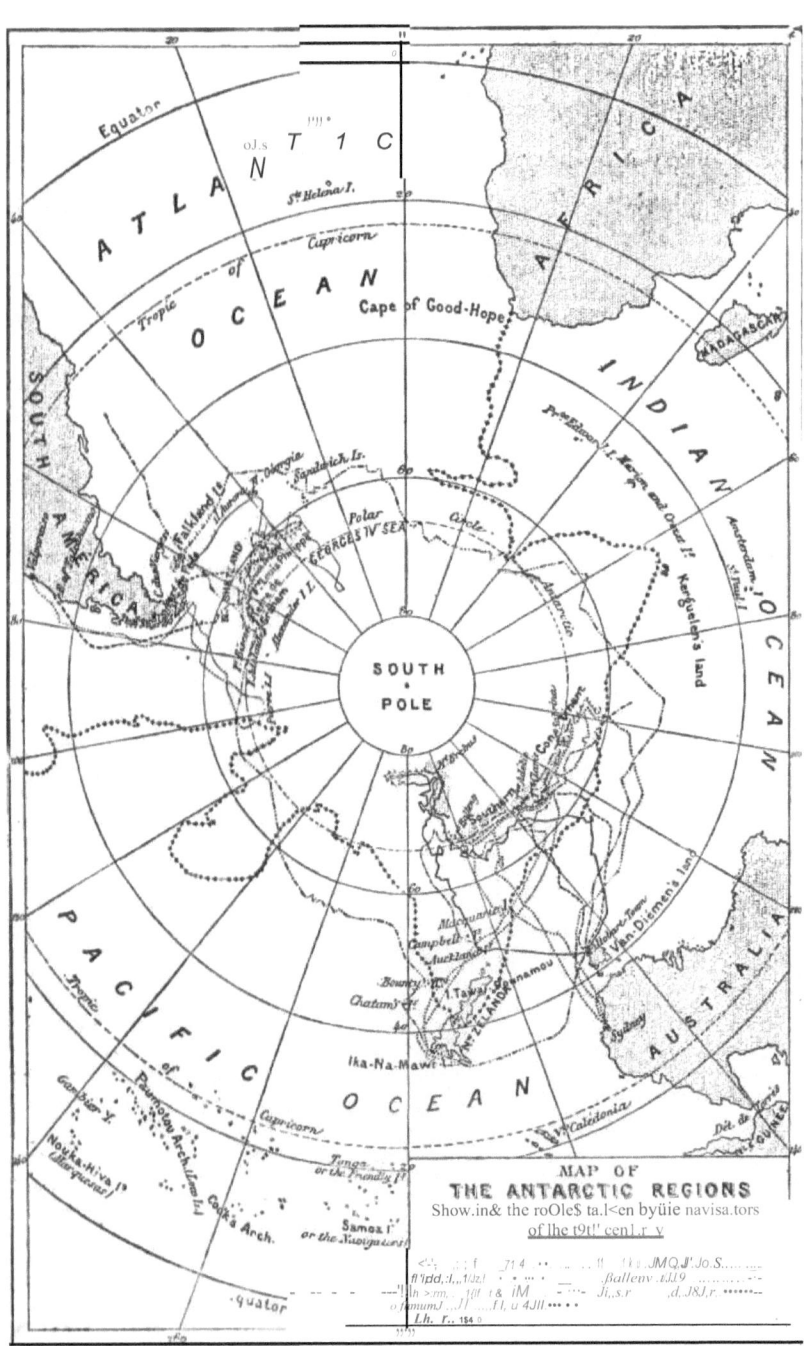

MAP OF
THE ANTARCTIC REGIONS
Show.in& the roOle$ ta.l<en byüie navisa.tors
of lhe t9t!' cenl.r y

Engraved by E. Morieu.

At the same period a master in the Royal Navy, James Weddell by name, was appointed by an Edinburgh firm to the command of an expedition, to obtain seal-skins in the southern seas, where two years were to be spent. This expedition consisted of the brig *Jane*, 160 tons, Captain Weddell, and the cutter *Beaufort*, sixty-five tons, Matthew Brisbane commander.

The two vessels left England on the 17th September, 1822, touched at Bonavista, one of the Cape Verd Islands, and cast anchor in the following December in the port of St. Helena, on the eastern coast of Patagonia, where some valuable observations were taken on the position of that town.

Weddell put to sea again on the 27th December, and steering in a south-easterly direction, came in sight, on the 12th January, of an archipelago to which he gave the name of the Southern Orkneys. These islands are situated in S. lat. 60° 45', and W. long. 45°.

According to the navigator, this little group presents an even more forbidding appearance than New Shetland. On every side rise the sharp points of rocks, bare of vegetation, round which surge the restless waves, and against which dash enormous floating icebergs, with a noise like thunder. Vessels are in perpetual danger in these latitudes, and the eleven days passed under sail by Weddell in surveying minutely the islands, islets, and rocks of this archipelago, were a time of ceaseless exertion for the crew, who were throughout in constant danger of their lives.

Specimens of the principal strata of these islands were collected, and on the return home put into the hands of Professor Jameson, of Edinburgh, who identified them as belonging to primary and volcanic rocks.

Weddell now made for the south, crossed the Antarctic Circle in W. long. 30°, and soon came in sight of numerous ice islands. Beyond S. lat. 70°, these floes decreased in number, and finally disappeared; the weather moderated, innumerable flocks of birds hovered above the ships, whilst large schools of whales played in its wake. This strange and unexpected change in the temperature surprised every one, especially as it became more marked as the South Pole was more nearly approached. Everything pointed to the existence of a continent not far off. Nothing was, however, discovered.

On the 20th February the vessels were in S. lat. 74° 15' and W. long. 34° 16' 45".

"I would willingly," says Weddell, "have explored the south-west quarter, but taking into consideration the lateness of the season, and that we had to pass homeward through 1000 miles of sea strewed with ice islands, with long nights, and probably attended with fogs, I could not determine otherwise than to take advantage of this favourable wind for returning."

Having seen no sign of land in this direction, and a strong southerly wind blowing at the time, Weddell retraced his course as far as S. lat. 58°, and steered in an easterly direction to within 100 miles of the Sandwich Islands. On the 7th February he once more doubled the southern cape, sailed by a sheet of ice fifty miles wide, and on the 20th February reached S. lat. 74° 15'. From the top of the masts nothing was to be seen but an open sea with a few floating ice-islands.

Unexpected results had ensued from these trips in a southerly direction. Weddell had penetrated 240 miles nearer the Pole than any of his predecessors, including Cook. He gave the name of George IV. to that part of the Antarctic Ocean which he had explored. Strange and significant was the fact that the ice had decreased in quantity as the South Pole was approached, whilst fogs and storms were incessant, and the atmosphere was always heavily charged with moisture, and the temperature of surprising mildness.

Another valuable observation made, was that the vibrations of the compass were as slow in these southern latitudes as Parry had noted them to be in the Arctic regions.

Weddell's two vessels, separated in a storm, met again in New Georgia after a perilous voyage of 1200 miles amongst the ice. New Georgia, discovered by La Roche in 1675, and visited in 1756 by the *Lion*, was really little known until after Captain Cook's exploration of it, but his account of the number of seals and walruses frequenting it had led to being much favoured by whalers, chiefly English and American, who took the skins of their victims to China and sold them at a guinea or thirty shillings each.

"The island," says Weddell, speaking of South Georgia, "is about ninety-six miles long, and its mean breadth about ten. It is so indented with bays, that in several places, where they are on opposite sides, they are so deep as to make the distance from one side to the other very small. The tops of the mountains are lofty, and perpetually covered with snow; but in the valleys, during the summer season, vegetation is rather abundant. Almost the only natural production of the soil is a strong-bladed grass, the length of which is in general about two feet; it grows in tufts on mounds three or four feet from the ground. No land quadrupeds are found here; birds and amphibious animals are the only inhabitants."

Here congregate numerous flocks of penguins, which stalk about on the beach, head in air. To quote an early navigator, Sir John Nasborough, they look like children in white aprons. Numerous albatrosses are also met with here, some of them measuring seventeen feet from tip to tip of their wings. When these birds are stripped of their plumage their weight is reduced one-half.

"Here congregate flocks of penguins."

Weddell also visited New Shetland, and ascertained that Bridgeman Island, in that group, is an active volcano. He could not land, as all the harbours were blocked up with ice, and he was obliged to make for Tierra del Fuego.

During a stay of two months here, Weddell collected some valuable information on the advantages of this coast to navigators, and obtained some accurate data as to the character of the inhabitants. In the interior of Tierra del Fuego rose a few mountains, always covered with snow, the loftiest of which were not more than 3000 feet high. Weddell was unable to identify the volcano noticed by other travellers, including Basil Hall in 1822, but he picked up a good deal of lava which had probably come from it. There was, moreover, no doubt of its existence, for the explorer under notice had seen on his previous voyage signs of a volcanic eruption in the extreme redness of the sky above Tierra del Fuego.

Hitherto there had been a good deal of divergence in the opinion of explorers as to the temperature of Tierra del Fuego. Weddell attributes this to the different seasons of their visits, and the variability of the winds. When he was there and the wind was in the south the thermometer was never more than two or three degrees above zero, whereas when the wind came from the north it was as hot as July in England. According to Weddell dogs and otters are the only quadrupeds of the country.

The relations with the natives were cordial throughout the explorer's stay amongst them. At first they gathered about the ship without venturing to climb on to it, and the scenes enacted on the passage of the first European vessel through the states were repeated in spite of the long period which had since elapsed. Of the bread, madeira, and beef offered to them, the natives would taste nothing but the meat; and of the many objects shown to them, they liked pieces of iron and looking-glasses best, amusing themselves with making grimaces in the latter of such absurdity as to keep the crew in fits of laughter. Their general appearance, too, was very provocative of mirth. Their jet black complexions, blue feathers, and faces streaked with parallel red and white lines, like tick, made up a whole of the greatest absurdity, and many were the hearty laughs the English enjoyed at their expense. Presently disgusted at receiving nothing more than the iron hoops of casks from people possessed of such wealth, they proceeded to annex all they could lay hands on. These thefts were soon detected and put a stop to, but they gave rise to many an amusing scene, and proved the wonderful imitative powers of the natives.

"A sailor had given a Fuegan," says Weddell, "a tin-pot full of coffee, which he drank, and was using all his art to steal the pot. The sailor, however, recollecting after awhile that the pot had not been returned, applied for it, but whatever words he made use of were always repeated in imitation by the Fuegan. At length he became enraged at hearing his requests reiterated, and, placing himself in a threatening attitude, in an angry tone, he said, 'You copper-coloured rascal, where is my tin-pot?' The Fuegan, assuming the same attitude, with his eyes fixed on the sailor, called out, 'You copper-coloured rascal, where is my tin-pot?' The imitation was so perfect that every one laughed, except the sailor, who proceeded to search him, and under his arm he found the article missing."

The sterile mountainous districts in this rigorous climate of Tierra del Fuego furnish no animal fit for food, and without proper clothing or nourishment the people are reduced to a state of complete barbarism. Hunting yields them hardly any game, fishing is almost equally unproductive of results; they are obliged to depend upon the storms which now and then fling some huge cetacean on their shores, and upon such salvage they fall tooth and nail, not even taking the trouble to cook the flesh.

In 1828 Henry Foster, commanding the *Chanticleer*, received instructions to make observations on the pendulum, with a view to determining the figure of the earth. This expedition extended over three years, and was then—i.e. in 1831—brought to an end by his violent death by drowning in the river Chagres. We allude to this trip because it resulted, on the 5th January, 1829, in the identification and exploration of the Southern Shetlands. The commander himself succeeded in landing, though with great difficulty, on one of these islands, where he collected some specimens of the syenite of which the soil is composed, and a small quantity of red snow, in every respect similar to that found by explorers in the Arctic regions.

Of far greater interest, however, was the survey made in 1830 by the whaler John Biscoe. The brig *Tula*, 140 tons, and the cutter *Lively*, left London under his orders on the 14th July, 1830. These two vessels, the property of Messrs. Enderby, were fitted up for whale-fishing, and were in every respect well qualified for the long and arduous task before them, which, according to Biscoe's instructions, was to combine discovery in the Antarctic seas with whaling.

After touching at the Falklands, the ships started on the 27th November on a vain search for the Aurora Islands, after which they made for the Sandwich group, doubling its most southerly cape on the 1st January, 1831.

In 59° S. lat. masses of ice were encountered, compelling the explorers to give up the south-western route, in which direction they had noted signs of the existence of land. It was therefore necessary to bear east, skirting along the ice as far as W. long. 9° 34'. It was only on the 16th January that Biscoe was able to cross the 60th parallel of S. lat. In 1775 Cook had here come to a space of open sea 250 miles in extent, yet now an insurmountable barrier of ice checked Biscoe's advance.

Continuing his south-westerly course as far as 68° 51' and 10° E. long., the explorer was struck by the discoloration of the water, the presence of several eaglets and cape-pigeons, and the fact that the wind now blew from the south-south-west, all sure tokens of a large continent being near. Ice, however, again barred his progress southwards, and he had to go on in an easterly direction approaching nearer and nearer to the Antarctic Circle.

"At length, on the 27th February," says Desborough Cooley, "in S. lat. 65° 57' and E. long. 47° 20' land was distinctly seen." This land was of considerable extent, mountainous and covered with snow. Biscoe named it Enderby, and made the most strenuous efforts to reach it, but it was so completely surrounded with ice that he could not succeed. Whilst these attempts were being made a gale of wind separated the two vessels and drove them in a south-easterly direction, the land remaining in sight, and stretching away from east to west for an extent of more than 200 miles. Bad weather, and the deplorable state of the health of the crew, compelled Biscoe to make for Van Diemen's Land, where he was not rejoined by the *Lively* until some months later.

The explorers had several opportunities of observing the aurora australis, to quote from Biscoe's narrative, or rather the account of his trip drawn up from his log-book, and published in the journal of the Royal Geographical Society. "Extraordinarily vivid coruscations of aurora australis (were seen), at times rolling," says Captain Biscoe, "as it were, over our heads in the form of beautiful columns, then as suddenly changing like the fringe of a curtain, and again shooting across the hemisphere like a serpent; frequently appearing not many yards above our heads, and decidedly within our atmosphere."

Leaving Van Diemen's Land on the 11th January, 1832, Biscoe and his two vessels resumed their voyage in a south-easterly direction. The constant presence of floating sea-weed, and the number of birds of a kind which never venture far from land, with the gathering of low and heavy clouds made Biscoe think he was on the eve of some discovery, but storms prevented the completion of his explorations. At last, on the 12th February, in S. lat. 64° 10' albatrosses, penguins, and whales were seen in large quantities; and on the 15th land was seen in the south a long distance off. The next day this land was ascertained to be a large island, to which the name of Adelaide was given, in honour of the Queen of England. On this island were a number of mountains of conical form with the base very large.

In the ensuing days it was ascertained that this was no solitary island, but one of a chain of islets forming so to speak the outworks of a lofty continent. This continent, stretching away for 250 miles in an E.N.E. and W.S.W. direction, was called Graham, whilst the name of Biscoe was given to the islets in honour of their discoverer. There was no trace either of plants or animals in this country.

To make quite sure of the nature of his discovery, Biscoe landed on the 21st February, on Graham's Land, and determined the position of a lofty mountain, to which he gave the name of William, in S. lat. 64° 45' and W. long. 66° 11', reckoning from the Paris meridian.

To quote from the journal of the Royal Geographical Society,—"The place was in a deep bay, in which the water was so still that could any seals have been found the vessels could have been easily loaded, as they might have been laid alongside the rocks for the purpose. The depth of the water was also considerable, no bottom being found with twenty fathoms of line almost close to the beach; and the sun was so warm that the snow was melted off all the rocks along the water-line, which made it more extraordinary that they should be so utterly deserted."

From Graham's Land, Biscoe made for the Southern Shetlands, with which it seemed possible the former might be connected, and after touching at the Falkland Islands, where he lost sight of the *Lively*, he returned to England.

As a reward for all he had done, and as an encouragement for the future,

Biscoe received medals both from the English and French Geographical Societies.

Very animated were the discussions which now took place as to the existence of a southern continent, and the possibility of penetrating beyond the barrier of ice shutting in the adjacent islands. Three powers simultaneously resolved to send out an expedition. France entrusted the command of hers to Dumont d'Urville; England chose James Ross; and the United States, Lieutenant Charles Wilkes.

The last named found himself at the head of a small fleet, consisting of the *Porpoise*, two sloops, the *Vincennes* and the *Peacock*; two schooners, the *Sea-Gull* and the *Flying-Fish*; and a transport ship, the *Relief*, which was sent on in advance to Rio with a reserve of provisions, whilst the others touched at Madeira, and the Cape Verd Islands.

From the 24th November, 1838, to the 6th January, 1839, the squadron remained in the bay of Rio de Janeiro, whence it sailed to the Rio Negro, not arriving at Port Orange, Tierra del Fuego, until the 19th February, 1839.

There the expedition divided, the *Peacock* and *Flying-Fish* making for the point were Cook crossed S. lat. 60°, and the *Relief*, with the naturalists on board, penetrating into the Straits of Magellan, by one of the passages south-east of Tierra del Fuego; whilst the *Vincennes* remained at Port Orange; and the *Sea-Gull* and *Porpoise* started on the 24th February for the Southern Seas. Wilkes surveyed Palmer's Land for a distance of thirty miles to the point where it turns in a S.S.E. direction, which he called Cape Hope; he then visited the Shetlands and verified the position of several of the islands in that group.

After passing thirty-six days in these inhospitable regions the two vessels steered northwards. A voyage marked by few incidents worthy of record brought Wilkes to Callao, but he had lost sight of the *Sea-Gull*. The commander now visited the Paumatou group, Otaheite, the Society and Navigator's Islands, and cast anchor off Sydney on the 28th November.

On the 29th December, 1839, the expedition once more put to sea, and steered for the south, with a view to reaching the most southerly latitude between E. long 160° and 145° (reckoning from Greenwich), bearing east by west. The vessels were at liberty to follow out separate courses, a rendezvous being fixed in case of their losing sight of each other. Up to January 22nd numerous signs of land were seen, and some officers even thought they had actually caught sight of it, but it turned out, when the various accounts were compared at the trial Wilkes had to undergo on his return, that it was merely through the accidental deviation before the 22nd January of the *Vincennes*, in a northerly direction, that the English explorers ascertained the existence of land. Not until he reached Sydney did Wilkes, hearing that D'Urville had discovered land on the 19th January, pretend to have seen it on the same day.

Dumont d'Urville.

These facts are established in a very conclusive article published by the hydrographer Daussy in the *Bulletin de la Société de Géographie*. Further on we shall see that d'Urville actually landed on the new continent, so that the honour of being the first to discover it is undoubtedly his.

The *Peacock* and *Flying-Fish*, either because they had sustained damages or because of the dangers from the roughness of the sea and floating ice, had steered in a northerly direction from the 24th January to the 5th February, The *Vincennes* and *Porpoise* alone continued the arduous voyage as far as E. long. 97°, having land in sight for two or three miles, which they approached whenever the ice allowed them to do so.

"On the 29th of January," says Wilkes, in his report to the National Institution of Washington, "we entered what I have called Piners Bay, the only place where we could have landed on the naked rocks. We were driven out of it by one of the sudden gales usual in those seas. We got soundings in thirty fathoms. The gale lasted thirty-six hours, and after many narrow escapes, I found myself some sixty miles W. to leeward of this bay. It now became probable that this land which we had discovered was of great extent, and I deemed it of more importance to follow its trend than to return to Piners Bay to land, not doubting I should have an opportunity of landing on some portion of it still more accessible; this, however, I was disappointed in, the icy barrier preventing our approach, and rendering it impossible to effect.

"Great quantities of ice, covered with mud, rock, and stone, presented themselves at the edge of the barrier, in close proximity of the land; from these our specimens were obtained, and were quite as numerous as could have been gathered from the rocks themselves. The land, covered with snow, was distinctly seen in many places, and between them such appearances as to leave little or no doubt in my mind of it being a continuous line of coast, and deserving the name bestowed upon it of the *Antarctic Continent*, lying as it does under that circle. Many phenomena were observed here, and observations made, which will be found under their appropriate head in the sequel.

"On reaching 97° east, we found the ice trending to the northward and continuing to follow it close, we reached to within a few miles of the position where Cook was stopped by the barrier in 1773."

Piners Bay, where Wilkes landed, is situated in E. long. 140° (reckoning from Paris), that is to say it is identical with the place visited by D'Urville on the 21st January. On the 30th January the *Porpoise* had come in sight of D'Urville's two vessels, and approached to within speaking distance of them, but they put on all sail and appeared anxious to avoid any communication.

On his arrival at Sydney, Wilkes found the *Peacock* in a state of repair and with that vessel he visited New Zealand, Tonga Tabou, and the Fiji Islands, where two of the junior officers of the expedition were massacred by the natives. The Friendly, Navigator, and Sandwich Islands, Admiralty Straits, Puget Sound, Vancouver's Island, the Ladrones, Manilla, Sooloo, Singapore, the Sunda Islands, St. Helena, and Rio de Janeiro, were the halting places on the return voyage, which terminated on the 9th June, 1842, at New York, the explorers having been absent three years and ten months altogether.

The results to every branch of science were considerable, and the young republic of the United States was to be congratulated on a début so triumphant in the career of discovery. In spite, however, of the interest attaching to the account of this expedition, and to the special treatises by Dana, Gould, Pickering, Gray, Cassin, and Brackenbridge, we are obliged to refrain from dwelling on the work done in countries already known. The success of these publications beyond the Atlantic was, as might be expected in a country boasting of so few explorers, immense.

Whilst Wilkes was engaged in his explorations, i.e. in 1839, Balleny, captain of the *Elizabeth Scott*, was adding his quota to the survey of the Antarctic regions. Starting from Campbell Island, on the south of New Zealand, he arrived on the 7th February in S. lat. 67° 7', and W. long. 164° 25', reckoning from the Paris meridian. Then bearing west and noting many indications of the neighbourhood of land, he discovered two days later a black band in the south-west which, at six o'clock in the evening, he ascertained beyond a doubt to be land. This land turned out to be three islands of considerable size, and Balleny gave them his own name. As may be imagined the captain tried to land, but a barrier of ice prevented his doing so. All he could manage was the determination of the position of the central isle, which he fixed at S. lat. 66° 44' and W. long. 162° 25'.

On the 14th February a lofty land, covered with snow, was sighted in the W.S.W. The next day there were but ten miles between the vessel and the land. It was approached as nearly as possible, and then a boat was put off, but a beach of only three or four feet wide with vertical and inaccessible cliffs rising beyond it rendered landing impossible, and only by getting wet up to their waists were the sailors able to obtain a few specimens of the lava characteristic of this volcanic district.

"Only by getting wet up to their waists."

Yet once more, on the 2nd March in S. lat. 65° and about W. long. 120° 24',
land was seen from the deck of the *Elizabeth Scott*. The vessel was brought to
for the night, and the next day an attempt was made to steer in a south-west

direction, but it was impossible to get through the ice barrier. Naming the new discovery Sabrina, Balleny resumed his northerly route without being able further to verify his discoveries.

In 1837, just as Wilkes had started on his expedition, Captain Dumont d'Urville proposed to the Minister of Marine a new scheme for a voyage round the world. The services rendered by him in 1819-21 in a hydrographic expedition, in 1822 and 1825 on the *Coquille*, under Captain Duperrey, and lastly in 1826-29 on the *Astrolabe*, had given him an amount of experience which justified him in submitting his peculiar views to the government, and to supplement so to speak the mass of information collected by himself and others in these little known latitudes.

The minister at once accepted D'Urville's offer, and exerted himself to find for him enlightened and trustworthy fellow-workers. Two corvettes, the *Astrolabe* and the *Zelée*, fitted up with everything which French experience had proved to be necessary, were placed at his disposal, and amongst his colleagues were many who were subsequently to rise to the rank of general officers, including Jacquinot, commander of the *Zelée*, Coupvent Desbois, Du Bouzet, Tardy de Montravel, and Perigot, all well-known names to those interested in the history of the French navy.

The instructions given by Vice-Admiral Rosamel to D'Urville differed from those of his predecessors chiefly in his being ordered to penetrate as near as the ice would permit to the South Pole. He was also ordered to complete the great work he had begun in 1827 on the Viti Islands, to survey the Salomon archipelago, to visit the Swan river of Australia, New Zealand, the Chatham Islands, that part of the Caroline group surveyed by Lütke, Mindanao, Borneo, and Batavia, whence he was to return to France *viâ* the Cape of Good Hope.

These instructions concluded in terms proving the exalted ideas of the government. "His Majesty," said Admiral de Rosamel, "not only contemplates the progress of hydrography and natural science; but his royal solicitude for the interests of French commerce and the development of the French navy is such as to lead him greatly to extend the terms of your commission and to hope for great results from it. You will visit numerous places, the resources of which you must study with a view to the interests of our whaling-ships, collecting all information likely to be of service to them alike in facilitating their voyages and rendering those voyages as remunerative as possible. You will touch at those ports where commercial relations with us are already opened, and where the visit of a state vessel will have salutary effects, and at others hitherto closed to our produce and about which you may on your return give us some valuable details."

In addition to the personal good wishes of Louis Philippe, D'Urville received many marks of the most lively interest taken in his work by the *Académie des Sciences morales* and the Geographical Society, but not unfortunately from the *Académie des Sciences*, although he had for twenty years been working hard to increase the riches of the Museum of Natural History.

"Whether from prejudice or from whatever cause," says D'Urville, "they (the members of the *Académie des Sciences*) showed very little enthusiasm for the contemplated expedition and their instructions to me were as formal as they would have been to a complete stranger."

It is matter of regret that the celebrated Arago, the declared enemy of Polar researches, was one of the bitterest opponents of the new expedition. This was not, however, the case with various scholars of other nationalities, such as Humboldt and Kruzenstern, who wrote to congratulate D'Urville on his approaching voyage and on the important results to science which might be hoped for.

After numerous delays, resulting from the fitting up of two vessels which were to take the Prince de Joinville to Brazil, the *Astrolabe* and *Zelée* at last left Toulon on the 7th September, 1837. The last day of the same month they cast anchor off Santa Cruz de Teneriffe which D'Urville chose as a halting- place in preference to one of the Cape Verd Islands, in the hope of laying in a stock of wine and also of being able to take some magnetic observations which he had been blamed for neglecting in 1826, although it was well known that he was not then in a fit state to attend to such things.

In spite of the eagerness of the young officers to go and enjoy themselves on shore they had to submit to a quarantine of four days, on account of rumours of cases of plague having occurred in the lazaretto of Marseilles. Without pausing to relate the details of Messrs. Du Bouzet, Coupvent, and Dumoulin's ascent of the Peak, we will merely quote a few enthusiastic remarks of Coupvent Desbois:—

"Arrived," says that officer, "at the foot of the peak, we spent the last hour of the ascent in crossing cinders and broken stones, arriving at last at the longed-for goal, the loftiest point of this huge volcano. The smoking crater presented the appearance of a hollow sulphurous semi-circle about 1200 feet wide and 300 feet deep, covered with the débris of pumice and other stones. The thermometer, which had marked five degrees at ten a.m., got broken through being placed on the ground where there was an escape of sulphuric vapour. There are upon the sides and in the crater numerous fumerolles which send forth the native sulphur, which forms the base of the peak. The rush of the vapour is so rapid as to sound like shots from a cannon.

"The heat of the ground is so great in some parts that it is impossible to stand on it for a minute at a time. Look around you and see if these three mountains piled one upon the other do not resemble a staircase built up by giants, on which to climb to heaven. Gaze upon the vast streams of lava, all issuing from one point which form the crater, and which a few centuries back you could not have trodden upon with impunity. See the Canaries in the distance, look down, ye pigmies, on the sea, with its breakers dashing against the shores of the island, of which you for the moment form the summit!... See for once, as God sees, and be rewarded for your exertions, ye travellers, whose enthusiasm for the grand scenes of nature has brought you some 12,182 feet above the level of the ocean."

We must add that the explorers testified to the brilliancy of the stars, as seen from the summit of the peak, the clearness of all sounds, and also to the giddiness and headache known as mountain sickness. Whilst part of the staff were engaged in this scientific excursion, several other officers visited the town, where they noticed nothing special except a narrow walk called the Alameda, and the church of the Franciscans. The neighbourhood, however, is interesting enough on account of the curious aqueducts for supplying the town with water, and the Mercede forest which, in D'Urville's opinion, might more justly be called a coppice, for it contains nothing but shrubs and ferns. The population seemed happy, but extremely lazy; economical, but horribly dirty; and the less said about their morals the better.

On the 12th October the two vessels put to sea again, intending to reach the Polar regions as soon as possible. Motives of humanity, however, determined D'Urville to change his plans and touch at Rio, the state of an apprentice with disease of the lungs becoming so rapidly worse that a stay in the Arctic regions would probably have been fatal.

The vessels cast anchor in the roadstead, not the Bay of Rio, on the 13th November, but they only remained there one day, that is to say, just long enough to land young Dupare, and to lay in a stock of provisions. The southerly route was then resumed.

For a long time D'Urville had wished to explore the Strait of Magellan, not with a view to further hydrographical surveys, for the careful explorations of Captain King, begun in 1826, had been finished in 1834 by Fitzroy, leaving little to be done in that direction, but to gather the rich and still unappropriated harvest of facts relating to natural history. How intensely interesting it was, too, to note how real had been the dangers encountered by early navigators, such as the sudden veering of the wind, &c. What a good thing it would be to obtain further and more detailed information about the famous Patagonians, the subject of so many fables and controversies. Yet another motive led D'Urville to anchor off Port Famine, rather than off Staten Island. His perusal of the accounts of the work of explorers who had penetrated into the Southern Seas convinced him that the end of January and the whole of February were the best times for visiting these regions, for then only are the effects of the annual thaw over, and with them the risk of over- fatigue to the crews.

Anchorage off Port Famine.

This resolution once taken, D'Urville communicated it to Captain Jacquinot, and set sail for the strait. On the 12th December Cape Virgin was sighted, and Dumoulin, seconded by the young officers, began a grand series of hydrographical surveys. In the intricate navigation of the strait, D'Urville, we are told, showed equal courage and calmness, skill and presence of mind, completely winning over to his side many of the sailors, who, when they had seen him going along at Toulon when suffering with the gout, had exclaimed, "Oh, that old fellow won't take us far!" Now, when his constant vigilance had brought the vessels safely out of the strait, the cry was, "The —— man is mad! He's made us scrape against rocks, reefs, and land, as if he had never taken a voyage before! And we used to think him as useless as a rotten keel!"

We must now say a few words on the stay at Port Famine.

Landing is easy, and there is a good spring and plenty of wood; on the rocks are found quantities of mussels, limpets, and whelks, whilst inland grows celery, and a kind of herb resembling the dandelion. Another fruitful source of wealth in this bay is fish, and whilst the vessels were at anchor, drag-nets, trammels, and lines captured enough mullet, gudgeon, and roaches to feed the whole crew.

"As I was about to re-embark," says D'Urville, "a little barrel was brought to me which had been found hung on a tree on the beach, near a post on which was written *Post Office*. Having ascertained that this barrel contained papers, I took it on board and examined them. They consisted of notes of captains who had passed through the Straits of Magellan, stating the time of their visits, the incidents of their passage, with advice to those who should come after them, and letters for Europe or the United States. It seemed that an American captain, Cunningham by name, had been the originator of this open-air post-office. He had merely, in April, 1833, hung a bottle on a tree, and his fellow-countryman, Waterhouse, had supplemented it by the post with its inscription. Lastly, Captain Carrick of the schooner *Mary Ann*, from Liverpool, passed through the strait in March 1837, on his way to San Blas, California, going through it again a second time on his way back on the 29th November, 1837, that is to say, sixteen days before our own visit, and he it was who had substituted the barrel for the bottle, adding an invitation to all who should succeed him to use it as the receptacle of letters for different destinations. I mean to improve this ingenious and useful contrivance by forming an actual post-office on the highest point of the peninsula with an inscription in letters of a size so gigantic as to compel the attention of navigators who would not otherwise have touched at Port Famine. Curiosity will then probably lead them to send a canoe to examine the box, which will be fastened to the post. It seems likely that we shall ourselves reap the first fruits of this arrangement, and our families will be agreeably surprised to receive news from us from this wild and lonely district, just before our plunge into the ice of the Polar regions."

At low tide the mouth of the Sedger river, which flows into Famine Bay, is encumbered with sand-banks; some 1000 feet further on the plain is transformed into a vast marsh, from which rise the trunks of immense trees, and huge bones, bleached by the action of time, which have been brought down by the heavy rainfall, swelling the course of the stream.

Skirting this marsh is a fine forest, the entrance to which is protected by prickly shrubs. The commonest trees are the beech, with trunks between eighty and ninety feet high, and three or four in diameter; Winteria aromatica, a kind of bark which has long since replaced the cinnamon, and a species of Barbary. The largest beeches seen by D'Urville measured fifteen feet in diameter, and were about 150 feet high.

Unfortunately, no mammiferous animals or reptiles, or fresh or salt water shell-fish are found on these coasts; and one or two different kinds of birds with a few lichens and mosses were all the naturalist was able to obtain.

Several officers went up the Sedger in a yawl till they were stopped by the shallowness of the water. They were then seven and a half miles from the mouth, and they noted the width of the river where it flows into the sea to be between ninety and a hundred feet.

"It would be difficult," says M. de Montravel, "to imagine a more picturesque scene than was spread out before us at every turn. Everywhere was that indescribable wildness which cannot be imitated, a confused mass of trees, broken branches, trunks covered with moss, which seemed literally to grow before our eyes."

To resume, the stay at Port Famine was most successful; wood and water were easily obtained, repairs, &c., were made, horary, physical, meteorological, tidal, and hydrographical observations were taken, and, lastly, numerous objects of natural history were collected, the more interesting as the museums of France hitherto contained nothing whatever from these unknown regions beyond "a few plants collected by Commerson and preserved in the Herbarium of M. de Jussieu."

On the 28th December, 1837, anchor was weighed without a single Patagonian having been seen, although the officers and crew had been so eager to make acquaintance with the natives.

The difficulties attending navigation compelled the two corvettes to cast anchor a little further on, off Port Galant, the shores of which, bordered by fine trees, are cut by torrents resembling a little distance off magnificent cascades from fifty to sixty feet high. This compulsory halt was not wasted, for a large number of new plants were collected, and the port with the neighbouring bays were surveyed. The commander, however, finding the season already so far advanced, gave up his idea of going out at the westerly end of the strait, and went back the way he came, hoping thus to get an interview with the Patagonians before going to the Polar regions.

St. Nicholas Bay, called by Bougainville the *Baie des Français*, where the explorers passed New Year's Day, 1838, is a much pleasanter looking spot than Port Galant. The usual hydrographical surveys were there brought to a satisfactory issue by the officers under the direction of Dumoulin. A boat was despatched to Cape Remarkable, where Bougainville said he had seen fossil shells, which, however, turned out to be nothing but little pebbles imbedded in a calcareous gangue.

Interesting experiments were made with the thermometrograph, or marine thermometer, at 290 fathoms, without reaching the bottom, at less than two miles from land. Whereas the temperature was nine degrees on the surface, it was but two at the above-named depth, and as it is scarcely likely that currents convey the waters of the two oceans so far down, one is driven to the belief that this is the usual temperature of such depths.

The vessels now made for Tierra del Fuego, where Dumoulin resumed his surveys. Low exposed, and strewn with rocks which serve as landmarks, there were but few dangers to be encountered here. Magdalena Island, Gente Grande Bay, Elizabeth Island, and Oazy Harbour, where the camp of a large party of Patagonians was made out with the telescope, and Peckett Harbour, where the *Astrolabe* struck in three fathoms, were successively passed.

"As we struck," says D'Urville, "there were signs of astonishment and even of excitement amongst the crew, and some grumbling was already audible, when in a firm voice I ordered silence, and without appearing at all put out by what had happened, I cried, 'This is nothing at all, and we shall have plenty more of the same kind of thing.' Later these words often recurred to the memory of our sailors. It is more difficult than one would suppose for a captain to maintain perfect calmness and impassiveness in the midst of the worst dangers, even those he has reason to imagine likely to be fatal."

Peckett Harbour was alive with Patagonians, and officers and men were alike eager to land. A crowd of natives on horseback were waiting for them at the place of disembarkation.

Gentle and peaceable they readily replied to the questions put to them, and looked quietly at everything shown to them, expressing no special desire for anything offered to them. They did not seem either to be at all addicted to thieving, and when on board the French vessels they made no attempt to carry anything off.

Their usual height is from four and a half to five feet, but some are a good deal shorter. Their limbs are large and plump without being muscular, and their extremities are of extraordinary smallness. Their most noteworthy characteristic is the breadth of the lower part of the face as compared to the forehead, which is low and retreating. Long narrow eyes, high cheek-bones, and a flat nose, give them something of a resemblance to the Mongolian type.

They are evidently extremely languid and indolent, and wanting in strength and agility. Looking at them squatting down, standing or walking, with their long hair flowing down their backs, one would take them for the women of a harem rather than savages used to enduring the inclemency of the weather and to struggle for existence. Stretched upon skins with their dogs and horses about them, their chief amusement is to catch the vermin with which they swarm. They hate walking so much that they mount horses just to go down and pick up shells on the beach a few yards off.

A white man was living amongst these Patagonians; a miserable, decrepit-looking fellow, who said he came from the United States, but he spoke English very imperfectly, and the explorers took him to be a German-Swiss. Niederhauser, so he called himself, had gone to seek his fortune in the United States, and that fortune being long on the road, he had given ear to the wonderful proposals of a certain whaleman, who wanted to complete his crew. By this whaleman he was left with seven others and some provisions on a desert island off Tierra del Fuego to hunt seals and dress their skins. Four months later the schooner returned laden with skins, left the seal-hunters fresh provisions, went off again, and never came back! Whether it had been shipwrecked, or whether the captain had abandoned his sailors, it was impossible to ascertain. When the poor fellows found themselves deserted and their provisions exhausted, they embarked in their canoe and rowed up the Straits of Magellan, soon meeting with some Patagonians, with whom Niederhauser remained, whilst his companions went on. Well received by the natives, he lived their life with them, faring well when food was plentiful, drawing in his belt and living on roots when food was scarce.

Weary, however, of this miserable existence, Niederhauser entreated D'Urville to take him on board, urging that another month of the life he was leading would kill him. The captain consented, and received him as a passenger.

During his three months' residence amongst them, Niederhauser had learnt something of the language of the Patagonians, and with his aid D'Urville drew up a comparative vocabulary of a great many words in Patagonian, French, and German.

The war costume of the Fuegans includes a helmet of tanned leather protected by steel-plates and surmounted by a crest of cock's feathers, a tunic of ox-hide dyed red with yellow stripes, and a kind of double-bladed scimitar. The chief of Peckett Harbour allowed his visitors to take his portrait in full martial costume, thereby showing his superiority to his subjects, who would not do the same for fear of witchcraft.

On the 8th January anchor was finally weighed, and the second entrance to the strait was slowly navigated against the tide. The Straits of Magellan having now been crossed from end to end, and a survey made of the whole of the eastern portion of Tierra del Fuego, thus bridging over an important gulf in hydrographic knowledge, no detailed map of this coast having previously been made, the vessels steered for the Polar regions, doubling Staten Island without difficulty, and on the 15th January coming in sight of the first ice, an event causing no little emotion, for now was to begin the really hard work of the voyage.

Floating ice was not the only danger to be encountered in these latitudes: a dense fog, which the keenest sight could not penetrate, soon gathered about the vessels, paralyzing their movements, and though they were under a foresail only, rendering a collision with the ice-masses imminent. The temperature fell rapidly, and the thermometrograph marked only two degrees on the surface of the sea, whilst the deep water was below zero. Half-melted snow now began to fall, and everything bore witness that the Antarctic regions were indeed entered.

Clarence, New South Orkney Islands, could not be identified. Every one's attention had to be concentrated on avoiding blocks of ice. At midday on the 20th January the vessels were in S. lat. 62° 3' and W. long. 49° 56', not far from the place were Powell encountered compact ice-fields, and an immense ice-island was soon sighted, some 6000 feet in extent and 300 in height, with perpendicular sides greatly resembling land under certain conditions of the light. Numerous whales and penguins were now seen swimming about the vessels, whilst white petrels continually flew across them. On the 21st observations gave S. lat. 62° 53', and D'Urville was expecting soon to reach the 65th parallel, when at three a.m. he was told that further progress was arrested by an iceberg, across which it did not seem possible to cut a passage. The vessels were at once put about and slowly steered in an easterly direction, the wind having fallen.

"We were thus enabled," says D'Urville, "to gaze at our leisure upon the wonderful spectacle spread out before our eyes. Severe and grand beyond expression it not only excited the imagination but filled the heart with involuntary terror, nowhere else is man's powerlessness more forcibly brought before him.... A new world displays itself to him, but it is a motionless, gloomy, and silent world, where everything threatens the annihilation of human faculties. Should he have the misfortune to be left here alone, no help, no consolation, no spark of hope, would soothe his last moments. One is involuntarily reminded of the famous inscription on the gate of the Inferno of Dante—

"'Lasciate ogni speranza, voi ch' entrate.'"

D'Urville now set to work on a very strange task, which, as compared with others of a similar kind, was likely to be of considerable value. He had an exact measurement taken of the outlines of the iceberg. Had other navigators done the same we should have had some precise information as to the direction taken by icebergs, their movements, &c., in the southern Polar regions, a subject still wrapped in the greatest obscurity.

On the 22nd, after doubling a point, it was ascertained that the iceberg was bearing S.S.W. by W. A lofty and broken piece of land was sighted in these latitudes. Dumoulin had begun to survey it, and D'Urville was about, as he thought, to identify it with the New South Greenland of Morrell, when its outlines became dim and it sunk beneath the horizon. On the 24th the two corvettes crossed a series of floating islets, and entered a plain where the ice was melting. The passage, however, became narrower and narrower, and they were obliged to veer round, to save themselves from being blocked in.

Everything pointed to the conclusion that the edge of the ice was melting, the ice-islands fell apart with loud reports, the ice running off in little rivulets: there was undoubtedly a thaw, and Fanning had been right in saying that these latitudes should not be visited before February.

D'Urville now decided to steer for the north, and try to reach the islands of New South Orkney, the map of which had not yet been accurately laid down. The commander was anxious to survey that archipelago thoroughly, and to spend several days there before resuming his southerly course, so as to be in the Antarctic regions at the same time of year as Weddell.

For three days the explorer coasted along the southern shores of New South Orkney without being able to land; he then once more turned southwards, and came in sight of the ice again in S. lat. 62° 20' and W. long. 39° 28'.

A few minutes before midday a kind of opening was discovered, through which the vessels were forced at all risks. This bold manoeuvre was successful, and in spite of the heavy snow, the explorers penetrated into a small basin scarcely two miles in extent and hemmed in on every side by lofty walls of ice. It was decided to make fast to the ice, and when the order to cast anchor was given a young middy on board the *Zelée* cried naively, "Is there a port here? I shouldn't have thought there were people living on the ice."

Great indeed was now the joyful enthusiasm on both vessels. Some of the

436

young officers of the *Zelée* had come to empty a bowl of punch with their comrades of the *Astrolabe*, and the commander could hear their shouts of delight from his bed. He himself did not, however, look upon the situation in quite the same favourable light. He felt that he had done a very imprudent thing. Shut into a *cul-de-sac*, he could only go out as he had come, and that he could not do until he had the wind right aft. At eleven o'clock D'Urville was awoke by a violent shock, accompanied by a noise of breaking, as if the vessel had struck on some rocks. He got up, and saw that the *Astrolabe*, having drifted, had struck violently against the ice, where she remained exposed to collision with the masses of ice which the current was sweeping along more rapidly than it did the vessel herself.

When day dawned the adventurers found themselves surrounded by ice, but in the north a blackish blue line seemed to betray the existence of an open sea. This direction was at once taken, but a thick fog immediately and completely enveloped both ships, and when it cleared off they found themselves face to face with a compact ice barrier, beyond which stretched away as far as the eye could reach AN OPEN SEA!

D'Urville now resolved to cut himself a passage, and began operations by dashing the *Astrolabe* with all possible speed against the obstacle. The vessel penetrated two or three lengths into the ice, and then remained motionless. The crew climbed out of her on to the ice armed with pickaxes, pincers, mattocks, and saws, and merrily endeavoured to cut a passage. The fragment of ice was already nearly crossed when the wind changed, and the motion of the waves in the offing began to be felt, causing the officers to agree in urging a retreat into the shelter of the ice-walls, for there was some danger if the wind freshened of the vessel being embayed against the ice and beaten to pieces by the waves and floating *débris*.

The corvettes had traversed twelve or fifteen miles for nothing, when an officer, perched in the shrouds, sighted a passage in the E.N.E. That direction was at once taken, but again it was found impossible to cut a passage, and when night came the crew had to make the ship fast to a huge block of ice. The loud cracking noises which had awoke the commander the night before now began with such violence that it really seemed impossible for the vessel to live till daylight.

After an interview with the captain of the *Zelée*, however, D'Urville made for the north, but the day passed without any change being effected in the position of the vessels, and the next day during a storm of sleet the swell of the sea became so powerful as completely to raise the ice plain in which they were imprisoned.

More careful watch than ever had now to be kept, to guard against the pieces

of ice flung long distances by this motion, and the rudder had to be protected
from them by a kind of wooden hut.

"The rudder had to be protected."

With the exception of a few cases of ophthalmia, resulting from the continual glare of the snow, the health of the crews was satisfactory, and this was no little satisfaction to the leaders of the expedition, compelled as they were to be continually on the *qui-vive*. Not until the 9th February were the vessels, favoured by a strong breeze, able to get off, and once more enter a really open sea. The ice had been coasted for a distance of 225 leagues. The vessels had actually sustained no further damage than the loss of a few spars and a considerable portion of the copper sheathing, involving no further leakage than there had been before.

The next day the sun came out, and observations could be taken, giving the latitude as 62° 9' S., and the longitude 39° 22' W.

Snow continued to fall, the cold was intense, and the wind very violent for the three succeeding days. This continuance of bad weather, together with the increasing length of the nights, warned D'Urville of the necessity of giving up all idea of going further. When, therefore, he found himself in S. lat. 62° and W. long. 33° 11', in other words in that part of the ocean where Weddell had been able to sail freely in 1823, and the new explorer had met with nothing but impassable ice, he steered for New South Orkney. A whole month passed amongst the ice and fogs of the Antarctic Ocean had told upon the health of the crews, and nothing could be gained for science by a continuance of the cruise.

On the 20th the archipelago was again sighted, and D'Urville was once more driven out of his course in a northerly direction by the ice, but he was able to put off with two boats, the crews of which collected on Weddell Island a large number of geological specimens, lichens, &c., and some twenty penguins and chionis.

On the 25th February Clarence Island was seen, forming the eastern extremity of the New South Shetland Archipelago, a very steep and rugged district covered with snow except on the beach, and thence the explorers steered towards Elephant Island, resembling Clarence Island in every respect, except that it is strewn with peaks rising up black against the plains of snow and ice. The islets of Narrow, Biggs, O'Brien, and Aspland were successively identified, but covered as they are with snow they are perfectly inaccessible to man. The little volcano of Bridgeman was also seen, and the naturalists tried in vain to land upon it from two boats.

"The general colour of the soil," says the narrative, "is red, like that of burnt brick with particles of grey, suggestive of the presence of pumice-stone, or of calcined cinders. Here and there on the beach are seen great blackish-looking blocks, which are probably lava. This islet has, however, only one true crater, although thick columns of smoke are emitted from it, nearly all of them issuing from the base on the western side, whilst in the north are two other fumerolles, thirty or forty feet along the water. There are none on the eastern or northern side, or at the top, which is smooth and round. The bulk appears recently to have undergone some considerable modification, as indeed it must have done, or it could not now resemble so little the description given by Powell in December, 1822."

D'Urville soon resumed his southerly route, and on the 27th February sighted a considerable belt of land in the south-east on which he was prevented from landing by the fog and the continuous fall of very fine snow. He was now in the latitude of Hope Island—i.e. in S. lat. 62° 57'. He approached it very closely, and sighted before reaching it a low-lying land, to which he gave the name of Joinville. Then further on in the south-west he came to an extensive district which he named Louis Philippe, and between the two in a kind of channel, encumbered with ice, an island he called Rosamel.

"Now," says D'Urville, "the horizon was so light that we could trace all the irregularities of Louis Philippe's Land. We could see it stretching away from Mount Bransfield in the north (62° W. long.) to the S.S.W., where it faded away on the horizon. From Mount Bransfield to the south it is lofty, and of fairly uniform surface, resembling a vast, unbroken ice-field. In the south, however, it rises in the form of a fine peak (Mount Jacquinot), which is equal perhaps, indeed superior, to Bransfield; but beyond this peak it stretches away in the form of a mountain chain, ending in the south-west in a peak loftier than any of the others. For the rest, the effect of the snow and ice, together with the absence of any objects with which they can be compared, aid in exaggerating the height of all irregularities, and, as a matter of fact, the results of the measurements taken by M. Dumoulin showed all these mountains, which then appeared to us gigantic and equal to the Alps and Pyrenees at least, to be after all of very medium size. Mount Bransfield, for instance, was not more than about 2068 feet high, Mount Jacquinot 2121 feet, and Mount d'Urville, the loftiest of them all, about 3047 feet. Except for the islets grouped about the mainland, and a few peaks rising above the snow, the whole country is one long series of compact blocks of ice, and it is impossible to do more than trace the outlines of this ice-crust, those of the land itself being quite indistinguishable."

On the 1st March soundings gave only eighty fathoms with a bottom of rock and gravel. The temperature is 1°9 on the surface, and 0°2 at the bottom of the sea. On the 2nd of March, off Louis Philippe's Land, an island was sighted which was named Astrolabe, and the day after a large bay, or rather strait, to which the name of Orleans Channel was given was surveyed between Louis Philippe's Land, and a lofty, rocky belt, which D'Urville took for the beginning of Trinity Land, hitherto very inaccurately laid down.

From the 26th February then to the 5th March D'Urville remained in sight of the coast, skirting along it a little distance off, but unable entirely to regulate his course on account of the incessant fogs and rain. Everything bore witness to the setting in of a very decided thaw; the temperature rising at midday to five degrees above zero, whilst the ice was everywhere melting and running off in little streams of water, or falling with a formidable crush into the sea in the form of blocks, the wind meanwhile blowing strongly from the west.

All this decided D'Urville against the further prosecution of this voyage. The sea was heavy, the rain and fog incessant. It was therefore necessary to leave this dangerous coast, and make for the north, where on the following day he surveyed the most westerly islands of the New Shetland group.

D'Urville next steered for Conception, and very arduous was the voyage there, for, in spite of every precaution, the crews of both corvettes, especially that of the *Zelée*, were attacked with scurvy. It was now that D'Urville measured the heights of some of the waves, with a view to the disproving of the charge of exaggeration which had been brought against him when he had estimated those he had seen break over Needle Bank at a height of between eighty and a hundred feet.

With the help of some of his officers, that there might be no doubt as to his accuracy, D'Urville measured some waves of which the vertical height was thirty-five feet, and which measured not less than 196½ feet from the crest to the lowest point, making a total length of 393 feet for a single wave. These measurements were an answer to the ironical assertion of Arago, who, settling the matter in his own study, would not allow that a wave could exceed from five to six feet in height. One need not hesitate a single moment to accept, as against the eminent but impulsive physicist, the measurements of the navigators who had made observations upon the spot.

On the 7th April, 1838, the expedition cast anchor in Talcahuano Bay, where the rest so sorely needed by the forty scrofulous patients of the *Zelée* was obtained. Thence D'Urville made for Valparaiso, after which, having entirely crossed Oceania, he cast anchor on the 1st January, 1839, off Guam, arrived at Batina in October, and went thence to Hobart's Town, whence, on the 1st January, 1840, he started on a new trip in the Antarctic regions.

At this time D'Urville knew nothing either of Balleny's voyage, or of the discovery of Sabrina's Land. He merely intended to go round the southern extremity of Tasmania with a view to ascertaining beneath which parallel he would meet with ice. He was under the impression that the space between 120° and 160° E. long. had not yet been explored, so that there was still a discovery to be made.

At first navigation was beset with the greatest difficulties. The swell was very strong, the currents bore in an easterly direction, the sanitary condition of the crews was far from satisfactory, and 58° S. lat. had not yet been reached when the presence of ice was ascertained.

The cold soon became very intense, the wind veered round to the W.N.W., and the sea became calm, a sure indication of the neighbourhood of land or of ice. The former was the more generally received hypothesis, for the ice- islands passed were too large to have been formed in the open ocean. On the 18th January, S. lat. 64° was reached, and great perpendicular blocks of ice were met with, the height of which varied from ninety to 100 feet, whilst the breadth exceeded 3000.

The next day, January 19th, 1840, a new land was sighted, to which the name of Adélie was given. The sun was now burning hot, and the ice all seemed to be melting, immense streams running down from the summits of the rocks into the sea. The appearance of the land was monotonous, covered as it was with snow. It ran from west to east, and seemed to slope gradually down to the sea. On the 21st the wind allowed the vessels to approach the beach, and deep ravines were soon made out, evidently the result of the action of melted snow.

View of Adélie Land.
(Fac-simile of early engraving.)

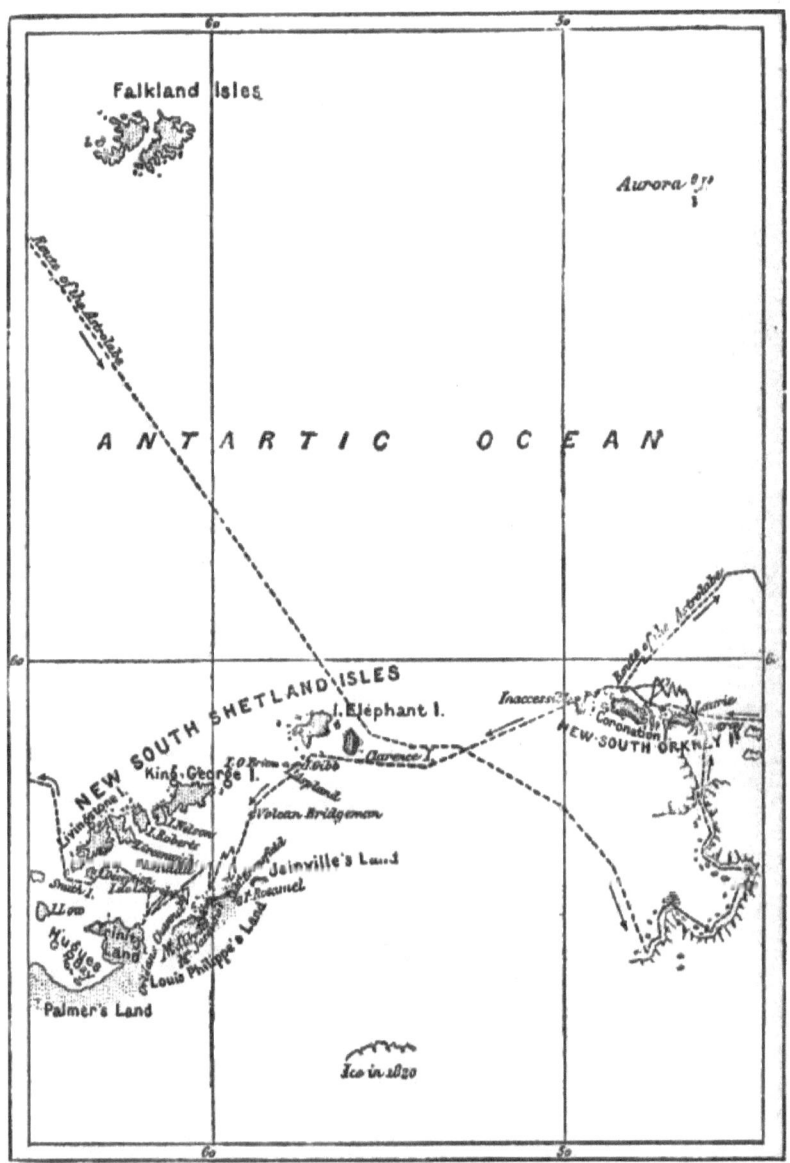

Reduced Map of D'Urville's discoveries in the Antarctic regions.

As the ships advanced navigation became more and more perilous, for the ice-islands were so numerous that there was hardly a large enough channel between them for any manoeuvring.

"Their straight walls," says D'Urville, "rose far above our masts, glowering down upon our vessels, which appeared of absurdly small dimensions, as compared with their huge masses. The spectacle spread out before us was alike grand and terrible. One might have fancied oneself in the narrow streets of a city of giants."

The corvettes soon entered a huge basin, formed by the coast and the ice-islands which had just been passed. The land stretched away in the south-east and north-west as far as the eye could reach. It was between three and four thousand feet high, but nowhere presented any very salient features. In the centre of the vast snow plain rose a few rocks. The two captains at once sent off boats with orders to bring back specimens which should testify to the discovery made. We quote from the account of Du Bouzet, one of the officers told off on this important survey.

"It was nearly nine o'clock when to our great delight we landed on the western side of the most westerly and loftiest islet. The *Astrolabe* boat had arrived one moment before ours, and its crew were already clambering up the steep sides of the rock, flinging down the penguins as they went, the birds showing no small surprise at being thus summarily dispossessed of the island, of which they had been hitherto the only inhabitants. I at once sent one of our sailors to unfurl a tricolour flag on these territories, which no human creature had seen or trod before ourselves. According to the old custom—to which the English have clung tenaciously—we took possession of them in the name of France, together with the neighbouring coast, which we were prevented from visiting by the ice. The only representatives of the animal kingdom were the penguins, for in spite of all our researches we did not find a single shell. The rocks were quite bare, without so much as the slightest sign of a lichen. We had to fall back on the mineral kingdom. We each took a hammer and began chipping at the rock, but, it being of granite, was so extremely hard that we could only obtain very small bits. Fortunately in climbing to the summit of the island the sailors found some big pieces of rock broken off by the frost, and these they embarked in their boats. Looking closely at them, I noticed an exact resemblance between these rocks and the little bits of gneiss which we had found in the stomach of a penguin we had killed the day before. The little islet on which we landed is part of a group of eight or ten of similar character and form; they are between five hundred and six hundred yards from the nearest coast. We also noticed on the beach several peaks and a cape quite free from snow. These islets, close as they are to each other, seem to form a continuous chain parallel with the coast, and stretching away from east to west."

On the 22nd and 23rd the survey of this coast was continued; but on the second day an iceberg soldered to the coast compelled the vessels to turn back towards the north, whilst at the same time a sudden and violent snow-storm overtook and separated them. The *Zelée* especially sustained considerable damage, but was able to rejoin her consort the next day.

Throughout it all, however, sight of the land had not, so to speak, been lost, but on the 29th the wind blew so strongly and persistently from the east, that D'Urville had to abandon the survey of Adélie Land. It was on this same day that he sighted the vessels of Lieutenant Wilkes. D'Urville complains of the discourtesy of the latter, and says that his own manoeuvres intended to open communications with them had been misunderstood by the Americans.

"We are no longer," he says, "in the days when navigators in the interests of commerce thought it necessary carefully to conceal their route and their discoveries, to avoid the competition of rival nations. I should, on the contrary, have been glad to point out to our emulators the result of our researches, in the hope that such information might be of use to them and increase our geographical knowledge."

On the 30th January a huge wall of ice was sighted, as to the nature of which opinions were divided. Some said it was a compact and isolated mass, others —and this was D'Urville's opinion—thought these lofty mountains had a base of earth or of rocks, or that they might even be the bulwarks of a huge extent of land which they called Clarie. It is situated in 128° E. long.

The officers had collected sufficient information in these latitudes to determine the position of the southern magnetic pole, but the results obtained by them did not accord with those given by Duperrey, Wilkes, and Ross.

On the 17th February the two corvettes once more cast anchor off Hobart's Town, and on the 25th set sail again for New Zealand, where they completed the hydrographical surveys of the *Uranie*. They then made for New Guinea, ascertained that it was not separated by a strait from the Louisiade Archipelago, surveyed Torres Strait with the greatest care, in spite of dangers from currents, coral reefs, &c.; arrived at Timor on the 20th, and returned to Toulon on the 8th November, after touching at Bourbon and St. Helena.

When the news of the grand discoveries made by the United States reached England, a spirit of emulation was aroused, and the learned societies decided on sending an expedition to the regions in which Weddell and Biscoe had been the only explorers since the time of Cook.

Captain James Clark Ross, who was appointed to the command of this expedition, was the nephew of the famous John Ross, explorer of Baffin's Bay. Born in 1800, James Ross was a sailor from the age of twelve. He accompanied his uncle in 1818 in his first Arctic expedition, had taken part under Parry in four expeditions to the same latitudes, and from 1829-1833 he had been his uncle's constant and faithful companion. Entrusted with the taking of scientific observations, he had discovered the north magnetic pole, and he had also made a good many excursions across the ice on foot and in sledges. He was, therefore, now one of the most experienced of British naval officers in Polar expeditions.

Captain John Ross.

Two vessels, the *Erebus* and the *Terror*, were entrusted to him, and his second in command was an accomplished sailor, Captain Francis Rowdon Crozier, companion of Parry in 1824; of Ross in 1835 in Baffin's Bay; and the future companion of Franklin in the *Terror*, in his search for the north-west passage. It would have been impossible to find a braver or more experienced sailor.

The instructions given to James Ross by the Admiralty differed essentially from those received by Wilkes and Dumont d'Urville. For the latter the exploration of the Antarctic regions was but one incident of their voyage round the world, whereas it was the very *raison d'être* of Ross's journey. Of the three years he would be away from Europe, the greater part was to be spent in the Antarctic regions, and he would only leave the ice to repair the damages to his vessels or recruit the health of his crew, worn out as they would probably be by fatigue and sickness.

The vessels had been equally judiciously chosen, stronger than those of D'Urville, they were better fitted to resist the repeated assaults of the ice, and their seasoned crews had been chosen from sailors familiar with polar navigation.

The *Erebus* and *Terror*, under the command of Ross and Crozier, left England on the 29th September, 1839, and touched successively at Madeira, the Cape Verd Islands, St. Helena, and the Cape of Good Hope, where numerous magnetic observations were taken.

On the 12th April Ross reached Kerguelen's Island, and there landed his instruments. The scientific harvest was abundant. Some fossil trees were extracted from the lava of which this island is formed, and some rich layers of coal were discovered, which have not yet been worked. The 29th was fixed for simultaneous magnetic observations in different parts of the globe, and by a singular coincidence some magnetic storms such as had already visited Europe, were on this very day observed in these latitudes. The instrument registered the same phenomena as at Toronto, Canada, proving the vast extent of these meteoric disturbances, and the incredible rapidity with which they spread.

On his arrival at Hobart Town, where his old friend John Franklin was now governor, Ross heard of the discovery of Adélie and of Clarie Lands by the French, and the simultaneous survey of them by Wilkes, who had even left a sketch of his map of the coasts.

Ross, however, decided to make for E. long. 170°, because it was in that direction that Balleny had found an open sea extending to S. lat. 69°. He duly reached first the Auckland and then the Campbell Islands, and after having, like his predecessors, tacked about a great deal in a sea strewn with ice-islands, he came beyond the sixty-third degree to the edge of the stationary ice, and on the 1st January, 1841, crossed the Antarctic Circle.

The floating ice did not in any respect resemble that of the Arctic regions, as James Ross very soon discovered. It consisted of huge blocks, with regular and vertical walls, whilst the ice-fields, less compact than those of the north, move about in chaotic confusion, looking, to quote Wilkes' imaginative simile, like a heaving land, as they alternately break away from each other and reunite.

To Ross the ice barrier did not present so formidable an appearance as it had done to the French and Americans. He did not at first venture upon it, however, being kept in the offing by storms. Not until the 5th January was he able to penetrate to S. lat. 66° 45', and E. long. 174° 16'. Circumstances could not have been more favourable, for the sea and wind were both acting upon and loosening the ice, and thanks to the strength of his vessels, Ross was able to cut a passage. As he advanced further and further southward, the fog became denser and the constant snow-storms added to the already serious dangers of navigation. Encouraged, however, by the reflection in the sky of an open sea, a phenomenon which turned out to be trustworthy, he pushed on, and on the 9th January, after crossing 200 miles of ice he actually entered that open sea!

On the 11th January land was sighted 100 miles ahead in S. lat. 70° 47' and E. long. 172° 36'. This, the most southern land ever yet discovered, consisted of snow-clad peaks with glaciers sloping down to the sea, the peaks rising to a height of from nine to twelve thousand feet. This estimate, judging from D'Urville's remarks on Graham's Land, may, however, possibly be an exaggerated one. Here, there, and everywhere, black rocks rose up from the snow, but the coast was so shut in with ice that landing was impossible. This curious series of huge peaks received the name of Admiralty chain, and the country itself that of Victoria.

MAP

discovered by **Jameli** Ross

Engraved by E. Morieu.

A few little islands were made out in the south-east before the vessels left this coast, and on the 12th January the two captains, with some of their officers, disembarked on one of the volcanic islets, and took possession of it in the name of England. Not the slightest trace of vegetation was found upon it.

Ross soon ascertained that the eastern side of this vast land sloped towards the south, whilst the northern stretched away to the north-west. He, therefore, skirted along the eastern beach, forcing a passage in a southerly direction beyond the magnetic pole, which he places near S. lat. 76°, and then returning by the west, thus entirely circumnavigating his new discovery, which he looked upon as a very large island. The mountain chain extends all along the coast. Ross gave to the principal peaks the names of Herschell, Whewell, Wheatstone, Murchison, and Melbourne. He was unable, however, on account of the ever-increasing quantity of ice about the coast, to make out the details of its outlines. On the 23rd January the seventy-fourth degree, the most southerly latitude ever reached, was passed.

The vessels were now considerably hampered by fogs, southerly gales, and violent snow-storms, but they managed to continue their cruise along the coast, and on the 27th January the English disembarked on a little volcanic island in S. lat. 76° 8' and E. long. 168° 12', to which they gave the name of Franklin.

The next day a huge mountain was seen, which rose abruptly to a height of 12,000 feet above a far-stretching land. The summit, of regular form, and completely covered with snow, was every now and then wrapped in a thick cloud of smoke, no less than 300 feet in diameter. Taking this diameter as a standard of measure, the height of the cloud, in shape like an inverted cone, would be about one-half of it. When this cloud of smoke dispersed, a bare crater was discovered, lit up by a bright red glow, visible even in broad daylight. The sides of the mountain were covered with snow up to the very crater, and it was impossible to make out any signs of a flow of lava.

A volcano is always a magnificent spectacle, and the sight of this one rising up from amongst the Antarctic ice, and excelling Etna and Teneriffe in its marvellous activity, could not fail to make a vivid impression upon the minds of the explorers. The name of Erebus was given to it, and that of Terror to an extinct crater on the east of it, both titles being admirably appropriate.

The two vessels continued their cruise along the northern coast of Victoria, until their further passage was barred by a huge mass of ice towering 505 feet above their masts. Behind this barrier rose another mountain chain, which sunk out of sight in the S.S.E., and to which the name of Parry was given.

Ross skirted along the ice barrier in an easterly direction until the 2nd February, when he reached S. lat. 78° 4', the most southerly point attained on this trip, during which he had followed the shores of the land he had discovered for more than 300 miles. He left it in E. long. 191° 23'.

But for the strong favourable winds which now blew, it seems probable that the vessels would never have issued in safety from amongst the formidable ice masses through which they finally worked their way at the cost of incredible exertions and fatigues, and in face of incessant danger.

On the 15th February yet another attempt was made in S. lat. 76° to reach the magnetic pole; but further progress was barred by land in S. lat. 76° 12' and E. long. 164°, i.e. sixty-five ordinary miles from the position assigned to it (the magnetic pole) by Ross, and the appearance of this land was forbidding and the sea so rough that the explorer gave up all idea of continuing his researches on shore.

After identifying the islands discovered in 1839 by Balleny, Ross found himself on the 6th March amongst the mountains alluded to by Wilkes.

"On the 4th March," says Ross's narrative, "they recrossed the Antarctic Circle, and being necessarily close by the eastern extreme of those *patches of land* which Lieut. Wilkes has called 'the Antarctic Continent,' and having reached the latitude on the 5th, they steered directly for them; and at noon on the 6th, the ship being exactly over the centre of this mountain range, they could obtain no soundings with 600 fathoms of line; and having traversed a space of eighty miles in every direction from this spot, during beautiful clear weather, which extended their vision widely around, were obliged to confess that this position, at least, of the pseudo-antarctic continent, and the nearly 200 miles of barrier represented to extend from it, have no real existence."[1]

[1] The Editor of the *Literary Gazette* adds the following note. "Lieutenant Wilkes may have mistaken some clouds or fog-banks, which in these regions are very likely to assume the appearance of land to inexperienced eyes, for this continent and range of lofty mountains. If so, the error is to be regretted, as it must tend to throw discredit on other portions of his discoveries, which have a more substantial foundation."—*Trans.*

The expedition got back to Tasmania without having a single case of sickness on board or sustaining the slightest damage. The vessels were here refitted, and the instruments regulated before starting on a second trip, on which Sydney and Island's Bay, New Zealand, and Chatham, were the first stations touched at by Ross to make magnetic observations. On the 18th December, in S. lat. 62° 40' and E. long, 146°, ice was encountered 300 miles further north than in the preceding year. The vessels had arrived too early, but Ross, nevertheless, endeavoured to break through this formidable barrier. After penetrating for 300 miles he was stopped by masses so compact that it was impossible to go further, and he did not cross the Antarctic Circle until the 1st January, 1842. On the 19th of the same month the two vessels encountered the most violent storm just as they were entering an open sea; the *Erebus* and *Terror* lost their helms, floating ice washed over them, and for twenty-six hours they were in danger of going down.

The detention of the expedition amongst the ice lasted no less than forty-six days, and not until the 22nd did Ross reach the great barrier of stationary ice, which was considerably lower beyond Erebus, where it was no less than 200 feet high. When Ross came to it this year it was only 107 feet high, and it was 150 miles further east than it had been on the previous expedition. The acquisition of this piece of geographical information was the only result of this arduous campaign, extending over 136 days, and greatly excelling in dramatic interest the preceding expedition.

The vessels now made for Cape Horn, and sailed up the coast as far as Rio de Janeiro, where they found everything of which they stood in need. As soon as they had laid in a stock of provisions they again put to sea and reached the Falkland Islands, whence, on the 17th December, 1842, they started on their third trip.

The first ice was this time met with near Clarence Island, and on the 25th December Ross found his further progress barred by it. He then made for the New Shetland Islands, completed the survey of Louis Philippe and Joinville Lands, discovered by Dumont d'Urville, named Mts. Haddington and Parry, ascertained that Louis Philippe's Land is only a large island, and visited Bransfield Strait, separating it from Shetland. Such were the marvellous results obtained by James Ross in his three expeditions.

To assign to the three explorers, whose work in the Antarctic regions we have been reviewing, his just meed of praise, we may say that D'Urville first discovered the Antarctic continent; Wilkes traced its shores for a considerable distance, for we cannot fail to recognize the resemblance between his map and that of the French navigator; and that James Ross visited the most southerly and most interesting part.

But is there such a continent after all? D'Urville was not quite sure about it, and Ross did not believe in it. We must leave the decision of this great question to the later explorers who were to follow in the footsteps of the intrepid sailors whose voyages and discoveries we have related.

II.

THE NORTH POLE.

Anjou and Wrangell—The "polynia"—John Ross's first expedition—
Baffin's Bay closed—Edward Parry's discoveries on his first voyage—
The survey of Hudson's Bay, and the discovery of Fury and Hecla Straits
—Parry's third voyage—Fourth voyage—On the ice in sledges in the
open sea—Franklin's first trip—Incredible sufferings of the explorers—
Second expedition—John Ross—Four winters amongst the ice—Dease
and Simpson's expedition.

We have more than once alluded to the great impulse given to geographical
science by Peter I. One of the earliest results of this impulse was the discovery
by Behring of the straits separating Asia from America, and the most important
was the survey thirty years later of the Liakhov Archipelago, or New Siberia.

In 1770 a merchant named Liakhov noticed a large herd of reindeer coming
across the ice from the north, and he reflected that they could only have come
from a country where there were pastures enough to support them. A month
later he started in a sledge, and after a journey of fifty miles he discovered
between the mouths of the Lena and Indighirka three large islands, the vast
deposits of fossil ivory on which have since become celebrated all over the
world.

In 1809 Hedenstroem received instructions to make a map of this new
discovery. He made several attempts to cross the frozen ocean on a sledge, but
was always turned back by ice which would not bear him. He came to the
conclusion that there must be an open sea beyond, and he founded this opinion
on the immense quantity of warm water which flows into the Arctic Ocean
from the great rivers of Asia.

In March, 1821, Lieutenant (afterwards Admiral) Anjou crossed the ice to
within forty-two miles of the north of the island of Kotelnoï, and in N. lat. 76°
38' saw a vapour which led him to believe in the existence of an open sea. In
a second trip he actually saw this sea with its drifting ice, and came back
convinced of the impossibility of going further in a sledge on account of the
thinness of the ice.

Whilst Anjou was thus employed, another naval officer, Lieutenant Wrangell,
collected some important traditions about the existence of land the other side
of Cape Yakan.

From a Tchouktchi chief he learnt that in fine weather—though never in the winter—from the coast and some reefs at the mouth of a river mountains covered with snow could be seen far away in the north; and that in former days when the sea was frozen over reindeer used to come from there. The chief had himself once seen a herd of reindeer on their way back to the north by this route and he had followed them in a sledge for a whole day until the state of the ice compelled him to give up the experiment.

His father had told him, too, that a Tchouktchi had once gone there with a few companions in a skin boat, but he did not know what they had discovered or what had become of them. He was sure that the land in the north was inhabited, because a dead whale had once been washed on to Aratane Island with spears tipped with slate in its flesh, and the Tchouktchis never used such weapons.

These facts were very curious, and they increased Wrangell's desire to penetrate to the unknown northern districts; but the truth of all the rumours was not verified until our own day.

Between 1820 and 1824 Wrangell made four expeditions in sledges from the mouth of the Kolyma, which he made his headquarters, first exploring the coast to Cape Tchelagskoi, and enduring thirty-five degrees of cold; and in his second trip trying how far he could go across the ice, an experiment resulting in a journey of 400 miles from the land. In the third year (1822), Wrangell started in March with a view to verifying the report of a native who said he had seen land in the offing. He now came to an icefield, on which he advanced safely for a long distance, when it began to be less compact and was soon not solid enough to bear many sledges, so two small ones were selected, on which were packed a wherry, some planks, and some tools. The explorer then ventured on some melting ice which broke under his feet.

"Two small sledges were selected."

"At the outset," says Wrangell, "I had to make way for seven wersts across a bed of brine; further on appeared a surface furrowed with great *crevasses*, which we could only succeed in clearing by the help of our planks. I noticed in this part several small mounds of ice in such a liquefying condition that the slightest touch would suffice to break it and convert the mound into a round slough. The ice upon which we were travelling was without consistency, was but a foot in thickness, and—what was more—was riddled with holes.... I could only compare the appearance of the sea, at this stage, to an immense morass; and indeed the muddy water which issued from these thousands of crevasses, opening up in every direction, the melting snow mixed with earth and sand, those little mounds whence numerous streamlets were issuing,—all these combined to make the illusion perfect."

Wrangell had advanced some 140 miles, and it was the open sea or the *polynia*—as he calls vast expanses of water—north of Siberia, the outskirts of which he had reached, the same in fact as that already sighted by Leontjew in 1764, and Hedenstroem in 1810.

On his fourth voyage Wrangell and his small party of followers started from Cape Yakan, the nearest point to the Arctic regions, and, after passing Cape Tchelagskoi, made for the north; but a violent storm broke up the ice, there only three feet thick, and involved the explorers in the greatest danger. Now dragged across some large unbroken slab, now wet to the waist on a moving plank, sometimes above and sometimes under water, or moored to a block serving as a ferryboat, which the swimming dogs dragged along, they at last succeeded in crossing the shifting reverberating ice and regaining the land, owing their life to the strength and agility of their teams of dogs alone. Thus closed the last attempt made to reach the districts north of Siberia.

The Arctic calotte[1] was meanwhile being attacked from the other side with equal energy and yet more perseverance. It will be remembered with what untiring enthusiasm the famous north-west passage had been sought. No sooner had the peace of 1815 necessitated the disarmament of numerous English vessels and set free their officers on half-pay, than the Admiralty, unwilling to let experienced seamen rust in idleness, sought for them some employment. It was under these circumstances that the search for the north-west passage was resumed.

[1] The word *calotte* here used by Verne is untranslateable. It signifies, literally, a particular kind of cap, frequently a monk's cap or cowl.—*Trans.*

The *Alexander*, 252 tons, and the *Isabel*, 385, under command of the experienced officers, John Ross and Lieutenant Parry, with James Ross, Back, and Belcher, who were to win honour in Arctic explorations amongst their subordinates, were sent by the Government to explore Baffin's Bay and set sail on the 18th April. After touching at the Shetland Islands, and seeking in vain for the submerged land seen by Bass in N. lat. 57° 28', the explorers came on the 26th May to the first ice, and on the 2nd June surveyed the western coast of Greenland, hitherto very imperfectly laid down in maps, finding it greatly encumbered by ice. Indeed the governor of the Dutch settlement of Whale Island told them that the severity of the winter months had been steadily increasing during the eleven years of his residence in the country.

Hitherto it had been supposed that the country was uninhabited beyond 75° N. lat., and the travellers were therefore greatly surprised to see a whole tribe of Esquimaux arrive by way of the ice. They knew nothing of any race but their own, and stared at the English without daring to touch them, one of them even addressing to the vessels in a grave and solemn voice the inquiries, Who are you? Whence do you come? From the sun or from the moon?

Esquimaux family.
(Fac-simile of early engraving.)

Although in many respects far inferior to the Esquimaux who had become to some extent civilized by long intercourse with Europeans, the new-comers understood the use of iron, of which a few of them had even succeeded in making knives. This iron as far as the English could gather was dug out of a mountain. It was probably of meteoric origin.

As public opinion in England subsequently confirmed, Ross, in spite of qualities as a naval officer of the highest order, showed extraordinary apathy and levity on this voyage, appearing not to trouble himself in the least about the geographical problems for the solution of which the expedition was organized. He passed Wolstenholme and Whale Sounds and Smith's Strait, opening out of Baffin's Bay, without examining them, the last named at so great a distance that he did not even recognize it. Still worse than that was his conduct later. Cruising down the western shores of Baffin's Bay a long deep gulf no less than fifty miles across gradually came in sight of the eager explorers, yet when on the 29th August the two vessels had sailed up it for thirty miles only Ross gave orders to tack about, on the ground that he distinctly saw at the further end a chain of lofty mountains to which he gave the name of Croker. His officers did not share his opinion; they could not see so much as the slightest sign of a hill, for the very excellent reason that the gulf they had entered was really Lancaster Sound, so named by Baffin, and connecting his bay with the western Arctic Ocean.

The same sort of thing occurred again and again in the voyage along this deeply indented coast, the vessels keeping so far off shore that not a detail could be made out. Thus it came about that Cumberland Bay was passed on the 1st October without any survey of that most important feature of Davis Strait, and Ross returned to England, having literally turned his back on the glory awaiting him.

When accused of apathy and neglect of duty, Ross replied with supreme indifference, "I trust, as I believe myself, that the objects of the voyage have been in every important point accomplished; that I have proved the existence of a bay, from Disco to Cumberland Strait, and set at rest for ever the question of a north-west passage in this direction."

It would have been impossible to make a more complete mistake. But fortunately the failure of this expedition did not in the least discourage other explorers. Some saw in it a brilliant confirmation of the venerable Baffin's discovery, others looked upon the innumerable inlets, with their deep waters and strong currents, as something more than mere bays. They were straits, and all hope of the discovery of the north-west passage was not yet lost.

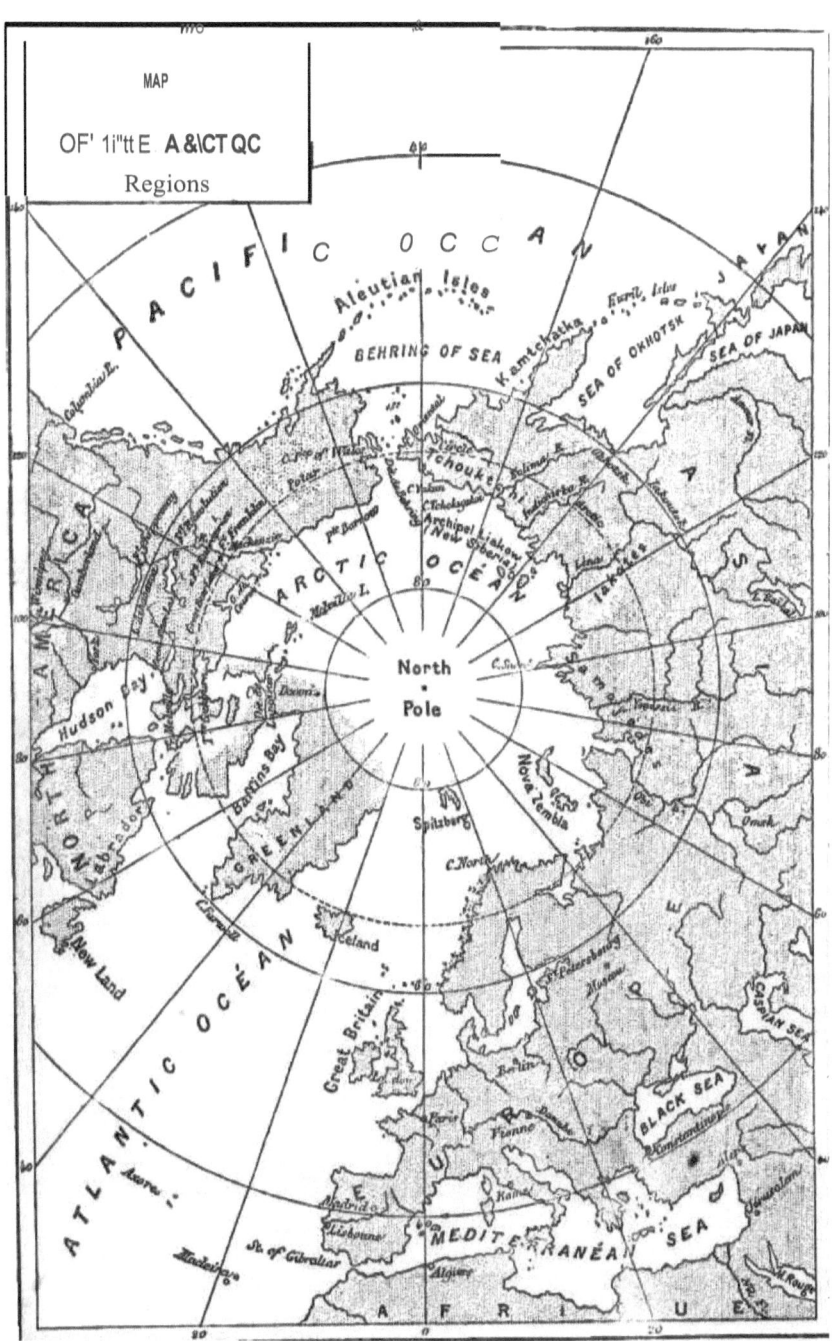

MAP
OF' 1i"tt E A&\CT QC
Regions

Engraved by E. Morieu.

These suggestions so far weighed with the English Admiralty as to lead to the equipment of two small vessels, the bomb-vessel *Hecla* and the brigantine *Griper*, which left the Thames on the 5th May, 1819, under command of Lieutenant William Parry, whose opinion as to the existence of the north-west passage had not coincided with that of his chief. The vessels reached Lancaster Sound without meeting with any special adventures, and after a delay of seven days amongst the ice which encumbered the sea for a distance of eighty miles, they entered the supposed Bay "shut in by a mountain chain" of John Ross, to find not only that this mountain chain did not exist, but that the bay was a strait more than 310 fathoms deep, where the influence of the tide could be felt. The temperature of the water rose some ten degrees, and in the course of a single day no less than eighty full-grown whales were seen.

On the 31st July the explorers landed on the shores of Possession Bay, visited by them the previous year, and found there their own footprints, a sign of the small quantity of snow and hoar frost which had fallen during the winter. All hearts beat high when with a favourable wind and all sails set the two vessels entered Lancaster Sound.

"It is more easy," says Parry, "to imagine than to describe the almost breathless anxiety which was now visible in every countenance, while, as the breeze continued to a fresh gale, we ran quickly up the sound. The mast-heads were crowded by the officers and men during the whole afternoon; and an unconcerned observer, if any could have been unconcerned on such an occasion, would have been amused by the eagerness with which the various reports from the crow's-nest were received; all, however, hitherto favourable to our most sanguine hopes."

The two coasts extended in a parallel line as far as the eye could reach, that is to say for a distance exceeding fifty miles, and the height of the waves together with the absence of ice combined to convince the English that they had reached the open sea by way of the long sought passage, when an island framed in masses of ice checked their further progress.

An arm of the sea, however, some twelve leagues wide, opened on the south, and by it the explorers hoped to find a passage less encumbered with ice. Strange to say, as they had advanced in a westerly direction through Lancaster Sound, the vibrations of the pendulum had increased, whilst now it appeared to have lost all motion, and "we now therefore witnessed for the first time the curious phenomenon of the directive power of the needle becoming so weak as to be completely overcome by the attraction of the ship; so that the needle might now be properly said to point to the north pole of the ship."

The arm of the sea widened as the vessels advanced in a westerly direction, and the shores seemed to bend sensibly towards the south-west, but after making some 120 miles further progress was again barred by ice. The explorers therefore returned to Barrow's Strait, of which Lancaster Sound is but the entry, and once more entered the sea, now free from the ice, by which it had been encumbered a few days previously.

In W. long. 92° 1′ 4″ was discovered an inlet called Wellington Channel, about eight leagues wide, entirely free from ice and apparently not bounded by any land. The existence of these numerous straits led the explorers to the conclusion that they were in the midst of a vast archipelago, an opinion daily receiving fresh confirmation. The dense fogs, however, made navigation difficult, and the number of little islands and shallows increased whilst the ice became more compact. Parry, however, was not to be deterred from pressing on towards the west, and presently his sailors found, on a large island, to which the name of Bathurst was given, the remains of some Esquimaux huts and traces of the former presence of reindeer. Magnetic observations were now taken, pointing to the conclusion that the magnetic pole had been passed on the north.

Another large island, that of Melville, soon came in sight, and in spite of the fogs and ice the expedition succeeded in passing W. long. 110°, thus earning the reward of 100*l.* sterling promised by the English Government. A promontory near Melville Island was named Cape Munificence, whilst a good harbour close by was called Hecla and Griper Bay. It was in Winter Harbour at the end of this bay that the vessels passed the winter. "Dismantled for the most part," says Parry, "the yards however being laid for walls and roofed in with thick wadding tilts, they were sheltered from the snow, whilst stoves and ovens were fixed inside." Hunting was useless, and resulted in nothing but the frost-biting of the limbs of some of the hunters, as Melville Island was deserted at the end of October by all animals except wolves and foxes. To get through the long winter without dying of ennui was no easy matter, but the officers hit upon the plan of setting up a theatre, the first representation in which was given on the 6th November, the day of the disappearance of the sun for three months. A special piece was given on Christmas day, in which allusion was made to the situation of the vessels, and a weekly paper was started called the *North Georgia Gazette and Winter Chronicle*, which with Sabine, as editor, run into twenty-one numbers, all printed on the return to Europe of the expedition.

In January scrofula broke out, and with such virulence as to cause considerable alarm, but the evil was soon checked by skilful treatment and the daily distribution of mustard and cress, which Parry had managed to grow in boxes round his stove.

On the 7th February the sun reappeared, and although many months must elapse before it would be possible to leave Melville Island, preparations for a start were at once begun. On the 30th April the thermometer rose to zero, and the sailors taking this low temperature for summer wanted to leave off their winter clothes. The first ptarmigan appeared on the 12th May, and on the following day were seen traces of reindeer and of musk goats on their way to the north; but what caused the greatest delight and surprise to the crews was the fall of rain on the 24th May.

"We had been so unaccustomed to see water naturally in a fluid state at all, and much less to see it fall from the heavens, that such an occurrence became a matter of considerable curiosity, and I believe every person on board hastened on deck to witness so interesting as well as novel a phenomenon."

Rain as a novel phenomenon.

During the first fortnight in June, Parry, accompanied by some of his officers, made an excursion to the most northerly part of Melville Island. On his return, vegetation was everywhere to be seen, the ice was beginning to melt, and it was evident that a start could soon be made. The vessels began to move on the 1st August, but the ice had not yet broken up in the offing, and they got no further than the eastern extremity of Melville Island, of which the furthest point reached by Parry was in N. lat. 113° 46' 13" and W. long. 113° 46' 43". The voyage back was unmarked by any special incident, and the expedition got back to England towards the middle of November.

The results of this voyage were numerous and important. Not only had a vast extent of the Arctic regions been surveyed; but physical and magnetic observations had been taken, and many new details collected on their climate and animal and vegetable life. In fact in a single trip Parry did more than was accomplished in thirty years by all who followed in his steps.

Satisfied with the important results obtained by him, the Admiralty appointed Parry to the command in 1821 of the *Hecla* and the *Fury*, the latter built on the model of the former. On this new trip the explorer surveyed with the greatest care the shores of Hudson's Bay and the coast of the peninsula of Melville, not to be confounded with the island of the same name. The winter was passed on Winter Island on the eastern coast of this peninsula, and the same amusements were resorted to which had succeeded so well on the previous expedition, supplemented most effectively by the arrival on the 1st February of a party of Esquimaux from across the ice. Their huts, which had not been discovered by the English, were built on the beach; and numerous visits paid to them during the eighteen months passed on Winter Island gave a better notion than had ever before been obtained of the manners, customs, character, &c., of this singular people.

The thorough survey of the Straits of Fury and Hecla, separating the peninsula of Melville from Cockburn Island, involved the passing of a second winter in the Arctic regions, and though the quarters were now more comfortable, time dragged heavily, for the officers and men were dreadfully disappointed at having to turn back just as they had thought to start for Behring's Strait. On the 12th August the ice broke up, and Parry wanted to send his men to Europe, and himself complete by land the exploration of the districts he had discovered, but Captain Lyon dissuaded him from a plan so desperate. The vessels therefore returned to England with all hands after an absence of twenty-seven months, having lost but five men, although two consecutive winters had been spent in the Arctic regions.

Although the results of the second voyage were not equal to those of the first, some of them were beyond price. It was now known that the American coast did not extend beyond the 70° N. lat., and that the Atlantic was connected with the Arctic Ocean by an immense number of straits and channels, most of them—the Fury, Hecla, and Fox, for instance—obstructed with ice brought down by the currents. Whilst the ice barrier on the south-east of Melville Peninsula appeared permanent, that at Regent's Inlet was evidently the reverse. It might, therefore, be possible to penetrate through it to the Polar basin, and it was with this end in view that the *Fury* and *Hecla* were once more equipped, and placed under the orders of Parry.

This voyage was the least fortunate of any undertaken by this skilful seaman, not on account of any falling off in his work, but because he was the victim of unlucky accidents and unfavourable circumstances. Meeting, for instance, with an unusual quantity of ice in Baffin's Bay, he had the greatest trouble to reach Prince Regent's inlet. Had he arrived three weeks earlier he would probably have been able to land on the American coast, but as it was he was obliged to make immediate preparations for going into winter-quarters.

It was no very formidable matter to this experienced officer to spend a winter under the Polar circle. He knew what precautions to take to preserve the health of his crews, to keep himself well, and what occupations and amusements would best relieve the tedium of a three months' night. Races between the officers, masquerades and theatrical entertainments, with the temperature maintained at 50° Fahrenheit kept all the men healthy and happy until the thaw, which set in on the 20th July, 1825, enabled Parry to resume exploring operations.

He now skirted along the eastern coast of Prince Regent's Inlet, but the floating ice gathered about the vessels and drove them on shore. The *Fury* was so much damaged that though four pumps were constantly at work she could hardly be kept afloat, and Parry was trying to get her repaired under shelter of a huge block of ice when a tempest came on, broke in pieces the extemporary dock and flung the vessel again upon the shore, where she had to be abandoned. Her crew were received on the *Hecla*, which, after such an accident as this, was of course obliged to return to England.

Parry's tempered spirit was not broken even by this last disaster. If the Arctic Ocean could not be reached from Baffin's Bay, were there not other routes still to be attempted? The vast tract of ocean between Greenland and Spitsbergen, for instance, might turn out less dangerous, freer as it of necessity would be from the huge icebergs which gather about the Arctic coasts. The earliest expeditions in these latitudes of which we have any record are those of Scoresby, who long cruised about them in search of whales. In 1806 he penetrated in E. long. 16° (reckoning from Paris), beyond Spitzbergen, i.e. to N. lat. 81° 30', where he saw ice stretching away in the E.N.E., whilst between that and the S.E. the sea was open for a distance of thirty miles. There was no land within 100 miles. It seems a matter of regret that the whaler did not take advantage of the favourable state of the sea to have advanced yet further north, when he might have made some important discovery, perhaps even have reached the Pole itself.

Parry now resolved to do what the exigencies of his profession had rendered impossible to Scoresby, and leaving London on the *Hecla* on the 27th March, 1827, he reached Lapland in safety, and having at Hammerfest embarked dogs, reindeer, and canoes, he proceeded on his way to Spitzbergen. Port Snweerenburg, where he wished to touch, was still shut in with ice; and against this barrier the *Hecla* struggled until the 24th May, when Parry left her in Hinlopen Strait, and advanced northwards with Ross, Crozier, a dozen men, and provisions for seventy-two days in a couple of canoes. After leaving a depôt of provisions at Seven Islands he packed his food and boats on sledges specially constructed for the occasion, hoping to cross in them the barrier of solid ice, and to find beyond a navigable if not an entirely open sea. The ice did not, however, as Parry expected, turn out to form a homogeneous mass. There were here and there vast gaps to be forded or steep hills to be climbed, and in four days the explorers only advanced about eight miles in a northerly direction. On the 2nd July, in a dense fog, the thermometer marked 1° 9' above zero in the shade, and 8° 3' in the sun; and as may be imagined the march across the broken surface, gaping everywhere with fissures, was terribly arduous, whilst the difficulties were aggravated by the continual glare from the snow and ice. In spite, however, of all obstacles the party pressed bravely on, and on the 20th July found they had got no further than N. lat. 82° 37', i.e. only about five miles beyond the point reached three days previously. Now, as they had undoubtedly made at least about fourteen miles in the interval, it was evident that the ice on which they were was being drifted southwards by a strong current.

Parry at first concealed this most discouraging fact from his men; but it soon became evident to every one that no progress was being made, but the slight difference between their own speed as they struggled over the many obstacles in their path and that of the current bearing the ice-field in the opposite direction. Moreover, the expedition now came to a place where the half-broken ice was not fit to bear the weight of the men or of the sledges. It was in fact nothing more than an immense accumulation of blocks of ice, which, tossed about by the waves, made a deafening noise as they crashed against each other; provisions too were running short, the men were discouraged, Ross was hurt, Parry was suffering from inflammation of the eyes, and the wind had veered into a contrary direction, driving the explorers southwards. There was nothing for it but to turn back.

This venturesome trip, throughout which the thermometer had not sunk beneath 2° 2, might have succeeded had it been undertaken a little earlier in the season, for then the explorers could have penetrated beyond 82° 4'. In any case they would certainly not have had to turn back on account of rain, snow, and damp, all signs of the summer thaw.

When Parry got back to the *Hecla*, he found that she had been in the greatest danger. Driven before a violent gale, her chains had been broken by the ice, and she had been flung upon the beach, and run aground. When got off, she had been taken to Waygat Strait. All dangers past, however, the explorers got back safely in the rescued vessel to the Orkneys, where they landed, and whence they returned to London, arriving there on the 30th September.

Whilst Parry was seeking a passage to the Pacific, by way of Baffin's or Hudson's Bay, several expeditions were organized to complete the discoveries of Mackenzie, and survey the North American coast. These expeditions were not fraught with any great danger, and the results might be of the most vital importance alike to geographical and nautical science. The command of the first was entrusted to Franklin afterwards so justly celebrated, with whom were associated Dr. Richardson, George Back, then a midshipman in the royal navy, and two common seamen.

The explorers arrived on the 30th August at York Factory on the shores of Hudson's Bay, and having obtained from the fur-hunters all the information necessary to their success, they started again on the 9th September, reaching Cumberland House, 690 miles further, on the 22nd October. The season was now nearly at an end, but Franklin and Back nevertheless succeeded in penetrating to Fort Chippeway on the western side of Lake Athabasca, where they proposed making preparations for the expedition of the ensuing summer. This trip of 857 miles was accomplished in the depth of winter with the thermometer at between 40° and 50° below zero.

Early in spring, Dr. Richardson joined the rest of the party at Fort Chippeway, and all started together on the 18th July, 1820, in the hope of reaching comfortable quarters at the mouth of the Coppermine before the bad season set in; Franklin and his people did not, however, make sufficient allowance for the difficulties of the route or for the obstacles resulting from the severity of the weather, and it took them till the 20th August to cross the waterfalls, shallows, lakes, rivers, and portages which impeded their progress. Game too was scarce. At the first appearance of ice on the ponds the Canadian guides began to complain; and when flocks of wild geese were seen flying southwards they refused to go any further. Annoyed as he was at this absence of good will in the people in his service, Franklin was compelled to give up his schemes, and when 550 miles from Fort Chippeway, in N. lat. 64° 28', W. long. 118° 6', he built on the banks of Winter River a wooden house, which he called Fort Enterprise.

Here the explorers collected as much food as they could, manufacturing with reindeer flesh what is known throughout North America as *pemmican*. At first the number of reindeer seen was considerable; no less than 2000 were once sighted in a single day, but this was only a proof that they were migrating to more clement latitudes. The *pemmican* prepared from eighty reindeer and the fish obtained in Winter River both run short before the expedition was able to proceed. Whole tribes of Indians, on hearing of the arrival of the whites, collected about the camp, greatly harassing the explorers by their begging, and soon exhausted the supply of blankets, tobacco, &c., which had been brought as means of barter.

Disappointed at the non-arrival of reinforcements with provisions, Franklin sent Back with an escort of Canadians to Fort Chippeway on the 18th October.

"I had the pleasure," says Back, writing after his return, "of meeting my friends all in good health, after an absence of nearly five months, during which I travelled 1104 miles in snow-shoes, and had no other covering at night in the woods than a blanket and deerskin, with the thermometer frequently at 40°, and once at 57° below zero, and sometimes passing two or three days without tasting food."

Those who remained at the fort also suffered terribly from cold, the thermometer sinking three degrees lower than it had done when Parry was at Melville Island, nine degrees nearer the pole. Not only did the men suffer from the extreme severity of the cold, but the trees were frozen to the pith, and axes broke against them without making so much as a notch.

Two interpreters from Hudson's Bay had accompanied Back to Fort Enterprise, one of whom had a daughter said to be the loveliest creature ever seen, and who, though only sixteen, had already been married twice. One of the English officers took her portrait, to the terrible distress of her mother, who feared that if the "great chief of England" saw the inanimate representation he would fall in love with the original.

On the 14th June the Coppermine River was sufficiently free from ice to be navigable, and although their provisions were all but exhausted, the explorers embarked upon it. As it fortunately turned out, however, game was very plentiful on the green banks of the river, and enough musk oxen were killed to feed the whole party.

The mouth of the Coppermine was reached on the 18th July, when the Indians, afraid of meeting their enemies, the Esquimaux, at once returned to Fort Enterprise, whilst the Canadians scarcely dared to launch their frail boats on the angry sea. Franklin at last succeeded in persuading them to run the risk; but he could not get them to go further than Cape Turn-again in N. lat. 68° 30', a promontory at the opening of a deep gulf dotted with islands, to which the leader of the expedition gave the name of Coronation, in memory of the accession of George IV.

Franklin had begun to ascend Hood River, when he was stopped by a cataract 250 feet high, compelling him to make his way overland across a barren, unknown district, and through snow more than two feet deep. The fatigue and suffering involved in this return journey can be more easily imagined than described; suffice it to say that the party arrived on the 11th October in a state of complete exhaustion—having eaten nothing for five days—at Fort Enterprise, which they found utterly deserted. Ill and without food, there seemed to be nothing left for Franklin to do but to die. The next day, however, he set to work to look for the Indians, and those of his party who had started before him, but the snow was so thick he had to return without accomplishing anything. For the next eighteen days life was supported by a kind of bouilli made from the bones and the skin of the game killed the previous year, and at last, on the 29th October, Dr. Richardson arrived with John Hepburn, only looking thin and worn, and scarcely able to speak above a whisper. It seemed as if they were doomed! We quote the following from Desborough Cooley:—

"Dr. Richardson had now a melancholy tale to relate. For the first two days his party had nothing whatever to eat. On the third day, Michel arrived with a hare and partridge, which afforded each a small morsel. Then another day passed without food. On the 11th, Michel offered them some flesh, which he said was part of a wolf; but they afterwards became convinced that it was the flesh of one of the unfortunate men who had left Captain Franklin's party to return to Dr. Richardson. Michel was daily growing more insolent and shy, and it was strongly suspected that he had a hidden supply of meat for his own use. On the 20th, while Hepburn was cutting wood near the tent, he heard the report of a gun, and looking towards the spot saw Michel dart into the tent. Mr. Hood was found dead; a ball had entered the back part of his head, and there could be no doubt but that Michel was the murderer. He now became more mistrustful and outrageous than before; and as his strength was superior to that of the English who survived, and he was well armed, they became satisfied that there was no safety for them but in his death. 'I determined,' says Dr. Richardson, 'as I was thoroughly convinced of the necessity of such a dreadful act, to take the whole responsibility upon myself; and, upon Michel coming up, I put an end to his life by shooting him through the head!'"

Many of the Indians who had accompanied Richardson and Hepburn had died of hunger, and the two leaders were on the brink of the grave when, on the 7th November, three Indians, sent by Back, brought them help. As soon as they felt a little stronger, the two Englishmen made for the Company's settlement, where they found Back, to whom they had twice owed their lives on this one expedition.

The results of this journey, in which 5500 miles had been traversed, were of the greatest importance to geographical, magnetic, and meteorological science, and the coast of America had been surveyed as far as Cape Turn- again.

In spite of all the fatigue and suffering so bravely borne, the explorers were quite ready to make yet another attempt to reach the shores of the Polar Sea, and at the end of 1823 Franklin received instructions to survey the coast west of Mackenzie River, all the agents of the Company being ordered to supply his party with provisions, boats, guides, and everything else they might require.

After a hearty reception at New York, Franklin went to Albany, by way of the Hudson, ascended the Niagara from Lewiston to the famous Falls, made his way thence to Fort St. George on the Ontario, crossed the lake, landed at York, the capital of Upper Canada (*sic*), passed Lakes Siamese, Huron, and Superior, where he was joined by twenty-four Canadians, and on the 29th June, 1825, came to Lake Methye, then alive with boats.

Whilst Dr. Richardson was surveying the eastern coast of Great Bear Lake, and Back was superintending the preparations for the winter, Franklin reached the mouth of the Mackenzie, the navigation of which was very easy, no obstacles being met with, except in the Delta. The sea was free from ice, and black and white whales and seals were playing about at the top of the water. Franklin landed on the small island of Garry, the position of which he determined as N. lat. 69° 2', W. long. 135° 41', a valuable fact, proving as it did, how much confidence was to be placed in the observations of Mackenzie.

The return journey was made without difficulty, and on the 5th September the explorers arrived at the fort to which Dr. Richardson had given the name of Franklin. The winter was passed in festivities, such as balls, &c., in which Canadians, English, Scotch, French, Esquimaux, and Indians of various tribes took part.

On the 22nd June a fresh start was made, and on the 4th July the fort was reached where the Mackenzie divides into two branches. There the expedition separated into two parties, one going to the east and the other to the west, to explore the shores of the Arctic Ocean. Franklin and his companions had hardly left the river when he met near a large bay a numerous party of Esquimaux, who at first testified great delight at the rencontre, but soon became obstreperous, and tried to carry off the boat. Only by the exercise of wonderful patience and tact were the English able to avert bloodshed on this emergency.

Franklin now surveyed and gave the name of Clarence to the river separating the English from the Russian territories, and a little further on was discovered another stream, which he called the Canning. On the 16th April, finding he had only made half of the distance between Mackenzie River and Icy Cape, though the winter was rapidly approaching, Franklin turned back and embarked on the beautiful Peel River, which he mistook for that of Mackenzie, not discovering his error till he came in sight of a chain of mountains on the east. On the 21st September he got back to the fort, after having in the course of three months traversed 2048 miles, and surveyed 372 miles of the American coast.

Richardson meanwhile had advanced into much deeper water with far less floating ice, and had met with a great many Esquimaux of mild and hospitable manners. He surveyed Liverpool and Franklin Bays, and discovered opposite the mouth of the Coppermine a tract of land separated from the continent by a channel not more than twenty miles wide, to which he gave the name of Wollaston. His boats arrived at Coronation Gulf, explored on the previous trip, on the 7th August; and on the 1st September they got back to Fort Franklin, without having sustained any damage.

In dwelling on Parry's voyages, we have, for the time, turned aside from those made at the same time by Ross, whose extraordinary exploration of Baffin's Bay had brought upon him the censure of the Admiralty, and who was anxious to regain his reputation for skill and courage. Though the Government had lost confidence in him, he won the esteem of a rich ship- owner, who did not hesitate to entrust to him the command of the steamship *Victory*, on which he started for Baffin's Bay on the 25th May, 1830.

For four years nothing was heard of the courageous navigator, but on his return, at the end of that time, it turned out that his voyage had been as rich in discoveries as had been Parry's first trip. Ross, entering Prince Regent's Inlet, by way of Barrow and Lancaster Sounds, had revisited the spot where the *Fury* had been abandoned four years previously; and continuing his voyage in a southerly direction, he wintered in Felix Harbour—so named after the equipper of the expedition—ascertaining whilst there that the lands he had passed formed a large peninsula attached on the south to the northern coast of America.

In April, 1830, James Ross, nephew of the leader of the party, set out in a canoe to examine the shores of this peninsula, and those of King William's Land; and in November of the same year all had once more to go into winter- quarters in Sherif Harbour, it being impossible to get the vessel more than a few miles further north. The cold was intense, and it was agreed by the sailors of the *Victory* that this was the very severest winter ever spent by them in the Arctic regions.

The summer of 1831 was devoted to various surveys, which proved that there was no connexion between the two seas. All that was accomplished this season was to bring the *Victory* as far as Discovery Harbour, a very little further north than that of Sherif. The ensuing winter was so intensely severe, that the vessel could not be extricated from her ice prison, and but for the fortunate discovery of the provisions left by the *Fury*, the English would have died of hunger. As it was, they endured daily greater and greater privations and sufferings before the summer of 1833 at last enabled them finally to leave their winter-quarters and go by land to Prince Regent's and Barrow Straits. They had just reached the shores of Baffin's Bay when a vessel appeared, which turned out to be the *Isabel*, once commanded by Ross himself, and which now received the refugees from the *Victory*.

But England had not all this time been forgetful of her children, and had sent an expedition in search of them every year. In 1833 Back, Franklin's companion, was the leader, and he starting from Fort Revolution, on the shore of Slave Lake, made his way northwards, discovered Thloni-Tcho-Deseth River, and settled down in winter-quarters, with the intention of reaching the next year the Polar Sea, where he supposed Ross to be held prisoner, when he heard of his incredible return journey overland. Back, therefore, gave up the next season to the survey of the fine Fish River, discovered the previous year, and sighted the Queen Adelaide Mts., with Capes Booth and Ross.

1836 found him at the head of a new expedition, which was to attempt to connect by sea the discoveries of Ross and Franklin. It failed, and the accomplishment of the task assigned to it was reserved to Peter Williams, Dease, and Thomas Simpson, all officers in the service of the Hudson's Bay Company, who, leaving Fort Chippeway on the 1st June, 1837, went down the Mackenzie, arriving on the sea-coast on the 9th July, and making their way along it to N. lat. 71° 3' and W. long. 156° 46', i.e. to a cape they named Simpson, after the governor of their company.

Thomas Simpson now made his way overland with five men to Port Barrow, already sighted in the direction of Behring Strait by one of Beechey's officers, so that the whole of the North American coast from Cape Turn-again to Behring's Strait was now complete, and there was nothing left to do but to explore the space between the former and Point Ogle, a task accomplished by the explorers in a later expedition.

Leaving the Coppermine in 1838, they followed the eastern coast, arriving on the 9th August at Cape Turn-again, which was too much encumbered with ice to be rounded. Thomas Simpson therefore remained near it for the winter, discovered Victoria Land, and on the 12th August, 1839, arrived at Back River. The rest of the month he devoted to the exploration of Boothia.

Discovery of Victoria Land.

The whole of the coast-line of North America was now accurately laid down, but at the cost of what struggles, devotion, privations, and sufferings? What, however, is human life when weighed in the balance with the progress of science? and with what disinterestedness and enthusiasm must be embued the savants, sailors, and explorers, who give up all the joys of existence to contribute to the best of their power to the progress of knowledge and to the moral and intellectual development of humanity.

With the voyages last recorded the discovery of the earth was completed, and with our account of them our work, which began with the first attempts of the earliest explorers, also closes. The shape of the earth is now known, the task of explorers, is done. The land on which man lives is henceforth familiar to him, and he has now only to turn to account the vast resources of the countries to which access has recently become easy, or of which he can without difficulty possess himself.

How rich in lessons of every kind is this history of twenty centuries of exploration. Let us cast a glance behind us and enumerate the main features of the progress made in this long series of years. If we take the map of the world of Hecatæus, who lived 500 years before the Christian era, what do we see? When it was published the known world did not extend beyond the basin of the Mediterranean, and the whole, with a terribly distorted outline, is represented only by a very small portion of southern Europe, the interior of Asia, and part of North Africa; whilst encircling them all is a river without beginning or end, to which is given the name of Ocean.

Side by side with this map, ancient monument as it is of antique science, let us place a planisphere representing the world as known in 1840, and on this vast surface we shall find the portion known, and that but imperfectly to Hecatæus, occupying but an infinitesimal space.

Taking these two typical maps as our starting-point, we shall be able to judge of the magnitude of the discoveries of modern times. Imagine for a moment all that is involved in thorough knowledge of the whole world, and you will marvel at the results achieved by the efforts of so many explorers and martyrs, you will grasp the importance of their discoveries and the intimate relations between geography and all the other sciences. This is the point of view from which can best be seen all the philosophic bearings of a work to which so many generations have devoted themselves.

Doubtless the motives actuating these various explorers differ greatly. First, we have the natural curiosity of the owner anxious to know thoroughly every part of the domain belonging to him, so that he may estimate the extent of the habitable districts, and determine the boundaries of the seas, &c.; and secondly, we have the natural outcome of a trade, which, though still in its infancy, introduced even in remote Norway the products of Central Asian industry. In the time of Herodotus the aim of explorers was loftier: they wished to learn the history, manners, customs, and religion of foreign races; and later, the Crusades, which, whatever else they accomplished, certainly vulgarized oriental studies, inspired some few with a fervent desire to wrest from infidels the scene of our Lord's Passion, but the greater number with a lust of pillage and a yearning to explore the unknown.

Columbus, seeking a new route to the Indies, came across America on the way, and his successors were only anxious to make rapid fortunes, differing greatly indeed from the noble Portuguese who sacrificed their private interests to the glory and colonial prosperity of their country, and were the poorer for the offices conferred on them with a view to doing them honour.

In the sixteenth century religious persecution and civil war drove to the New World the Huguenots and Puritans, who, whilst laying for England the foundations of colonial prosperity, were to bring about a radical change in America. The next century was essentially one of colonization. In America the French, in India the English, and in Oceania the Dutch established counting-houses and offices, whilst missionaries endeavoured to win over to the Christian faith and modern ideas the unchangeable "Empire of the Mean."

The eighteenth century, ushering in our own, rectified received errors, and surveyed minutely alike continents and archipelagoes; in a word brought to perfection the work of its predecessors. The same task has occupied modern explorers, who pride themselves on not passing over in their surveys the smallest corner of the earth, or the tiniest islet. With a similar enthusiasm are imbued the intrepid navigators who penetrate the ice-bound solitudes of the two poles, and tear away the last fragments of the veil which has so long hidden from us the extremities of the globe.

All then is now known, classed, catalogued, and labelled! Will the results of so much toil be buried in some carefully laid down atlas, to be sought only by professional *savants*? No! it is reserved to our use, and to develope the resources of the globe, conquered for us by our fathers at the cost of so much danger and fatigue. Our heritage is too grand to be relinquished. We have at our command all the facilities of modern science for surveying, clearing, and working our property. No more lands lying fallow, no more impassable deserts, no more useless streams, no more unfathomable seas, no more inaccessible mountains!

We suppress the obstacles nature throws in our way. The isthmuses of Panama and Suez are in our way; we cut through them! The Sahara interferes with the connexion of Algeria and Senegal; we will throw a railway across it. The Pas de Calais prevents two nations so well fitted for cordial friendship from shaking each other by the hand; we will pierce it with a railway!

This is our task and that of our contemporaries. Is it less grand than that of our predecessors, that it has not yet succeeded in inspiring any great writer of fiction? To dwell upon it ourselves would be to exceed the limits we laid down for our work. We meant to write the History of the Discovery of the World, and we have written it. Our task therefore is complete.

FINIS.

LONDON:
GILBERT AND RIVINGTON, PRINTERS,
ST. JOHN'S SQUARE.

www.ingramcontent.com/pod-product-compliance
Lightning Source LLC
Chambersburg PA
CBHW030041130726
47901CB00005BA/1259